NJANDEJARA LOVES SCANDALOUSLY

The universe is barreling toward heat death. Interdimensional energy beings see matter-based life forms as an energy-consuming plague—and to support their case, sentients do have a habit of destroying every world we touch. Either matter-beings will be forced to give back the energy we've co-opted, or we need someone else to fill that deficit.

Njandejara is the Progenitor energy being, and the only life-form with enough juice to stop the drain. Unlike the other inter-dimensionals, he's deeply in love with matter, and would gladly give all of himself to save these little worlds.

But Njandejara can't die. It's physically impossible. If he could, the universe that depends on him would spiral into noth-ingness—not nonexistence, but a harsh, hellish meaninglessness.

There's a little bioship hopping from planet to planet trying to stop the heat death, though, and on board they have Njande-jara's greatest vulnerability. With death at the end of the road, either they're about to save the universe ... or they'll be the ones to damn it forever.

NEODYMIUM APOCALYPSE: PART 2

NEODYMIUM APOCALYPSE: PART 2

NEODYMIUM CHRONICLES
BOOK 5

JEN FINELLI, MD

EBook ISBN: 978-1-68057-705-1
Trade Paperback ISBN: 978-1-68057-706-8
Dust Jacket Hardcover ISBN: 978-1-68057-707-5
Library of Congress Control Number: 2024947010
Cover design by Janet MacDonald
Kevin J. Anderson, Art Director
Published by
WordFire Press, LLC
PO Box 1840
Monument CO 80132
Kevin J. Anderson & Rebecca Moesta, Publishers
WordFire Press eBook Edition 2024
WordFire Press Trade Paperback Edition 2024
WordFire Press Dust Jacket Hardcover Edition 2024

Printed in the USA
Join our WordFire Press Readers Group for
sneak previews, updates, new projects, and giveaways.
Sign up at wordfirepress.com

Dedicated to the ones who died.
Especially the little boy whose name began with a K.

CHAPTER ONE

Laaru

LESS THAN TWO WEEKS TO THE ALL-IMPORTANT SOLSTICE, AND Laaru was having doubts.

This evening found him in the engineering office, a cave just off the main mineshaft at the root of the Structure, running a bare finger along a compuwall slab hung kind of haphazardly on the blueish-black rock jutting out from the wall. It was warmer in here, with two portable heaters going, but both Laaru and his sharpshooter bodyguard still wore parkas. The fluorescent lights pinned to the ceiling cast a harsh, eerie light that made both youths look pale and ill.

Laaru sometimes wished he did believe in gagging the Frelsi terrorists. Reise—his bodyguard—talked almost nonstop, pressuring him with questions he didn't know how to answer and filling his head with grand philosophical soliloquies. And it was hard to argue with him. The work on the Structure was on schedule to finish late tonight—the Turned bodies did what they were supposed to—but it was almost impossible to restrain the brutality of the blitzer guards when mocked by their now-voiced prisoners. After the first beating incident Laaru had demanded a camera feed at every workstation so he could supervise everything at once, and occasionally he had Reise watch the feed to warn him if something was happening so Laaru could keep his hands free for tunneling.

On this occasion, Reise stood with his weapon at the ready, staring at the control panel on the workstation table while Laaru checked some of the recent geological findings against the Structure's blueprints. Near the pocket of neodymium crystal his guys were mining they'd hit something that seemed a lot like a lamproite pipe: a diamond repository. *But the space around it's all wrong—diamond doesn't form like this, in sheets more and more like ice the deeper we go.* It was like the planet itself had a clear gemstone layer under its most superficial crust, and this was a problem: both the Turned workers and the machines struggled to carve accurate space into the hard material, and the shape of the underground portion of the Structure needed to be perfect. Bricandor had given Laaru some advice—"This is why we chose Bijou," the old Counselor reassured him—but the practical *doing* was still tricky.

Laaru's holopen dinged—he drew a quick square in the air to read the message. Oh, yeah, and then there were the reports of this strange buzzing sound that grew louder as they dug deeper by the lamproite … but so far ultrasound hadn't revealed anything.

Reise cleared his throat. "What are the moving cameras?" he asked. "Some of the views on your control pad aren't stationary, and they flicker every few seconds."

"Those are feeds directly from Frelsi eyes," Laaru said, not looking up from his work. He'd devoured the Standard Operating Procedure manual for the mind-control units the day after he confiscated the main panel. "The dart has a special—uh, connector—just for the optic nerve, the oculomotor nerve, and the visual cortex. It's supposed to wind past all the other cranial nerves on the brain stem without disrupting them, but it doesn't actually make it to the optic nerve in everyone. Just some people."

Reise's voice was heavy with discouraged epiphany. "So while you're running an active software command that requires those nerves, those people wouldn't have the capacity to shut their eyes, then—I mean shut, not just blink," he realized. "Like the programmed sequence for 'shoot': that order requires vision, so it'll keep eyes open even if the control panel doesn't need the feed—even if the controller's not the one aiming and the program's only lining up shots using the Turned person's instincts. Because there's a separate tendril for vision."

"I'm—not sure what you mean," Laaru said. "But the PL will be back soon, and you know he thinks I tell you too much. I'm not trying to get shot in the back here."

"You haven't revealed anything tactical," Reise assured him. His tone darkened into the customary accusatory grumble: "You've just let me know how filked I am."

"You're saying you can't control your eyes when you shoot?" Laaru asked. "Huh. Your dart's really in there, then." *This pocket of neodymium crystals has the wrong chemical make-up for the southern end of the Structure. We'd need to move that over to—*

Laaru realized suddenly how matter-of-fact he sounded. What'd happened to his empathy? This guy just confirmed to him that when he had to *kill* or capture his comrades, he couldn't look away. And that felt totally reasonable to Laaru: of course you wouldn't want your military device to shut off its visual feed the moment it fired. But it was scary that this felt reasonable. Because the reality was that they were talking about a *person* carrying the weight of dozens of deaths he couldn't unsee.

What else had become normal to Laaru that wasn't actually okay?

He'd *had* to toughen up to get things done with the other officers, though! The revolt in the mine changed everything. If Laaru wanted the Frelsi workers treated humanely, he needed military authority: had to talk like the officers, strut like the officers, threaten like the officers. He wasn't as good at it as they were. He needed to get better at their game, their culture. He always felt their eyes on him—eyes that despised him, that saw him as weak … vulnerable …

He shivered. "I'd like you to stay with me again tonight," he said. His paranoia about assassination had started as a warm dread in his stomach the night after the revolt, but now it'd become so constant he almost *felt* nothing about it—threat was just another iron fact. He needed a Turned guard because he couldn't trust anyone he couldn't remote control.

"You say it like I have a choice," Reise grimaced. "You know I'd choose to stay near my comrades."

"That'll only endanger your people. There are microphones in the cages now, and if the officers figure out who you conspired with, they'll kill them, and it'll be hard for me to do anything about it," Laaru said. *What if we move these drills here? We may even have enough polishing equipment to process some of the diamond for drill bits to speed up the neodymium work.* "They're already suspecting the kitchen staff—they can't prove it, though, since I was on my way to the mine anyway—Gideon's the only one they can prove, and they're only keeping him around because he's such a fantastic physical laborer and the darts are expensive. They're running out of healthy settlers to poach." Laaru looked up from his work now to stare the Frelsi guard straight in the face. "I was there when the logistics lead literally sat down and calculated the financial cost to kill him versus keep him alive. It came very close."

"Gideon'll be glad to know his muscles saved him," Reise said with a sardonic grin. "He's already said he wants people to start calling him Candy Biceps."

"I'm definitely not calling him that," Laaru smirked back; Reise chuckled.

Footsteps clinked on the ladder above them. Laaru jumped—

he and Reise looked too friendly. He snatched the control panel off the table and clutched it under his arm, pretending to run his other hand over the compuscreen in front of him with great interest.

"Permission to enter?" said the friendly voice just above.

"Granted," Laaru called back, eyes still on his screen.

"How's everything going?" the platoon leader asked, walking into the room. He'd brought two orbs of brewed herb from his Alpinoan home planet; he handed one to Laaru now. Laaru glanced over at Reise. "Before you scold me, sir, I've tried sharing a drink with him on multiple occasions," the PL said. "He bites."

Reise smiled—a vicious, toothy grin. "I *bite*? Oh no and goodness me, I wonder why someone might do something like that."

"Look, I've got nothing against you personally," the PL said. "I've always treated you well—you know that. And I'm the one who provided Major Fpokmmud with the numbers on your big friend—the numbers that kept him alive?"

"The fact that you need to justify yourself only confirms your guilt," Reise said. "Just release us. The Growen only drain you of that which makes you yourself."

The PL sighed and turned his back to Reise, facing Laaru. "The platitudes get a little annoying, don't they, sir?"

"A little," Laaru admitted. "Would you mind looking over this? I think we need to move the bulk of your platoon over here." He pointed—

Out of the corner of his eye, Laaru saw a dark, reddish cloud cross Reise's face. "You know why Bricandor initially wanted you to have a Turned guard, Laaru?" Reise asked.

Laaru tried to ignore him as the PL entered Laaru's data into his compupad.

"You ever wonder why he specifically told you to get a sharpshooter?" Reise went on.

Laaru's stomach tightened. The PL made eye contact with

him, raising an eyebrow. "He's fine," Laaru said. "Do you have what you need?"

"I'll go move my men, sir." The platoon leader nodded his head toward Reise. "You sure you don't want a muzzle back?"

"If we can't handle what they say, do we really have a right to be in charge of them?" Laaru asked. "I'll see you in a couple hours once your platoon's moved. We're still rotating shifts—a quarter of your guys should sleep every six hours so everyone stays sharp and we keep work going around the clock. I'm going to grab four myself and I'll be back to relieve you for yours. Sound good?"

"Too easy, sir." And the platoon leader left, his boots cling-clanging back up the ladder just outside.

"You probably shouldn't say that—'sound good.' It's weak, like you're asking if he likes your order," Reise reminded Laaru. "'Tracking?' always works."

Reise had been helpful to Laaru with a lot of military culture stuff, but at the moment the young Stygge just felt irritated. He whirled on his bodyguard, snapping against his better judgment: "What are you trying to say with the sharpshooter thing?"

"They didn't want you to obtain the panel because I was supposed to be your insurance. So if you decide to grow a pair and stand up to the Growen, I can ensure your permanent servitude." Reise nodded his head toward his rifle, still loaded with one of those expensive change-bullets or freedom-darts or whatever they were supposed to be calling them.

Laaru didn't answer. This sounded like one of those ugly true things that'd started to make tactical sense lately. *But Father Bricandor would never do that to me!* a piece of him immediately piped up; another piece reminded him they threw Xunst out on a deserted planet for the "greater good." *But he wouldn't do that to me. He trusts me—I have an in with him. I can influence him for the better.*

Laaru glanced at the time on the side of his holopen. By the time he got back and got to sleep, he'd lose half an hour of his four. And he was pretty sleep-deprived—maybe that was why he felt so jumpy. He'd pulled all-nighters in school at Beryllia, but this long, slow military drain was something else. *Like a marathon of moderate stress and bad sleep punctuated with moments of terror.*

At least efficiency had gone up since he'd started having the platoon leaders rotate their soldiers every six hours. Instead of trying to "tough it through" with 25-hour days, actually working with the science of the human body made work faster. Who knew.

"You're staring into space, man," Reise said.

"We're sleeping here tonight," Laaru announced. "I want to get right back to work in a few hours, and I don't want to deal with walking up there and saluting every idiot I walk past who thinks he knows my job and doesn't, while I also *take* salutes from everybody I outrank that knows way more than I do." He ran out of breath halfway through, and tried to ignore Reise's grin as he added, "There are spare sleeping systems in the corner, we'll move the shelf over the doorway and sleep against it. Understood?"

"Yes sir," Reise's grim voice almost cheered. "Just listen to all that untapped rage!"

"Shut up."

"You can make me, but you won't."

Laaru sighed. He set Reise on guard near the compuwall and dragged the heavy metal shelf over the opening to the room. *Toss two sleeping systems on the floor, and voila.*

Laaru actually liked the Growen sleeping systems. They were basically two fluffy, self-heating bags with a ground pad under them that then fit into another waterproof bag—apparently rated even for sleeping in Alpinoan snow. Laaru dropped Reise kind of on/in one sleeping system—it was really difficult to make the smaller maneuvers without just turning the mind control off—and sat about a meter away on his own.

Before Laaru lay down, though, he reached into his vest pocket for the purple gas Bricandor had recommended for his nerve health.

Reise scowled. "Why are you inhaling the sedative the Growen use to make people more receptive to being Turned?"

"What?" Laaru closed the vent on the vial's breathing tube. "What are you talking about?"

"We bring that shyte with us to sedate the colony first, so it's harder for them to put up resistance," Reise said. Anger bubbled underneath his tone, but he remained calm. "We ran out recently, but that's the gas—I've Turned enough people to recognize it."

"You're mixing this up with something else," Laaru said, opening the vent to inhale again. "This is something Counselor Bricandor recommended me for my powers." He closed the vial, wrapped its breathing tubing around it, and tucked it back in one of his vest pockets.

Reise's grin wasn't pleasant. "Do you feel tranquil and benevolent after taking it?"

"… yes," Laaru admitted. "But that's to help my mind focus."

"Are you supposed to take an extra dose before training with him or calling him?" Reise asked.

"… yes."

"He's sedating you so you'll do what he says," Reise said. "You told me the other day you think he didn't know about the mind-control project. But how long have you had the sedative gas? About a year?"

"About that long … yes." Laaru didn't like how Reise spat facts rapid-fire like he knew everything about everything—but Laaru didn't have any defense.

"So almost a year before you informed him about the project, Bricandor recommended you ingest something developed *for* the project," Reise said. "So he knew."

Laaru didn't answer that. The purple felt calming, and Reise's words did not. "But it really does help me focus," he said.

"If a substance truly enhances function, I'm usually in support of that substance," Reise said. "But this is given to you by someone with power over you who profits from your good behavior. You have to see that merits at least a little scrutiny!"

Laaru said nothing. He rearranged his jacket, and squirmed into his sleeping system, patting the fluffy pillow-like attachment at the top of it as he shifted to find a restful position. "You don't know for sure it's the same thing," he said. "For all we know this was developed first, and the rogue leaders just stole it to use for mind control."

"You have access to research files as a Growen scientist, don't you?" Reise said. "Look it up."

"It's not that easy." Laaru pulled the poofy material up over his mouth, comforted by the wet heat of his breath against it. "Besides, Bricandor's been really helpful to me with some—personal—issues. I understand he's not perfect, but this is war. It makes people do things that aren't perfect. He legitimately wants peace with everyone."

"What a nice guy," Reise mocked. "Sorry if I don't feel the same way. Something in my spine, just, oh, I don't know."

Laaru sat up on one arm to look over at Reise. "All right, supposing you're right—which you're not. If he's mind-controlling you to do things that are for your own good—for everyone's good—isn't that—okay, though?"

"That's presupposing, a), that he knows what good is for each person, and b), that 'good' is more important than 'free.'" Reise answered right away, like it was a quiz at school and he needed this grade to impress a girl. "Each person's needs and values may differ and change over time, so it's intrinsically impossible for 'greater good' to be known by one person, or even a group of people or a data-based algorithm. There is such a thing as absolute good, but it's discovered by Reason, not Force: All decisions made 'for the greater good' can always only approximate 'good' for a majority, not for every individual, so if you truly want a granular selection process for 'good,' you need to involve the most people possible in that process with as little oversight possible, giving each individual as much leeway as possible to dissent and live their own 'good.' For the second presupposition—"

"Okay, I can't do this with you." Laaru raised a hand. "It's just too much and too fast. I can post you outside the room overnight to keep watch or you can give me a break. Please."

Reise glowered. "It's a coward who won't answer logic with logic," he said.

"Well, this coward is really tired," Laaru said.

"Subjugating peoples really does take it out of you," Reise yawned. "As a mass murderer myself, I know exactly what you mean."

Laaru groaned, rubbing a hand over his weary face. "Look, if I were to let you go, you would all immediately kill every Growen person in this camp—including me."

"How do you know that's true?" Reise asked.

"Can you really tell me it isn't?" Laaru clapped back.

Reise paused; behind his spectacles he seemed to be calculating something. After some time he answered, his words slow and even: "Those who have treated us foulest would definitely die. For the rest of you, worst case you'd be taken prisoner according to Frelsi standards, which is more humane than you deserve. More likely, because we're in a wasteland with no resources, someone could come up with some kind of joint survival agreement. A truce. Best case scenario, you could all join us in destroying the blockade."

"That's impossible," Laaru said.

"So you've just determined that for us without even giving us a chance," Reise spat. "Who gave you the right? Who are you protecting? The logistics lead who would shoot you himself if he could?"

"I have to protect—everyone." Laaru hesitated. "All life is sacred."

"No, it's not," Reise almost laughed. "Trust me, it's not."

"Go to sleep, Reise," Laaru growled.

The bodyguard sighed. "Fine," he said. "I almost feel bad for you. I may be under mind control, but at least I know it. You can't even see yours."

Laaru was very, very afraid that Reise might be right—but if Laaru wanted to keep feeling more and more okay with himself and his Thought, he needed Bricandor, and if he needed Bricandor, he needed to make sure the terrorists didn't destroy the Growen. If conflict came from inequality and poverty, then completing the Structure's energy solution would solve it—and if mind control was the only way to make sure as few people got hurt as possible, then Laaru had to do this.

Somehow, without ever making a conscious decision, he'd taken sides.

CHAPTER TWO

Nathan

It was a few days before Gideon rejoined Nathan in the cage. Nathan was half-asleep, curled on his belly with his head in his elbows, when boots crunching on icy rock woke him over brutish laughter. The cage door clanged—he lifted his head—

"The kitchen lead's compliant; maybe he'll be a good influence on the big guy," a rough blitzer silhouette was saying as he shoved Gideon forward. Still on the control program, Gideon couldn't catch himself when pushed—he fell face-first toward the heated metal floor—

Nathan dashed forward, pushing off on his hands and knees. A thump knocked the wind out of him as the larger guy fell on top of him—he didn't quite manage to catch his friend, but he did break his fall, get squished, and get laughed at.

"Aw, how cute," mocked the largest silhouette. "This your boyfriend, kid?"

"No. I love him too much for that," Nathan answered almost without thinking.

"What the hell?" A thinner blitzer lowered his balaclava and spat on the ground. "Filking prude."

"Me? You're the one mocking me for my theoretical

boyfriend," Nathan said. But as he rolled Gideon to a seated position against the side of the cage, he saw his friend shake his head. *No comebacks, no jokes!* Nathan switched to a tone of deference. "Thank you for not killing him. We'll work extra-hard to be useful to make up for everything."

"Yeah, you better thank," someone laughed. But then they left—no one stayed around a suck-up too long.

Gripes, what'd they done? Even in the shadows of the sheltered ice cave Nathan could see blood trickling down the side of Gideon's face, a smear matting his golden hair. "I thought the Stygge was supposed to be preventing this," Nathan grumbled.

"He can't be everywhere at once," Gideon breathed. "He's only got cameras at the workstations. The logistics lead's quarters isn't a workstation."

"Do you want to sit up, or lie down?" Nathan asked. They hadn't turned off his friend's software. *They probably left it on while they swung at him, too.*

"Neither," Gideon murmured. "I want to evaporate."

"Don't talk like that!" Nathan snapped. He heard the fierceness in his voice—*that's fear*—and dialed it back. "I mean—you can't evaporate before I do, Gideon, my boiling point's lower than yours. Everyone knows you're too chill."

Gideon raised an eyebrow. "Was that a really nerdy attempt at a joke?"

"No," Nathan said. "You're thinking of Captain Calloway's presentation this morning in formation. That was a joke."

"What's gotten into you?" grunted Gideon.

"Mostly processed food and panic," Nathan said truthfully. "Although I think that guard who just left wants to—also—get into me." The attempt at crude humor felt uncomfortable the moment it left his mouth, and Gideon protested.

"Holy shyte, Nathan, calm down," Gideon said. "I'm not gonna die. You don't have to try to speak my language or some shyte. They had their doc check me over to make sure they hadn't ruined their equipment." His last sentence melted from reassurance into bitterness.

Gideon's head drooped toward his chest. "Can I lay you on your back?" Nathan asked.

"Yeah. Thanks." Nathan pressed a shoulder under Gideon's armpit, shifting his weight to help the larger guy down. Gideon hissed in pain, but said nothing. The distant fluorescent lights in the Growen quarters reflected off the ice all along the outside passageway; in the dim rays that reached their cage Nathan could see bruises along Gideon's jaw and cheekbones, and his breathing halted on every exhale like his ribs hurt.

"Shyte, I hope they haven't made it too hard for you to work tomorrow," Nathan muttered. "That'd get you killed now."

"Shyte? Did you just curse?" Gideon asked. "Where's my soft little buddy who's always getting me in trouble for unprofessional behavior?"

"Where's my uncouth idiot who's got a quip for every situation?" Nathan retorted.

Gideon smiled—a pained smile, but a smile. "My man, is it gonna weird you out if I say something—weak?" he asked, his voice as quiet as a tree-cat's whimper. He didn't give Nathan a chance to say yes or no. "Shyte, it weirds me out, but I just—the last couple days all I could think about was getting back here. Not back here to the cage, but back here with—well. Back to ..."

Back to you. Gideon couldn't finish the sentence, and Nathan saved his pride. "It's been the same here," Nathan said. He pitched his voice down, a little more masculine, a little less intimate, so Gideon didn't have to fear the closeness. "Missed my friend, nonstop."

It was time for him to share his own secret. He couldn't say it aloud; Angela had overheard that the blitzers had mic'd the cages. Nathan showed his palm to Gideon and tapped on it to demonstrate how he was going to communicate. *"Microphones,"* he mouthed.

Gideon nodded, understanding. *Good*—the last thing Nathan wanted to do was touch the guy's hand when he couldn't move and already felt vulnerable. Assured he wasn't going to freak the guy out, Nathan slipped his thin, soft fingers into Gideon's rough palm, and tapped Frelsi code.

I'm a chemosynth, he tapped, spelling out chemosynth—it took a while. There was no shorthand for that. *My body's adapted to the mind-control dart. I can move on my own.*

Gideon couldn't tap back, and it seemed to take him a while to spell everything out in his head. After a couple seconds his eyes widened, and he nodded, brow furrowed.

It's because of you. Nathan didn't know how to say too much more without making Gideon uncomfortable, but he wanted Gideon to have hope, to know the little things he did for the other prisoners each day mattered. *I'm releasing some kind of endorphin in response to humor.*

"That's weird," Gideon said. "But cool."

That's you.

Gideon sighed. "Don't give me too much credit. I filked up. Should've been able to get those guys off me, keep control of the panel—I wanted to get you all free. Now they've got me gagged so tight around them it's hard to breathe. And you better bet that microphone's off when I'm around now." He lowered his voice to mutter under his breath. "Shyte, I'd die for a chance to re-do that."

I know. And maybe you're freeing us a different way. I just need to get to a Frelsi scientist somehow with my blood.

He paused, and then spoke aloud—he wanted the people in nearby cages to hear, and didn't care if the blitzers did. "In real life, resistances aren't made by one great person heroically standing up to be a legend," Nathan said. "Those things happen, but they're not why movements succeed. They succeed because many little people all do their little part. One guy's an assassin, maybe, but who hides his gun from his family? Another guy smuggles refugees, but who's supplying him the cart for free, or getting the guards looking the other way? Who's printing the leaflets that get passed from person to person so people know what's going on? Who's calming people down, keeping heads level—

"We all have to make our decisions alone, and sometimes we *stand* alone, but in the end, it's not big people alone, but little guys building off each other, that make resistances that survive."

"Reise would disagree with you," Gideon chuckled, groaning a little as he did.

"Well, Reise's not here." Nathan withdrew his hand and tilted his head toward the cage on the other side of them, with other people in it. Gideon nodded. They needed to keep trying. He needed to get to someone who could figure out how to get this cure out of his blood.

CHAPTER THREE

Jake

As Jake squeezed into the small, human-sized tunnel through the ice, dragging himself forward with his arms, pushing with his toes, and feeling his breath freeze on his slipping balaclava, he thought of his brother.

If this was the way the Growen originally took Reise and the guys—well, wow. Reise *hated* small spaces. Had he panicked? He'd been locked in the Turned body, so he couldn't have fought. Couldn't scream, while his insides shrieked. What—what was that like? Nefesh said that based on Lev's intel the tunnel was smaller now than last year—it'd started to freeze shut. A full-grown blitzer couldn't fit anymore.

But like, even when a blitzer could fit, this had to have been *bad* for claustrophobia.

"You've disconnected the earbud-clip from your wristband, right?" Nefesh asked in Jake's ear. "It's silence from here on out."

Jake scrawled the affirmative symbol on the face of his wristband and kept crawling. That was Nefesh testing to see if he answered out loud. Nefesh had made him promise to bail out if he failed any checkpoints along the way. She couldn't *physically* stop him from doing this anyway, but she was the only one who had the data from Lev's private explorations to make this possible—if Jake just ran in blind without her he'd die.

He was probably too young to be useful Turned.

It was weird that Lev hadn't told Jake about his night-time expeditions. *Probably to keep me from seeing him Turn, if that happened.* Apparently Lev had spent the first six months here running missions and resupply for the colonists before disappearing off into the tunnels like some yellowing liver-failure superhero. *Lactulose-Man!*

Jake had to get lactulose. That was the stuff Lev needed to keep living, Nefesh said.

Jake approached the end of the tunnel pistol-first. "Are you tired yet?" Nefesh asked. It'd been a three mile walk just to the entrance of this tunnel.

Jake scribbled the negative symbol on his wristband, then the question symbol. Next?

He could hear beeps and taps as Nefesh dragged windows and charts around her compuscreen. "Stand fast for about three minutes. There should be a blitzer patrol that comes out below you in a bit. We want them to *just* past you before you come out." *Maximize the time I have to get by before they come back around.* If Nefesh felt nervous about this first danger—and Jake doubted she believed in him—her voice didn't show it.

Jake talked in his head to his new invisible friend while he waited. *So, like, I really appreciate you being with me back there with the ursa-fly. I don't know if you answer back? I've been told by other people who hear you that it almost takes practice, like opening up a part of your brain and making it quiet.* He paused to see if he could do that. Nope. But that warm feeling was still there—that, like, warm thing, next to him. Even though there was no "next to him" except the wall. *Anyway, uh. I wonder if anyone ever asks you if you're doing okay. Is that rude, since you're all big and stuff? Sorry if it is. I just feel like you care, and I kinda wanna care back.*

"Go," Nefesh's cool voice interrupted. Jake jolted forward—

cleared the entrance with his weapon first—saw the blitzers disappearing around the corner to his left—and squirmed out into a cavern. He landed on a wide ledge overlooking a series of cliffs and walkways, and in the distance below, brown and grey blotches and holes at the foot of a huge metal tower with construction vehicles parked nearby.

He turned his head to make sure the camera on the earbud-clip could pick up what he was seeing, and then dashed to the right into a tall rectangular tunnel to get out of the open.

"There should be a service ladder at the end of that hallway you're in. The hallway's narrow with no cover, so get through it fast," Nefesh said. "I'm making note of the structure you're seeing there."

This hallway had lights pinned to the ceiling. Jake hated that! *Too blitzery.* He ran through, came out onto another ledge, and saw military vehicles traveling across one of the bridges below him. He felt so exposed up here, and he wasn't happy to see the ladder Nefesh had mentioned trailed down a bare cliff face.

I'm going to get shot if I go that way. He made sure Nefesh could see the problem, and scrawled the negative symbol on his wristband, followed by a death symbol.

"You're not wrong," Nefesh said. "It's busier than it should be. We'll have to find another way down. Lev mentioned a ... all right, how are you with dark spaces and weird smells?"

Jake scrawled an affirmative symbol. He raised his pistol toward the ceiling of the cavern—looked back behind him down the hallway, then forward across the ledge—there was a boulder-y bit he could hide behind there while Nefesh calculated. He couldn't stay here.

Thump, scratch, thump, scratch. His boots made such an obvious *him* sound. It seemed so loud. He ducked into the nook behind the boulder—and heard voices. *Oh man, I'm so easy to see if they're coming from the hallway behind me, or above—please be coming from up ahead!* He backed tighter into the crevasse and pointed the pistol first up—didn't see anyone on the ledge above him—then back the way he'd come.

The voices neared—thank goodness. They were coming from up ahead—now they were beside him—his heart got *way* faster than he really thought it needed to—and then he saw them passing him and heading off into the nasty hallway with the lights in the ceiling. Two blitzers, fully armored—his weapon honestly wouldn't do much to them unless he was lucky enough to hit the joint of their necks or the seam under their arms.

"Good. Are you steady, cadet?" Nefesh asked.

He swiped the affirmative. Nefesh didn't waste time asking if he was sure. "Keep going right along the ledge, and hang a right at the first dark, unlit hole you see. There's an unused tunnel that should take you all the way to the bottom of the cliff. It's where they've been storing the dead."

Ooh. Oh, huh. Jake hated that. He flared his nostrils, imagining eyeless soldiers with their jaws hanging off, uniforms tattered, rising to follow him in the darkness ...

Jake clenched his jaw and squeezed his eyes shut. *Lev. Lev is going to die. And then I will die. I am doing this for Lev!*

"You're holding your breath cadet. We can still bail out."

Jake swiped no, held his pistol out around the boulder ahead of his face—keeping his head low, below eye level—and then scrambled down along the ledge. He saw the dark cave almost immediately. *Dark is good, right Njandejara? Can I call you Njande? I'm going to call you that. Let me know if that's not okay.*

He was not alone. That was all that mattered—he was not alone.

An acrid smell hit him when he broke into the shade. It was warmer in here—the hair on the back of his neck stood up straight. To his right, no wall—only a low ceiling stretching far off into a bumpy uphill darkness his eyes couldn't penetrate. To his left, no wall—only a low ceiling sloping downward, following the downhill curve of the floor into the depths. Ahead the path dove into grey dusk—and far, far away, there was a small light, so tiny it was like a distant star.

He could only tell there was a path here because of the scattered sharp stalagmites to the left, and suspicious mounds he couldn't make out piled up on the right.

"Bloodseas," Nefesh muttered, breaking her perfect professionalism for a moment.

She brought it back immediately. "You see the small light, cadet? That should be the opening to their excavation project, cadet."

Affirmative.

"Roger. But you'll break off to the left before you get down there. Keep your wristband light off for now for OPSEC. But I don't want you wandering off into the darkness and falling off some kind of hidden cliff or anything. It's a honeycomb in here, and we have to take exactly the right entrance. I'll have you turn on your light if we start to get lost."

We. Like she was here, too. It would've been so cool if she had been—sharp blue Draconian markings framing take-no-prisoners eyes, her sharp fingers gripping her pistol, bat-wings tucked close to her back—*Lev. Lev is so lucky. Also, I'm like nine years younger than her. Geez.* Jake was surprised his brain was calm enough to wander.

That didn't last long. There were sounds in the darkness. Dripping. His boots—*short, long, good leg, bad leg, step, drag*—roared in the quiet. He stopped—was there something walking behind him, dragging itself along, too?

It echoes in here, he almost said aloud—but fortunately his tongue stuck to the roof of his mouth, dry now, fat, and his jaw was like one of those metal clamps at the weorkshop back home.

Before "home" started to kill itself. The flickering lights, the guns popping out of the walls, the walk-in refrigerator slamming itself on one of the adults and switching to flash freeze—the agonized scream from in there, as the kids like Jake scrambled away into an old vent after Cinta—the tiny tunnel started to heat up once someone passed a sensor, as if trying to cook them out. The kid behind Jake got burns on his paws.

Darkness was better than light. You could hide in the darkness.

Step, drag. Good, bad. Long, short. He *hated* how empty the left-hand side of the path was: spiked nothingness sandwiched by ceiling and floor that grew ever closer to each other but never seemed to touch—like at the school back home, in math class, when the two sides of $1/x$-squared tried to reach infinity on the y-axis, and never did. Did the blackness there break off into a cliff, or was there a wall somewhere? Or a … den? His vision strained—was he seeing those little fake blips that show up when you squeeze your eyelids shut too tightly, or did he see lights like eyes down there?

A clattering, crunching sound, like a step, as a rock shifted—Jake whirled his pistol to the right and without thinking fired.

"Jake!" Nefesh snapped as, for an instant, the darkness lit up and the inscrutable mounds became bodies, bodies of every shape and size—mostly Frelsi bodies, frozen, contorted, mostly unclothed, with jaws gnashing at the ceiling. One matted Bichank corpse jerked, limbs flopping as Jake's oxidizer cartridge shot into it. One thin, almost skeletal form face-down had grey matter and cord jutting out the back of its neck, like something had been ripped out from its spine. One body with a smashed blitzer helmet, thrown sideways atop the pile, seemed like it was crouching, staring at Jake with vicious eyes.

It was like Jake's heart was trying to swim up his throat and flee. He dashed off the path to hide to the left—behind one of the stalagmites—out of the view of those awful, awful eyes still staring this way—!

"Jake, your pulse is too elevated. You've failed trigger discipline. It's time to turn back."

"No," Jake croaked aloud. Oh no! Oh no he was so loud.

They could hear. Everything and everyone could hear. *They're dead. They can't hear. They're dead. Blitzers don't come this way because they're scared. I'm not. I'm going this way.*

"Cadet."

"I can't!" Jake hissed, looking up and down the path for signs of any *alive* people who might hear him. "The tunnel you took me through? It's too high up in the slippery wall for me to pull myself back up. I have to go through the Growen camp and take another road back."

"You're talking about the path through the Frelsi settlement," Nefesh realized.

"I was listening during your mission brief, ma'am." His voice was so, so hoarse. It was like someone was choking him. "One of the escape options, you said."

Her tight-lipped voice allowed a small sigh of relief. "Better hurry then."

"… And I might as well pick up medications along the way," Jake whispered. He could feel his chest punching him a little less now.

"Jake … Jake, I said no! This is an order!" *You're a child,* she meant—despite his "authorized-on-offensives" age. *You haven't proved your manhood, you're not a soldier! You're a handicapped child we can't trust!* She was barking into the microphone, almost screaming in his ear. "You are ordered to return to your camp!"

"If you have someone else who can do this instead, please let me know," Jake squeaked. "But Lev can't die. He definitely can't die now that I know he was doing all this stuff for the settlement."

Her yelling faded to the back of his mind. Oh, he didn't want to move. He wanted to hide behind the stalagmite forever.

Lev is turning yellow.

Best to just run. Jake took off, tripping over a few small rock formations as his feet found the path. Run, run, to the light at the bottom of the cliff. Run, and the bodies couldn't catch him. They were broken anyway. They were dead. And he wasn't.

Eventually Nefesh stopped berating Jake, and he ran out of stamina. He walked in silence. He could hear her transmitter crackling every now and then—she was still there. And, despite the mind-bending terror and the ridiculous shame over his random corpse-shooting—so was Njandejara. Maybe the interdimensional had always been there. Maybe he was the hugging darkness where a kid could hide without a blitzer or a machine finding him.

After some time, Jake began to hear a buzzing to the left. He ducked instinctively.

"Report, cadet," Nefesh ordered—not strained, not mad, like nothing had happened.

Jake swiped the symbol for danger, then for okay—he was okay, but there was a threat to investigate. They were always supposed to clear every room, check every scene for safety, first things first. He crouched—galaxies it was hard to do that. The unit physical therapist had tried so hard to get him to crouch-walk. He still couldn't. Whatever. He kind of crawled, kind of crouched, down the slope to the right, scuttling from stalagmite to stalagmite. It was better to sneak up on the thing—to be the scary monster in the darkness himself—than to be stalked.

Jake came to a wall. Not rock—this was ice, with maybe some rock in it. Hm. He looked back to the path toward the mine—he could still see the light at the bottom of the hill. He followed along the wall—it curved inward toward the path, and soon traced along it.

"You need to turn here. There should be a hole that opens up."

Jake scribbled the affirmative; he'd found it. A winding passageway opened up in the wall, twisting toward faint light with the soft scent and whispery touch of outside air—*that'll take me to their storage complex.*

But the buzzing was louder further down the hill to the mine, past this opening. And it was a buzzing Jake recognized.

Jake found himself possessed with a curiosity he'd never felt before. He needed to see where the ursa-flies were. He definitely didn't want to meet one. But he wanted to know—

"Stand fast," he scrawled. There were a lot of basic symbols he'd forgotten, but he remembered that one. Nefesh said nothing; Jake progressed down toward the mine. There were many openings after the one he was supposed to take—like a honeycomb, as Nefesh had said, all the way down to the mine.

Suddenly the wall dropped away; Jake's hand slipped. He stumbled, body leaning toward nothingness—no! He flung himself backward to fall on stone and not off the surprise cliff.

His back hit rock with a stinging thud. "Report!" Nefesh snapped.

Jake squirmed back away from the edge and scrawled his okay—he was definitely too close to the Growen mine to talk aloud now. Then panting, Jake rolled over on his belly and slowly, slowly, hands out in front of him, crawled back to the ledge to look down.

There was an enormous writhing mass down there in the black. Some thin sheen of something lay at the bottom of this cliff—ice, maybe? It was really hard to see—but underneath it something, or many somethings, squirmed. Either the Growen were digging into a nest, or their excavation had frightened a huge population of ursa-flies this way. Maybe the ursa-flies smelled the dead and hadn't figured out yet how to get up through here. Lev didn't think they dug the tunnels they lived in —something else bigger, or older, or worse had to have done that.

Either way, whatever mystery brought the horde here, it would only take just the wrong heavy thing to fall down there, and an apocalypse of lightning-fast, spine-targeting, fire-causing, wire-eating demon-bugs would swarm through here and out into the valley.

Jake shuddered and turned back to take the tunnel that would put him out near the Growen supply tents. Nefesh said according to Lev's old intel the polymerwall at the back of the storage corral would probably let Jake through—the Turned had to work here, and no one wanted to give *them* DNA control over the entrances. Forced labor had its inherent security risks, Reise would've said. And today was stocking day, when the Turned moved supplies from the storage area to different workstations. Ideally Jake could nick medicine right off the open vehicles as they loaded.

Jake's heart was still pounding as he left the warmer darkness behind, but nothing really seemed that terrible now. Not compared to what he'd just left. And no matter what happened, at least Jake wasn't the poor unsuspecting fool who'd be first to dig into that ursa-fly hive.

CHAPTER FOUR

Reise

REISE AWOKE ENRAGED TO SOMETHING ROUGH AND COLD PRESSING into his mouth and around his head—he was silenced before he could protest. The gag. The filking gag. Who—what—he blinked furiously at the rough flint-blue ceiling, unable to even wipe the sleep out of his eyes as his internal fight instincts screamed at him to attack.

He scanned the room for threats. To his left, the Stygge lay still, mousy hair and smudged forehead just peeking out from his sleeping system. His chest rose and fell in deep, slow motion —alive, but asleep.

The platoon leader knelt above the Stygge, reaching for the mind-control panel peeking out by his pillow—

A smooth, expert motion slipped the prize away without so much as a twitch from the sleeper. A finger brushed the pad, and Reise's muscles stung; his palms pressed hard against the rough floor, shoving him to standing in two quick, jerky motions as if he wasn't exhausted and sore.

What the filk. He was being stolen.

The platoon leader led Reise out into the mine; with a soft, almost imperceptible grunt he replaced the barricade shelf behind them, closing Laaru back in.

"I don't want to disturb his sleep," the PL whispered once they'd turned a corner. "No one can deny he's worked overtime."

Reise couldn't believe Laaru hadn't woken up. *Clearly his soft civilian upbringing deprives him of unconscious perception.* Whatever the young Stygge's failings, Reise did not want to leave him behind. Reise didn't trust the other Growen not to disturb, harm —or worse—frame him. And Reise preferred Laaru infinitely to these other mass-produced facsimiles of sapience the Growen called soldiers.

Where the filking galaxy are you taking me? Reise tried to snap with his eyes. The fact that he had his sniper rifle loaded at the ready had not been lost on him. He was almost surprised the platoon leader hadn't turned him on the young Stygge.

The platoon leader took Reise through the camp, away from the huge valley near the Structure, and into the well-defended thoroughfares under the white, luminous ice where more sensitive operations took place. They passed the hive of Growen sleeping quarter caves and made their way to the small weapons depot. Reise's stomach tightened. The platoon leader was having him add incendiary rounds to his magazine pouch.

As they were leaving the depot they came across a Frelsi Turned Bichank with one of the lower-ranking Growen soldiers.

"Hey, he's not supposed to be muzzled," the Bichank growled, nodding toward Reise. "Orders from your Stygge."

The blitzer's shifting discomfort was apparent even through the orb'd, space-capable helmet and full winter gear. "Sir, he's right. Mass order for the whole installation. Authorized uniform only."

The platoon leader opened his mouth—Reise could imagine a hundred excuses or threats, because even though this blitzer wasn't under this PL's chain of command, the PL did outrank him; Reise had seen entitled officers intimidate lower-ranking soldiers out of following regs simply by asking for the name of the lower soldier's commander.

But the PL was in too much of a hurry to be petty, apparently —he glanced at the chronometer on his wrist, and, without a word, untied the muzzle with one hand.

"Sorry, sir, just obeying the guys at the top," the blitzer said as they left. Reise gave his fellow Frelsi a grateful nod and followed the PL through another tunnel.

"Why are we going toward the Frelsi settlement without any other blitzers?" Reise croaked, his morning voice thick with sleep and apprehension.

"Someone just stole some meds from supply," the platoon leader said. Reise knew the PL didn't have to explain himself to his vassal, but he maintained the facade of teamwork. "With this deadline coming up, literally everyone is either guarding the tower or working on it. We don't have time to be distracted anymore with that settlement, and we're unlikely to get any more good workers from there. You and I are just going to bomb it and be done with it. I've cleared it with the commander, and I just need someone who can hit their far generator from the crow's nest. So, you."

Reise's eyebrows shot up as if to kiss his hairline. Without slowing his stride, the platoon leader angled the control panel so Reise could see a still captured from one of the camera feeds. "Stygge Laaru asked for this camera to be moved over a few meters," the platoon leader added. "For a better view of the workers. And it's a good thing: we were ripped off several times a few months back, and we thought they came through the road to the settlement. But here we can see the culprit coming out of the graveyard, see? We'll catch up with him at the settlement, and I need someone who can shoot him at a good distance without damaging the small med-crate."

A surge of overwhelming emotion shoved words out of

Reise's mouth almost before he could process what he was seeing. "He's just a kid," he protested.

He was seeing Jake. Jake, more built and paler than Reise remembered, clothed in some kind of thick, white bristly leather, emerging through the wall with frightened determination on his face and a pistol in his hands. Jake was alive, as of this recording. And if Jake was stealing meds—actually looking pretty healthy himself—that meant somehow Lev had survived, too.

The platoon leader hadn't picked up on the begging in Reise's voice. "Yes, just a kid—with an injury, too, I think," he continued, pulling the panel back. "They're obviously running out of able-bodied people. I don't know how he got in there— there's only bad terrain between the settlement and the entrance to that side of the valley. That's where we've lost a number of men to wild animals and unsteady ice—thin sheets just break under you and for no reason you're falling into a cavern. Anyway."

Reise found his fingers unloading the mind-control darts from his weapon, tucking them into his coat, and loading a live flayer cartridge. *Oh shyte. Oh, absolutely never.* Reise struggled to hold the panic out of his voice. "He's a kid. I don't need to kill him. I can Turn him. Let me just—"

"He's injured and too young to be useful. Plus, all the ethical issues of child imprisonment, putting him in contact with our soldiers—you know we've got some bad ones," the platoon leader shrugged. "He must be miserable on this planet anyway. First person under your age I've seen all year."

"He's not too injured. Look how strong he is with that whole medicine crate! He's only two years younger than I am. He'll be worth it!" Reise begged.

"I thought death was better than this for you," the platoon leader said—as casually as if pointing out what Reise had for dinner—and it was true, this was a huge break from Reise's logic, he believed in decreasing the Growen workforce at any cost, he believed this mind control was the highest form of sapient abuse—but he couldn't think! His mind was only screaming *Jake is alive* and *I am not killing my brother!* After blocking Jake and Lev out of his head all year to hold back the weakness of grief, Reise's memory was taking violent revenge. He'd still loved the annoying Jake back on Luna-Guetala who pinned him in wrestling but whined like a baby about leaving their parents, and now *this* Jake he'd just glimpsed, this tight-jawed survivor wearing what looked like dyed ursa-fly hide— Reise *needed* to meet this Jake, this new brother on his way to manhood, and find out how he'd survived, and share a drink, and bump his fist after a story while staring off into a flame— he loved his brother and hated the platoon leader with the most vicious agony he'd ever felt. All the best and worst embers of the past and possibilities of the future flared up into a desperate fiery *hope* as painful as if he'd broken a leg, it'd set wrong, and now someone had rebroken it to repair it. He heard himself roaring expletives and pleas, and the platoon leader's sickening sympathetic face sent blood hurtling into Reise's temples, his forehead, behind his eyes—*maybe I'll have a stroke!* A part of him wished. *Maybe then I'll die and can't shoot anyone!*

As they stopped, well out of range of the Growen camp, and the platoon leader put Reise at attention to retie the gag, Reise calmed down enough to lower his voice behind gritted teeth. "If you make me do this one," he hissed, his voice trembling. "It doesn't matter how long it takes me, but I will slaughter you belly-up like a fang-fish for a dinner plate. Even if the war ends and you're pardoned and you have a family—no matter what good should befall you—I will find you and end you in screaming agony."

The platoon leader grunted with exertion behind Reise as he struggled to fasten the gag around Reise's gnashing jaw. He cursed as Reise got his teeth into his thumb. *I bite, remember?* But the platoon leader had had a year of practice with this, and the sniper was soon silenced.

LAARU

When Laaru awoke to find both the control panel and his bodyguard gone, he panicked. He scrambled out of his sleeping system, kicked it to the side, and knocked the shelf out of his way—stupid, had he really thought it'd be too heavy for a soldier to move without making noise? The first Turned Frelsi person he met in the main corridor of the mine told him Reise had gone with the platoon leader—"it looked like he had a gag in?"—and Laaru took off fuming toward the road to the Frelsi settlement. He'd never been there, but he had the map everyone else had, and where else would the platoon leader take Reise, muzzled and armed? The platoon leader had to work with Laaru—they'd gotten along more or less, Laaru thought, right?—maybe not—but even if the PL truly didn't like Laaru, Laaru was still alive, and the platoon leader liked to avoid conflict, so he would only risk taking Reise for something important. And what important thing would you need a sniper for? Either the camp was under attack from terrorists— which it didn't seem to be—or someone needed sniping. And Laaru—

For a moment, Laaru's run slowed to a jog. What did he think he was going to do? Stop Reise from killing a terrorist? No … this was war, and a few people had to die, even if Laaru hated it, even if he hoped the army's more humanitarian missions would end the poverty that made people vulnerable to recruitment by fundamentalist ideologues. If Reise needed to kill someone, that was because they were a threat to enough other people that the calculation added up to the least suffering for the most people.

Except Laaru didn't trust the people doing the calculating anymore.

Renewed vigor pumped into his legs; his soft boots punched the rough excoriated ice as he dodged through the camp. He didn't have time to be returning salutes or talking to anyone. He needed full control of that panel. Did other people know he didn't have it? Anything could be happening to the Frelsi Turned if he wasn't watching. *They tried to cut out that one guy's tongue ...*

He hadn't even seen that guy around the mines since.

Oh no ... Laaru's pounding heart gave him panic power. He never got lost around the tunnels—experience with the Beryllian underground mazes helped with that—so this turn—that glance at the map—across this open space—past this beehive of sleeping quarters—onto the main settlement road—and Laaru found the tunnel to the little cliffside sniper point that overlooked the main road and the Frelsi base. The "crow's nest," they called that point.

Did he hear screaming? Faintly. It was gone now. That was an unhappy guy. Oh man, poor Reise. But Laaru was going the right way.

Without a weapon. Why didn't he bring a weapon? He didn't even have that dumb mace Bricandor had told him to practice with—that was in his room somewhere.

I am the worst soldier in the whole galaxy.

At last Laaru's failure of a self reached the narrowing path that sloped up to the crow's nest. The hill was so steep at first the only thing visible at its other end was a view of the "poor man's sky," the thick icy ceiling of the world beneath Bijou's uninhabitable surface. But as Laaru got closer, chest heaving with heavy breath, he saw the nest—a round, ribbed outcropping just big enough for three or four people—and Reise flat on the ground with his cheek to his rifle under the shadow of the platoon leader.

The platoon leader whirled on Laaru, gun drawn—*weapon, not gun,* he corrected his brain, *they call it a weapon in the military* —strange the things that shouldn't be flashing through your head when at gunpoint.

"Oh—it's just you," the platoon leader said. "You should have alerted me via transmitter first. I could've shot you."

Laaru still couldn't see what Reise was aiming at. "Are you gonna put that away, or are you thinking about shooting me anyway?" Laaru asked the platoon leader. "Because Bricandor definitely knows where I am. And he's patient, but—"

"But everyone who pisses him off suddenly disappears, I know," the platoon leader smirked, holstering the pistol—aware, as Laaru was, that evoking Bricandor's name was basically an admission of Laaru's weakness. *My Daddy will get you!* Ugh. But this felt like an emergency.

Except—*everyone who pisses him off suddenly disappears? What?*

But Laaru didn't have time to sort out conspiracies, because just as he stepped forward, Reise fired.

Something on the other end of the valley exploded. As Reise reloaded, flame leapt from one abandoned polymerwall structure to the other as if the fort was made of paper. The platoon leader pointed to two dark tunnels in the far cavern wall that descended into the floor; fire blocked them now, and if there was anything in there, it'd die of smoke inhalation soon.

"They're mostly living in those two caves now." The PL sounded like he was explaining the biology of a terrarium. "We barricaded them into this valley pretty much as soon as we arrived. The only other way out is toward an awful wasteland near the surface, that way—ah, see, one's running that way now." The platoon leader whispered something into the control panel, and Reise's rifle swiveled toward—

Shyte, just a boy with a limp, no older than the little first years back at school.

"Whoa!" Laaru dove on the rifle and jerked it to the side. It burned his hands; the shot veered into the cavern wall, sending a shower of ice and rock down over the wasteland exit already weakened by intense fire. The boy jumped back, looked around for the shooter, then dashed toward "cover" near the cavern wall, hugging it as he ran back the way he'd come toward the main road. Fire leapt behind him and the wasteland exit closed with an echoing clatter.

"You idiot," the platoon leader muttered. He tried to line up the shot again; inspired by the pain in his fingers Laaru jumped up and—without thinking—thrust a "bear-strike" palm into the officer's chest.

The platoon leader's armor exploded with Laaru's Thought, splitting like a plate—fragments shot to the sides, around Laaru and Reise—the platoon leader fell backward, panting.

As he hit the wall of the nest Laaru snatched the control panel from him, took Reise's rifle, and stepped away from both combatants.

"That's 'you idiot, *sir*,'" Laaru corrected.

Then three things happened almost simultaneously. Laaru released Reise's hands to allow him to remove his gag; the dutiful platoon leader, unfazed, tapped the side of his visor-less helmet, about to warn the blitzers guarding the pass of the incoming free Frelsi; Reise, instead of removing his gag, swung his upper body toward the prone officer, grabbed a nearby shard of splintered armor, and stabbed him in the face.

The platoon leader just managed to get his hands up to save his eye; the shard sliced into his cheek. Reise smashed his helmet's transmitter mic with the other hand; the platoon leader kicked him and squirmed away, toward Laaru, just as Laaru's terrified fumbling managed to freeze Reise at attention.

"Holy …" Laaru breathed.

All three men did nothing for a moment. Just stared, chests heaving, not one trusting the others. Blood trickled down the platoon leader's face, harsh and dark against the white ground.

The *evil* in Reise's eyes—did evil exist? Laaru thought this was evil. He knew Reise hated his captor, but the animalistic frenzy—he'd never seen anything like that. Something had snapped.

"What did you do?" Laaru panted to the platoon leader. He almost couldn't speak above a frightened whisper. "What did you do to him?"

"I think he knows that guy," said the PL. "Am I allowed to go back to base and warn them the supply thief's coming their way, or are you both going to kill me here?"

Come to think of it, if they pushed the platoon leader off the crow's nest, Laaru would have one less social anxiety to worry about.

But he needed all hands on deck to finish the Structure in time. He said so, backed up until the passageway widened enough for people to pass him without getting near him, and waved the platoon leader ahead of him. Laaru sent Reise behind the PL to keep him honest, and then, rifle in hand—Laaru didn't want to get near this rabid version of Reise, even under full control—Laaru fell in at the rear and marched his two captives back to base.

CHAPTER FIVE

Jake

JAKE HAD ORIGINALLY BYPASSED THE BLITZERS GUARDING THE MAIN road to the Frelsi settlement by crawling into one of Lev's hidden "thief tunnels" blocked by boulders on both ends; for a while these little passages had been the settlement's only way to nick food and medicine for survival.

But now, as Jake fled back that way from the fire and the sniper, he heard voices almost as soon as he ducked into the thief tunnel. And when he crawled to the other end, he heard voices there, too. Voices that just … stayed there. It didn't matter what they were saying—it mattered that they were clearly speaking through the tinny, mechanistic speakers of blitzer helmets, and they weren't leaving.

"Hold steady," Nefesh said in his ear. She sounded so far away. So unafraid, so perfect. Meanwhile Jake was flaring his nostrils and squeezing his jaw shut to keep from breathing like an old-fuel generator as his chest heaved so hard he thought it might explode. He wasn't really thinking anything—he felt kind of far away himself—but as he looked down, he saw his hands trembling wildly.

Nefesh picked it up on the earpiece's camera. "That's just you crashing from the adrenaline. That's perfectly normal. It's not because you're scared necessarily."

Jake scrawled the affirmative.

"Lev told me one time he had to wait in one of the thief tunnels for almost a day before he could get out and come home to you," Nefesh added.

Jake remembered. He'd thought Lev had died hunting. He scrawled another affirmative.

"I can see the sniper on the video your camera caught," Nefesh said.

Jake hadn't seen. But he knew she meant Reise. He and Lev hadn't talked about it much, but he knew the Frelsi soldiers had tried again and again to get up to the sniper's roost to blow it up, block it off, or straight up kill his brother so they could come out for food without being Turned. Jake had overheard that much.

"He doesn't usually miss," Nefesh said. "I don't think he ever has."

Jake's trembling slowed a little. His auburn-brown knuckles were ashy from clenching the medpack so hard; he sat up—he had just enough room to sit cross-legged in here—and laid it down on the ground, leaning his head back against the wall. Somehow it was kind of cool that Reise had managed to miss him. Or maybe that was one of those Njandejara things.

"If you can't pull yourself up into the return tunnel, we'll need to get you something to stand on. I'd tell you to find a small stepladder, but from that conversation outside it sounds like they know things have been stolen by now. I think you'll have to break off a large rock in the crypt when you go back through there."

Jake scrawled the affirmative. He felt so numb. So numb and shaky. His whole body felt hot and cold. The air coming out of his nose was like fire. He'd thought people were exaggerating when they talked about adrenaline crashes after their first offensive. But oh, it was so real.

"You can't take the return tunnel by the supply closet to get back into the graveyard. They're definitely watching that. There's another hidden tunnel—pretty close to where you are—that comes out in the mine just below it."

Jake nodded, squeezing his eyes shut, face tilted toward the ceiling.

"I can't see you nodding. I'm just guessing here," Nefesh said.

He scrawled the affirmative. The voices had gone away. He hadn't heard footsteps leaving, though. Then again, he hadn't been listening. He scrawled the sign for danger, and the swipe for question.

"I heard three voices, and three separate cadences of steps, cadet," Nefesh answered.

So—they should be gone. Jake strapped the medpack to his chest and crawled to the boulder blocking the entrance. Gosh, he couldn't shake the feeling that someone was still watching out there. He squeezed his eyes shut again. *Njandejara, my new friend, you're going with me, right? To capture or death or whatever? I have had a very crazy day.*

But, Jake realized, not an altogether terrible one. He had the lactulose. That was half of saving Lev. And Reise probably knew that he was alive now. That meant something—proving to his older brother he could do things.

Jake laid his gloved palm on the freezing stone and pushed it just a bit. He waited—nothing. He pushed a bit more until he could just see out a crack in the side. Then, with a deep gulp of air, he crept out of the thief tunnel and sealed it back up behind him.

It was easy going finding the next tunnel and making his way to the mine. He was almost to the graveyard. Almost out of Growen territory. It should've been easy, this part. He even listened for a good minute before breaking out into the mine and taking a right toward the crypt. It was quiet, except for the buzzing of the ursa-fly nest below him.

But as Jake stepped into the mine—its floor glittering and littered with strange, purposeful piles of pink and brown crystals—he stepped on a sleeping Frelsi soldier.

Jake stumbled forward as the soldier cried out. There were several of them, lying there—gripes and butter-hats, they'd been put on their sleep cycle *here* rather than sent back to their cells. The moment they saw him—a *free* Frelsi—they squeezed their eyes shut, as if the Growen could see through them.

"Run, kid!" coughed the woman he'd stepped on. "Run!"

Jake's bad foot stumbled over the uneven ground as he fled. The straps holding the little med-crate to his chest decided now was a good moment to come undone, and Jake dropped the whole thing. He tripped over it—fell—

As Jake looked up, he saw the Turned rising to pursue him, their limbs jolting like puppetry. Most of them had their eyes closed; their shouts and pleas to him to *run, run!* made them *much* more disturbing as they lurched towards him. Jake gathered up his pack: one of the lactulose packets had fallen out, and his knuckles scraped against the floor in his hurry to snatch it—he resealed the small chest—and he ran again. The fastest Turned swiped at him, dirty fingers just missing his coat; a blitzer rounded the corner and fired on him just as he ducked into the crypt.

Step, slide, good leg, bad leg. Jake reached the honeycomb of tunnel entrances—grey light filtered through some of them, but as he passed doorways into complete darkness, impenetrable to light, his heart climbed back into his throat, certain something dead would leap out at him from one of those black holes at any minute. *We're fine! We're running!* Jake sped up, made it past the honeycomb—looked behind himself—reached the side of the drop-off to the sealed ursa-fly nest—

And ran up on what must have been two whole squads of blitzers.

They were blocking his path, too close to the wall before the drop-off. For a second, they didn't see him. If they'd only been five steps further back, he could've ducked into the forest of stalagmites on the side and waited for them to pass. But he was between them, his pursuers, a wall on the left, and the cliff down to the ursa-flies on the right. He had nowhere to turn.

Blitzers don't have a sound that can make them flee, but ursa-flies do.

Jake drew his pistol.

This is a terrible thing to do, but I have to save Lev.

The blitzers up ahead saw him.

Maybe they can't paralyze the Turned—the Turned already have something in their spines.

Jake fired into the abyss and hummed.

The ice cracked.

As the swarm sprung out like a geyser of rot and claws the blitzers in front of him jumped back and Jake dashed into the stalagmite forest and pressed his back against the wall, clutching the med-crate and his pistol and hissing the sound the creatures hated with all his might—

Two braver ursa-flies zipped over to investigate him, their proboscises twitching and huge compound eyes almost glowing in the dark as they reached curious paws past the stalagmite in front of him—but Jake hissed the sound and hissed the sound, frozen in place and stone digging into his back but throat vibrating like a broken air-rider as he stared them down, and they went away, following the rest of their horde.

The swarm streamed out into the graveyard, out into the mine, out into the valley, and gunfire and screams filtered back to Jake, almost inaudible under the horrendous buzzing. All light from the entrances was soon completely blocked out. Jake couldn't see the stalagmites or the ursa-flies any more than he could see his fingers clutching the pack of lactulose in front of him. He hated that—a monster, a dead person, anything could be right in front of him, leering at him, and he wouldn't know—but he kept making his sound, breathing as evenly as he could so he didn't have to pause it. He turned on the speaker on his wristband so Nefesh could make it too, and she did, covering his silences so nothing pounced at his throat when he inhaled. He heard slashing and slurping as some of the beasts stayed to liquefy and devour the discarded dead, but there wasn't room for all of them, and they poured out into the sapient world like trapped underworld spirits jealous of the living.

Jake didn't have control over his thoughts anymore—his brain seemed so far away, and he felt so numb. How had the flies become trapped, he wondered? Had the Growen construction caused a cave-in somewhere? Had the seasons changed on the surface so even they couldn't go out anymore? Was there something about the valleys they feared, or had they just never been able to get in? Many of the cavern networks didn't overlap: most of the Frelsi hadn't even encountered an ursa-fly, because no one ventured into the wasteland where Lev and Jake lived. Had something *else* once lived here to frighten them away—some other civilization, or some more terrible predator?

Jake was grateful for the numbness. He was going to make it back to Lev no matter what. He knew that now. He just hoped his split-second decision to flood the world with monsters didn't make him one himself.

CHAPTER SIX

Jaika-Lem Benzaran

MY STOMACH FLUTTERED AS WE APPROACHED BIJOU. IT WAS STILL just a small twinkling blip, but already much bigger than any other light around us—we'd be there in less than an hour at our current clip. And right now I wanted nothing more than a private room to hide in and maybe hyperventilate a little.

But Biouks don't really do privacy; in this bioship everyone could see everyone at all times unless you pulled the wall around you to deposit waste for the ship to eat. And after spending almost twenty-four hours trapped in the doppelgänger Shadow's polymerwall statue, I didn't really need to be in any small spaces for a while.

So I sat in the front, by the controls, leaning back on the right wall of the ship, and stared into space while everyone else milled around in the back. Cinta was organizing the passengers into their own squads, trying to figure out how many refugees we could transport from Bijou and how to ensure the safety of our civilians. Everyone was leaving me alone—everyone knew what I had to do.

That kind of made it worse. If I failed, I failed in front of everyone despite perfect conditions for my success. Jei, Jei should've been here for this kinda thing. He could've stood atop the bioship and crushed the blockade just by curling his fists. At the end, he was maybe the physically most dangerous electromagnetic across the known solar systems. My abilities, worth saving? Of course I knew it wasn't just for me that he'd taken the dive with Diebol—Diebol had gotten too strong, and with mind control on the table, Jei was a liability for the cause. The Growen would run every planet by now if he hadn't died. But I wanted so badly to trade places with someone who could actually do this.

"She's erratic at best, a traitor at worst." I remembered the curtains at the hearing—burgundy. I remembered the room—dark except for a light in front of me embedded in the obsidian-colored table, and lights in front of the witness seat, and the hearing officers. I remembered the intense desire in my chest to hide under the table so they would all stop looking at me. I was still just a couple months out from *basically dying,* so my whole body ached, my chest most of all, and despite my pretty epic recent win over Diebol, I felt so, so weak.

It was Lt. Seria's testimony that screwed me most. I'd stared her down the whole time. She couldn't make eye contact with me. She described my abilities in a level of detail I was surprised she knew, and then recounted the machine apocalypse at Fort Jehu that I wasn't around to stop. She'd figured out that I was the blitzer Jei'd pursued in the woods during the tank siege, and she accused me of leaking entrance codes to the Growen—because she and Jei were the ones that found my helmet, like I wanted them to when they tricked the Growen into bombing their own ground vehicles. I didn't lie: I did leak those passwords that day. So I could get to Diebol. So I could get to Sterba. So I could stop her from wiping us off every planet like she did with Skraeli and Burbura.

How do you explain that, though? How do you explain that Jei couldn't have escaped Mera without me? There were things Jei didn't want to reveal, and things I couldn't. He tried to testify for me. He was in deep shyte himself, and not allowed to attend in person—but his recording was my only relief after hours of listening to one acquaintance after another rant about what a horrible person I was. I was almost stunned at how many people I'd pissed off over the years. I almost cried when I heard his voice.

But Lt. Seria—Captain now, I guessed—had managed to get Jei's testimony dismissed by implying he was compromised both by my rescue after his capture and the irrational feelings that had him chase me down in the first place. He was being investigated himself, so how could anyone trust anything he said? I was dangerous and erratic, a zealot playing on the border of insanity, and he was irrational, emotional, and deceived. That was the story. He had a stellar record before that, and just before he chased me down, he'd destroyed a Growen transit center with his bare hands, so while they turned his life into an open-air prison, they at least wanted to keep him.

I wasn't valuable enough for that. Shyte, I narrowly escaped execution: the Frelsi only kill you if you've sexually assaulted someone or killed someone unprovoked, and Seria and a few others made the argument I'd killed with the codes. But my assigned advocate interrogated them about all the times I'd saved this or that Frelsi mission over the last year, and not even Seria could argue my whims hadn't rocked miracles. My unit physician, Dr. Patti Loylan, argued that I'd become ill. That this was my delayed mental breakdown after imprisonment and torture. That I just wasn't fit for this work, and since I was a little too erratic and dangerous to keep in a Frelsi refugee base, I should go away from any conflict zones to "heal."

She wasn't wrong. But even a sick mind can *know things*, and

I wasn't too broken to save the world—wasn't so broken they had to bury me.

Not even my assigned advocate believed in me at the end.

Sometimes I thought about what I'd do if I saw Seria again. The first six months after they exiled me to Beryllia I'd fantasized almost nonstop about smashing her face in. I was so much stronger than she was. Njandejara didn't like that, though. So I tried to fight it. Eventually I was too busy trying to stop Diebol to think much about idiots like her. But I still cared what she'd said, no matter how much I reminded myself she knew nothing.

"What happened to my bold sister, full of emunah, chutzpah, spark, with no care what the world thinks?" Cinta had asked me. *"Who would charge through a wall before she knew she could?"*

"She died."

Because ... the people who decided I wasn't worth keeping— I mean, they were experts over legions of soldiers, people who lived and died rescuing people. Mentors, leaders, heroes. They were the good guys.

And *they'd* decided I wasn't. So I wasn't.

After my exile I'd played with the idea of going back to the Growen. Of seeing if Diebol would have me, since I'd basically handed him the High Counsel, as he put it, on a silver platter. Maybe we could reform the Growen together.

But there was always the problem of Njandejara, and of Jei.

Now my family didn't know I was alive, and I really didn't think they cared. Like—they probably missed me some, but if anything, me being dead was probably a relief from the shame that fell on my parents after my hearing. I didn't think they'd put it that way, but they did believe at least half of Command's bull—they decided to "love me anyway." I didn't want to be loved "anyway." I didn't want anyone's pity or mercy. I wanted justice.

I felt like my brothers understood, though. They believed me, last time I'd called them. I'd pushed the little sister I adored mostly out of my head—it was too painful, after how close we were three years ago, when she decided I'd "abandoned" her by going to Beryllia for involuntary exile. *"Why couldn't you just move into the forest with Cinta, then, if you're kicked out? You left us!"* I couldn't make her understand that spaceship rides are one way if you don't have money or a freedom fighter network behind you. *"If it were me I would find ways to take civilian transport!"* she'd snapped.

Except I was also hiding from the Growen, who definitely did not want me in this universe.

No one wanted me in this universe.

And maybe that was why it had been so easy to believe that I would somehow be responsible for the apocalypse.

I sighed. Shyte, I was filked. I stared at the stars, but my eyes actually watched a future where I failed today and the bioship exploded, where everyone unlucky enough not to incinerate instantly found themselves frozen in space, bits of iced gut exploding out of them from the negative pressure—I watched Cinta float by, and Masha, and the reptilian passengers who were apparently now the last vestiges of their species. Shyte, if I messed up, it was basically like I'd completed their genocide.

I couldn't tell if my thoughts came from the Accuser or from myself, or from all those other people. They coalesced just below my lungs and hurt like someone had knocked the wind out of me, and I just could not get that wind back. Jei had wanted me around? He'd died for *this*? "What an idiot," I muttered under my breath.

I curled up into a ball, pressing my back against the warm bioship wall, and wished I could go to sleep, and not wake up. I wanted to punch myself for thinking that—I'd come all this way to get here, and what, I was going to whine and choke at the finish line? Weak.

"'Ey—uh, lass, can I tell you something?"

I sat up. Lark Scrita crouched down by my side. "What's up?" I asked.

"I heard about what happened at Fort Tapiz, you know," she said. "And Retrack City."

In both cities the "blue juice" had super-powered my innate electric field to become that crazy EMP shield. "Yeah?"

"So I know you can punch a lovely old hole in that blockade just fine, lass," she said. "And Cinta says you'll charge up before we get there so we can turn tail if there's a problem or what-not. But—eh, this may be the wrong thing to say—" She paused and scratched her matted hair. "Look even if you don't, or can't, and we all go belly-up to stardust, every single person on this ship would be dead already if you hadn't butted in to their rescue some way this week. So even if you've just bought us another day, another few hours—well, that's more than most of the galaxy's done for us right now, innit?"

I blinked, staring at her. "I wish there was somewhere habitable on the way we could put you all off instead of flying you into danger. I wish we had more time."

She bopped me on the forehead. "You not listening, lass? Our collective time already ran out. What with K'arl, and the Pit-God, and the Growen, and the Aliash I guess, and apparently you lot had a run-in with some nutter Biouks on Forge—well. We're already all meant to be dead, we are; you've already bought us more time than we were meant to have. You've done more than your bit, whatever 'appens here."

The hard knot at the base of my lungs softened a little. I looked away from her earnest, crescent-moon eyes down to my long fingers. I still felt like shyte, but the logic of her words helped. "Hadn't thought of it like that," I grunted.

"'Course you hadn't. That's why I'm here, lass." She slapped my shoulder and stood up. "Have fun."

"Thanks."

She backed up; Cinta trotted over to the controls with a nod in my direction. I picked my space-capable uniform off the floor and zipped halfway up.

"It is time, Jaika," Cinta said.

I took Jei's transmitter off my neck and handed it to Cinta to drop into his Faraday pouch. No electronics, where I was going.

His soft little clawless paws closed under my naked fingers.

Then I snapped open the canister on my belt and emptied it into my palm.

My world turned violent azure and electric sapphire as I closed my suit, gloved up, snapped my hood shut, and turned the mechanical valve on my oxygen supply.

"See you on the other side," I said. My hood hardened, and I punched the ceiling. It slurped me up into it, sealing airtight around and behind me like my own temporary decontamination chamber; I clawed my way through the thickness and felt a blast of cold on my face and chest as I emerged into space with a splatter.

I tapped the bioship's roof before even trying to stand—it wound tendrils around my legs, affixing me in place as the edges of my visible static field spread like an orb around us with the invisible EMP blast behind it—I enveloped the ship, sparking out to double, triple our size—

"I don't know how it's possible for the magnitude of power either you or I generate to exist in one organism," he'd said.

"Bigger," I muttered. "This needs to be bigger." My EMP needed to reach the blockade well ahead of our ship. "More!" It shot out into the distance until I almost couldn't see its edge. A weight lifted off me; whatever inhibitory neurons keep me normal most of the time were completely asleep with my blue serum.

"You seem to have something built up inside you, like when you carry something to the top of a hill, and it's just itching to roll down."

To shrink the field, I had to transform or fire off energy. To make it grow, I just had to *inhale*—to build, and build, and let the pressure expand in my chest—

"Potential energy driven by entropy I think, is your thing."

I gathered my entropy. I raised my left hand, and my Sterba appeared; I raised my right, and summoned the vicious little black and brown Biouk with the torn ear. I cried out, and Diebol's shadow flitted in the periphery of my vision. I took the mess I am, the fear, the grief, the paradoxical ecstasy and bitter resistance to shame, and instead of trying to fight or erase or justify them—I could always do that later—I sat with them, no thoughts, no judgment, and let them breathe. Feeling everything I suddenly felt nothing, like a yoke had shattered on my shoulders. Out here in space, control wasn't needed anymore, responsibility disappeared, and there was no Bricandor, no laser, no trial, no passengers who needed protecting—only the feeling and the sky.

"If it's true that you have something to do with the thermodynamics of entropy—heat death—then maybe anisotropy matters to you like EEG signals matter to me. After all, heat death is essentially just the perfectly isotropic arrangement of all matter in the universe."

Bring all photons into the same energy state—a laser—to power down. Gather energy in wild, diverse states to power up. I breathed, and let my heart ache, and let the piercing pain from the canyon on Forge return, along with all the conflicting feelings about Jared who was called Diebol, and all the enraged, stilted compassion that'd become my sense of justice, and the euphoria of connecting with Sterba before she died, and the guilt and longing for my family, and the loneliness and abandonment of my people, and the warmth of nearness with Cinta and Masha, and—

Sometimes what we call chaos is nature's most ordered state.

A guided missile approached. Guided by electronics. Its cap fizzled; it veered around my field. Its family followed. Each one lost its tracking system as I concentrated bursts of static, plumes blooming at the edge of my orb, to push them away. Some exploded, some floated, some continued on their journey into nowhere. We plunged through the hailstorm like a land-shark parting earth, an ichthian parting water, and as we approached the blockade, darkness rippled out from us: the lights on the ships were extinguished and, uniform with the coldness of space, their heat was dead.

CHAPTER SEVEN

Reise

Sweat soaked the inner garments of Reise's cold-weather uniform, cooling into an unpleasant sticky moistness as he, Laaru, and the PL marched along the road from the settlement back to the Growen camp.

But Reise's shivering wasn't from cold. He'd never had so much adrenaline left over after action before. His eyes seemed clearer. His whole body wanted to pounce on something.

Laaru was ordered to Major Fpokmmud's office almost the moment the wayward trio passed the two boulders at the entrance to the camp. The PL flagged down the first sentry to send soldiers after Jake; Laaru scrambled to keep a grip on the rifle and the control panel while *also* pressing the voice button on the side of his softened space-ready hood.

"I'll be there in a bit," he told the logistics lead over his transmitter. "I have to take the PL to medical treatment."

"No, you'll report now!"

"He's bleeding from his face."

"You're a consultant, not a commanding officer. Bricandor notwithstanding, by regs you still fall under my chain of command. You will report now."

"He's bleeding though?"

Reise would've found it humorous if he wasn't still heated from attacking the platoon leader who'd dared to aim him at his brother. As his heaving chest slowed its fiery bellows, however, Reise begrudgingly admitted Laaru had managed to handle the situation at the crow's nest with exceptional strategic … savvy.

The ever-present buzz in Reise's fingers and arms ceased; his feet continued their Turned march behind the PL, soft boots crick-crunching across the frozen ground. "You can take off the dumb gag now," Laaru said.

Reise was too far away from the PL to try anything else murderous. He did reach out a glove to check—Laaru shook his head. All right then.

Reise untied his gag with a small nod, acknowledging Laaru's problem-solving. *Creativity consistent with his values there.* With his mouth now free, Reise's upper body snapped back into a straight-backed perfect military march; Laaru set him on the program to carry a weapon and laid the rifle back in his obedient arms.

Laaru didn't want the weapon. Obviously. Laaru wanted both hands gripping the control panel. His sleep-deprived round eyes darted from around him as if any and every icicle might steal it again. Angry red smears crossed his palms—mild first-degree burns from grabbing the rifle as it fired—but he seemed too hopped up to notice.

"You haven't seen them kill kids before," Reise noted.

"I didn't believe you," Laaru admitted. "Let's turn here for medical."

"It's not a bad cut," the PL argued over his shoulder. The cloth dressing he held against his face was soaked with crimson, and his fingers stained. Not a bad cut? Reise had felt the shard of armor hit bone. The mini med-kits tucked into every soldiers' uniform almost didn't have enough dressing to stop this bleed.

But the PL's voice remained as even and professional as ever, still full of that cold *"this is for your own good"* compassion. "I'm fine," he insisted. "I'll take myself to medical after I talk with Major Fpokmmud. With you. About you."

"You do that," Laaru snapped. "I'm sure he'll want to discipline you for trying to kill an injured kid instead of Turning or capturing him."

"You'll never get it, will you?" the PL laughed. "A quick cartridge to the head would've been kind. Now the kid starves to death over time and we lose supplies. Your way, he'd be locked up with dangerous adults who'd do who-knows-what to him, and we'd lose an extremely expensive dart on someone who's not productive. Do you know how much life-saving equipment we can buy for the cost of one dart?" The PL shook his head as they reached the hive of bright ice caves that made up the barracks and offices. "You've never had to make the call between supplies for the mission and supplies to keep soldiers alive. In the old days before the freedom-darts went into production, ordering *any* extra shipment came with added risk to your men from constant Frelsi ambushes. Things have calmed down now, but these logistics are still much more complex than you're making them. You're dangerous because you don't know what you don't know."

Reise almost couldn't let the man finish before he opened his mouth to argue—so many flaws in his Reason came from incorrect presuppositions about value when calculating the worth of a life. But they'd reached the polymerwall draped over the entrance to Major Fpokmmud's cave, and there was no point: the platoon leader ignored Reise's existence, clapping three times to announce their presence.

"You're done," he mouthed to Laaru as the logistics lead called them inside.

"Reporting, sir." Inside Reise and the PL jumped to attention and saluted, each raising the outer blade of his right hand toward the major, elbow bent.

Laaru's salute followed more slowly as his other hand hugged the control panel against his body; Major Fpokmmud frowned. He held them all there for a few seconds instead of returning the salute, looking Laaru up and down as if cataloging his deficiencies.

Out of habit Reise's gaze scanned the frivolous self-aggrandizing ornamentation of the officer's chambers for exploitable weakness. No alterations since his last visit, apparently. Three blitzers with glowing badges on their chests stood like decorative statues in small alcoves along the back wall. The silver floating bed was tucked away, flipped to be the floating desk—*why the hell would any furniture need to float*—adorned with an expensive metallic representation of the solar system. Beside the solar system, a small hollow plaque held luminous badges of all colors commemorating the logistics lead's service.

Major Fpokmmud ran his finger absently across the plaque now before putting down his holopen to return the salute. "Thank you both for your prompt attendance," he said, nodding at the PL. "You can be dismissed to medical."

"I have something to report, sir," the PL said.

"Stand fast, then. But first"—the logistics lead turned to Laaru—"where were you during the officer mess tonight?"

Laaru blinked in confusion. Reise laughed out loud. "Are you his *mother*? 'Oh no, he missed dinner!'" Reise spat. "He was busy constructing your enormous priapic folly, you tumescent numbskull. During your dinner party he was most likely snatching an hour of rest to maintain the functioning of his mind."

"Where's this one's gag?" Major Fpokmmud asked.

"I've disposed of it," Laaru lied.

"Well then." The logistics lead sighed, averting his eyes from Reise as if hoping that would make him disappear. "Laaru, you've failed to listen to anything we've tried to teach you," he said. "Your discipline's nonexistent. I've had multiple soldiers report you running like a wild person through the camp, hair unkempt, not returning a single salute. One of the mine workers found your sleeping system thrown around the geological office and shelves out of place. And now you're skipping mandatory officer wellness."

"Wait, *what*?" Laaru blurted, all pretense of decorum dead. "We're finishing a project that could change three solar systems *tonight*. We've got teams literally made up of people who want to kill each other, with zombies working for us against their will. We've got starving Frelsi supply thieves, and soldiers aiming weapons at children. We have so much more important stuff going on, and you're on me about—not making my *bed*?"

"You're in trouble for missing the wellness meeting to do your wellness, Laaru," Reise smirked.

Major Fpokmmud's stern voice lowered in pitch and raised in volume. "Young man, discipline is the foundation of readiness—"

"Permission to speak, sir?" the PL asked.

"One moment! Stygge, this is not a discussion," the logistics lead thundered. "You will attend mandatory meetings. You will correct your bearing. And I think it's time you turned over the control panel."

Laaru shook his head, actually taking a step back now. "We're making faster progress since I've taken over. And I can't trust your section leads not to take their exhaustion out on the Tur—the converts."

"The individual workstation leaders know best what to do with their workforce," Major Fpokmmud said.

"I'm not interrupting any of the relays," Laaru protested. "I'm literally just making sure no one hurts anyone."

"Sometimes discipline is necessary to teach uniformity. It's not out of malice," the logistics lead said, nodding to two of the blitzers in the back.

Reise's gut clenched as they approached.

"All of our recruits undergo brutal training so they can

survive brutal wars, young man," Major Fpokmmud went on. One blitzer began to roll up Reise's sleeve. "Do you think the Frelsi anarchists and zealots would treat you any differently on the battlefield?"

"I'm on a noncombat contract," Laaru squeaked, suddenly even more pale than normal. He looked like he wanted to pretend he didn't have guesses about the blitzers' intentions.

Reise didn't need to guess.

"So we teach the Frelsi with the language they understand, just as we teach each other," the logistics lead said. "Physically punishing a disobedient recruit is just a more rapid form of memory enhancement." One blitzer opened his personal med-kit to take out a small medbot, while another rubbed disinfecting alcohol on Reise's left forearm. "Even the Contaminated have texts about physical retribution for physical crimes."

Laaru's knuckles trembled.

"And some people cannot be taught," Major Fpokmmud said. "Some individuals best serve the community by returning their matter to the universe, so it can continue to care for the rest of us." The blitzers overrode the medbot's automated setting for a manual one: cautery. The little white orb lit up. "It's no more cruel than when a parent euthanizes a child. You've studied on Beryllia. You're familiar with that form of household planning."

The logistics lead leaned forward across his desk, his deep-set eyes locked on Laaru as if they could pierce his mind. "Everyone believes that some people shouldn't exist. All political debate is just settling the question of who those people are, how we make them disappear, and at what stage in their lifespan we do it."

"I'm going to report you to Bricandor," Laaru croaked.

"Go ahead," Major Fpokmmud smiled. "You're a bit too special to teach via physical retribution. But you can be trained psychologically." One of the blitzers took Reise's rifle out of his hands; the other activated the medbot. The little white egg sprouted legs and clung to Reise's arm like an elegant, fat spider. *Awaiting manual command* glowed in green letters on its back.

Reise wanted to beg Laaru to turn off the control panel so he could fight back—but what would that do? He fixed his glare on the logistics lead and visualized force-feeding him his light-emitting badges, snapping his desk solar system in half and forcing it with a bloody crunch into his eyes—

The blitzers activated the medbot, and it began to sear a line into Reise's skin. He focused all of his hatred on silence, clenching his teeth until his jaw ached and his stomach roiled with effort. His arm screamed, but he did not.

Laaru's cry began with a stammer. "Stop—stop it or I'll set him loose!"

Shrieking arm, skin roasting—

"You don't see the pistol pointed at him from across the room?" Major Fpokmmud raised a humoring eyebrow. "Loose or not this is happening. Unlike you, he's a soldier. He understands."

I am burning his eyebrows off his face—all the agony of his arm, focused on that brutish round forehead—Reise's breath rushed through his flaring nostrils faster, faster—

"What do you want from me?!" Laaru begged.

"Compliance, and the control panel. You fall in like the other officers and you toe the line."

Now Reise spoke—with effort, as if he needed a crowbar to pry open his teeth. "Keep the panel," he growled. "Better you than them." He wheezed a deep breath, chest tightened to hold. In. The. Scream—shyte, the burning cut stretched almost to the back of his wrist now. "You have powers, kill him," Reise hissed.

"Maybe we should try his tongue next," the logistics lead wondered.

That was it. "What the filk is with you people and mouths?" Laaru screamed. "Here, take the panel!"

But Reise saw Laaru's hand brush over the controls as he dashed over to the desk, and Reise felt his whole body go free.

CHAPTER EIGHT

Laaru

LAARU'S HEART WAS SKIPPING SO FAST HE WONDERED IF IT WAS beating at all. Growen, Frelsi, right, wrong, he couldn't think. He only wanted the smell of burning human flesh to *stop*. He raced to the desk, and as he laid the control panel on it, his other palm reached for the mineral-rich surface of the table—

"Don't let him touch that!" A sharp twinge shot through Laaru's elbow, and before he knew what had happened his cheek pressed against cool faux-rock and his hands were twisted behind his back: the PL had rushed Laaru almost before he approached the table. "Sir, we still need the sniper intact for other missions, if they can please turn that off?" the PL asked. "And there's an additional security risk you should know about. The Stygge intentionally caused the sniper to miss today when ..."

The PL stopped talking suddenly. Everyone did. Everyone heard it: a loud, buzzing roar outside over gunfire and scattered screams.

"We're under attack. Mobilize," Major Fpokmmud said, jumping to his feet and drawing his pistol. "Lock the Stygge in here—he'll be safer—and bring the sniper. You, check with comms—why haven't they sent out an alarm?"

Laaru looked over at the holopen in front of his face on the desk; everyone else checked their wrists and helmets. Everything glowed pale yellow with the "no signal" sign.

"Something's destroyed the tower ship," the platoon leader realized. "Something's broken through the blockade."

Bent over the desk, Laaru couldn't see what happened next behind him—but in his line of sight the blitzer holding Reise at distant gunpoint looked down for just a second to check his transmitter.

Distraction was death. A grunt, a squelch, and a scream followed—a firearm went off, and when the PL released Laaru to reach for the control panel, Laaru glimpsed Reise shoving the medbot's hot needle into someone's throat. That person became a shield as Major Fpokmmud and his nearest blitzer switched their ammo to stun cartridges and fired at the rogue Turned. The second blitzer by Reise's side couldn't get his weapon out of his holster—Reise had already taken it to shoot him in the neck.

Laaru and the platoon leader both snatched the control panel. "Let go!" Laaru cried. "I want him shut off as much as you do!" They tumbled onto the ground, both trying not to break the device while peeling the other's fingers off of it. In all the rustling of fabric and weight and heat, still Laaru blocked his Thought, and the PL didn't draw the pistol hanging on his hip by Laaru's face. There was hope here—*he doesn't want to hurt me, maybe he could listen, please*—"You know I'm right!" Laaru wheezed with the PL's knee on his stomach. "I can't trust you with it anymore!"

Then a foul-smelling inky blur smashed through the unlocked polymerwall.

Reise screamed and threw himself on the floor under his dead human shield. The blur darted first to the blitzer firing on

Reise—the blitzer clutched the back of his neck and collapsed like a bag of groceries. The blur shot across the table toward Laaru and the platoon leader. They untangled from each other— Laaru kept the control panel, the PL drew his pistol—Laaru saw huge eyes and a long needle-nose—

A weapon fired; the blur whirled on the logistics lead who held the smoking gun. A torn wing fluttered from its hulking bristled back, but it had more. Two hairy paws with claws like steel knives slashed the logistician's chest as he fired again. The platoon leader raced to his master's aid, emptying a clip and reloading. Weapons flashed again and again—the beast's buzzing intensified—blood splashed on the wall as Major Fpok-mmud roared for the glory of the Unification—

And man and beast fell still.

Laaru was standing. He didn't know when he'd gotten up. His dizzy brain had about reached its limit on its two hours of sleep. He heard the platoon leader yelling at him, reaching for him. Laaru turned—

To see the platoon leader clutch his chest and drop his gun. The seared pink of an oxidizer cartridge hole glowed under his fingers. "You're such a fool, Laaru," he scowled.

And with that, he fell to the floor dead.

"You're the fool who lowered your weapon." Reise smiled from under the dead blitzer, where he lay on his belly with both hands clutching a freshly discharged pistol. "*Sir.*"

Laaru sliced his fingers across the quick-freeze button to lock Reise in place. "What the hell!" he shouted. "He's the only person in the room who didn't want to kill you!"

"But I wanted to kill him," Reise said.

"He wasn't a threat to you!"

"Neither were most of the people he had me shoot."

Laaru ran over and took the pistol out of Reise's hands. Between the giant—bug-mammal—with arms like a mutated

Bichank—sprawled on top of the logistics leader as his dead, blood-splattered face scowled to the ceiling—and the platoon leader's dead scorn staring up at Laaru from the floor where he'd crumbled—and these other dead people everywhere, so dead—wow, he *was* a fool.

"I wanted the least number of people to get hurt," he murmured. "Maybe one or two people have to die sometimes so others can live, but—" Laaru looked at Reise with realization. "It's you. If *you'd* died, the least number of people would've been hurt."

"I suppose you're in a position to make that happen to me now." Reise glared at the control panel. "But you'd better figure out what the filk is happening out there first."

Laaru collapsed to a cross-legged seat on the floor next to the frozen Frelsi and looked at his cameras.

Those—things—were everywhere, a giant cloud spilling into the air and dashing from person to person like buzzing bullets. Cameras blinked out as Turned people—died? Stopped seeing? —and the control panel's view switched to other heads; proboscises and mirrored eyes and leathery, bristly skin flashed in and out of view. Blitzers ducked behind cover, firing in scattered squads; it looked like some units had rigged up old-fashioned radio, but it was all chaos without the communication satellite.

Reise's hard stained-oak face softened and paled. "Shyte, you don't have the Frelsi on a unified fighting program. The workstation relays only have commands for basic defense—you have to let us all go!"

"Let—I can't do that!" Laaru gasped. "You'll all kill people!"

"More people than the ursa-flies are killing?!"

"No—no, there's another way," Laaru stammered. "I'll—" He had read the manual. He could send—squads—here and—

"Laaru, let us go!" Reise roared. "You're not a combat strategist, you can't coordinate our attacks! We can't defend ourselves if you don't release us!"

"It'll be chaos." Laaru's throat was so dry. Another camera blinked out and reloaded. In one camera an unarmored blitzer was torn to pieces by four bugs. Huge eyes rushed at another camera. It blinked and reloaded.

Then, Reise said the magic words. "Laaru. This is the kindest thing."

Laaru shut off Bijou's mind control panel—and before he could do anything else, Reise grabbed the gun from him and destroyed it.

JAIKA-LEM

We'd busted through the blockade.

I climbed back inside the bioship before we breached atmosphere. The walls slurped me through, embracing me like swaddling cloth—I didn't power down, and I didn't talk to anyone. I still needed all of this potential energy built up to smash the Structure.

As I knelt to buckle myself in, the ship's spongy, tongue-like floor seemed to shrink away from me just a tad, and the wall trembled. "It's okay," I told it. "I'll be normal soon."

We escaped from the quaking rumble of re-entry into an open sky so pale it seemed almost white over a flat, frigid world that sparkled like clear gemstone. The thick, frozen rock below was so translucent you could see shapes moving underneath its thinner places—otherwise, layers of cerulean and Maya-blue faded under brighter and brighter shades of ivory and ghost as the thick depths plunged into indeterminable mystery. You couldn't quite tell what was hollow and what wasn't from up here.

"It's beautiful," my Sterba murmured.

"It's hideous and dead," sulked my torn-eared Biouk.

"Nefesh says we shall fly over Lev's cave now," said Cinta. "Soon we will see the entrance where the Growen ships fly into their base." He sounded so far away and warbly compared to the citizens of my electrical mind. I couldn't see him—I'd powered up too far for that. My mind was protecting my visual cortex from overload as I neared my unknown limit, like a computer browser choosing not to load unnecessary images so an intranet site would load faster.

As we swooped toward the surface, though, I did see a tiny figure below the ice, near the surface, running back the way we'd come. A triangle of life forms stretched behind it—was it leading them, or fleeing?

"Nefesh says that is Jake," Cinta said. "He is fine, she says, and will reach his safe haven soon."

"What's following him?"

"Chasing, not following. But he is able to handle it, she says. She says he has perhaps disrupted the entire Growen camp for us."

"Is that the base?"

A huge vent in the ground lay up ahead, approaching fast. Tiny fighter ships twinkled in the cold light as they streamed out from it, surrounded by a flowing cloud of something like—bees?

"What are those?"

"Nefesh calls them ursa-flies."

Some ships fired on the swarming mass; some crashed as blobs of swarm rushed them, driving them to the ground; others simply fled into space.

"Can you shrink your field, Jaika?" Cinta asked me.

"No," I said. "Why?"

He didn't answer.

"Because there might be Turned in those little fighters, and you'll make them all crash," hissed my little palette-swapped Cinta-me. "*Ratschica*. Everything's awful."

"It is unlikely that the fleeing Growen pilots have decided to bring their captives along," soothed my patchwork Sterba.

"Cowards," snarled my inner Biouk.

"Sacrifices made for the greater good," said she.

A burst of blotches turned and zoomed toward us, their vrooming buzz like a blood-sucker opening a concert for an engine. Compound eyes, long sharp snouts, two strange front paws, so many clear wings—maybe six? Some of the creatures veered away from my field with twitching wings, scratching themselves as if itchy or ticklish—others charged right through, aiming for our bioship with palpable hunger.

"Masha?" Cinta asked.

"I have it," Masha answered. I heard her rustling through the Faraday bag; her compupad turned on inside it with a ding, and she began to play a really irritating high-pitched squizzly sound from it at full volume.

"I hate that," I growled.

"So do they," said Masha.

"From the video footage Jake gave Nefesh," Cinta said. "The Growen have hidden the Structure in a valley beyond the entry cavern. The passage into the Structure's valley is low, and a ship cannot fly from the landing area into the construction site—this is most likely on purpose to prevent sabotage or accidents. You will have to get out and go through on the ground. I will try to get you close. The ground is too cold for the bioship to land for long—we will circle and look for your brothers. If we can steal space-ready armor without freezing their human skin Lark and the Shadow will join you."

"Shouldn't be hard with all the downed pilots, lad," Lark said. "Oop—there goes another one, there."

"Once you return, we will fly back for Jake and Lev, and leave," Cinta finished.

"Roger," I said.

Our stomachs tilted and twisted as Cinta maneuvered through the congested air; ships and creatures parted before us like the waters of a stream around a rock.

Then our front window dove into darkness—we were blinded for a moment by fleeing flies—and we finally broke into the Bijou Growen camp.

CHAPTER NINE

Gideon

Gideon wanted to make a beeline for the kitchen to protect Nate the moment the insect apocalypse took off. But it happened on the lift, on the way down to the mine: he was sharing the rickety hand-pulley elevator system with two other Turned and a relay-holding blitzer while the rest of their workstation team waited for them below. The second the ursa-flies poured out of the mine, the blitzer fumbled the relay and dropped it off the lift, so for about five minutes before the mind control cut out none of Gideon's group could do anything but stand at attention in the swarm, each at the mercy of the next fly's random decision: you, or the person next to you?

Gotta give the guy a tiny bit of credit, though. The grease-fingered blitzer emptied his rifle and two pistols protecting his Turned crew still stuck on the ground. He fired in rhythm like Reise would—breathe, fire, breathe, fire—picking off the beasts below one by one like it was a video game he'd practiced all night.

That was why Gideon didn't slide-kick him off the ledge when the mind control peaced out. Before anyone could fight anyone, he ripped the gag out of his bruised mouth and shouldered between his comrades and the blitzer. "Don't anyone freak out!" he shouted, sore hands by the blitzer's elbow to keep his weapon from swiveling toward them. "We can all kill each other later, but right now since we can all move, let's try to not die to bugs! I'll recharge your weapons, Sergeant. Jikky, my gal, can you man the lift so we can ferry people out? I figure those Turned forearms aren't just for show."

The swarm was so thick by the foot of the Structure that no one who wanted to live had time to argue. The blitzer's orb'd helmet hid his expressions, but the sweat on the man's wrists where gloves met uniform spoke pretty loudly: he was more scared of the bug-eyed winged things than the mostly unarmed and kinda malnourished prisoners. He continued pumping cartridges at the ursa-flies like an automated turret. Jikky—a big human woman from Nathan's homeworld—began cranking the lift down to the other Turned, who'd picked up mining gear to fight back against the swarm. Gideon's fingers picked their way across the recharging slides of weapon after weapon almost without thinking—*yank, prime the manual pump, fill the cartridge tank with oxidizer, it lights up*—each thrust transforming mechanical energy into the chemical reaction that filled the cartridges with burning explosive.

The horde thinned out some as it spread out into the valley. With electric picks, laser cutters, rock blasters, and other nasty mining equipment in hand the lift and the area under it was actually pretty defensible if you kept your back to the cliffside and your head down. Several of the Turned that'd been stung in the neck got back up—the bugs punched the mind-darts instead of their spines, maybe? It was the claws you had to worry about.

But the firearms were eventually going to run out of redox tubing for the cartridges. You could prime the chem reaction all day even without a charging station if you had to, but once you ran out of substrate and bullets to fill, well. After that, the guns would just spit hot burning fluid—something for last ditch survival, not long-range wins.

And Gideon didn't have all day.

Nathan. Nathan's got the mind-control cure.

Several Frelsi opted not to go out into the unprotected open above the mine shaft—better to hole up where they could survive. Others made breaks for freedom and ships—forget underground monster-bugs, they were ready to battle blitzers. So after the second or third elevator ride it wasn't hard for Gideon to hand the next weapon to someone else to charge and slip off the elevator.

"I've gotta find my squad leader," he said with a salute.

It was chaos above ground. Wings droned behind Gideon; he threw himself on his stomach and a stench like rotten Smung-wurm sailed over him. The distracted shadow flitted to its next target. Gideon crawled to a paralyzed Growen officer, yanked his pistol out of his holster, and wished the ground under him wasn't so filking cold.

The above-ground crews had been crazy unlucky. Dead or paralyzed bodies littered the open field. Ursa-flies swooped, and gunfire sprayed in all directions. The kitchen was just through that distant arch, outside the construction site for the Structure. Gideon could see it from here—polymerwall cube leaned up against a cavern wall.

There was just a long stretch of *no cover* between here and there.

Gideon crawled. Then dashed behind a body. Then crawled to another. Then fired to get a fly off some girl. Then rolled under another body as the enraged fly whirled on him.

He almost wanted to stay hidden there, under this reassuring pressure, the dead person's long hair draped like a curtain over his view as he kept his head perfectly still under hers. He breathed hard to psych himself up for the next dash. Shyte, it was insane out there. This was all insane. If you thought about it too much you might—

A heavy weight *thunked* on top of the carcass on him. Blood from it sprayed onto the rock beside him, wet on his wrists, splashing his uniform. Holy shyte. One of the bugs was feeding. Claws mashed the corpse. Through the hair he saw a proboscis lower right in front of his face. It withdrew its sharp tip; a dripping ribbed straw extended instead. The proboscis raised out of sight again—he felt the jolt of the impact as it stabbed into the body above him—*filk, the slurping sound.*

Gideon eased his hand to the side, just—didn't want to get claws in his wrist, just—aim the pistol—

He fired. The ursa-fly jumped back with an enraged hum; Gideon shoved himself to his feet, holding his dead rescuer out in front of him like a shield. Wow she was heavier than she looked. Wow, yeah, this was why he'd worked out so much, sure. He fired past her on the fly again. He hit its gut again. It threw itself at him—at her—flailing its claws into her ribs—

"Get out of my way!" he roared, pushing back. "I've got somewhere to be, bro!"

A *thwick*—Gideon and the fly both looked right. Then the fly didn't look anywhere anymore. Reise was standing across the field, against the right cavern wall with the little Stygge tucked behind him and his rifle in both hands. The ursa-fly fluttered a little, then plopped to the ground with a hole through its eye.

Gideon didn't have Reise's sniper eyes, but he could see Reise mouth *where's Nathan?* Gideon pointed his gun toward the kitchen and the hangar bay. "Obviously!" Where everyone else was going. Through the archway, where Frelsi and Growen soldiers scrapped over escape vehicles.

Reise shook his head.

Filking hell, that meant Nate was in the cages.

"Will you dance with me a little longer, ma'am?" Gideon asked, plowing forward across the field with his new "friend's" body. Her head flopped on her neck. "I'll take that as a yes! Sorry I'm not exactly dressed to the nines. I won't assume you want me, if that helps."

Gideon, stop! Nathan would've snapped.

With Reise covering him Gideon made it to his side. "Kitchen's empty!" Reise shouted over the din.

"Cages, then!" Gideon answered. *Through the arch to the parking area, then take the side tunnel …*

"Who's this?" Reise yelled, taking the front. The dead Turned soldier still dangled by her uniform collar in Gideon's grip.

"I'm gonna call her Julie, and get a super-great plaque put up in memory of her when I get home," Gideon yelled back, stepping behind the Stygge to take the back. He swiveled so "Julie" could protect everyone's rear as they hugged the wall along the edge of the cavern. "Julie, say hi!"

"Hi Julie!" Reise cleared another ursa-fly out of their path.

"She's been dying to meet you!" Gideon said.

"What is wrong with you people?" the Stygge screamed.

"We grew up hunted by you people and then spent a year without being able to decide when we piss!" Gideon shouted back. He'd take flak from Nate, but not this guy. If he didn't crack irreverent nonsense right now his brain would definitely break and end him screaming in the middle of the field like that guy over there. "Forgive the darkness of serf humor, me-lord!"

"'Julie' wears a Frelsi uniform, Laaru," Reise snapped, somehow still managing to fit in a lecture to the Stygge while sniping monsters. "We all prefer to save our comrades in death if we can. You can only hope to have such a noble purpose as hers!"

"So you're just going to keep carrying her like a shield?!" the Stygge cried.

Three ursa-flies suddenly dive-bombed them at once. Reise had time to shoot two. The third reached the Stygge, claws just grazing his arm—before Gideon body-slammed it full force with

"Julie." The ursa-fly fell back, stunned, and he fired at its eye. This time he got the kill.

"Would you still like Julie to leave?" Gideon asked him. "I'm sure she'd oblige!"

"No—no she's fine," the Stygge squeaked.

"Say thank you to Julie for saving your life!"

"Thank you—Julie?"

Gideon grinned, despite himself. The Stygge's voice gained some confidence as they reached the arch. "You came from the mine," he called. "Is our Structure okay?"

"Glad you asked!" Gideon shot back. "My bone structure's definitely been better, you know, before it got smashed a lot by your buddies. Julie thinks it's still pretty great, though, don't you Julie? As a friend, of course. She says *your* bone structure on the other hand could use some work, guy. Not even as a friend." He relished the Stygge's frustrated panic as they rounded the corner into and through the arch. "Oh, did you mean *that* Structure, back there? I guess I forgot to check on my favoritest forced labor project when it started belching rib-cracking neck-stabbers."

Gideon wasn't going for quality laughs. Just mental survival. And his brain thanked him for it, because suddenly as the trio made it out into the lot where the spaceships parked they were met with a crackling blue electric forcefield—and in its center marched a girl with glowing blue eyes, black hair frizzing around her head like an electric storm, and four neodymium maces.

CHAPTER TEN

Jaika-Lem Benzaran

My brother saw me before I saw him.

I was kinda hard to miss, not gonna lie. The moment I'd jumped out the bioship I fried six oblong Maggot fighters and, from the sound of it, a whole bunch of electrically-charged flayer rifles stopped working. Despite what I'd said to Cinta on the bioship, I was doing my absolute best to try to hold my field closer to me without leaking energy I'd need for the Structure. It felt like I was crushing my stomach, but I didn't want everyone's weapons to stop working while stinking hairballs with eyes attacked them. I didn't want to down everyone's ships, either. I just wanted to kill the Structure, get my brothers, and go home.

"You don't have a home, remember?" Diebol whispered in my ear.

I almost jumped. "Filking—stop it, Jared. Help me with these guys." The distorted ultraviolet of his mace disoriented the flies; they flitted in dizzy circles around me, dashing away each time I successfully managed to mimic that annoying sound they hated. Diebol's and Mera's maces became my stabbing missiles flung and retrieved with static charge; Sterba's mace, and mine, spun in my hands—

And Jei's hung from my hip beside the compacted and sheathed lightning rod I'd brought in case anyone tried to power me down by hitting my nervous system with an outside shock. But I didn't need to draw the rod. No one could shoot me once my EMP field crossed their weapon. A few blitzers managed to switch their electronic firing mechanisms to the slower manual back-up—

"Stupid people," spat my little torn-ear imp. "Looks like their manual setting is shyte with modern ammunition. What, they hoping someone's carrying gunpowder and metal?"

"They're only saving their shots, little one, because they mustn't waste cartridges," said Sterba. "They cannot recharge with blown electronics."

"Sounds like us being here makes it easier for the bugs, then," smirked my angry Biouk.

That's not true!

"You carry death in your wake," Sterba said to me.

I'm so sorry. The faster I could get to the Structure and get this over with, the better. My maces sliced wings and severed paws as I passed; as the flies leapt person to person, I leapt fly to fly, always toward the archway, always toward the Structure.

I was jumping on the head of a fly, yanking the staff end of Sterba's mace out of its brain, my boot pushing off against it to leap toward another bug, when I looked left. For a split second, as my brain treated him like a threat, I saw Reise, sniper rifle aimed—

Over my shoulder. I smiled, and he blinked out of existence.

He was alive. And the fly behind me wasn't anymore.

I landed near him, sheltered by the arch for a moment. My heart almost broke from longing: I wanted to find him, to grab him, but I couldn't see him. I pointed at Cinta's ship touching down on a ledge above. "Get there!" I shouted. "Let's go home!"

"Jake's alive!" his voice yelled back.

"I know! We're picking him up on the way out!"

"Wait—" I recognized Gideon's voice. "Reise, close his ears, will you?" Reise apparently obeyed as a softer voice I only half-recognized protested. *Who* ... "Ma'am," Gideon pleaded, apparently not recognizing me; anything near my face was a threat, and I saw him briefly as he spoke as close to my ear as he could get. "Please don't leave without a guy called Nathan Peter on board. We have a cure for the mind control."

"We do?" Reise was as shocked as I was.

A *cure*?

I looked through the archway to the translucent metallic trunk of the Structure, and then back over my shoulder to the bioship. It had just finished another loop and set down on the ledge again. Any heavy artillery that could've hit it had fried when I landed, but Cinta was keeping it out of reach anyway. It was ... kinda far for someone carrying sensitive information who smelled like blood. Should I escort them—?

My stomach squealed at me; I clenched my teeth. No. I needed to get to the Structure.

"Can you handle it?" I asked Reise.

"Aye aye."

"See you at the ship, then. Make this noise to keep the flies away!" I produced it, gave him a very unmilitary two-fingered half salute—the most happiness I could show right now—and stepped off to pass the archway. I heard a scuffle as Reise released his—captive, or whatever, and footsteps followed after me.

"Wait, where are you going?" asked the third voice.

"To save the universe," I said over my shoulder.

Reise and Gideon both shouted something I couldn't hear— they were already moving in the other direction, and I was already on my way, and a huge ursa-fly zoomed between us, and there wasn't time for anything else. I turned to throw Mera's mace like a hammer through the head of the fly and heard the third voice again just before it caught up with me.

"Please, I'd rather not die," he pleaded. "But I have to go that way, too."

"This ain't a bodyguard mission, buddy," I said, still running along the wall with my eyes fixed ahead. "I've got to fix that mess over there." I pointed Sterba's mace at the Structure; three more ursa-flies dive-bombed me and took my other three maces to their faces.

"What mess?" And as I recognized his voice, Laaru appeared beside me.

Holy shyte, Laaru—my little human classmate from the mines of Beryllia. The guy Diebol said Bricandor had taken. To train.

Bricandor had tortured Jei and Diebol to train them. Poor Laaru—who knew what he'd gone through.

But why could I see him?

If he was a threat, Gideon and Reise obviously thought I could take care of it. It seemed like they'd been protecting his life. But the quick way they ditched him without making sure he was going to be okay with me—they clearly didn't like him that much.

"What the filk are you doing here, man?" I asked.

"I was put in charge of the Structure! Bricandor said the other Stygges wouldn't be needed, so I'm surprised but of course really glad you're here to help. It's been awful lately. Some of these guys have been beating up on or even torturing the Turned —I mean the converts—and I saw one try to kill a kid."

"Yeah, they do that," I said.

My Sterba scowled. "Was he not less irritatingly talkative, during your school time?" she asked.

"Nah, chill-out, witch," said the me-Biouk. "He's the same sweet stammering thing. Sucks what's happened to him."

It also sucked that this kid kept leaving his back exposed to bugs, even though we were running along a rock face, and I was having to do a helluva lot of spinning to protect my own tush already. There was a lot of screaming in this field; the ursa-flies seemed to be coming from a big hole around the Structure's root. I didn't know whether to be glad or pissed I couldn't see the injured Frelsi being devoured. *Just need to get this over with, then we can help everybody.*

"You're—not surprised," Laaru realized. "That the blitzers here do those awful things."

"Nope." I put Sterba away, keeping Diebol and Mera afloat over me.

"You're—not okay with it, too, are you?" he squeaked.

"Nope." I deactivated my mace and started gutting it for its neodymium crystal.

"Okay, good … so wait—wait, what are you here to do? If you already knew about the blitzer abuses, did Bricandor actually send you, or—"

I was close enough. I stopped, eyeing the spires and spindles for the shape's weakest point—it looked like it tapered a little in the midsection. That was where I'd hit.

"You're not here to help, are you," Laaru realized.

"Nope." I raised my hand, imagined a weight about to roll down a hill, and pushed it as hard as I could.

At the same time, Laaru punched the side of the cave and screamed.

I went flying with the force rippling from the exploding rock. My laser veered into the side of the cavern, across the valley, then up into the thick sloped ceiling as I fell, reflecting wildly off the mirrored rock above us. The entire cavern collapsed in front of me. Boulders and ice showered down around Laaru, each one missing him as I scrambled backward, cursing like a Vibrant pirate. There was something disturbing in the kid's eyes—a shame, a pleasure, a weariness, surrender? *What the filk has Bricandor done …* The ground shook. The thundering roar drowned out all the screams and gunfire. The cold gritty itch of ice shavings and smashed dust filled my nose. A frigid wind gushed in through the opened crack to the sky, even colder than the already unbearable chill of the hidden valley. Before the Structure completely disappeared from view, I could see the hole around it collapsing and filling in.

Oh no. My whole body trembled as my maces clattered down beside me. I could still get to it. Right? There had to be a way. It wasn't totally blocked off now by an entire mountain. Explosives —did this camp have enough explosives? They'd been mining for a while, they should have some—

Enough explosives to go through a mountain in less than a week? The gunfire was picking up in the distance, and I heard buzzing approach. How quick could we mine with a fight on our hands?

I'd recharge, though. I could burn through it then, right?

But this side of the mountain was mostly made of some kind of reflective rock from the surface. My "laser" would mirror right off.

Laaru collapsed to the ground, leaning against his finished avalanche with sweat pouring from his face, as wan as an Alpinoan winter moon. I was lying on my back in the ice. Another fly tried to land on me; I impaled it with Diebol. My arm raised, weak as a blade of grass, to point my crystal again, but it didn't even spark. I couldn't even throw a small static charge. I'd put everything into that one shot.

My arm flopped to the ground beside me. Filk. Filking … I couldn't cry. I couldn't scream. My stomach was so heavy. Like I was melting. My chest wept, so—empty, like my lungs didn't even care about holding air anymore. It was like someone had drained my blood and replaced it with sand.

I knew the kid couldn't understand about the Structure. He probably didn't know what it did. But sapient life, he should understand. Everyone should.

"You just buried anyone who was left in that mine," I groaned. "How are you better than the blitzers you just told me about?"

His jaw clenched; terrified rebellion burned in his grey eyes. "I've just sealed off one of the sources of the swarm. If anyone did die—one or two people—I calculated the loss of the least people to save the most. It's three solar systems we're talking about." A choking, hacking breath, like a withheld sob, interrupted him and he gritted his teeth. "Sometimes you have to make those calculations."

"Three solar—wait, so you know what it does?"

"How can you be against it, if you do?" he croaked.

"The heat death of the universe?"

"What? No!"

Oh my filking … this. The doubt. I couldn't take this. I was possessed with an overwhelming urge to just lie there until a bug ate me. Everything. I'd put everything into this. Twice now, catastrophic nonsense blocked me. Me, against two apocalypses? Why? I could feel my heartbeat slow. My eyes begged to close, to just—not see anymore. I just wanted to go home, wherever home was, somewhere far away from here.

"Njandejara," I whispered. "I am so tired."

A fly flitted toward me, then turned suddenly. I heard the kick of a flayer rifle on mechanical back-up; a slender, elegant and kind of malnourished Bichank snout appeared above me.

"The package is secure, ma'am," said the Frelsi soldier. "You need to leave."

CHAPTER ELEVEN

Nathan

It wasn't blitzers who put Nathan in the cage.

When the swarm hit, Angela and the rest of Nathan's kitchen crew were still at the stoves and chopping boards, their lower halves frozen in place and their hands busy while Nathan, closest to the entrance and their degenerate guard, desperately tried to pretend mind control still worked on him.

Their lazy blitzer stepped out for a second for some fresh air. He never came back in. There wasn't even a scream—just some kind of grunt. Entranced as ever with his naked people videos, he probably wasn't paying attention when the buzzing judgment hammer fell.

The kitchen crew noticed something was wrong when the guard's hand fell back through the unlocked polymerwall—clenched—unclenched—shuddered and spasmed—and then lay still.

Then a huge round shape like a two-chambered heart bulged through the wall, popping to reveal a head with antennae, giant compound eyes, and a long stinger dripping blood. The head swiveled like a curious children's toy.

Nathan recognized the ursa-fly—no one else knew what it was.

"Heads up!" he yelled, wishing his voice wasn't so thin. "Keep something sharp on you and throw everything else!"

Pots and knives hit the creature's eyes—a couple stuck, but most clinked and fell to the ground. An angry buzzing began outside, and the creature brought a thick paw inside, shaking off its head.

"It's shielded by some kind of clear chitin!" shouted the Bichank girl who'd once worked with her unit doctor in medical zoology. "Throw heavier stuff!"

She ripped up the entire top of her stove with her enormous paws. "Duck!" she roared as she hurled it.

The stove top smashed into the creature's eye, actually denting it. A spurt of clear goo trickled from a crack by the dent; the thing cringed, and its buzzing almost sounded like a whimper as it backed out and left.

"Nice. Why'd they put you on kitchen duty, again?" cheered the suave little Biouk guy on chopping duty.

"Leg, I guess," the Bichank medic, Kola, pointed at her right stump. "I think they didn't notice my prosthetic when they Turned me. And then it broke."

Nathan ran to the polymerwall and—without putting his head directly against it, for fear of getting stabbed or something —listened. A thrumming chorus of wings kept an ominous tune under the tinkly soprano of screams and whizzing oxidizer cartridges.

"It sounds like there are more out there," Nathan said.

Angela wiped off her hands and took off her gag. "I don't think he's going to mind if I talk anymore." She nodded to the dead hand. "Can you get the relay, Nathan?"

"Aye." Nathan dropped to his hands and knees, gripped the blitzer's hand, and pulled him inside. He was very, very heavy with all his armor, and Nathan immediately wished Gideon were with him.

No relay—*he must've dropped it outside*. But the dead guy did have two pistols strapped to his thighs. Nathan gave one to Angela and one to Graap, the Sailfin on sauces, then—head as close to the ground as possible just like in stealth training—he poked through the polymerwall to look outside.

He almost got stepped on by a fully armored blitzer plunging into the kitchen for cover. The blitzer stumbled over him and fell on his back on the floor; when the soldier saw himself surrounded by Frelsi holding knives and guns, he flipped out. "This is all your fault somehow," his tinny transmitter crackled. Both pistols came up.

But the Frelsi were more afraid than he was, and they fired first. They weren't sharpshooters, but with enough people shooting at the same time they managed to hit his neck and the seam under his arm, and he died.

Around this time the mind control turned off.

"Are we all—better?" asked Graap.

"No," said Kola. "Someone's hit the mind-control panel. Whether by accident or on purpose, there's a force here to liberate us."

"We'll try to cross the parking bay to get Nathan to a ship," Angela said. "We have four more pistols here. He stays in the center of our formation. If there's no cover, we're the cover."

"Yes, chef," the kitchen team said in unison.

"If we don't make it," Nathan said. "I'm really honored to have known you all."

"You'll make it," said Kola. "That's your duty."

And the team of seven grabbed their coats and gloves and plunged into the fray.

It wasn't the chaos that was the problem—it was the organized people. Closer to the Structure the blitzers seemed more focused on surviving the swarm, but here by the vehicles they were mostly mowing down Frelsi ex-Turned making for escape ships. Graap went down almost immediately with a flayer cartridge between his eyes. An ursa-fly swooped down and literally lifted the small chopping station Biouk away into the air. He saluted goodbye as the giant claws pierced his chest.

Nathan felt that loss more than the cartridge that hit his arm. His adrenaline was up so high, his eyes so wide and primed on battle, he almost didn't feel pain. But Angela saw and made the call.

"We can't go straight through!" she shouted. "There's another tunnel that lets out by the back of the bay—everyone see it, over there, across the clearing?"

"There isn't a direct passageway from here to that outlet!" Kola yelled. "We have to go through the whole maze literally under our feet, then back up."

"We better hurry then!"

So they backed away from the parking bay, passed the officer mess hall with its tables overturned and silverware scattered, and ducked into the wide tunnel mouth behind them.

As they passed the huge row of sleeping cages in the hollowed-out ice cave to the left, they came face to face with what must have been thirty feeding ursa-flies.

"Shyte on a pigstick sandwich," Kola muttered.

"I wouldn't use that term exactly, but yes," Angela said.

"Stow him in the cages," Kola said. "Stay with him. Me and the girls will clear the way."

"Aye."

Nathan wanted to protest; it took everything in him not to rush after Kola and the rest of the team toward the flies. He didn't want anything to happen to them. He couldn't let everyone do this for him. *It's not for me. It's for the Frelsi. My duty is my blood.*

Angela closed the cage behind Nathan and herself, pushed him toward the back, and knelt between him and the door with her gun drawn. She tried to cover the other girls with firepower as best she could, but soon they'd disappeared around the bend.

Angela and Nathan didn't see their crew again until Kola, roaring in the names of her city and her family, backed into view with two pistols flaring. Six ursa-flies followed her. One went down. Angela managed to kill another through the cage bars.

The other four reached Kola. She fell on her back; they pounced on her, claws swinging. Angela rushed to leave the cage and help her—

"No!" Kola screamed. "He needs a guard!" Her voice gurgled as blood spurted from her muzzle. "Just help me take some with me," she spat, punching an empty pistol through an ursa-fly's eye.

"Aye aye, young lady," Angela whispered back. She stayed put, peppering the ursa-flies with cartridges; each time one fell another took its place. Kola thrashed and fired and fought with their claws in her chest as her guts and theirs splattered on the walls—until a claw finally pierced her neck, and she lay still, and they fed.

"This isn't working," Nathan groaned. He hadn't had time to mourn the others, but literally a captive audience to Kola's—end —he felt everything. His throat tightened. He thrust his gloves under his hat into his curly hair, gripping it like he needed to keep his head from falling off. "This isn't okay."

"They'll thin out," Angela said. Her voice was somehow still so calm and soft. Maybe that came with the age she had on him —she'd faced who-knew-how-many battles and uprisings to survive at least a decade past normal Frelsi life expectancy. Her steady arm wrapped around Nathan's thin shoulders even as she kept her pistol and her eyes pointed at the ursa-flies outside the cage. "Wait."

She worked on them steadily, one at a time. Nathan recharged her pistol for her. The whole team should've stayed in the cages, he thought.

"I think Kola bought us just the time we need," Angela said, firing again, stabilizing her pistol with both hands and her elbow on her knee. "We may be safe from the bugs in here, but we're sitting ducks for any blitzers who come past—if we'd all waited in the cages we'd never have gotten through. Hear the buzzing?"

"Not as much, no," Nathan said.

"The girls did a good job further down the tunnel, too," Angela said. "I don't think we'll find any of them alive, though. Be ready for that."

One or two of the last ursa-flies eating Kola charged the cage, irritated by the flayer fire. But in seconds everything in the area was dead, and Angela opened the door, motioned Nathan to keep to the wall of the cave as she led the way around the bend.

"Nate!"

Nathan whirled; Angela swiveled, then lowered her weapon. Gideon and Reise ran up, Reise with a sniper rifle and Gideon holding a pistol and a dead human girl whose cratered ribs and back showed she'd clearly been shielding him while he brute-forced his way through bugs. They both backed against the opposite side of the tunnel to face Angela and Nathan, weapons pointed away from them but ready.

Reise's mouth moved ten meters a second as the group dashed through the tunnel. "My sister's arrived with transport for Nathan," he panted.

"Dude, that was your sister?" Gideon gasped.

"Yes. There's also a sound to make to scare the flies away," Reise said. "It's like—like this."

Angela repeated it; Reise repeated and confirmed.

"I thought you told me you overheard from the officers your sister was probably dead," Gideon said. "Big electromagnetic battle on Forge?"

"I must've heard wrong," Reise said. He nodded his head toward the parking bay outside. "Most people's weapons were disabled by the EMP blast. I'm on manual firing, but I'm running out of cartridges. Is your weapon fresh?"

"There are—two freshish ones here." Nathan darted to Kola's body—the pulped torso with its exposed ribs didn't even have a face anymore, wasn't even her, and suddenly didn't bother him. "Thank you," he whispered, to her, not it, as he grabbed her pistols.

"Fighting's shyte around the ships," Gideon said, switching out his pistol—apparently empty—with one from Nathan. His encouraging smile was the best hello Nathan could've asked for. "Blitzers up here didn't get the memo our blitzers down at the mine did."

"Apparently the worst of the flies are in other parts of the camp or by the Structure," Reise said. "Up here, the Growen seem to think there's a Frelsi attack. There's a ledge up at the top of the parking bay we need to get to. Do any of you know which tunnel can get us there?"

"Ledge?" Angela tilted her head. "You must be talking about the sentry roost. Yes. We need to go down into the maze first, but there's a branch that'll take us straight up from there. It's a little steep."

"Too easy," Gideon said, and they were off.

The tunnel was almost entirely quiet except for one or two stray bugs here and there. The bodies were piled so thickly the team had to climb over ursa-fly carcasses in some places.

"There were a *lot* of bugs here," Gideon whistled.

"Yes. Whoever cleared this performed phenomenally," Reise said.

"Yes, they did," Angela agreed.

CHAPTER TWELVE

Gideon

THE TEAM JOGGED, SPRINTED, AND CREPT THROUGH A WINDING series of downhill tunnels, soon leaving the bright ice caves behind for dark rock passages. Ursa-flies kept away from them, and they only saw one blitzer, who took the long nap as soon as Reise saw him. It was starting to get so quiet Gideon almost thought about ditching his poor human shield—almost, because he just had a very strong gut feeling they'd run into an area with no cover at some point. Still, Gideon's arm was getting tired. They crossed a wide, really unpleasant dark space into a bright burrow lined with deep, translucent white crystal, and the burn started to remind him of maxing his weight regimen back on Alpino. It was hard to even think about that, about a life without …

"Hey Reise," Gideon asked. "We going to stay free? Or will the first control panel we walk past suddenly—you know, make it puppet city up here?"

"Only if they capture you. They have to resync each device manually," Reise said.

"There isn't some kind of back-up server or some shyte?"

"Apparently they're working on something like that," Reise

said. "It's not that easy. It's more like tuning to an ancient radio frequency, or like Bluetooth, than like—inter or intranet."

"That's cool, then."

Gideon walked in front; Angela, right behind him, directed his steps. Nathan was behind her, and Reise took up the rear. Gideon suddenly really wanted to talk to Nathan alone, though.

Safety first, though.

He sighed. "Hey Nathan," he said.

"Yeah?"

"Your arm okay?"

"Yes—I'm very fortunate. I'm fine."

"Good."

Gideon heaved a sigh. "I'm still really bothered about—when we first got into this mess," he said.

"What do you mean by that?"

Reise interjected from the back. "He means when the Growen made him shoot you." The rancor in Reise's voice reminded all three of them that Reise often thought about what lives might've been saved had he just let Nathan die. Maybe, Gideon realized, that was why they'd butted heads even harder this year than normal. Maybe they both wished …

"If we can get a cure home to the Frelsi, it'll all be worth it," Nathan said. His voice trembled a little. He didn't have much "positive psychology" left; over the past year his oppressive almost-whiny scold had pretty much disappeared.

Gideon almost expected a scoff from their bitter sniper, but Reise said nothing. Everyone had more hope, maybe, when they could control their own bodies.

"We just have a few more turns," Angela said, pausing the weird thrumming sound to take a breath. Gideon took it up for her instead. "I'll tell you," she panted. "I was one of the original settlers here, for you two who don't know—and we never had problems with these—what you're calling ursa-flies—before the Growen arrived. I heard of someone who saw one, like once. The

Growen definitely made them aggressive drilling all willy nilly. I almost don't feel bad for any blitzers who got eaten. I respect all life, but—well. It's tough."

"Nature's justice is harsh," Nathan ventured.

"Nature has no justice," Reise answered. "And all life does not merit respect."

Gideon almost laughed. He loved these guys. These sad, bickering, silly buddies of his. They couldn't see the sparkle on the ice around them or the humor in a spilled dish or anything little, really, with all their big ideas. They only saw planets where he saw rocks and grass, and that was cool and okay. He was so glad to have known them.

Because suddenly as Angela flashed the leading mirror on the edge of her pistol around the next corner, then held up her hand for a silent halt, Gideon realized he wasn't going to hear these guys fight much longer.

"Seems like the Growen guessed people would try to come through here," Angela whispered. "Just a left turn after this and you'd have a straight shot to the ledge."

Everyone else spread out a bit to get a look at the tiny mirror without revealing themselves. There was like no cover up ahead. *Scratch that*, Gideon told himself. *Not "like" no cover. Actually just, no cover.* The tunnel was long and straight and curved upward. In the distance knelt two fully armored blitzers in protected alcoves on either side of the passage, the edges of their orb'd helmets just visible through the square "windows" on which they leaned their rifles. Otherwise, it was a straight tunnel with only enough room for one person at a time—single file only. Another quick, floor-level peep and Gideon could see a room to the left with at least fifteen more fully armored guys waiting to take their buddies' place.

"They do *not* want anyone getting the high ground above the parking area," Gideon muttered.

"They're scared of snipers getting up behind their guys," Nathan mouthed.

The four looked at each other, and back down to the maze behind them. Not even Reise could hit a blitzer's neck if it was tucked behind solid stone, and even if you did manage to shoot both guys eventually, then what? Two more would wait for you until you ran out of ammo or gave up. The Turned didn't have much time. They didn't know when Benzaran's ship was going to move, and the longer they waited the higher the likelihood of that transport getting damaged or shot down. Then what? Try to scrap it out for another ship with the Growen still mowing people down across the parking bay?

"We've got another problem," Reise whispered, nodding his head back behind them. The characteristic click of blitzer boots— maybe ten minutes behind, but definitely blocking the way back.

That was when Gideon knew his time was up. He was big enough, wide enough, to fill the hallway. Shyte, he was big enough to block that doorway at the same time. His buddies needed cover.

He'd provide it.

"Hey, Nathan," he said, and held out his hand for a shake goodbye. Nathan looked at him for a second, then down the hallway, and somehow understood. He threw his arms around his neck and hugged him hard.

Reise looked at them quizzically. Gideon saluted him with a grin, and dropped the quick finger-signal to let everyone know to follow behind him.

Then Gideon hoisted Julie up one more time, and charged down the hall with his pistol flashing under her arm.

Julie took the first five or six shots. But she was thinner than Gideon. It didn't matter much when something grazed his arm, or just whistled through the skin of his right side, but his left thigh, he needed to run. *Push. It didn't hit bone. I've got a lot of muscle around it. This is just another rep. Just taking this set to muscle fatigue. Maxing out.*

He made it to the two blitzers in the alcoves. He barreled into one of their friends who popped out from the door, knocked him down sports-ball style, shot him in the neck, and kept himself in the hall just for the second it took for Angela and Reise both to reach under his arms and close-quarters-shank those alcoves guys in the necks. Then he swiveled and became a door, blocking the other blitzers from getting into the hallway. His pistol sprayed in at them with the randomness of a wildfire.

"Go go go!" he yelled as his companions squeezed past his back. "Don't get caught! I'll catch up!"

He wasn't going to catch up, though. He allowed himself a glance down the hall after them; Reise turned to salute him. Gideon wished he could've seen his buddy Nathan's face one more time, but the curly hair disappeared to the left ahead of Reise, and then they were all gone.

He couldn't let anyone pursue them. He backed out of the doorway and started firing into the ceiling of the hall. He didn't care that his lungs were on fire. That his stomach was screaming like it was spilling acid. He wasn't trying to hit blitzers. He was trying to bring down the ice.

The tunnel collapsed. It wouldn't hold them forever—it was just ice and a little rock, after all—but it would hold them long enough. He found himself sinking to his knees—shyte, he was getting dizzy. He inched backward on the ground. "Julie" fell down next to him. She had pretty eyes. He emptied his pistol into the hall ceiling, knocking down more debris, and inched backward again. He charged it and emptied it again.

"Look, Mom, I'm building a snow fort," he grinned. He'd never really known his parents. Maybe he'd get the chance now.

He couldn't charge the silly pistol anymore. Something was wrong with his arms. The floor was really slippery.

"I'm also making a painting, apparently," he noted, looking

at all his blood being not where it was supposed to be. "It's abstract. Some artists have a blue period. I'm going through my red period." He chuckled. "Hmm. That doesn't sound right."

He had to lie down.

Wow, she did have pretty eyes. She didn't look mad, either, or scared. Maybe she'd just been happy to be free. "Well, Julie, I'm really glad we got to meet," Gideon murmured. "Thanks for helping me save the Frelsi. I'm sorry it was a super-disrespectful way to do it. But we did good."

The adrenaline was—was it crashing now, or still rising? He'd never been any good in science training, really. Whatever the adrenaline was doing, he was suddenly feeling a lot of pain he hadn't been feeling. He was also so incredibly cold. Shyte. And—scared?

"Hey, Julie," he croaked. "Since you know what it's like to be dead already … you got any advice for me?"

His vision was fading for some reason. That was weird. Shyte, his whole body felt like it was on fire. He couldn't really—couldn't really breathe. That was terrifying.

"Maybe we'll meet for real," he gasped. "Lev used to say Njandejara saves his friends'—programming and electricity and stuff—to set them up somewhere else." *Air. Breathe.* "Somewhere good. Maybe you were his friend. I haven't been a good friend to him. But Njandejara's always been good to me. If this is all because we talked to him sometimes, I say it's worth it."

Shyte. He couldn't really talk anymore. *Please, please, please Njandejara, make it stop. Please, the air—I need the air. I'm so scared. Please don't let me be scared.*

"Maybe I'll look you up, Julie," Gideon whispered. "Maybe we can go out."

Then the hallway was quiet, and Gideon wasn't there anymore.

CHAPTER THIRTEEN

Jaika-Lem Benzaran

BLOODSEAS, I HAD TO MAKE THIS MESS WORTH IT SOMEHOW.

Rakao, my Bichank messenger, filled me in as we ran across the field of gore. After relying on nothing but word of mouth to communicate over the last year, the Turned had become very good at passing information fast. Gideon and Reise had shared my anti-fly sound with everyone they could on the way to Nathan—the guy with the cure—and most of the Turned apparently already knew about Nathan's blood. The only reason Reise didn't was that he'd been Laaru's bodyguard, apparently.

Laaru. I'd been weak when I'd stood back up, but not as weak as he was. I didn't want to carry his sorry ass across the field, but I sure as hell wasn't letting a threat like him run around free until he recharged. I thought about killing him with a quick burning stab through the forehead—I really didn't want to, even though I was so mad my body couldn't handle the feeling and decided to just blank it out with numbness.

In the end I made the split-second decision to bind his hands with the fabric of the soft cloth belt under my atmo-suit and shove a gag in his mouth—Rakao had one with her for some reason.

Because, my foggy brain decided, Laaru would know where and how I could get to Bricandor. Might even be good bait. If I was gonna kill him, I should've done that *before* he filked up my entire mission, not now when I could use him.

And … maybe I could still help him. Maybe what I did now kept a Jared from becoming a Diebol.

I recited his prisoner-of-war rights under Frelsi regs to him as we ran. The whole thing, the thing Jei had said when arresting me, with the part about trial for war crimes, and protection from torture, the whole spiel. Because we did this shyte different. Rakao paused her report for it.

"It's getting really bad over by the parking bay," she went on when I'd finished, dropping to her belly to duck an ursa-fly—I smashed its eye in with my Sterba mace—as she fired on another one. She didn't kill it, but she at least gave its victim a fighting chance. "The bugs have actually thinned out, but the blitzers are managing to organize; we'll have an all-out old-fashioned battle on our hands soon. There's talk they might be getting reinforcements and comms back-up from the surviving ships in orbit soon. If you don't get out now you might be stuck here for weeks. But the *package* has to leave *now*."

"Roger," I said. I was too tired to really say anything else. I almost couldn't think. I was so defeated I felt totally fine letting the adult make decisions for me. All I could do right now was slash at anything that tried to eat me. I could only hold my mace and Sterba's now—with my abilities totally powered down Diebol and Mera had to wait on my outer belt with Jei.

"We'll work on blasting through the rubble so we can destroy the Structure for you," Rakao reassured me. "It's not something we can use ourselves, is it? It's been a lot of work to build."

"I don't know if you'll believe me if I tell you what it's for," I said. Laaru grunted in frustration behind his gag.

"Well, the point is, I don't think we can get through to it in a week, even with you, and the Growen've made that deadline seem really important in a not-good-way," Rakao said. "Another reason to get the filk out of here fast: there should be another piece of it on Luna-Guetala you can hit faster."

"Roger." I slid to knock a young human out of the path of a dive-bombing ursa-fly—the bug dove face-first into the staff end of my mace instead. Rakao showed the guy how to make the sound, then covered him as he ran.

We didn't make the sound. We let the ursa-flies come to us as we crossed the field of death. It was an unspoken decision between us—yes, I had to get out of here ASAP, but on the way out, we were going to save some lives by attracting some flies.

We ended up back-to-back in the middle of a circle of five now. "You're Lem Benzaran, right?" Rakao panted. "Luna-Guetala Command screwed you to cover their butts after you went undercover when they didn't believe you?"

Shyte, that was a mouthful. "Yeah," I said. I hadn't heard anyone put the story that way. I'd only heard it the other way.

"A couple of the guys told me about you. Glad to meet you."

We'd almost rounded the archway back to the parking bay when I saw a familiar face getting thrashed by an ursa-fly against the wall. *Speak of the little witch herself.*

Wow. I waved Rakao forward—she had more bugs to shoot— and I marched over to that familiar face, smashed the bug's head in, and handed the wound-wrap from my med-kit *to the woman whose testimony had done me in.* "Better plug that up, Captain," I said, nodding to the row of gaping claw wounds in her right side. She was too skilled for anything to get the drop on her from behind, but from the front, once you ran out of ammo and it became those claws versus your knife—well. I could see the results littered across the field. *Shyte* I wanted to box Laaru around the ears—look at these people! He'd basically voided the entire reason I'd let my EMP kill everyone's charging mechanisms in the first place. He'd made any extra deaths pointless. *Filking idiot.* "Did you drop a lung, Captain?" I asked Seria.

"No," she panted. "But actually it's major now."

"Congratulations." I didn't even care enough to say I didn't care. Wasn't like her rank protected her from Turning. I didn't know how she'd come to be stationed here, but she was stick-skinny, with blotchy bags under her eyes, and thin hair—no longer the super-hot model who'd tried to climb Jei to success, as he'd put it. Her misery didn't make me feel better, or her success, worse; I didn't feel compassion or pity either. I no longer felt the need or desire to hurt her back.

Because seeing her wasn't the horrible reminder of the trial I thought it'd be. That was such a different time. She might even be a different person now. Probably not, because she didn't apologize—but she was suddenly so insignificant next to all this carnage, all the weight on me, all these heroes dying amidst the heat death it turned out I actually did need to stop.

An insignificant person clinging to insignificant things.

I didn't want to be like that.

"It's me, by the way—Lem Benzaran," I did say. I did want her to know.

But then I left, and replaced all the old images of her in my head with this one, and never thought of her again. The whole interaction took maybe fifteen seconds.

Rakao and I broke through to the parking bay, and shyte, Rakao was right. The conflict when I'd landed had been more scattered and chaotic—bad, but not bulletstorm bad. Now organized battle lines had formed. Behind us, near the tunnels and what was probably a mess cube, we mostly had Frelsi. On the other side, ahead of us, we had rows and clusters of armored blitzers hunkered down behind cold-weather-equipped tanks, land-cars, and ships. I could see engineers huddled behind artillery, desperately trying to replace blown circuits.

We needed to get to the Growen side and the ledge behind it. Cinta definitely couldn't land down here now, or even swoop down where he'd let me off earlier.

"They used to use us as shields." Rakao nodded toward Laaru. She wasn't suggesting we do that, but she wasn't *not* suggesting it. "They'd send Turned in ahead of themselves to take shots from the settlement."

"No, I need him for something," I said, noting his grey eyes widening. "But actually—"

I raised my voice as loud as I could over the firepower. I've never had trouble being heard anywhere, and here I echoed through the cavern: "Yo, idiots, I have your Stygge guy, and Bricandor's gonna be *pissed* if he gets shot, so let me pass!"

Some folks stopped—some didn't. But enough did that I could at least drag Laaru over behind the nearest Maggot fighter for cover. Someone tried to get smart and quick-climb over top of it; Rakao shot them down.

"I am serious!" I roared. "This is also the guy who just protected all your filking work from the last several months, if you wanna look to your right. My left, your right. See that mountain thing? Totally ruined my day. So be nice and do not shoot him!"

I heard murmuring. I wasn't good at spinning my mace into an forcefield without at least some "em-hance" still tingling in my system, so I had to sheath Sterba, push Laaru over to Rakao, and spin my personal mace with two hands to shield us some as we crossed to the next "checkpoint:": a converted Frelsi supply ship. Again, someone tried to get smart and shoot under the feet of the ship. Rakao shot them instead.

"Play stupid games, win stupid prizes!" I shouted.

We were almost halfway across the parking bay when Rakao took a shot to the leg, and Laaru took one to the shoulder. Shyte. His eyes squeezed shut with pain as he yelled into the gag—he'd definitely never been shot before. Rakao clenched her teeth and returned fire to our right. I backed them both against the nearest Maggot to protect our rear; my fingers, warmed by my staff despite the cold air, spun to keep a forcefield in front of us.

If I squinted, I could kind of tell that the people still shooting at us outranked those who didn't.

"You didn't make yourself very popular among the Growen officers here, did you," I said to Laaru. He shook his head, wincing.

Rakao quick-wrapped medical bands around his shoulder while shots scattered off my forcefield. I was not doing a good job. Cartridges pinged against the ship behind us, way too close to our heads, and more cartridges were going to get through. We were pinned down.

My frustrated gaze clung to the ledge above the blitzers. How the filking shyte were we going to get up to where Cinta could get us without just swooping down into everyone's gunfire? I could see a construction lift nearby that could get high enough … we'd be huge targets then, though.

Suddenly, officers and upper enlisted Growen started dying. You could just kind of see the side of a face—like mine, but male —hugging a rifle behind a boulder on the ledge. Reise had made it to the bioship. And he was pretty mad. You could just kind of sense it in the rhythm of the shots, like the gun itself was screaming expletives.

I didn't see his friend. I did see what were probably Lark and Carl firing beside him. At some point during the thinner fighting, they'd managed to get full blitzer armor.

The Growen confusion at getting shot in the back—and by blitzers—gave another Frelsi squad a chance to rush the field behind us, laying down enough suppressive fire to get us a better position behind a different vehicle. Rakao sat, threw a tourniquet on herself, and rolled on her belly to return fire again, too. "That thing can cut, can't it?" she shouted at my mace. "Carve out a plate off this ship and get the filk onto that lift, kid."

I obeyed. Age still had its advantages over me. One of the Maggot's scales came off for me. I stowed my mace, grabbed

Laaru's shirt with one hand, and held the big plate of metal with the other. It was a much better shield. Two Frelsi rushed forward with me, and hidden behind the base of the lift, started cranking it manually as soon as we got on. Reise, Lark, and Carl disappeared into the bioship, and it swooped over just under us. I shoved Laaru into its open side, and on its second pass, I jumped in, too.

And then, my system finally crashed. I barely remember picking up Jake and Lev—Lev was so, so yellow. Reise gave Jake the fiercest, most tearful, most warrior-like hug I've ever seen a guy give someone. I passed out.

CHAPTER FOURTEEN

Jake

JAKE SAT CURLED AGAINST THE BIOSHIP WALL WITH THE BIG transmission-booster attachment on his wrist, sharing Nefesh's wonderfully clear video with his still-faint mentor. Lev languished on the floor, strapped in by what seemed like tongues wrapping around his body and a single ribbed, blue plant-vine around his waist. They'd both taken off almost all of their clothes except for the jumpsuit trousers that went under their uniform: it was *so hot* in the tropical plant-mobile after living a year in the cold.

Lev was going to be okay. Probably. As long as they could get him to Luna-Guetala soon. For now, he wasn't going to die this week. The lactulose Jake had stolen was holding off the brain damage, and Jake had packed enough anti-toxin for the doctors to analyze or use if they needed it, too.

"He'll need a transplant when he arrives," Nefesh said. "I'm flying out to LG to meet you. I'm bringing Dr. Loylan and a fresh liver for immediate surgery."

"Thank you," Jake said, double-checking the flicker of Lev's eyelids for the umpteenth time, because without the throes of delirium—his long lashes closed in quiet rest—Jake's exhausted mentor seemed too peaceful to be alive. "The Frelsi liked our lair, by the way."

"I saw that," said Nefesh.

The bioship crew had dropped off a lady named Angela to set up base in Lev and Jake's home when they left. *"We need somewhere we can safely evac and stage,"* she'd explained as she helped load Lev into the bioship. *"Ooh, he's not very heavy is he? Anyway, if we can keep your ursa-fly herding secrets to ourselves, the wasteland will be a good place to regroup against the Growen while our main forces vie for the camp by the Structure. The armored blitzers will fall right through the false ice bridges while Lev's map keeps us solid."* She'd nodded toward Lev. *"Met him a few times, actually, when he was our own personal superhero."*

Nathan had given her a big hug goodbye—it was quick, because for some reason there wasn't time, everyone said. Nate looked so sick to Jake—not as sick as Lev, but pretty sick, not at all like Jake remembered. *"Thank you for everything,"* Nathan said. *"Are you sure you're going to stay?"*

"I signed up for Bijou, and I'm going to make Bijou free," the woman said. *"I'll see you when the orbits permit, my friend."*

When they took off, giant bat-wings pounding the air, the settler's fluffy hair rolled in the wind over a smile and a wave that was just as calm and casual as if they'd be back in time for dinner.

Lev's bony, ridged hand reached up now to stabilize Jake's wrist so he could see his mate better on the screen. He looked like he wanted to say something to her, but when he opened his mouth, nothing came out. Nefesh stared back at him with her electric eyes as sharp as if she could see into his soul, and Jake again found himself thinking how *lucky* Lev was.

I need to get over this, he told himself. He started to unstrap the transmitter so they could talk alone when the little Biouk lady came over with her child.

"He looks quite bad," Masha told her son. "Can you help him, Joshua?"

The Biouk cub, Joshua, laid a hand on Lev's forehead, and then touched Jake's hand. "But he already has, Mali," he said.

Lev's red fist suddenly flashed out to grip the cub's paw; his mother gasped, but the cub smiled and laid the other paw over the Draconian's hard knuckles. "It's good to see you, Lev," the cub said.

"My *go'ali*, and my leader," Lev croaked, his tongue suddenly free. "Have I died? I can't believe it's you."

"Shh," the cub answered. "It's a secret. You're not dead, though. Nefesh needs you."

"Who is that?" Nefesh asked over the video—but the cub scampered away with his confused and frustrated mother following, and Lev, overwhelmed, held on to Jake's wrist and shook his head.

"I—" he began. "Did you see?"

Jake frowned. "I think he needs to rest, Nefesh, ma'am," he said. "He's still acting weird."

"No, he's not," she snapped. "He's seen something. But Lev, as long as you're all right, you take your time. There's no rush to talk."

He nodded; his breath was really loud through those dry, scaling lips. "I'm going to get you some water," Jake said.

Lev nodded. Jake got up to follow the little Biouk mother across the ship—she seemed to know where and what everything was.

Before he reached her, though, Jake paused, holding on to the wall to whisper one last question to Nefesh.

"Hey, Nefesh—I'm just getting him a drink, and then I'm going to put you on his wrist so you can be alone," he said. "But —" He glanced around the room for listening ears, and then lowered his voice. "Was it wrong what I did?"

"We don't have to talk about it," she said.

"People got hurt. I wanted to live and save Lev, though."

"And you did."

"Did I do it just because I'm afraid?" he asked. "I feel all trembly and hot still. Was that just me going back to being a coward?"

"Well. Coward is a strong word, and you exceeded my expectations. Why do you think you did it?"

"I really didn't want Lev and me to die," he said.

"You don't have to be afraid of taking steps backward as long as you keep looking forward. As Lev would say, 'He who has begun a good thing in us will see it through as always.' For now, I doubt the Turned would have gone free without your swarm. So, was it wrong? I would normally consider weaponizing animals a bioterrorist war-crime. I wouldn't do it again if I saw other options. But it was going to happen sooner or later, and if you'd died instead, what would that have accomplished? We did what we had to."

We. We did what we had to. Jake sighed. He was part of the "we" now, the warrior "we." He was also Contaminated now—he'd definitely talked to a thing from another dimension, and he planned to keep talking to it until he could hear better, too. Until he could become what he needed to be. It didn't matter so much how tired or scared he was, or had been. He had jobs to do now.

But for now, his job was just to get his teacher water.

K'ARL

Setbacks just make the fans want me more.

K'arl was in the middle of uploading the edited footage of his epic defeat of the witch. He'd scoured the dunes for a while looking for the nasty tumor-ship and its child inhabitant; a sandstorm plus the biological make of the vehicle had made it hard for either his radar or his heat detection to find the thing, and at this point he knew it might have gone off-world. Without a very clear idea of its objective beyond "don't get killed," it was hard to predict its next move. But if it landed in any registered dock, independent, Growen, or Frelsi, it was an odd enough anomaly that he'd know where it was right away.

"Feel free to let me know if you see this nasty mutation-lump anywhere," K'arl finished into the camera. *A quick upload to follow the longer witch video.* The anonymity and drama of the videos really helped build the mystique of the Ebon Shadow—Carl hated them, but he benefited from them as much as K'arl did. They definitely brought in more jobs. They also sometimes generated tips. And it was a service to war-torn and bored civilizations alike, something exciting and personal to take them out of the daily grind.

In the meantime, he'd do another sweep of the Forge Biouk colony for leads. Their prophecies culminated in a return to Luna-Guetala, so he'd made sure to fuel up enough to take him there just in case. He just needed a registration hit on a dock somewhere, or one reported sighting—

"Silver Knight Six to the Ebon Shadow, baby," hummed the *Empress*'s onboard AI, K'arl's sometimes space-girlfriend. Someone else had definitely used her during the time his ship spent impounded while he languished in Revelonian prison, so she still had some quirks to work out.

"Put him through," K'arl said. "And I say baby, not you."

"You have failed me, but may yet prove useful," was Stygge Counselor Bricandor's opening line. "Tell me when you last saw the Child."

"Big nasty Biouk bioship," K'arl smirked. "You saw the video."

"Yes. Well, a 'big nasty Biouk bioship' has appeared on Bijou and threatened the Structure. And who does this look like?" A small video appeared next to Bricandor's face on the 180-degree curved compuwall that made up the front view of the *Empress's* cockpit. K'arl would've laughed if it didn't make him look so bad: someone's low-grade sentry camera showed a shivering, cyanotic loincloth-clad primate dangling from a nasty, dripping bioship tendril, shooting a blitzer, and then snatching the poor soldier up into the slurping walls of the ship. The soldier's body fell out unclothed onto corrugated ice a few minutes afterward.

"I mean, you know that's not me," K'arl said.

"I know it is the brother you claimed was locked in a reptilian cage half-paralyzed, if not dead," Bricandor said.

K'arl bit his lip. He'd only claimed Carl was dead—he'd kept the rest of that shyte to himself. At this point, the mind-reader rumors made a lot of sense.

"So I go to Bijou, then," K'arl said.

"No. Cease your attempts to ingratiate yourself through initiative." Bricandor laughed—a harsh, coughing, angry laugh. "There is little time, so hear me once and record this. They attempted to destroy the Structure, and with the solstice almost upon us the next target must be Luna-Guetala—Skraeli is too far. Satellite video data from the blockade confirms a Guetala heading. You must not damage the ship, as my student is now hostage on board. I am sending you his file now. Understood?"

"Sure boss." K'arl kept a cool, friendly demeanor—no stiff Growen blitzer respect shyte—as the old man hung up. He wasn't really bothered by the Counselor's rudeness. The wheezing medley of skin and bones always paid well so long as you let him think he was in control.

All in all, K'arl was pretty excited as he took off. "Aces to spades," as Lark Scrita would say, he was about to see her again.

CHAPTER FIFTEEN

Reise

Reise usually had words for every situation—poetic philosophical prose produced easily by an overactive mind. He had no words for the moment he could no longer see Bijou behind him, when they'd plunged far enough into the tapestry of stars that it became just another meaningless dot in a void of sparks.

He had no words, because even in the pain as Gideon disappeared into the vastness of that space and time, Jake—long, long dead in his mind—lived, and Reise could move on his own, and his year of so much forced silence would soon fade with the rash around his mouth from long days of icy, wet cloth crushed against his skin.

This was why he took Laaru's gag off almost immediately after the little Biouk female strapped him to the wall. Because Jake lived, and Laaru had done that for him.

"I'm assuming there's an excellent reason your hands are bound," Reise said.

"I saved the Structure," Laaru said, wiping his face on his shoulder. "From her."

"Ah." Reise leaned back. He didn't like the weird gooey

texture of the wall, and he sat back up again. He didn't have anything more to say to the Stygge who'd come so close yet so far from virtue.

Nathan was a distraught ball of feelings beside him, face buried in his knees. Reise wanted to have something to say to him, but Reise had found any encouragement frustrating during his moments of deepest grief, and he didn't want to return that slight to Nathan, however many times the man had inflicted it on him. He raised a hand—paused—and placed it firmly on Nathan's shoulder.

Nathan curled into him, gripping his shirt, his tearless face contorted in a grimace of purest agony. Reise was conscious of the awkwardness, and the eyes on them, but he gave Nathan a firm squeeze, then turned his attention to the little female Biouk and the strange, slender sail-less Sailfin hovering over them with medical tape. "You've got a cartridge lodged in your arm, I think," Reise said.

"I think that's just the burn, actually," the little Biouk said. "I'm Masha, by the way. May I take a look?"

Nathan assented. He clenched his teeth, shivering now as he tried to swallow his terribly obvious distress with distraction. He nodded toward Lem, passed out on the floor. "She looks a lot like someone who used to train at our base—almost like your sister, actually. But your sister was built differently. And she had brown eyes, right?"

Reise laughed. "That is my sister, you nincompoop. The blue's a reaction to her overcharging her powers. Don't ask me how: it's absolutely *incomputably* stupid to suppose her neuronal action potentials could affect the amount of melanin her iris produces, but here we are."

"Don't blue-eyed mutants still have brown pigment in the back? Aren't blue eyes just because light is reflecting weird? Maybe it has something to do with light energy," Nathan said.

"Also, I think you made up 'incomputably,' I don't think that's a word."

"Shyte, I must still be under mind control." Reise strained for something like a quip. "I didn't make anything up, my overlords did."

Nathan squeezed his thin lips together—it wasn't quite a smile, and his eyes were bleeding misery, but he managed.

When Lem woke up, she did in fact have brown eyes again. Reise didn't ask her if her training partner was in fact dead, as he'd heard—her changed face, matured by wind and sun and grief spoke to a lot of time on Forge where the supposed death had occurred, and Bereens would have certainly accompanied her here for something as important as the Structure seemed to be. Once he'd let her settle in and greet everyone properly, he did request strategic clarification: "Lem—"

She didn't seem to hear him. "Jaika," Masha repeated.

"What is the purpose of the Structure?" Reise asked when she looked over.

She glanced at Laaru, and then back to Reise. "Bricandor wants to channel heat energy out of the known universe into another dimension," she said.

"That's ridiculous!" Laaru cried. "What do you mean, another 'dimension'?"

"We know there are other planes of existence beyond ours, because interdimensionals do exist, and they come from there," Reise corrected him. "They're just evil, and you've been fortunate never to encounter one."

Lem and Cinta both gave him suspicious glances, but Lem focused on answering Laaru. "Laaru, do you actually remember me? From Beryllia? I feel like you have to have known I talked to interdimensionals back then."

"So you are Pele, then." Laaru's eyes widened. "I wasn't totally sure, because you've—you've changed a *lot*. But—" His brow wrinkled. "Bricandor said you were one of us. Undercover to stop the Frelsi, not help them."

"Did he now." Lem glowered. "I'm getting real tired of people lumping me in with the bad guys."

"*Bad guys?* We're trying to create a sustainable energy solution that'll solve all energy crises for all time," Laaru protested. "How is that bad?"

Lem actually laughed out loud. "Yeah, I guess heat death would solve all energy inequality forever."

Reise squinted. "Laaru, are you not familiar with any of the technological advancements out of Skraeli, already in production, for improving matter-to-energy conversion? The Growen aren't needed for that."

"This will be better than that! You're—you're trying to blow up a sustainable energy solution because you think some invisible sky beings don't like it?"

"That's a huge oversimplification, man," Lem groaned. "No. I'm trying to blow up a planet-spanning scale model of a laser crystal because—how to put this in mining school elitist-speak—"

"Hey, you went there, too," Laaru said.

"—because it'll cause environmental catastrophe across all the planets where it operates," Lem finished. "And the chain reaction across the involved solar systems could accelerate the thermodynamic collapse of our universe."

"*How?* Do you have blueprints, equations, a white paper, for any of this?"

"Do you?"

Laaru paused; doubt flickered across his forehead. "M-my part is the geological part," he stammered. "The environmental engineers and the civil engineers—and the energy experts—they've done all that other work."

"Laaru," Reise interjected—he'd picked up on at least two

logical fallacies from either side of the discussion, but he tried to focus on contributing instead of correcting. "I have significant doubts about whether the Growen's environmental engineers performed a survey before beginning construction on Bijou. One of the early settlers told us the ursa-flies never disturbed the colonists, not even out in the wasteland, before the Growen began drilling. A real survey would've avoided their habitat. The site was selected because of mineral deposits, full stop."

"They can make mistakes, and I'll freely admit—I mean, I saw the corruption, too." Laaru cringed. "But that's because of Major Fpokmmud and the other Bijou leadership. The project itself is still valid!"

"Okay," Lem said. "So, let's put aside the fact that the Growen have never invested this much money and manpower into anything that wasn't some tool for subjugation. You say there are blueprints demonstrating this thing's use—blueprints that would justify slavery, disastrous local environmental effects, all that shyte. So where are they?"

Laaru looked out the window as he answered. "I'm sure they're publicly available."

Lem sighed. "Laaru, we've had a team on this for two years. What's publicly available is a few scant interviews between Growen-friendly Burburan media and Growen scientists about some vague invention to 'end scarcity, property, and war through equitable energy distribution.' There's no data. The public doesn't even know where these construction projects *are*, man."

"That's—to protect the Structure from terrorists, though. Which is obviously a real concern, apparently." He motioned with his bound hands toward Lem with a pointed glare.

"All I'm saying is you're relying on blind faith more than anyone," she said. "The only complete internal blueprint we've found clearly shows the involved planets aligned to make the shape of a neodymium laser crystal, and Bricandor's last partner —the guy you replaced, did you know that happened?—told me he's angling for heat death. I happen to know if you put a powerful enough electromagnetic person with the right abilities at the helm, you can in fact use neodymium to transform enormous amounts of energy from one state to another, and Bricandor's got interdimensional advisors who understand quantum states of heat and consciousness I don't. Isn't—I mean, didn't Bricandor say *something* to you about the changing universe?"

Laaru opened his mouth, then closed it again. When he spoke, he halted a great deal: "He says the universe is undergoing puberty. A change in its underlying energy fields that— well, that's why everyone's powers are getting—bigger in the past few years."

Cinta made eye contact with Lem over his shoulder from the front of the ship. "And?" Lem asked. "The Awakeners fit into that, don't they?"

"The—the Awakeners help people tap into those energy fields and—accelerate them," he said.

"I mean, it fits," she leaned back, speaking to Cinta, not Laaru now. "With the whole—expenditure thing. Energy's not created or destroyed, just transformed, so maybe that was part of his thing with the Stygge super-soldiers all along. Maybe in his deluded head he thought he'd make a dent toward heat death somehow by spending it all."

"But that was always impossible," Cinta said. "People are too small."

"True. He's never been practical. But maybe he's always been on the look-out for the *right* person. Laaru, didn't he say, like—" She seemed to be gathering information now, not arguing. "There isn't some powerful electromagnetic person who's supposed to meet him at the core of the thing, like on Luna-Guetala, at the solstice?"

"… I am, actually," Laaru muttered.

Lem looked over at Cinta again, her eyes widened like she was expecting a slightly different answer, but satisfied nonetheless. "Wow. It does fit, doesn't it? Instead of our person causing the heat death, they inadvertently awaken the person who does."

Reise didn't understand who she was talking about, but Cinta did. "Yes," he said simply.

Lem leaned forward. "Look, Laaru, I know my sources. I trust your predecessor and I trust the threats of the interdimensionals who hate us. Even if the interdimensional part doesn't work, the *giant space laser* part will, and on the solstice he will fire it at *someone*. Forget heat death. It's a giant space laser. I don't want the Growen to have a giant space laser."

That was all Reise needed to hear. He motioned to Masha to ask about food. He did hear Lem throw Laaru one last concession: "Hey. I wouldn't want to rely on character witness and guesses, either, in your shoes. Bricandor's not an engineer. There must be some actual calculations somewhere, and probably, just like you, each person's been misled about what their part does. Why don't we—try to put it all together. Masha can help you if you can get the data."

"How am I supposed to do that?"

"You trust Bricandor, apparently. Why don't you ask him?"

"She took away my holopen so I can't," he nodded at Masha, who handed Reise a fruit that reminded him a lot of lechichi from back at Fort Jehu.

"I just don't want him tracking us," Lem said. "But when we get to Luna-Guetala, I can drop you off, and we can go talk to him."

Reise saw Cinta staring at his sister with ears laid back and muzzle tight. Reise shrugged: it did in fact sound like an excellent set up for an assassination plot, and if that was where Lem was angling, more power to her.

Laaru picked up on it as well. "But if you know where he is, you could kill him."

"He can read any plans I might have right out of your mind. He'll be fine." She stood up to stretch. "But give him a call when we land."

CHAPTER SIXTEEN

Jaika

THE RIDE TO LUNA-GUETALA WAS MUCH LESS—STRESSFUL—THAN the journey to Bijou. I felt defeated, yes, but I'd found Reise and Jake, and maybe a cure for the mind control. Maybe the Frelsi leadership would even be happy to see me. Not that I cared, but.

I did, actually.

Cinta approached me one evening—or afternoon, it all kind of blended together—with his ears pinned to the back of his head. "What'd I do now?" I sighed.

"Is it so obvious?" He tilted his head.

"I mean—" I flopped his judgmental ears with the back of my hand. "Come on, brother."

"Well." He raised his ears in an effort to look less critical. "You should not have told the little Stygge who you are."

I glanced over to the sleeping kid. His bound fists gripped the parka he'd balled up to use as a pillow; his face was covered by his shoulder-length hair—stringy like grass instead of thick and mossy like mine. The rumpled grey vest, with all its pockets, still reminded me of the Stygges back at the training center.

"If you're—Lem Benzaran—I've heard of you," he'd said today. *"I've heard you were dead, though. But also—a lot of not good things.*

You killed like two of the Growen's most valiant heroes a couple years ago."

"Bricandor actually gives me credit for Sterba and Morda? Wow. That's more than the Frelsi did."

I shrugged. "Cinta, he already knew. One of the Frelsi Turned outed me in front of him."

"I see." Cinta rested on his haunches and collapsed against me. "It seems a pity. Your human brother did not even use your last name for a year, to protect himself, and could have kept the secret."

"You've mind-read my plan for the kid, right?" I asked Cinta.

"No … you have not thought very loudly," he said.

I nodded over to Masha; she scampered over. "It is done," she said, drawing Laaru's holopen and Jei's gutted wristband out of her pouch. "His GPS now will not send information to the Growen, only to you. Even if he escapes you will know where he is."

"Excellent," I said. I leaned back against the wall as Masha cuddled against me on the other side from Cinta. "Shyte, I really do talk like a villain, don't I?"

Cinta didn't answer. I tapped his spine absently with my long fingers. "Hey, buddy?" I asked. "You guys haven't filled me in yet on why the Ebon Shadow tried to kill Joshua, not you."

"He did not say," Cinta said. His ears lay flat again, their warm, leathery flaps pressing against my hand on his back. "Perhaps hired by those wicked royals from Masha's clan," he spat.

"They're not all wicked," Masha protested. "And I doubt it. He didn't seem to care about them when he came trampling into the community hearing."

"Where they pervert justice," Cinta growled.

"They didn't intend to," she said.

"Except for your employer," he said.

"That's one person."

"Maybe they're all crappy and insular because Forge sucks

for them, Cinta," I interjected, trying to slow him a little from hating on Masha's people. "It took years in that space station before Forge would let them land."

"Yes," Cinta assented. "I understand immigration rules were very strict before the Growen forced the planet open. Masha told me her grandparents lived in orbit for at least ten years before Forge let them land."

"Why is it people do that to themselves?" I smirked. "Please, have friends and then maybe imperialists won't run you over. Xenophobia only works until someone bigger than you wants your shyte. I mean, Burbura sucks but no one invades them. Why? Because everyone likes and needs them." I glared at the ceiling, remembering how the solar systems didn't make a peep when the Growen annexed the isolated Luna-Guetala Bichanks on my first mission with Jei. "Everyone's got a relative on Burbura so everyone gives a rat what happens there. Immigrants are an insurance policy. People should understand this."

Masha's little rib cage pushed against my side as she sighed. "Politics aside, I don't think the Shadow double was sent by my clan. They don't have that kind of money. I'm afraid Bricandor might have something to do with it. Because all this talk about interdimensionals and the energy of the universe sounds familiar. In a bad way." She nodded over to where Joshua was seated politely next to Szizzle—reptilian cultures don't cuddle, in general, because it's considered stealing someone else's warmth. Joshua's excited little black and white nose hovered millimeters from the compupad Masha had lent the reptilian: Szizzle was enthralled with the manuscript scans previously forbidden to her, and Joshua was eager to explain everything.

"*Look, Elitsza,*" the reptilian intellectual had exclaimed earlier. "*It actually prohibits self-harm in worship. The polar opposite of what the Pit taught.*"

"*What about the day to afflict our inner energy?*" Elitsza had pointed out. "*That's in there, too.*"

"That is a day to see where you have turned away from my Pali, and turn back to him, as he turns to you, like the sun and its planets." Joshua countered. *"Your inner energy does not need torture to be afflicted. It should be afflicted just from your distance from the Progenitor of all energy. That is the natural way of all things. Things become cold distanced from heat."*

"May I ask with what priesthood you studied the Being Beyond, little mammal?" Elitsza had asked, restraining the flash of red that jumped to her snout with a polite—if slightly passive aggressive —lavender. *"And what is this term you use, Pali?"*

"The translator does not say? Hm. It must be incomplete." Joshua had run to get his mother to fix the compupad then, and never gave the reptilian leader an answer—probably for the best. I got the vibe from Lark that Elitsza wasn't really safe for him to be around, much less to spout heresy at.

"He has said to me that Njandejara cannot die," Masha continued. "I overheard him telling Lark Scrita that he is a version of Njandejara that can. He *knows* about the metaphysical energy crisis you and Bricandor believe in. Without anyone telling him. These aren't normal things for someone so young to think about."

"I mean, he was never going to grow up normal after you told him he didn't have a male to make him," I smirked. She stiffened and drew away from me.

"I know what happened," she said.

"I'm sorry," I said. "I'm still—not sure you do. I want to believe you. But I'm also—sorry."

I got up and untangled myself from them. I needed to leave them alone. She could criticize her son's weird beliefs about himself if she wanted, but I still wasn't totally cool with the social shame she brought on Cinta, or the fact that she didn't have the guts to tell him she liked him when she'd tangled him up in her weird future like this.

Oh shyte—wasn't supposed to think that aloud. I turned to see Cinta looking at me. He'd definitely heard.

I threw my hands in the air. *Fine, the sneaky girl wins.*

CINTA

Cinta filled the space by Masha's side that Jaika had left, just to let Masha know, with his shoulder, that he believed her, even if no one else did. "One moment. I need to explain something to my sister," he said.

Cinta chased after Jaika and tackled her leg, like he used to when they played together. She fell with a smirk. "What?" she grumbled.

"Jaika," he whispered by her ear. "I am not trapped by Masha. And I will pay you back the money you lent me for the mating pact when I can."

"I don't care about the cash, man," she spat. "Don't insult me."

"I know, but I do not want you to think she is a burden on myself or on you," he said, settling on his belly beside her.

Jaika looked up at the ceiling and laid her hands on her stomach with another wordless grumble, hiding her mouth from him on purpose so he would read her thought. "I don't think she's a burden. I just want you to have a future with someone you love. I know you sell yourself short because of the stupid claws thing, and I guess I feel … responsible."

"Oh, Jaika," he said pushing his nose under the back of her neck. "My declawing was not your fault. That was also my choice. I told you not to give in, remember? And I heard you, in the storm on Forge, about Jared Diebol. We need not speak of it again."

"Are you sure?" Jaika thought.

"I am sure. And …" He tilted his head to the side. "Do not be like our parents, please. I know this is not normal, and one should know someone for at least ten years before deciding on a mate, but I actually can love someone I have only known for one."

Jaika spoke aloud now. "I understand that. It's not the same—I've never—I don't have a mate. But it doesn't always take that long for someone to get so deep in your electricity you'll never get them out." He heard her remember Jei and Mera, and, in a different way, herself and Jei. That was true, he realized—they had only worked together for three years.

"It seemed much longer," he agreed.

"It really did." She laid a fist over her chest, as if stanching a bleed there. "We're going to make this all worth it," she whispered finally.

"Will you be all right?" he asked.

"Once this is all over," she said.

What does that mean? But her mind did not tell him. Only that Bricandor would die, and after that—nothing. "I believe I am afraid of you for the same reason Masha fears Joshua," Cinta admitted.

"Well. At least I don't think I'm from outside of space," she grinned. "And—like with her and him—you're the one who started the weird ideas in my head."

"We sow the wind, and are surprised when we reap hurricanes," Cinta murmured.

His human hurricane ruffled the fur between his ears with a friendly pat, and Cinta was free to return to Masha's side with jubilee in his breath.

"Do you have something you need to tell me?" he asked her immediately.

"I don't want to burden you," she answered, trembling suddenly. She lowered her head like an Elder submitting after a duel. "I'm not a coward, you know. I just don't want to lose what we have. My son needs you."

"I do not make promises lightly. You will not lose me," he said. "But I also—as we get older, Masha, I cannot take from you what you do not *tell me* you agree to give."

She lay on her belly with a sigh; he dropped next to her. "It feels like it's not allowed to tell you," she said.

"There are many rules that we follow that are not in the manuscripts," he said. "As I am sure Joshua will gladly point out."

"But what happens after this?" she whispered. "With—is it really the end of all things? And what does it all have to do with my son?"

"I do not know," Cinta said. "But I would not like to waste the days until the end, no matter how long or short, with uncertainty between us."

"Why don't you just read my mind, then?" Masha exclaimed, sitting up straight. "You're the one male for whom understanding females should be easy!"

Cinta almost laughed; his back jerked him upright. "You truly want that?" he asked in wonder.

"You read everyone else's!" she cried out—then looked around, embarrassed. But no one had noticed her outburst. "You read everyone else's," she repeated with a quieter voice. "What's the problem? It doesn't seem invasive or painful or perverse. So why not me?"

It was, indeed, foolish when she put it that way. He covered his nose with his paw and dropped one ear. "Because … I feel I have so much power over you already. With—with what could have happened to you when they discovered Joshua."

"But that's power *I* gave you," Masha said. "I'm not just hunting any random male to cover my son like some dunehorn in heat. I want *you*. So why shouldn't you *know* me?" She lay back down, ears flopping down the side of her head in sadness as her voice quieted. "Am I too … tainted?"

Cinta did laugh now. "Oh, Masha." His belly filled with warmth, and his shoulders softened as nature made his next step so clear to him. He lay down beside her, nuzzled his nose by her cheek, and gently licked the fur at the side of her mouth. This, only for mates and children, she returned with a shy shimmy of her rump. "I have believed I am the one who is too tainted," Cinta whispered. "My tribe hates violence, and I have become a man of blood. All tribes value strength, and I have no claws. You know this."

"I hated it when they said that to you, earlier," she growled. Her neck's fur bristled, and Cinta hid his face in it. "They have clawless hearts and *nefesh* with no teeth. It's easy to face danger with strength handed to you by nature. It's much harder when you have to conjure your strength yourself. I know. I've been a small pregnant female working alone in a factory staffed by giant lizards and furless mammals. What clawed person stepped up for me when my clan threw rot at me and raided my tent? Besides, claws are overrated. I've heard—" It was her turn to hide her nose with her paw as her voice shrunk to the squeak of an embarrassed cub. "I've heard clawed males draw blood when they—make young."

Cinta shifted away from her, his ears upright on his head and eyes wide. Scandalously bold subject notwithstanding: "My tribe would consider that abuse," he gasped.

"It's not on purpose," Masha protested. "I've just heard during passion males can't—"

"We are too young for this," Cinta batted her ear with his paw. "When we are Elders, we will. And I do not mean to pass judgment on your clan's culture. But *I* do not intend to hurt you. Certainly not in that moment."

She batted his ear back. "Now you have me worried I'll hurt *you*," she grumbled.

"Masha, I have escaped Growen prisons that have driven seasoned warriors mad." His muzzle twisted with humor. "I have killed an electric sabertooth and a forest cephalopod. I believe I can handle mating with an 18-kilogram Biouk female."

She snuffled, shy at his boldness, and hid one of her eyes with her ear now. "Well. That's good, then." She cleared her throat, both paws over her muzzle hiding a surprised smile. "So. Can you see things when you read minds?"

"Sometimes. If I close my eyes," he said.

"There's something I want to show you," she said. "How will I know if you can see?"

"Unless you can read minds, too, I would have to tell you," he said. "But if you close your eyes, I can whisper to you, and then you will see in your mind what I say, and then we can both see the same thing."

"Okay." She nuzzled her head under his chin, one ear down under him, and one ear perked and waiting. He smiled, laid his head down on hers, and closed his eyes.

"I see a storm of every color, lit with a jubilant sun—a storm dangerous in its majesty, but safe for me," he whispered. "May I walk through it?"

"Yes," she said, and then he saw her there with him, the oranges and pinks of the wild sunset reflecting in the black sky of her shining pupils as her long fur spun in the wind. She licked his muzzle, and they ran off together into the most wonderful secret dawn.

CHAPTER SEVENTEEN

Jaika

IT WASN'T THAT LONG BEFORE I BEGAN TO UNDERSTAND MASHA'S fear better.

My first unease was emotional. I could tell Reise *bristled* every time Cinta or Masha mentioned Njandejara to each other, like the idea of our interdimensional friend literally disgusted him—*hurt* him. He'd never been good at masking his emotions —neither of us were—and finally I decided to try to talk to him.

I took the chance to sit beside him while everyone else was resting—mostly sleeping, some still eating, but all off doing their own thing. Reise was cleaning one of the pistols, and he seemed happy to see me, at least.

"So Lem," he said, turning that intense gaze on me. His cherry-wood eyes were so much darker than mine now—they almost seemed mahogany. "How are you doing?"

"Woof, that's a loaded question, man," I said. "I, uh—well, I'm not dead, as you've noticed."

"Yeah—Jake says he wasn't sure, either, even though he maintained contact with the Frelsi the whole year," Reise said, eyes back on his scrubbing. "I wouldn't have known, obviously.

But it was kind of cruel that you allowed our whole family to believe you'd perished."

"I figured it'd be better for you all if I died trying to do something right than if I lived doing nothing," I answered. I'd planned for this question. "I hadn't stopped the world from going to shyte. I didn't want to be alive until I'd fixed it."

His answer surprised me, though. "You were under no such obligation. We're living our own lives. I owe the universe nothing, and neither do you."

I tilted my head. "Why do you say that?"

"Because I despise all forms of control," he said. "That should be obvious." He tapped the back of his neck, where keloids rose over the slight bulges of something that stretched like fingers along his spine before disappearing into the base of his skull. My stomach twisted. How could I comfort or be any use at all to someone who'd gone through something so horrible, that I hadn't?

"It's—so filking awful what happened to you," I said quietly. "Is that why you're mad at Njandejara?"

"No," he laughed. "My capacity to reason is not dictated by trauma. Maybe you lost faith when no one came to save you, but I wasn't begging invisible brainworms for salvation." He spun the polished pistol over his wrist before plunging it into the plundered holster on his hip. "I will say you can't claim to be friends with someone or to love justice if you don't come to their aid when in peril. You came across the solar system to my aid, as I came to yours on the ledge, because we are actually friends, and we do love justice."

I returned his nod of respect, but I didn't like where this was leading.

"I'm not angry at Njandejara, because he doesn't exist in our dimension." Reise's eyes traced the curves of his weapon for a moment before shooting back up to mine almost like he was trying to get me to fight him. And I wanted to. "If he were in this dimension, I would kill him, though," Reise added.

"For the casualties he didn't save," I pressed, repeating the issue—trying to focus on his pain, not the fact that he'd just threatened someone I loved.

"No, I wouldn't kill him for people he didn't save," he scoffed—his friend across the ship gave him a look, and Reise cooled his tone. "Listen. You can't punish someone for what they didn't do. No one owes anyone else their action of their services. That mere idea is the basis of a socialized slave economy."

I disagreed with that—the Sterba within me disagreed hard, and she churned my stomach like the time Cinta accidentally fed me rotten peacock guinea pig—but Reise continued before my brain and tongue could come up with an exception to his hard and fast rule.

"I'd kill him," Reise said. "For the children he killed himself."

I narrowed my eyes. "Excuse me?"

"You haven't read it? In your manuscripts?" he said. "He ordered the mass slaughter of several civilization's children."

"Except in those stories, he literally carried the lifespan of every person on that planet. So not just children, but *everyone* who ever died, died at a time he knew beforehand, so they could finally rest. If he's choosing between all possible timelines—"

"That's worse, not better," Reise interrupted. "Inventing death? I've heard that timeline drivel a thousand times, and I reject it." He picked up another weapon to clean and jammed a small ramrod into its barrel. "You cannot truly believe this is the ideal timeline out of millions of other permutations."

"I do have my doubts," I admitted. "But I'm also not going to blame someone I can't see when there are blame-worthy folks I can. Those kids were going to be burned to death by their parents. Being quickly wiped out is a lot better."

"Those are ridiculous alternatives, and no offense, but they're exactly what Bricandor's saying about Contaminated people right now," Reise said. "Die via genocide, or be murdered slowly by your parents' evil mind disease. A being outside of space and time couldn't come up with *any* other option? You're assuming there weren't other possibilities."

"And you're assuming there were! Between millions of us making our own choices, I can understand how we could paint ourselves into a corner where our leaders have so destroyed our world and ourselves that there's nothing to do but take all our programming to a better plane and start over. Bricandor doesn't actually know what's best! Someone who knows everyone's choices would."

"But what about the victims' right to choose?" Reise cried. "They didn't ask for that. And don't tell me any more versions of 'bad things happen for a good reason.' I've heard that one, and after losing Gideon, I'm not really buying it."

Reise's friend walked over and sat down cross-legged in front of us. "I, uh. I want to say something."

"Shoot." I nodded; Reise's raised shoulders lowered, and his rigid spine relaxed.

"Go ahead," he said.

"I can't speak for a dead person," Nathan murmured. "But I think you and I both know Gideon wouldn't want his death to be seen as a tragedy. And I can't speak for all the people you had to—kill or Turn—but if you asked them, how many of them would say it would be worth it to die on Bijou if you could bring a cure to the rest of the planets? My blood wouldn't make it if we hadn't Turned."

Reise didn't want to argue with Nathan. I could see that. I spoke up for Reise, trying to be gentle. "I think maybe Reise would still say that's a false dichotomy," I said. "Like that there's a possible universe where we could've had both. No mind control, and no dead people." Reise nodded. I turned to him now. "But that's—that's impossible when there's free will, because each choice has rippling consequences. And you can't *be* sapient unless you have the ability to choose something bad. Non-sapient animals generally choose what's best for them, as far as they know, until we teach them good and bad. Like reina bees and their perfect hive. We're not like that. If we're sapient, there has to be a bad for us to choose."

"I continue to insist that by focusing on the choice of the wrongdoer you're overlooking the choice of the victim." He looked at Nathan. "Respectfully."

"That's fine," Nathan said. "I just don't think the world is victims and perpetrators. I think there are also heroes, and that maybe most people who've died innocent would choose that if they knew the full picture." He wrung his hands, then stood back up, suddenly looking very small. "That's all I wanted to say. I'm—going to go lie down."

Shyte, poor guy. He didn't seem to be holding up as well as Reise was. He squished against the wall of the ship and folded his parka over his face and ears to shut out the world.

Reise followed my gaze. "What would any of us choose, if we knew everything?" I asked him.

"Not this."

"Does it help to know Njande's angrier about this than you are?"

"Then he should fix it. But he doesn't, does he?" Reise's teeth flashed like knives. "He prefers to punish people with the law of cause and effect. He'd rather not stop a crime—he'd rather punish the murderer afterward. Except if you're right, and the entire timeline's pre-chosen, then the murderer can't help that he turned out that way. So now there's a double crime: the loss of the victim's free will, and of the murderer's."

"You're forgetting reference planes, though, man. What's predetermined outside the timeline wouldn't be predetermined inside it, because time only moves in here, right?" He didn't seem to buy it. "I mean two things can be true, Reise. It's sometimes true that we can't help but do evil because we give up that free will over time in exchange for other things. Like how addiction works. But then it's still true we're responsible for it, because we *could have had* the free will to stop ourselves, if we valued our own will enough."

"I didn't really choose to lose my free will," Reise said, eyes cold. "I didn't want to Turn."

"Not what I'm talking about," I groaned.

"It's the same tyranny," Reise spat. "Njandejara, the Growen —they're the same."

My chest heated as I struggled to ignore the insult. *Calm down. Don't be mad. He just doesn't know.*

But I finally understood what we were talking about: Reise wasn't the victim in his argument. He was the murderer.

"The Turn wasn't your fault," I said. Shyte, my voice sounded weak. "What if—even though the universe tries to sap our ability to choose—if we connect with the Energy Outside, we get the ability to survive other peoples' choices? And the ability to choose better ourselves?"

"That's a what-if. It's not real. I've seen plenty of Contaminated people go to their deaths screaming while Clean people kept their heads on," Reise muttered.

I looked over at Joshua playing in the corner with some of the flowers growing by the back of the ship. "Do you—you've never heard Njandejara then, Reise?" I asked.

He sprayed solvent down the gun barrel and rubbed it in. "I used to think I did. I was imagining things, most likely," he said.

"What if—what if someone could tell you in real time what he said?"

"I'd say they were lying."

"What if—" I didn't know if I could say something I wasn't a hundred percent sure I believed myself. "If there was like a— matter—option—like—"

"What if Njandejara became something I could talk to in this dimension, with a body?" he filled in for me.

"… yeah?"

"Then I would kill him," he shrugged. "For creating the death code and killing us all for things we couldn't control. Death isn't a solution."

"It's not that it's a solution, it's a consequ—"

But he'd already gotten up and stepped away to sit with his friend, and as much as I wanted to argue with him—as much as I *hate* not getting the last word—it was exhausting trying to defend something I wasn't sure about myself. He needed his friend.

But the conversation did leave me deeply uneasy about Joshua, because it scared me that my brother didn't have a connection with the one being who might actually be able to store his programming somewhere safe after death, if that was a thing, and it also scared me that if Joshua *were* somehow part of Njandejara, and my brother believed it, Reise could actually kill him.

My *other* unease was more personal. I saw Joshua's very deliberate look at Laaru when he walked over to the young Stygge and asked him if he'd like to see something. It was a look that knew exactly what he was doing. It was a dangerous look, and I didn't like it, because I *didn't* know what he was doing. I walked over to them just in time to see Laaru's jaw drop; some colors dissipated outside.

"What'd I miss?" I asked.

"He can—holy shyte," Laaru gasped. I remembered Laaru as a "good kid," not someone who cursed like me. Was it just from being around soldiers, or had Joshua just shown him something really shocking? "That's some electromagnetic ability you've got, little guy."

Instead of correcting him with some Pali this or Pali that, Joshua just thanked him and scampered away. *Why.*

"What was it?" I asked.

"It's—hard to describe," Laaru said. "He definitely just

moved an asteroid field around, though. And then—split it into a shower of colorful chemicals."

"What." I narrowed my eyes and chased after Joshua. "Excuse me, young man," I said, stepping over him. He ran through my legs, and then around them, laughing. I reached down for him, and he dodged out of my grasp with a squeal. "Joshua …"

"Yes, Auntie Jaika?" he giggled, rolling over on his back as I tripped and fell over myself next to him. "How can I help you?"

"Well, for starters, if you can levitate shyte, why did I have to save your butt in the marketplace at Forge?" I asked.

His tone became somber; the little child disappeared under the parthenogenetic being. "Because with you protecting us it was just a little fight, not a big prophecy-fulfilling event for my clan," he said. "And it took the Ebon Shadow longer to find us because it was just a little fight. It would have been worse for us and the Watchers if news about me traveled faster."

"I don't know how it could've possibly gone worse for the Watchers," I said.

"It could have," he said. "You and Cinta led him away quickly, though."

"Well, okay, then there's that!" I cried—and without meaning to, my complaint began to sound like an accusation. "We—*I* had to fight the Shadow. Why am I running around trying to save you and everyone else if you're able to move giant space rocks? Filk it, why didn't you help me down on Bijou?"

"You didn't let me," he said. "Even if I said I could, you would not have believed me. Even if I showed you, Mali would not let me."

"That didn't stop you before," I growled. Was I growling?

"Because it wasn't time for me now," he said. "It was time for you."

"Filk you very much," I spat. Shyte, what was wrong with me? I could feel moisture at the edges of my eyes. I threw my forearm over them and swallowed the sticky pudding in my throat. "Sorry."

"It is okay." He tapped my forearm. "Jerusha-Lem, do you know what I mean by that?"

I lowered my arm. I didn't call him out for violating Biouk honorific language. I found myself using it for him instead. "What do you mean by that, teacher?"

"I mean it is *actually* okay. You'll see at the end of this."

"I don't know how it could be. Two apocalypses on two different worlds with so much loss of life, Joshua. If you'd have been there—well. You were there. But actually been there, shown up, with all of you." I rolled over and raised myself on my forearms. "Joshua, one of my little brother's best friends died down there."

"I will tell you a secret about Gideon one day," Joshua said. No one had told him the kid's name. "In fact—" He looked out at the stars. "In about four days, I will tell you."

"All that cryptic shyte is really hard for those of us living and dying down here in the blood and sweat and violation of the real world, Njandejara." I didn't mean to say that name—it just kind of slipped. I didn't really believe he was related, did I? I definitely didn't mean to get both Elitsza and Reise looking over at me with so much scrutiny. "Come here," I said to Joshua. I wanted to hide in the back of the ship, but on the back right sat Laaru, and on the back left—well. We could go over behind Lark and Carl. That was fine. "Come here, please," I repeated.

Joshua sat next to me, and we stared out the back window. "Look," I said. "I remember Njandejara telling me about the electron and the wave. About being in sync with him, and about how sometimes he doesn't rescue because we're the rescue. And I know he told Jei about how sometimes evil is allowed to exist because what looks evil at first turns out to be good, and we just didn't know it, because we were so stuck in our own right and wrong. But … there is a real problem of suffering in the universe beyond those things, Joshua. When evil is actually evil, and it's not going to turn out to be good, and when we aren't the rescue, no matter how synced with him we might be."

Shyte, my chest hurt. I coughed to keep myself from choking on my words, and I lowered the pitch of my voice to sound stronger. "So then I'm just left with the mystery promise about a *go'ali* to buy back the universe, but then, then what? We're going to go on doing wrong for a long time. So maybe I work my butt off trying to be better, but inside there's still this desire to destroy, to consume, because the Accuser's always just a little bit right, you know? So suffering is going to continue, because even if I don't do something wrong, someone else still does something wrong, that filks up the environment, and then I get eaten by an ursa-fly. Right?"

"What is your question, Jaika?" Joshua asked. His tone seemed stern to me.

"Why am I damned no matter what I do?" I asked.

His ears dropped down beside him, almost reaching the floor past his little shoulders. His sigh was so deep, I thought for a second his chest hurt, too. "If I say you're not, will you believe me?"

"I guess not," I said.

"So if I tell you what I'm going to do with my body and how it works—because mine also has rules, just like yours, where you can't just keep firing lasers whenever you want—and if I tell you my plan to fix all this, will you listen to me, or will you and Mali lock me all up?"

I crossed my arms over my chest, and realized it looked more like I was hugging myself—because I was. I wanted comfort, and I was getting a nebula instead.

"I know to you it looks like I just do whatever I want all the time," Joshua said, tilting his head sideways like any creature with eyes on two sides of its head will do when it wants to look at you square in the face. "But I can't. I have to do what Pali says. The matter-being in front of you is still under the one outside of time and space."

"It must be nice to be told exactly what to do instead of having to figure it out," I muttered.

"There isn't much freedom in that," he said. "Most Turned will tell you they'd rather someone give them data and let them go from there—not decide every move for them. You have data: the historical manuscripts first, and then nature second, and Reason to help you parse it all. You haven't been set adrift without a guide. And Pali does talk to you. You just don't always hear." He turned to look back out at the stars. "Here inside time and space you have a kind of freedom we don't have out there, because out there, the whole timeline's just one static image, one place where everything's already happened. There everything that will be already is, from the first moment the Progenitor spoke. Don't envy me a throne whose cost you can't pay."

My ribs hurt so much, and my forehead seemed—full. Had I burned myself out that badly? I just couldn't understand. "I'm so confused," I whimpered.

"I know." He kept his gaze out the window, and for a second I thought he might pat me on the knee, but I didn't really want anyone to touch me right now, and he didn't. He sighed again, and looked over his shoulder at everyone, then back out the window. "This is a really confusing life. I feel like a solar system stuffed in a sausage casing most days."

A snort of laughter escaped me despite myself. "What?"

"I'm serious, Jaika," he said. "I'm really … scared. Of what I have to do. You're not the only one the Accuser talks to, you know."

I furrowed my brow. "What does he say?"

"It's a pretty painful belief, that you're destined for evil," he answered. "Perhaps the worst lie is that you're not destined for anything at all. Not a villain—not even a part of the story. 'Do you really know who you are?' he asks us, right? 'Little narcissist, if you are what you say you are, why don't you live up to it?' Over and over, just hoping we'll forget and stop believing what Njandejara told us about ourselves. That's why the greatest thing Pali can call himself is Someone Who *Is* What They *Are*.

"Because that's the most impossible thing to be."

CHAPTER EIGHTEEN

Lark

"WE WILL ARRIVE IN LESS THAN THREE HOURS," CINTA FINISHED TO the utter hodgepodge of sapient life now crowding the bioship. The tyke took control well these days, Lark thought—not that he'd been shy when they first started working together, but he gave orders like a military ship's captain now, not like some polite manager corralling consultants. Now when he said things, you knew by golly that was how things were going to be.

He'd obtained landing permission, prisoner transfer for the young Stygge, medical prep for the Draconian, and quarantine procedures to protect the reptilians from a new atmosphere and its diseases: everyone on board knew exactly what they needed to do when they hit dirt. The Benzarans would make sure the skinny lad got to whatever science bunker the Frelsi needed him in, and everyone else would head out to recon the center of the Structure. The Benzaran squad and Cinta and Masha would leave right away; Carl and Lark would supervise unloading and admin until the ship was secure and Frelsi child support could come for Joshua, and then they'd follow. The ship couldn't land in the current Frelsi base, so it'd touch down instead on a pad just by Fort Jehu's ruins: each person had to be checked individually for mind-control hardware, and to keep the Frelsi calm about former defector Lem Benzaran waltzing in with two known Turned soldiers, Nefesh would greet them on landing with an armed escort.

And Carl and Lark would handle the other Ebon Shadow, if he showed.

"Cinta sounds so bloody certain of us," Lark chuckled to Lem Benzaran as they buckled in. "You'd almost follow his plans to the edge of the known systems, you would."

"Well, you know what they say," Benzaran sighed. "Every plan's shyte when you make first contact with the enemy."

"Not sure that's what they say, mate," Lark smirked.

"Well, it's true. Real quick on the Shadow's double, though—just thought you should know the timer's not expiring on your disguise slips. So he's just whoever he wants to be, for however long he wants to be," Benzaran said.

"Timer?" Lark asked, one eyebrow raised.

"Yeah, timer. When I borrowed them for undercover shyte with the Growen I had time limits before they had to, like, recharge," Benzaran said. "He didn't have that problem. Am I crazy or something? Why you looking at me like that?"

"Beans," Lark gasped. "I'm so sorry, mate—got stuck on demo mode, you did."

"Anything I could've done about that?" Benzaran asked, crossing her arms—she seemed pretty peeved for someone talking tech issues that'd happened almost two years ago.

"No, not really, mate," Lark said. "It happens if they don't come back to me to get recalibrated over time, it does. You should've called me."

"Couldn't. Mind-readers and shyte," Benzaran grumbled.

"Well then, it is what it is, innit?" Lark said.

"Guess it is," Benzaran growled; her anger included the ship, apparently, and the hollow seat it'd formed around her. She unbuckled and reformed it with frustrated fists. "Beginning to think I'm just the *bika* hunting with all the bad wind," she muttered.

The Bioukism about bad fortune, Lark got. But: "What's a *bika*?"

A half-grin popped out the side of Benzaran's grumpy mouth. "Ah. Literally, it's a mating-age female who can't afford a canopy home," she said. "Which—ironically—both Masha and I are barreling toward becoming." She laughed; the Biouk girl overheard and chuckled, but Cinta looked annoyed. "It's used as an insult for like a dumb or lazy woman, or some poor little thing with nothing to offer. But younger folks like us use it the way you use 'lass' or whatever, just a little more rude."

"Beans, guess I'm a *bika*, too, then," Lark said.

"Are you?" Benzaran squinted. "Pretty sure the ship where you live's more expensive than a Biouk canopy home."

"It blew up, mate," Lark said. "'Sides, wasn't mine, was it?"

"Wasn't it?" Benzaran repeated.

"Keep narrowing your eyes like that, mate, and they'll be thinner than mine," Lark laughed. "What are you getting at?"

Benzaran shook her head with a sneaky little smile and got up. "Yo, Shadow, get over here and switch with me," she said, heading for the cockpit. "I need that spot you're sitting in. This one's messing with my back."

Carl looked a mite confused, but he didn't seem to see a point in arguing, and soon he'd settled into a new hollow beside Lark. As it formed a backrest and armrests around him, Szizzle and Joshua came over—Szizzle, apparently curious as ever, to investigate what could be wrong with *this* part of the ship, and Joshua carrying his mother's compupad in his mouth behind her.

"I don't feel any difference in the floor density here," Szizzle said through the translator, tapping with her long feet. "I hope that doesn't mean I'm becoming less sensitive."

"I think that's just Benzaran being a mite precious, lass," Lark said. "She's still peeved about all the things that've ever gone wrong in her life."

"Sounds familiar," Carl said. He didn't look at her when he said it; she couldn't tell if that was a twinkle or a grudge in his eye, or if he meant Lark or him. *You'd think without a mask on he'd be easier to read.* Being able to see his face still—that was Lark's doing. She'd noticed how jumpy the Frelsi boys got, what with Carl wearing a blitzer helmet on top of the armor, so she'd let him know to lose it for now. She had to admit a teeny tiny ulterior motive there: Carl had borrowed the clippers Cinta used for his fur, and he was right pleasant to look at now, all trimmed up but not quite clean-shaven.

Lark suddenly realized her inspection of her cage-mate's bone structure had made her miss something. "Wait, Szizzle, what's that mean, you're worried you're becoming less sensitive? What's that matter, lass?"

Szizzle waited a second for the translator—it was still utter bollycock they couldn't hear Lark, when she could pretty much speak their language—and answered: "When our population declines, a percentage of females will often change into male. I've heard lower skin sensitivity is an early sign. I don't *think* it'll happen, since we have Rizzt, but it could if his pheromones aren't strong enough."

"You lot can switch out your whole bodies?" Lark turned to Joshua. "So why is it okay for them and not us?"

Szizzle answered, apparently not understanding the eye contact. "Our Progenitor gave us these abilities for times of starvation to protect our species. Your kind has been given other tricks. Mammals usually have lower hatching death rates, for example, and can make milk so their young don't have to hunt to feed."

"But what if I don't want these things? Milk and shyte, yuck." Lark hugged herself, immediately conscious of her breasts even through the blitzer armor—the reminder literally sent a disgusting tingle across them like peroxide on an open wound.

"You are equally good." Szizzle tilted her head, confused. "You've proven we were wrong to treat you less than us. Clearly we can see now there's no goal we can achieve that you can't, at its core. We survive starvation, so do you. We teach our young, so do you. We invent, you do, too. You can already shape-shift with your special scale, the one that made you look like a mutated Allperson."

"A Bont reptilian, you mean," Lark nodded.

Szizzle nodded again. "If anything, with your minds making this technology, I should want to be like you. So why would you need my means, when you've proven you can reach the same ends without me?"

Lark didn't like how she put that. She didn't like the pained way Carl excused himself to go stand by the back window, either. "Because it's really hard to believe that I can," she sighed. She couldn't say more without hurting the Veterinarian's feelings—because beans, did this make Lark remember how much faster they could've escaped had she been Bont.

No one answered for a moment; in the quiet, Lark overheard a snippet of the conversation going on in the front of the ship. "Just because someone can make you do something doesn't mean you want it," said the human with the big, messy lighter curls. "The body can betray you."

"It is different, though," Rizzt answered through the updated translator on the human's wristband. "Because I chose my subjugation." He shuddered. "When the Bright One—when it got into me, I could taste—I don't know. It wasn't *completely* different from how I already felt. Like a hatred for my form. But this was —like a hatred for my very molecules."

Here you will be happy, and here you will be accepted for who you are, the Pit-God had said. *Because who you really are doesn't have matter. Aren't you tired of that body, Lark? Isn't that why you made me in the first place?*

"There's always a hidden desire for every desire," Joshua said finally. "A lot of people make the mistake of thinking the surface desire or even a twisted version of the deep desire will satisfy them. And then it doesn't. But if you can find the core of your desire, and fulfill that, you'll have peace."

Lark leaned back against the warm ship and wrapped her hands around her knees. What was her deepest desire? What did she want? She imagined being able to change her body, to be stronger and faster—why *did* she need to be stronger?

That receiver she couldn't reach and the gun shots in her parents' house flitted through the back of her mind, but so did the schoolyard competitions where other children wouldn't play with her, and the powerful feeling of her first catch as a Bont bounty hunter. Underneath it all, something hollow and warm and aching welled up in her stomach, and she looked over to where Carl was leaned up against the back wall, gazing out the clear window-like plating. His forearm rested against the wall, supporting his head like a pillow—with his arm raised like that, his whole side open, Lark could imagine the shape of the lats and ribs and long obliques now hidden by blitzer armor.

She hadn't seen him as him, when he lay on the forest floor with his back contorted and burns streaking his face and hands. She'd seen him as herself. She was glad of that somewhat. She'd taken the toxic drink to be what she wanted to be. But she'd also taken the drink because ... well, beans and blasted bloodseas, no one would listen to a human when they could have a reptilian, and Carl needed out of that bloody cage.

Because with him she'd found the closest thing to belonging, and no matter what happened to her he at least needed to survive. She smiled. Beans, she still remembered the shiver when he walked into the bar on Luna-Guetala that first time—

Lark furrowed her brow. Beans, had she always liked him, from that first time she'd tried to poison his beer? Strange that he'd never held that against her. That had been *why* he'd shot her—second strike, stealing his catch, after trying to assassinate him. The Ebon Shadow couldn't have people wandering around who tried to kill and rob him. She remembered why she'd done it, too. She'd listened wide-eyed to the legends about him, and copied his moves from the leaked videos—beans, she'd hate-watched the uploads for a while, because she wanted to save the kind of people he killed. But the fascination for his prowess had felt a little like watching the top athletes in her class and longing for their Bont legs.

But once she actually worked with him—beans, what a relief when he wasn't like in the videos. Those were K'arl's. Carl's Ebon Shadow was scarier, a thrilling, spine-tingling silent enigma, someone who took control without apologies but didn't overturn a whole blasted mountain about it. He didn't take down innocent targets anymore like in the videos, either. And he didn't have that massive insecurity so many blokes did where they couldn't take orders: Carl only cared about whether or not the shots Lark called made logical sense, and he didn't mean that in some stereotypical Burburan "lads think and lasses feel" way, either. The computer decided, the facts decided, and most of the time, Lark knew all sorts Carl didn't.

Even the thing she hated most about him was something she loved: how unlike everyone else in the botched-up universe, she couldn't read him *at all*. He kept her on her poor little, short non-Bont toes, and he also kept her out.

He was too far out of her league, he was, and so she'd settle for someone who thought she was a dime piece and told her nice things.

"Beans, I've been playing myself," Lark said aloud, unbuckling herself now. "Stay here and be comfortable, mates, I think my back doesn't favor this spot either."

"What? Why can't I feel this problem everyone else can?" Szizzle complained behind her.

CHAPTER NINETEEN

Lark

LARK DASHED TO CARL'S SIDE BY THE BACK WINDOW AND THREW her arms around his ribs—the tightest and highest hug her shortness could manage. He tensed; she realized with a chuckle his hand had leapt to the holster on his thigh before he forced himself to relax.

But his arms lowered, and he looked down at her, and squeezed her back. She realized when he stepped away that his body almost seemed—afraid.

"I'll ask you something, mate, and if you like me, I hope you'll open your blasted mouth and do your best to speak my language," she said, summoning all the game and bravado she could muster into her puffed-out chest.

His lips pursed, but one side rose a little—both nervous and curious, looked like. "All right," he said.

"First question: did she hurt you some other way, your ex?" Lark asked. "I'm not asking for details, mate, and I'm not about that prying. But your ribs"—she poked him as he sat down; even through the armor he twisted away a bit—"are scared."

He grimaced. "Very direct question. I'm not refusing to answer. But may I ask why?"

"Because, mate, I never wanted to ruin your life—certainly not a second time—and it broke my little heart right in two when you used past tense, 'liked,' about me," she said. She didn't love blatant honesty, but she knew how the law of equivalent exchange worked in conversation. "I didn't kiss you earlier because I didn't want to put world-digesting goo into you, not because I didn't want that kiss. You said you'd like to spend the end of the world with me. Then you said we're not compatible. I want to know what I'm s'posed to do with that, mate, and I want to know what you're working with."

He looked at her, processing. She waited. "I don't have any diagnosed physical or mental trauma from my ex, no," he said.

"So she's not why you never made a play at me," Lark said.

"No."

"So why not? I was on your ship for almost four years."

"Two reasons. One, I'm almost five years older than you."

Lark laughed out loud. "Who bloody cares, mate?"

"I do. That should be obvious. I'm the one who said it." This was the closest to an actual pet peeve rant Lark had heard from him lately. "Why are obvious things never obvious to people?"

"Well, mate, I don't care," Lark shrugged. "To be honest, I thought you were much older. Beans, you must've been a teenager with your first marriage."

"Yes. She was about five years older than me. She had experience I didn't in every way—a distinct uneven advantage." He cleared his throat. "Also—when it wasn't about my identity as the Ebon Shadow, she seemed to like my youth itself to an—obsessive—degree."

"You felt used in the end," Lark translated.

"Yes."

"But it's not like that now," Lark said. "I'm older than you were by a good bit, and I'm the younger one, not you. I'm not afraid of being used. Beans, I've—I've made you feel used, in fact." She lowered her voice. "That the second reason you never made a play, lad?"

"No," he said. "I didn't want to bother you with something you didn't want. The universe has too many frauds who say and do anything to 'conquer' people who just want to be left alone."

She threw her hands up in the air, well and truly frustrated. "Well, mate, how could you know I wanted to be left alone if you didn't ask?"

"I could say the same," he said. "I did show interest. I don't do the things for everyone that I do for you."

"Mate, I figured that's because I'm the only business partner you've never killed." Lark scowled. "Beans, we're stupid. We could've been together all this time. What a filking waste. Look, you've got to tell me stuff!"

He looked away from her at the wall—she caught his grin before he could completely hide it. When he turned back, he'd erased it with cool sobriety. "One could say this is an example of an incompatibility. Communication matters in relationships."

Lark didn't want to plead. She wanted to be wanted. But she couldn't help retorting: "Communication can be learned."

"Do healthy relationships generally start with bilateral attempted murder?" Carl asked.

"Mate, what is a healthy relationship for people like us? I grew up without parents and spent the last ten years pretending to be a lizard. You grew up all psycho and your main relative tries to kill you at least once a year. We're lucky not to be eating people's faces, mate," she laughed. "Much less live four years with someone and actually accomplish good like we have."

He looked away from her again. "I don't like how it sounds like I'm arguing with you," he said.

"How's that, mate?"

"I don't like proving a case against something I want." His eyes returned to hers with predatory intensity. She shivered—it was a good shiver. He blinked, and the burning quieted. "You did just mention another very serious incompatibility, however. I'm not my brother."

Hoo beanpods. "I'm daft, I know," Lark said. "At my most daft, I let myself believe he would become you. Grow a brain, stop killing kids. It was nice to have someone support what I feel inside, but … I just can't, mate. Even if the last two months hadn't happened to us, I'd have had to stop the wheels before getting to the destination, if you get my drift."

"I don't want a relationship that depends on him not changing to exist," Carl said. "I hate him. I would like to stop hating him. I would like him to improve, for the universe's sake, and so I can hate him less. And I hate him much more with you involved."

Lark pursed her lips. He was right: they couldn't have a life if Carl always felt he'd lose her if K'arl reformed. No one wants to be the budget option. He wasn't, though. How to actually reassure him she'd decided what she wanted …?

"Mate, what if I—what if I promised," Lark said, "that no matter what happens to him or anyone else, it's you for me. You want a signature? You want—one of those mating pacts like the Biouks do, with witnesses?"

He raised an eyebrow. "You're describing marriage."

"Not like the nutty legal tax shield what's used on most of Burbura," Lark said. "I mean an actual vow. Like what someone would be cursed if they break."

He leaned back in his seat with a heavy breath and crossed his arms. She'd seen him think like this when they'd gotten stumped on a target. "What's your quandary, mate?" Lark asked.

"I'm considering the possible outcomes of your scenario," he said, still staring straight ahead. "I'm aware this is not very romantic of me."

"I dunno who decides what's romantic and not, mate, but I'd rather be taken seriously than romanced," Lark said. "I've had a little bit enough of someone selling me easy street."

"What would be your expectation of me with regards to your dysphoria?" he asked, tilting his head to face her.

"Oof." Now it was her turn to get serious. She thought aloud: "It'd be a pretty botched thing to do to you, start one way then change on you, wouldn't it. I do want to be wanted for who I am, though, and I don't want to be abandoned for choosing something what you believe is wrong, because even staying human I'm going to do things wrong in my life. But maybe I don't actually know who I am. I thought I did. What's a little scary, mate, is that I think it really was working." She pointed to her scarred cheek. "A part of me still wants it finished. But I've been talking to—" She jerked her head back toward Joshua. "Do you know who he is, mate? Really is, I mean?"

"Yes," he said.

"Well if I'm honest with myself, mate—and I don't want to be —it's a little speciesist to believe there's a 'Bont' soul or a 'human' soul or a 'male' soul or a 'female' soul, what belongs with its body match," Lark said. "The world treats people unequal that way. But maybe it's the world's what's wrong, not me. I'm—I'm going to try to just learn what it means to be Lark."

He furrowed his brow. Her thoughts were confusing him. "I guess my expectations," she said. "Would be that you'd hear me when I talk about Bont stuff what I care about. And you'd tell me, with words, that what I am is made just exactly for my mission in life, when I feel like I'm not enough. I don't know if I need psychological treatment, but I might need help finding that, too. Because this bully hurts sometimes. I'd like to be held when it hurts."

"I can do that," he said.

She folded her hands on her lap. She suddenly needed to look very proper, because the earnest seriousness in his voice made her silly happy. The Ebon Shadow still wanted her—better than that, *Carl* wanted her. *I can do that* had all the assurance of the missions he never failed, all the safety of his shielding her when they'd rescued little Juju, and no mask, no armor, no facade. "So, 'til the end of the world, then?" Lark asked.

"You really wouldn't rather have him?" he asked.

"Mate, I've wanted you forever. You just made it seem impossible to have what I wanted," she said.

He looked away from her again with another deep breath—this one victoriously overwhelmed. "I'm uncertain whether or not I'm dreaming," he said.

Lark leaned in with a wicked smile right next to the side of his mouth, just close enough to *almost* touch. "I can show you you're not," she said.

His hand lashed out for her arm, gripping her like he'd lost his oxygen tank in space and she was his only line back to his ship. She stifled her gasp; her breath caught in her chest as his body rose to meet hers, bending her backward—

He stopped himself with the loveliest small laugh, touching his forehead gently to hers. "We need to be alone," he said.

"Very badly," she breathed. "Let's make this promise before you kill me."

CHAPTER TWENTY

Carl

CARL WAS NOT SURPRISED TO OVERHEAR THE EATER COMMENTING ON the promiscuity of mammals to Szizzle—with a side-eye toward him and Lark—as Carl took a knee to talk to Joshua. The Biouk cub was reading with Szizzle again, pointing out places the translator didn't make sense. He sat like a human at the moment, his little hind legs flat out in front of him, while Szizzle curled into an egg beside him. The youngest Benzaran boy sat beside him, watching over the ill, half-conscious Draconian.

Joshua rested the compupad on his hind legs as Carl approached.

"I've been waiting for you to come talk to me, Carl," Joshua said. "Why have you been avoiding me?"

Carl hadn't expected that question—he should have, he realized. Perhaps then he would've cornered Joshua alone. Instead, he found himself in front of the two reptilians and Lark, where he didn't want to answer that question. But Joshua held his gaze, and it suddenly seemed very correct to forget anyone else existed. "You know why, Presence," Carl said. "I'm matter covered in innocent blood, and you're radioactive energy full of goodness. A glimpse of you made your servant's face glow so brightly his people asked him to wear a veil." He still remembered that story little Juju Benzaran had told him; he still remembered that first night when his mind awoke and he'd so keenly sensed the *hatred* the Presence had for what he was doing to people like her. "I'm a house of wood, and you're fire."

"What should be done?" Joshua asked.

Carl's survival instinct flared, demanding silence: he looked down at his hard armored knee and forced himself to answer with logic, not desire. "In a just universe, I would be executed," he said. "I haven't really known what to do. It took me years to feel anything about my actions, and I've only recently realized I can't make up for them. Even now, if you hadn't peeled my armor off forcefully, I would've died inside it—the same cold machine just under a different emblem."

"At your trial, who would condemn you?" Joshua asked.

"There are no witnesses left other than my employers," he said.

"Do complicit criminals have the right to execute a criminal?" Joshua asked.

"No," Carl said.

"So only the energy you've sent to the Other Place—the blood on the ground—can speak against you," Joshua said.

"That is correct."

Joshua sighed, laying aside the compupad and folding his little paws together. "Something will have to be done to return the higher energy you've stolen from this plane," he said. "Your own would usually be required, spun into the engine of eternity. But I will take care of it. You'll hear about it in about three days, when it is done."

It was such a strange statement, but with his eyes fixed on the shining black pools of stern sympathy in Joshua's, Carl could think of nothing more natural. "What should I do?" he asked.

"Steal no more. If a planetary authority takes you in for a past evil, tell the truth, and pay what they ask, even including blood,"

Joshua said. He rose with another long sigh to place his paws on either side of Carl's face, and again it almost seemed to Carl as if the Biouk had human tears welling up in his eyes, or reptilian color under his skin. "But I won't let you pay your *self*," Joshua whispered. "I'll save your programming, no matter what happens, and you'll be okay. Because I really like you, Carl. We have to repay the victims. I like them, too, and the universe you broke. But I liked you even when I hated the Shadow you cast."

Carl bowed his head, so conscious of his slow pulse, his quiet heart. "Thank you. Please—forgive me," he said. "My mind calculates the value of what you're saying, and knows it, but my body—it's logically upsetting, something I don't like about myself, but I still don't feel everything I should, and I know you can tell. Please know the disrespect is unintentional."

"I don't ask people who can't walk to walk unless I plan on healing their legs," Joshua said. "Go and walk." Joy washed over his face—it didn't erase the sternness. "And love your lady! May I tell you both a story?"

Lark sat down now, the glowing pillows of her cheeks awash with concern. She gripped Carl's hand; he rubbed a thumb over her small, hard knuckles, then let go to keep the beast at bay. Her touch stirred the one thing in him that was too easy to feel since the cage.

"As you've suspected, Njandejara is the Progenitor being," Joshua said, standing back against the wall now. "From outside of time he's seen the whole thing from the moment his first sound wave punched energy into matter for the explosion that started the universe. That's kind of why the other interdimensionals hate him—creation is a betrayal, and he locked them in a timeline full of it. But he can't help it. He loves matter."

He grinned, a naughty grin wholly appropriate for his age, like a boy learning about reproduction. "And Njandejara made matter that can transform. Creatures that can take a plant, and make it energy, or take energy, and make a baby. He began to teach some of this matter to speak, and think, and want more. And that matter began to teach other matter, populating worlds with sapients."

He waved his paw, eyes sparkling as if they contained galaxies. "He gave them all of himself, and it was beautiful. But …" He darkened his tone. "You cannot *really* know you have something unless you know what it's like not to have it, and you cannot really be someone's lover, instead of their slave, if you didn't choose them."

"So that is why the first mother was given a choice," Szizzle said in awe. "To elevate her consciousness."

"It was a calculated risk, giving her that choice," Joshua nodded. "Because if you choose against oxygen, you cannot breathe, and if you choose against food, you will starve. By giving them the choice between himself, and not himself, he gave them the choice between the Wellspring of All, and death."

"So was the death code an accident, then?" Benzaran asked. She was standing over them now, leaning on her extended but deactivated mace like a walking stick.

"Not an accident," Joshua said. "An effect with safety measures included. You know the Burburan clownfish that lives with the stinging anemone? It rubs against the anemone to make itself secrete protection from its toxin. But if it stays away from the anemone too long, it'll become like other fish, and the anemone's sting will kill it." He wiggled the little bean-toes of his paws as if they were underwater life. "But away from the anemone, the clownfish will be eaten by larger fish. So no matter what, at some point, distance kills."

"I always thought the death code was deliberate so that we don't live forever and torture each other for eternity," Benzaran said.

"That's not wrong. But *how* you die is that with your protective covering gone, your telomeres begin to shorten: even the oxygen you need for life makes free radicals that kill your cells without their protection, and over time your life span decreases until both Njandejara and no Njandejara become poison to you," Joshua said. "It's a natural result of the distance."

"Shyte, you sound as science-y as your Mali," Benzaran laughed, flopping to the floor besides them all.

"So when the first mother chose to learn from the tree instead of Njandejara," Szizzle asked, "why was that—what does that mean for someone like me, who learns from every tree?"

"Your learning is precious, because your trees teach you Njandejara in everything." Joshua smiled. "This tree taught only one thing: binary morality. Good and evil. You can learn many things from the trees. But not good and evil. If you learn law without Njandejara, you will only learn the law of natural selection. There are good things in that law. But it will teach you, first and foremost, that you are naked, *arumim*, next to the tree's bark, and weak, next to its trunk. That you as you are, are not enough. That's what the Accuser told her, you know: 'learn from this tree, and you will be like an energy being, a power, not the matter you are.'"

"But it is good to know your deficiencies, so you can correct them, and our matter is flawed," Elitsza interjected, her snout flashing red. "The wrong was that she learned this without Njandejara, not that she learned her nakedness."

Joshua gave her a little smirk. "You have no deficiencies when you are wrapped in Njandejara. Nakedness was unity, and this is why I am telling you this story, Carl and Lark. Because animal nakedness is knowing, and trusting, and coming together in a rhythm of giving and receiving, entering and holding, taking turns in Yin and Yang to bring joy to two secret, exclusive creatures, harmonizing in their differentness. It can even transform more matter into new energetic life.

"But when the first mother and her mate chose *other* than Njandejara, it was like they found themselves in the ocean without their anemone—unsafe. They weren't naked like that before, because like the clownfish they were covered in his connection of trust. Under the law of natural selection, there isn't that kind of trust, and nakedness becomes dangerous. And so they tried to cover themselves with leaves, like the trees taught them. But armor could never replace trust.

"This choice opened the universe to danger and armor, and to morality without Njandejara, like Lady Elitsza said." He gave the reptilian a nod; her red snout didn't fade. "We can't be hard on those parents: it is likely a choice one of their descendants would have made, if they hadn't."

Joshua reached out again and lifted Carl's much bigger hand in his little paw, and put it to Lark's again; he gave Carl a pointed look that let the mercenary know the little Biouk knew about Carl's reaction to the feeling she caused. "Happy mates cover themselves and each other *only* with the one Covering that lets them stay naked with each other. I heard you'd like to make a promise. Did you understand my story?"

"Yes," Lark said, rising from her cross-legged seat to a kneel. Carl nodded—in the pause that followed, a nod seemed insufficient.

"I understand," he said aloud.

"What's your promise, friends?" Joshua asked.

Lark laid her hand on Carl's knee. "I swear it's only you, mate," she said. "I want to take you to the end of the world, and no one else. I want you to believe me."

Carl cleared his throat. "Mine is the same. And I will walk with you through your—" He doubted she'd want her dysphoria mentioned with everyone looking at them. "Through your battle. I'll learn what I can, and you won't be alone. I'll make sure you have a place to belong, and I'll let you know you're—" He glanced at Joshua. "Covered."

"I also like the story," Lark said. "I do want to keep nothing between us. No more—intrigue from me. Just—mate, it's weird to say it this way, but he started it—nakedness." She laughed, and Elitsza scowled and bounced away to the cockpit, where the two Turned and their Stygge slept by Cinta's feet, and Rizzt greeted her. "I choose that with you, and just with you," Lark added.

"Same." Carl gave a short nod to let Lark know he agreed and had nothing to add.

"I think that's it," she said for both of them. "Is that specific enough?" she asked, looking around. "It's really not anyone else's business, but maybe promises this dangerous need witnesses or they didn't happen."

"Yes, you have witnesses." Joshua smiled; then his eyes hardened a bit, and the fur on his muzzle became smooth and sober. "The lands, the planets, the bacteria on our skin and stars in the sky, are witnesses, too. They will uphold the law they know, and if you abandon your promise, they may draw disease and tragedy to you. If you keep it, they may celebrate with you. They don't make promises, but they will respond to your energy, and this law is their right."

"I accept that," Lark said. "We good, mate?"

"Yes," Carl said. They both stood; Benzaran approached to give Lark a firm handshake, and then Joshua waved everyone about their business, declaring they should all eat before they landed. They'd break atmosphere soon—everyone needed to strap in.

Lark leaned against Carl for a second. "That was odd. Nutty, even."

"Yes."

"But I'm into it," she said. "Will you kiss me before the world ends? When we're alone. I've had enough of being stared at for one day."

He looked down at her, touched his finger to his lips, and then with the lightest tap touched hers. He was so tired of using words; he was grateful when she understood the gesture and nodded in return. They strapped on weapons and pulled down fruit from the ceiling as if nothing had happened, prepping for the next mission. Carl did feel his heart beat a little faster, and his face glow a little warmer. It wasn't much, but it was enough. Lark wasn't the only one who was "botched up," as she put it. And he looked forward to finding healing together.

CHAPTER TWENTY-ONE

Jaika

WHEN I BROKE THROUGH THE BIOSHIP WALL ONTO THE LANDING PAD outside the ruins of Fort Jehu, the heat didn't "beat down" on me so much as "suffocate my whole body in a sweaty embrace." Home. For the first time in … almost three years? Shyte. Felt longer.

In the distance, past a rusting temporary fence, pinkish-green vines grew up the fort's translucent wall: the jungle was hugging us all. When I sighed, hot, wet air rushed into my throat like a super tongue-y kiss.

My home planet's clingy welcome felt weird. And not just because I'd served time in the cold, dry underground of Beryllia's crystal mines. *There's moss on the landing pad.* When Jei and I took off from this pad years ago it was squeaky clean. Uptight "Cadet Commander Bereens" wouldn't have it otherwise.

I opened and closed my fist, and chunks of deep green and rooty brown blasted into the air as the moss flew off the pad, lit up by sparks. I lifted my hand, gently, like an orchestra conductor, and the moss floated through the air to land in a puddle by the fence.

"Grow there," I said. "Not here."

It obeyed.

My crew went about their business. I overheard Joshua arguing with Cinta and Masha as they left for the Structure. Reise, Nathan, and Jake greeted their squad leader, Nefesh, then posted up by me as we waited for the Frelsi to inspect us so we could deliver Nathan, and I could talk to the Frelsi leadership about back-up for Cinta. A medical team checked Lev's neck at gunpoint for any signs of Turned darts, then carried him away for surgery. Atmosphere suits arrived for the reptilians—they couldn't leave quarantine until we knew neither they nor the planet would hurt each other with foreign germs. I trusted Lark and Carl to guard Laaru until another contingent of Frelsi could arrive from the detainment camp—apparently they didn't keep prisoners on base anymore.

Meanwhile, a Frelsi soldier patted me down, looking for a control panel while two others held Nathan and Reise at gunpoint. Reise and I shared a tired, punished look.

"It sucks to feel like a bad guy," I said.

I drew the line at stasis collars. "All right, look, the boys can't hurt you without weapons, and if you want you can give me a good shock, and I'll be powered down," I said. "These guys have gone through hell already. Don't filking insult them."

People don't usually volunteer to get tasered. The Frelsi sergeant called back to their superior to check whether that really worked for electromagnetics, and I got my shock with minimal swearing.

With that, we marched home to deliver our mind-control cure. *Hurry up. Today's the solstice.*

The new base was hidden, not far from Fort Jehu. I'd heard rogue machines still wandered the old fort, rusting, shooting anything that moved, still powered by the few renewable matter-to-energy cores the Frelsi had at that time. Scavenging parties from the new base still risked their lives for scrap metal and computer parts. I couldn't see anything like that, though—the wall in the distance still hid the fort like a pearl as we marched into the jungle in the direction of …

"Wait, we're going to the Biouk settlement," I said.

"They took our soldiers in and hid them during the last wave of Sterba's apocalypse," said one of our Frelsi escorts. "The base is under their homes. We got an EMP shield up around their town as soon as we could to protect them, too."

"Shyte. I used to live there."

I didn't recognize any of these soldiers. They were Frelsi—their wristbands, and Nefesh's presence, had confirmed that. But everything was different. Their faces were so much more stern and cold. As we hurried under the canopy houses, I looked for the Mali and Pali who raised Cinta and me for so long … usually around this hour she'd wash and clean animal skins on the porch high, high above our heads. Our home seemed empty when I passed under it, though—and above the trees, if you looked at just the right moment, you could see the shifting gleam of the EMP field.

The marks of war had come to my haven somehow.

My chest hurt again. *Just need to finish the mission. Deliver Nathan, kill Bricandor. Get a drink, take a nap.* I figured if the others failed to destroy the Structure, eliminating the person who wanted to turn it on would probably do the trick, too.

"The lift's up ahead," said one of the soldiers. I could see it—a polymerwall door in the carved center of a thick many-trunked Bangla tree. A young girl stood in its shade, about twelve revolutions old. The ethereal white dresses she used to wear had made way for combat fatigues, and the long, wispy hair that used to stand out from her head like a halo had been close-cropped. It still peeked out from the edges of her patrol cap, a yellow frame to the deep sky of her skin, echoing the glowing hazel of her eyes. She and Jake were both a few shades darker than Reise and I, and people had always said they would be the best-looking, but it still felt so weird to see these two handsome young soldiers, so grown-up, with faces just barely reminiscent of the children my little sister and brother technically were. I'd completely missed these changes in their lives, and now I lived in a world where what was couldn't be anymore.

Juju Benzaran was happy to see Jake. They wouldn't let her hug Reise and me, and the smile she flashed me was reserved. *Would my chest please stop aching?* I didn't think she'd ever know how much my heart suffered because of her in the Stygge training center, as day after day Diebol reminded me he'd have the Ebon Shadow kill her if I wouldn't comply. I'd had night-mares. I'd intentionally blocked her out of my mind after our last angry talk, but that just made this moment worse. She was so pretty. I hoped people had been good to her while I was gone.

"Are you still mad at me?" I asked as we passed.

"No," she said in a tone that said she was. "I just don't know you that way anymore. It's still good to see you."

"You too." *I love you, little one!* I wanted to blurt. But it felt like something she'd see as just a meaningless formality and wouldn't believe. And there wasn't time.

"Jake's rejoining our family squad," Juju said. "I'm here to bring him home."

Jake looked at Reise and Nathan, then back to Juju. "What about them?" he asked.

"I don't know. You'll have to ask Command," she said. She didn't say if this was because they were Turned. It wouldn't have been weird to add Nathan in—orphans got added to family squads all the time—but with the cure in his blood, who knew where they'd want to keep him, and what that meant for their squad with Nefesh and Lev, with Gideon dead.

"It's all right." Reise nodded to Jake. "I'm sure I'll see our parents soon, too. You'll need to check on Lev, though, when his surgery lets out, in case Nathan and I can't. Find out from Nefesh what's happening to *our* squad, if she knows."

"Too easy," Jake said. He seemed so proud to be able to give the "good soldier" answer honestly. Shyte, Reise trusted him now.

"Roger." They saluted each other, and Jake followed my sister through the trees until I couldn't see them anymore. I'd seen cities burn, but for some reason these little family rearrangements—so insignificant, right?—were what actually let me know we'd never really been safe after all. I was grateful she spoke to me, at least, and they were both alive. Maybe one day I would take her up to Retrack City to see the acrobats, like she'd always wanted.

"There's really no such thing as home, is there?" Reise said, straightening his back and chest, as if bolstering himself against a wind.

"No," I said. "There isn't." We stepped into the hollowed-out tree, and its polymerwall curtain hardened like bark behind us, and a small glowing floorlight flickered as we descended into the base.

NATHAN

The underground medbay was quieter than the one Nathan remembered at old Fort Jehu—no singing lizards outside, no big windows in the pulsing blue walls, just the silence of earth covered in simple polymerwall. Tree roots and peacock guinea pig burrows decorated the rich black earth in arabesques behind the transparent wall, and Nathan let out a long sigh.

Even sitting here shirtless on the grey-green medical cot, Nathan finally felt safe and warm.

"We need the both of you to test this, actually, Reise," Dr. Patti Loylan was explaining. Her magenta human fingers adjusted the glittered headwrap that marked her nationality from one of Luna-Guetala's southern continents, then flitted back to the hand sanitizer station beside her. "When I was stationed on Forge last year, Cinta's squad brought me a mind-control panel from what he's called the Duel of the Giants."

"Is that the storm event, where Bereens died?"

"Yes," Dr. Loylan said. She laid her hand on a DNA-locked case, and it popped open.

Upon seeing its contents, Nathan's body stiffened without his permission, and his heart rate rose—*it's off. It's off, it can't control you. You're safe. You can move.* His breath held. *Breathe. No freezing.*

Dr. Loylan's mind-control panel had burnt edges like it'd been fried and smashed; wires crisscrossed it, their ends rooted in blobs of untidy welding. "We've repaired it, and it works for some basic commands. One of our plans was to kidnap Turned people and sync them to this panel, under us instead—a person can only sync to one panel at a time after all, so then they'd be free as long as no one accessed it. We haven't been able to replicate the signal engineering to build a complete one, since this was so badly damaged, but that's one of the temporary 'cures' we've been working on."

"The prisoner on our ship read the manual," Reise said. He was leaning back against the wall, seated on a simple metal storage crate with his arms folded, legs stretched out to cross at the ankles. "Your engineering team should talk to him."

"A wonderful idea, and I'll pass it along. In the meantime, this panel is how we'll test your cure."

Reise's eyes narrowed. "You intend to re-Turn us, in other words," he said.

Nathan slouched. He missed Gideon more when Reise's tone burned like that. It made him want to cover his head and go to sleep.

"If we can replicate the effects you claim in a Turned person, we'll be on to something—we don't have a lot of other Turned available to us at this base. So in short, yes," Dr. Loylan said. She'd always been a chatterbox, Nathan remembered, and just like in the old days she prattled away while her fingers adjusted dials, moved test tubes from one centrifuge to another, and checked the oxysat monitor on his finger again. "Your blood tests show high levels of pro-opiomelanocortin, Nathan—POPM. I only checked that because I found a different opioid-like chemical in your blood I didn't recognize. POPM comes from your pituitary—it's for making endorphins," she said conspiratorially, as if this was quite naughty of the pituitary. "Another little prick here—" The "sticky" material of her glove pressed against the back of Nathan's neck, and with a thick, cold needle—*ouch!*—she took another tissue sample from the dart.

"POPM's also related to your immune system," she went on. "And I think that's where you became resistant to the foreign tissue from the dart. The Growen worked hard to engineer something that wouldn't cause inflammatory storms in your brain and kill you or the graft, but that's come with a trade-off that your immune system might have figured out how to exploit."

"What is the foreign tissue?" Reise asked, cracking his knuckles and crossing his arms. He'd jumped to his feet when she took out the needle—Nathan smiled. *Seems like I have a bodyguard.*

"It's actually cloned skin tissue from an electromagnetic person," said Dr. Loylan. "They're specialized secretory skin cells, with two functions. One, they release a series of neurotransmitters that hit targeted areas of the motor cortex—one of the reasons we've been struggling to find a cure is these particular neurotransmitters hit receptors used by your body's neurotransmitters, but they're actually not the same chemicals. They're new, and poorly understood.

"The second function's more effective: the tendrils actually block spinal access from your motor cortex, essentially acting like a second motor cortex to order your body around at the peripheral level. It's not so different from how some fungus controls insects."

"Skin cells, though?" Nathan asked.

"The original specimen would touch you to give the order. She had additional organs and pheromones that, in conjunction with personal persuasion, created a much more natural mind-control effect directly into your peripheral nervous system," Dr. Loylan said.

She pushed aside the rolling table with her lab equipment and pulled up a crate to sit in front of Nathan with both hands on her knees. "I'd like to run a PET scan with C-carfentanil to see exactly how receptor uptake is varying across the foreign tissue versus your own brain; your functional MRI already shows increased activity across your thalamus, caudate nucleus and putamen, and the insular, cingulate, and frontal cortices—and decreased in your middle cingulate cortices."

Nathan looked to Reise for help; none of this meant anything to him. Reise shrugged.

"It's similar to what we'd expect with laughter," Dr. Loylan clarified. "You've also got high levels of beta-endorphins in your blood—they're released with laughter, too, and this new chemical in your blood seems to be derived from them."

Nathan gave Reise a sad smile now. *I'm making the chemical because I've laughed so much.* Nathan knew this—he'd suspected it, anyway, but hearing it aloud, his shoulders relaxed, and his chest breathed more freely. This, this brought some sense to everything. It *had* to be him and Gideon, together, joking in captivity, or his body wouldn't make this stuff. It couldn't be anyone else. He didn't understand the rest of the whys. And he didn't really need to.

His parents' invisible friend did see him after all.

Reise clearly didn't feel the same way. He quickly broke eye contact to glare at the floor. He ran his forearm across his eyes, and blinked, and coughed.

Dr. Loylan was still talking, "I believe the new endorphin you're synthesizing is either directly poisoning the graft through an immune system effect, or blocking its signals. The former would mean a more permanent cure, and it's more biochemically likely given the diverse structures of the foreign neurotransmitters. We may have a combination of both mechanisms." She took a deep breath and gave Reise a nod. "Either way, it's highly likely a person has to take several doses of the cure over time for it to work, so Reise, you'll be Nathan's testing buddy. And I do, in fact, need to sync both of you up to this control panel."

She paused to let that thought marinate. The sniper was glaring at the wall, his arms crossed over his chest over the kind of shoulder-width stance Nathan had seen on civilian bouncers during his first mission into Retrack City. Shyte, they'd never get Reise under mind control again. He'd clearly rather die.

"So it'll make him immune, when we're done?" Nathan asked.

"Not immune," Dr. Loylan said. "This would be like an antibiotic, not like a vaccine. If you get shot again, there would be a new, non-poisoned graft in you, and you'd need to take it again to kill it. Of course, the mechanism of action isn't at all like an antibiotic, but that's the best way to explain it."

"That's still good, right, Reise?" Nathan pressed.

"That's the plan," Loylan said. "I promise we'll keep the panel under lock and key. You'll carry it yourselves. And if the cure doesn't work on Reise for some reason, we'll unsync you."

Nathan bit his lip. Would Reise—how would he even agree to anyone resyncing him to a panel again, after all they'd made him do, and the trust he couldn't—

Reise coughed; his intense eyes turned on Dr. Loylan. "Well, what are we waiting for?" he snapped. "We've got several million Turned casualties across four planets. Hurry up and sync us."

"Oh—oh, well then." Dr. Loylan hopped back up, apparently surprised by his reaction. "We're actually waiting for resupply of some reagents I need to extract the chemical from your friend's blood. I have some more tests I need to run just on Nathan, first, before I feel comfortable hooking you up to something we haven't proven we can undo."

"What can I do to make it faster?" Reise asked.

"I will absolutely give you some work to do, don't you worry." Her wristband flashed. "Ooh, that's a call coming in from the lead scientist over on Revelon. We're a team of about two thousand, you know, all analyzing the chemical formula I've gotten from Nathan here—once we've proven Reise suffers no ill effects, we'll all be running tests on whatever Turned we have across the solar systems. Providing that goes well, we're hoping to have the final cure shipped out by the end of the week. Oooh, hold on." She rushed through the polymerwall out into another room.

Reise relaxed and sighed. He plopped down on the cot beside Nathan; his weight bounced Nathan a bit, and Nathan almost chuckled despite himself. "All this responsibility's starting to make you heavier, I see, Reise," he said.

"Well one of us needs to gain weight around here." Reise smirked, giving Nathan a fake punch in the ribs. "Someone has to be able to grab you by the ankle and hold you down when the first blitzer breath blows your light ass away."

"Fair enough." Nathan half-smiled. It was weird, sitting here doing nothing in the middle of the day, and not having any orders, especially with the rest of the bioship crew out trying to solve a crisis.

It was also weird because neither he nor Reise moved at all when seated—he'd noticed that, on the ship, looking around at everyone else. Everyone normal fidgeted just a little. But Reise and Nathan, once sat down, sat completely still, like a machine powered off, or a trap-beast waiting for its prey. That was how the control program had worked, and that was what they were used to now. If they chose to move, it was very deliberate, with purpose.

"Hey Nathan," Reise asked, still not moving, still looking straight ahead. "You okay?"

Nathan shook his head. "I'm not okay, but I know things are okay, if that makes sense," he said.

"It does not," Reise said.

"I know." Nathan breathed; Reise breathed; a peacock guinea pig outside rushed past in its tunnel, and then disappeared down a bend they couldn't see. For a moment, the tunnel became white in Nathan's imagination, and at the end of it, his friend and a dead girl blocked a doorway. Gideon's back jerked as a cartridge hit him from the front, but he didn't even seem to notice. He was fine. He was so alive. Then they left around the bend, and that was it.

"I think the thing that's worst," Nathan said, "is that—I know he's dead. But he was alive when we left."

"You know there was no way to rescue him. Someone had to go down," Reise said.

"I know," Nathan said. "That's not how I mean it. I mean—I can't say goodbye, inside, because my brain doesn't believe he's actually dead. I saw my other people go. Kola, I know one hundred percent she's gone. Like my parents. With Gideon, my brain thinks we just left, and he's back there, but then of course, he's so *okay* that he could definitely find a ride on someone's ship, and he might already be here, just down any of those corridors we passed. I keep waiting for him, and he's not going to show, and that's the worst." Nathan heard his voice crack. His stomach forced a painful laugh. "Like maybe I'll be in the gym for weight-training, and he'll walk in and ask me to pass him the ones I can't lift."

"That can never happen." Reise wiped wet eyes and then flashed a sad grin. "Because you'd never go to the gym."

"Ouch," Nathan squeaked, his voice unable to choose between the cry and the chuckle fighting each other in his throat. It felt awful, but it also felt okay. He put out his fist; Reise knuckled it. "I think," Nathan said, "Gideon would've approved."

CHAPTER TWENTY-TWO

Lem

I CLAPPED OUTSIDE THE GREY SLAB POLYMERWALL—THE ENTRANCE
to the Admiral's office—and it softened to let me pass. Even
mid-wall I was thinking up a billion mannerisms, a trillion
possible things to say: I discarded "flipping him the three-
fingered-bird," "screaming," and "punching that sucker in the
face." After a year of bearing Jei's memory like an iron jacket, I'd
play it cool with his dad. His dad, who exiled me, who didn't
pick up when Jei called, right before—

Shyte!

I choked, and now I was through the wall without an
opening line, and here stood the short old man with his feathery-
looking hair and straight nose and wrinkly version of my battle-
buddy's eyes peering out of a greyer version of my battle-
buddy's face. His uniform was as crisp and neat as his son's
used to be.

"I wanted to see the last person to see my son alive," he said.

And I filking wanted so badly to talk about it, but the Jei in
me wanted the mission more. "Today is the day of the solstice,
sir. I need an airfleet mobilized to take out Bricandor's Structure
ASAP." I didn't have to use sir. I did anyway.

The Admiral sighed and leaned forward, folding his hands on his desk. "I still don't have those blueprints Lieutenant Belaran said he'd send," he said, using Cinta's family name. "We're *this* close to the cure—"

"That my team brought."

"—that Lieutenant Belaran's team brought. This isn't a military consultation. This is a social call."

I stepped back and bowed my head. I was getting so tired of this. I must've looked more humble than I intended, because he softened his tone. "Look, Benzaran, we're so close to being able to mobilize again. We can't risk leaving this base even one man short while we guard such a precious charge. Our current intel suggests we have enough people tasked out to the Structure—at this point, it's just an energy source we don't want them to have to power their military industrial complex."

I rubbed my face and sighed. "Look, if Bijou's got comms up, you should be able to call them and get more info. They'll at least tell you there's a deadline—"

"Stop. Stop! You're not Frelsi," he said. He wasn't used to being argued with, and he didn't like it. "I don't think you ever really were. You know as well as I do your record was soaked in insubordination."

"Too free for the freedom fighters," I quipped. "Trial's over, remember? I'm Jaika Belaran. Lem Benzaran's dead, so you can drop it." I cut my hand through the air as if decapitating my human self. "If I can get you a read-out in a few hours, how soon can you get me bombers?"

Now he sighed. He was tired, too. "It depends on what you send, and the progress of the cure."

"Roger," I said. I turned to go. My filking mouth stopped me at the exit. "He tried to call you, you know," I said, turning back.

"Yes," he said. "He left a message. I saved it." He tapped his wristband—

A strangled cry leapt from my throat. "Don't!" I cleared my

throat and lowered my voice. "Don't play it. Shyte." I leaned over, hands on my knees, like I needed to catch my breath. "I can't hear any of that right now. I have to go kill Bricandor. By myself. With no back-up. I can't be reliving the worst day of my life."

He ran a hand over his grizzled chin, leaning back. "You didn't, by any chance …"

"No, I didn't kill Jei," I grunted. "If you wanted to send forensics down to Forge once the universe isn't in danger, I'm sure Cinta can tell you where they're both buried. Shyte." I straightened. "I have so many questions of my own, man, and no time. Why'd you send him away to live with someone else when he got back from the cage as a kid? Why'd you never tell him what happened to his mom?"

The Admiral rose; his polished shoes clicked like blitzer boots on the dull grey floor with his brisk steps to the polymerwall. "She disappeared when he was taken," he said in a quick, "mission brief" tone as he unlocked the wall for me. "She could have wandered off a cliff, she could have run back to Burbura. I don't know. The marriage wasn't—she wasn't sure about being Frelsi, and when the cause took her son, she left me a message letting me know she was gone. I wouldn't want his damaged mind to know any of that, so I simply erased her from our lives."

"But he used to have this burnt-out image of her in his head. Was he taken from her, with her, you mean?" I asked.

"That I also don't know. I'd have thought I'd find a body, if that were the case," he said. "You know, I wouldn't have sent him away to the volcanoes if he'd fought me a little more for the bodyguard position he wanted. But he needed to be away from all this military mess anyway." He waved a hand around the underground room. It gave me a little mean satisfaction, despite everything, that they'd banished me to live underground and now so did the Admiral. Shyte, at least I didn't have to live not knowing what happened to a lover. I'd bet anything the Admiral sent Jei away to train with his Draconian mentor because he couldn't handle looking at his wife's son after that.

I wasn't even mad. The Admiral sucked, but the world sucked—this was just how things were. I stuck out my hand for a shake. "I'm sorry for your loss," I said, sincerely. "He loved you, you know. All he wanted at the end was for you to hear Njandejara like he did. And he didn't resent you. Not one bit."

A bony hug suddenly snatched me up. By my ear I heard the Admiral choke back a sob into my shoulder as his old, solid fingers dug into my spine like if he hugged me hard enough, I'd be Jei, instead. Shyte, was everyone trying to kill me with feels? My eyes misted as I patted his thin back. *Jei always getting me involved with people who love him that I hate. Jared. Mera. Filking ...* My chest ached, and I wanted nothing more than to give the Admiral his son back. With that squeeze, I knew he knew I wished he could give me back my friend, too.

"Goodbye," I said, as we split, eyes brushed on sleeves like it was dusty in here as we both pretended that didn't happen. "I'll be in touch."

I knew I likely wouldn't be. My pendant beeped when I made it out into the hall with my Frelsi escort. The little dot in the center was on the move, and not toward where they'd told me the detainment camp lay.

Laaru had escaped.

"Excellent," I said aloud, waving to the soldier to hurry up as I broke into a jog. *Lead me right to your master.*

Lark

Everyone but the Stygge knew about the tracker in his holopen. But that wasn't why Lark and Carl didn't bother when the little bugger escaped. K'arl was why.

From inside the bioship, under the trees, they didn't see the *Empress* break atmosphere.

"Just got the new chinwag from Benzaran," Lark announced to the reptilians as she strapped up her blitzer armor, its plates clicking into place. "Frelsi won't take you in. Wouldn't say why."

Carl was spraying Joshua with the bacterial balance serum formulated for his species and home planet—Cinta and Masha had said the bioship's organic tech should naturally adjust a mammal's microbial biome to a new planet when they pushed through its sopping walls, 'specially on Luna-Guetala where it came from, but better safe than sorry with these extra-terrestrial transitions.

And they hadn't a bleeding idea what the ship'd do for non-mammals.

"The rejection's for microbial risk," Carl answered. "No space travel history in their species. Too much trouble to determine bio-security on base. Once the Frelsi take their prisoner we'll head to the nearby civilian transition facility instead."

"Used to be they'd take you in anyway, figure it out best they could," Lark complained. "Unfriendly people these days." To Szizzle: "Ready to go? We've got some hurrying to do, lass, Carl and I, to go merc a space laser." Szizzle nodded. "The country town nearby's a mite small for any armies to badger and their sheriff's a faffing laggard, too. You'll be safe there, you will. The docs there'll just take your blood and some scale samples to figure out what kind of bacteria inn't compatible between you and here. You'll take Masha's compupad here, for translating, all good? I've loaded a map, here, in case we get separated."

Carl waved to the Stygge kid sitting in the corner with a bag over his bound hands. "Up," he said.

"You're lucky you are, lad." Lark smirked as she popped on her helmet. "You're the first Growen target we've taken care of who gets to live."

"Lovely," the Stygge grumbled.

"Don't be down, lad, we just don't give quarter to child-killers," she said. "We mostly do rescue missions anyway."

Joshua sighed as everyone headed for the walls. His ears drooped. "What's wrong, young master?" Lark asked.

"Oh, I'm just frustrated Cinta and Mali still don't believe in me," he said. "I'll have to find my own way to the Structure."

Lark pursed her lips. She did believe in the little tyke. How irresponsible would it be to take him with her …?

Carl suddenly stiffened; he'd had eyes on the window, but whatever he saw no one else could. "Hide," he said to Joshua, ripping a vine off the wall and handing him both ends of it. Then he snatched the polymerwall film lying on the ground—the one what had trapped Lem Benzaran—gripped Szizzle's hand, pressed it against the film, and mussed the seam of the wall to set its DNA filter to hers. "Only you can unlock this," he said. He snatched the Stygge's parka and stuffed it around Joshua to make a round lump-shape, then wrapped the wall over the Biouk before anyone could say anything.

"What the—you'll suffocate him!" the Stygge protested.

But as the wall hardened, Carl snatched a discarded fruit husk from the ship's digestion tube and punched out the bottom of the husk to make a ring. He stuck that ring into the closing wall, leaving a little open porthole for air in the hard bag he'd just made, and handed the vine handle of the lumpy ovoid bag to Rizzt. "You go for the town, now." He grabbed the scruff of the Stygge's collar and plunged through the bioship's wall.

A huge rumble shook the bioship, and a black mass obscured the front window.

K'arl's here.

"You'll go this way, mates," Lark said, escorting the reptilians to the other side of the ship from where Carl had exited. She cut herself through the wall first, kicking her way through that unpleasant slurping birth; she rolled to a kneel, rifle raised. She swiveled to both sides—and up—nothing but trees. As the reptilians followed her, she motioned for quiet—

Elitsza began to ask what that sign meant—Szizzle grabbed her snout closed, and made their sign, a circle around her own snout. *Oh. Obviously.* Lark repeated it, and pointed them into the underbrush.

Gunfire rang out on the other side of the ship. Something hit it, and it squealed, and shuddered. Rizzt hoisted Joshua's bag across his thin chest and ran into the jungle in the direction of the town, his atmosphere suit rustling against the thick, almost-plastick'ed leaves. Szizzle and Elitsza followed with the map.

Around the edge of the ship, Lark saw the Stygge run off, hands still bound, not a second glance behind him; she could hear K'arl's taunting voice now. She crept around the other side, heart pounding, hoping to get the drop on him. He had proximity sensors and a rear-view camera, but she knew its blind spot because she knew Carl.

She dropped low to the ground, peeking around the curved corner. K'arl's ship was just a couple meters away. If she could get Carl into it, they could access all its weapons with his DNA. *May also take it and K'arl to space—give Joshua time to get distance.*

Carl was on his back on the ground in front of K'arl's ship, two Growen-issue pistols pointed up at K'arl; the doppelgänger had his back to Lark, as she'd hoped, and two of his pistols pointed at Carl. Both fully armored; both also fully aware of each other's weak spots. Carl's blitzer armor had chinks at all the joints, and K'arl's was thinner around his neck—and that Ebon Shadow armor would take gobs more hits. Even in the neck it'd take at least two in the same spot to get through. In the next couple seconds, the question would be about superior aim and faster repeat trigger finger. And K'arl had an aim-bot.

So Lark lifted her rifle and aimed at the back of his neck.

The boys pulled triggers at the same time—Lark was a little faster. K'arl's head knocked forward, messing up his bot's triangulation; Carl rolled sideways; cartridges zipped into the armor on K'arl's shoulder, and Carl's thigh.

Both men cursed with the heat of the impact. K'arl whirled, keeping one weapon trained on Carl, firing over and over, while the other pointed backward toward "whatever anonymous nobody thinks it's charming to sneak up on someone like that."

Lark backed up, hidden by the side of the bioship. Her blitzer helmet reflected the forest around her like confusing mirrored camouflage, and K'arl hadn't seen her. She heard Carl's armor taking thwacking and pinging hits—

Lark rolled sideways into the underbrush to where she could see K'arl again, and fired on the side of his chin. There was an infrared sensor there. She didn't need him using it to see her in the underbrush. Best overheat it for a moment. Two shots, but she got it. Almost hit him in the neck, too, that. K'arl swore. Good. She needed him to get mad enough to forget Carl for just a wee second, and they were getting there.

"You've got some cowardly back-up," he told Carl. That laugh had an edge of irritation to it; he fired blindly in Lark's general direction—a cartridge *thwing*ed into the earth about a meter away from her. "I liked Lark better. Where is she by the way? I didn't see her in the video of you on Bijou."

Next sensor—the left pointer knuckle, the one that sat on the front of his pistol when he fired, and fed the aim-bot its data. That one she could break—it was thinner material over the fingertips, normally hidden by a fist. No one shot at anyone's fingertip, so it wasn't reinforced like the back knuckles.

It took a couple shots, but she hit it.

"You've leaked all our intel?" K'arl's voice scowled, almost dropping his pistol. "You're getting desperate, brother. What happened to 'no matter how much we hate each other, we keep this secret'?"

Carl answered only with return fire. He'd managed to duck

himself sort of behind a rusted iron maintenance chest on the landing pad.

Then Lark heard the click of K'arl's backpack grenade launcher engaging, poised to target the space behind Carl and his make-shift cover—

Beans beans beans uh oh—

Lark fired as the grenade lobbed into the air. She hit it. It exploded over K'arl. Fragments shot into the trees; the flash blinded Lark for a moment; the shock wave threw dirt and leaves and bark all over her, and she heard the iron box that was shielding Carl buckle—

Blood-like goo splattered in all directions as the front end of the bioship cratered inward.

"Oh, Benzaran, lass, I am sorry," Lark muttered, scrambling to her feet. She ran past K'arl, who'd been lain flat, and met Carl at the side of the *Empress.* Carl'd been closer to the blast than she had—the force had shoved him and his shield backward almost a meter—but aside for a slight limp, he seemed whole.

"We good, mate?" she asked, stepping under the ship's belly with him.

"I'm not dead," he said, ripping off a glove and activating the elevator. "Well done." And she had done well, hadn't she? Blitzer armor was far too weak to save him from the grenade had it landed behind him.

At Carl's touch, the *Empress'* elevator sucked them both inside; he ripped off his helmet to make sure the first line of defense cameras in the main hallway recognized his face.

"So to the cannons, then?" Lark asked.

"No, we need him to get into the cockpit," he said, striding into the weapons' closet. "Twins' irises aren't the same. The iris scanner's to keep each other out. If it didn't take so long to load during combat we'd have them outside, too." Ah. That one Lark didn't know.

"So that's why he didn't just execute you in your chair last month," she said, grabbing *her* laserwhip K'arl had stolen and holstering two fresh pistols. "How long've we got?"

"Five minutes. The fluid tech in his armor will have prevented most brain damage, hollow blast injuries—he might have a few fractures, if we're lucky."

"That's insane, mate," she said. "He took a grenade to the face and we've got five minutes?"

"I fell from the sky and lived," he said. "It's good armor. Besides," he added, strapping a rifle to his back, "it wasn't to the face. It was a full four meters in the air from him."

"Mate, you know what I meant," Lark smirked.

"I'm trying to communicate more," he retorted.

She laughed. "Shyte, I will be very mad if he kills you before we can kiss," she sighed.

He stiffened like he hadn't considered this possibility. "Shyte," he said.

"Why you think I'm so willing to blow him up, mate?" she smirked. "I'm not blood thirsty. I'm just thirsty."

Beans, she wished she could see his face right now. She'd seen it enough in the last month that she could imagine a little half-grin right now, but who knew.

"Wait—you're actually *with* him?" a voice in the hallway exclaimed.

"Not even five minutes!" Lark cried. She rushed the hall to avoid getting trapped in the closet—her whip swung ahead of her in both directions before she stepped out. It snagged K'arl's weapon, and she yanked as she slid out in front of him. The pistol clattered to the floor.

"Are you actually Lark, in that blitzer get-up?" he asked, pulling two more pistols.

"That's me, mate," she said, firing hers to disorient him. If she could get her whip around his wrist and pull him past the weapons closet doorway, Carl could get behind him for his helmet. "Sorry."

"But you were actually willing to kill me out there," he realized.

"Mate, I'm not daft. I don't want you to die, but it's going to be you or him, innit, so," she said.

"So you chose him." His head tilted forward, and the mechanical voice deepened.

Uh oh. "Now look, mate, you said all's fair in—" She yelped as he charged. Pistol cartridges smashed against her armor, stinging her chest—she fully expected him to hit a chink soon and bleed her out. She backed up, whip swinging, trying to use the field it generated to muss with his aim—

He grabbed her whip and yanked her to him, ignoring the burn as his gloves sizzled. Carl's fingers grazed her shoulder too late to grab her as she stumbled past the closet. K'arl's finger slipped under her glove—

"Oh, bloodseas," she said.

They fell backward into the galley just behind the cockpit, and when Lark recovered from the shock of hitting the deck, she found herself in her own arms.

"What are you playing at, mate?" She smirked, shoving her laserwhip toward his neck—the heat on the thinner part of his armor made him let go of her, and she scrambled to her feet. "You can't be a better me than I can."

"Can't I?" he asked. "Beans, mate, guess I'd best give up then."

It sounded—disturbingly—right.

CHAPTER TWENTY-THREE

Carl

CARL CHARGED INTO THE GALLEY TO FIND TWO LARKS AND NO K'arls. Normally, this would've been a preferable ratio of Larks to K'arls in the universe. It was not today.

"You're daft as bollocks, Jester, and here's why," one said to the other. "It's easy to tell the difference between us. You've got better armor on."

"Wait, what—"

The one on the left fired into the seam behind the knee of the one on the right. Carl expected to see no injury, confirming K'arl's identity.

But the shot one groaned and fell to the floor gripping her leg. "What the blasted bloodseas—"

"He's bloody fine," the other said. "Beans, good actor, though, in't he?"

The shot one threw a loop of laserwhip around the other one's neck with a snarl, yanking her to double over. The choked one screamed in pain.

"I don't have patience for this." Carl switched his pistol to stun and shot both of them. The one on the floor passed out. The one ripping a whip off her neck and swearing like a Bont pirate didn't. Huh. Interesting double-bluff from K'arl. Carl ripped off his glove, closed the distance, and helped "her" with the whip—yanking it to spin "her" toward the door—and removed the invisible helmet with a press of his palm's DNA against the back of the neck.

K'arl's head showed as his helmet receded into the fluid of the melting armor; the iris scanner picked up his face as he struggled against Carl's full nelson. Carl quickly reached up to the seam of the polymerwall and removed its DNA lock. He shoved K'arl in ahead of him, shot him before the armor closed back up, and raced to the cockpit to start take-off procedures. Too bad he hadn't had an arm free to set the weapon to kill. Never mind. He had about half an hour before either other passenger woke up. He still needed to secure or kill K'arl—*but Lark's shot.*

The ship began to rumble. *Lark's shot.* Carl stepped out of the pilot's seat to go get Lark and strap her in. He passed into the galley and crouched beside her to remove her blitzer helmet; her chest rose and fell in slow, even breaths, and her head tilted back, and her mouth hung just a bit open, showing her little tongue. Her strong carotid pulse was visible in the pale pink of her exposed neck. That was good. He grabbed a med-kit from the cabinet over the counter, threw a quick tourniquet above her knee—there was blood dripping to the floor around the burn—and carried her to the cockpit to lay her in the co-pilot's seat. Three little medbots happily got to work on the back of her leg as he strapped her in. He tapped some take-off directions for low orbit into the dashboard compuwall, and turned to secure K'arl.

K'arl was getting up. *What?!* Carl drew his pistol and fired on K'arl's neck. But the ship jolted; his shot went wide. K'arl closed the distance and got his forearm on the inside of Carl's weapon before Carl could stabilize himself. K'arl's armored knuckles smashed into the blitzer helmet; the material shattered like ice under a club. Pain and light flashed through Carl's face as his survival brain assessed. *The helmet broke the impact. It broke the impact, or I'd be dead, face caved in. I can still see. No shards in my eyes. I'm functional.* His pistol-arm twisted around K'arl's to try to fire on the neck again. K'arl kneed him in the stomach. The ship shook again, roaring now as it began to penetrate upper atmosphere. K'arl twisted to throw him away from the pilot's seat—Carl stumbled, catching himself before he hit the floor—and K'arl held his own pistol to Lark's unconscious temple.

Carl lay his own weapon on the floor immediately.

"Funny side effect of the mind prison," K'arl said. "I developed a really high tolerance to paralytics. Regular strength stun cartridges just don't do it for me anymore."

Carl raised both of his hands, bending to maintain his balance as the floor rattled.

"What would it take for you to drop her off unharmed after I'm dead?" he asked.

"I think maybe we're past that, Carl!" K'arl laughed. "I think I'm going to have you watch me kill her—awake—and then I'll kill you, as her."

"Your target's escaping in the meantime," Carl snapped. "This is completely illogical."

"But fun." K'arl shrugged. "I've been such a good guy. Maybe it's time I started my villain arc."

Jaika Belaran

For a moment, I was almost actually home. I was running through the treetops—stumbling a bit, a bit out of practice—soft boots gripping bark—hands gripping branches—hot air drowning my lungs in humidity that somehow also felt good, like a wet sauna on my Forge-dried skin—

And I remembered the hunts, with Cinta, as my chest

stretched and expanded with rich, powerful breaths that felt *good*. I'd never liked killing the little peacock guinea pigs—I just tried to be merciful, and eat—but the big game, the scale-deer with their spiked venomous tongues, the huge sharp frills flaring off the back of their necks in all colors—I didn't like killing things that didn't deserve it. But I liked *finding*.

And I'd found Laaru. I crept above him, mind quiet, every thought empty and blended into the jungle around me. There was no Jaika or Lem. There was the bare lechichi vine dangling from a branch, and the singing day-lizard flitting overhead, and Laaru's voice. It didn't matter if Bricandor read my mind, because there was no mind to read, only the jungle, and its wet, earthy, fresh musk.

"I've escaped," Laaru panted. His long hair clung to his neck and face, and the odor of teenage sweat permeated the air as he talked into the projection he'd drawn in the air with his holopen. The humidity was so intense here that the projection on the air droplets came out crystal clear, with deep, saturated colors like something out of a children's book. "I'm on my way to the Core now to prepare for the solstice, Father," Laaru said.

"Excellent," Bricandor said. "But I sense doubt, my child."

"I'm—yeah," Laaru sighed, wiping a muddy sleeve across his forehead, leaving a long streak. "I'm so sorry. I've been over-hearing some wild things."

"The terrorists have their merits," Bricandor admitted. "And we have evil among our ranks. This would cause doubt in anyone. Have you been practicing your Thought?"

"About that," Laaru said. "I—you know I saved the Structure on Bijou, right?"

"Yes," he said. "Well done."

"Well—the Thought was—really strong there, like it *owned* me," he said. "And it felt right. Really right. But then, when I was in the—bioship—there was this—young, like, teacher there. I could swear with his eyes on me he knew the Thought. And he

—they were stern eyes. Like there'd be consequences for it. But not eyes that hated me. Not like any of the cold or fake or professional or desperate or—despicable—eyes I've seen on either side in this fight. These were eyes like I was the enemy, but—worth something. Severe, but—love can't be the right word, can it? It was like he knew me, and he understood all the things that've gotten me to this point, and he also knew all the choices *I'd* made, so you can't lie to him or make excuses, but—"

"Enough!" Bricandor hissed. Laaru stiffened, and Bricandor softened his tone with a wheeze. He tried to speak, but the words came out as a vicious babble, and he gripped his chest, rage streaking his face. After a few deep breaths, he forced his wrinkles to smooth. "I am sorry to interrupt, but we haven't much time, I'm afraid. Was this a young Biouk—black and brown, white nose—"

"With a little black on it, yeah!" Laaru said. "Is he—I guess it wouldn't surprise me if you knew him, with the powers."

"What powers?" Bricandor leaned toward the camera.

"Well, I mean—I've never seen anything like it. He was rearranging an asteroid field in front of me." Laaru's overwhelm, even so long after the fact, came out now as a breathy laugh. "You want to talk about someone who could power the Structure, I'm nothing next to that."

Bricandor leaned back, nodding into the fingers over his cracked lips. "Thank you for your humility, Laaru. You've always been one to put the project above yourself."

"Well, I mean, I don't know if he'd willingly—he seemed pretty chummy with the terrorists," Laaru said.

"You'd be surprised," Bricandor said. "Where is he?"

"He was heading—I think north, with three reptilians—they looked like Sailfins with no sails, basically. They're looking for a civilian transition facility, since they've never been away from their homeworld before."

Bricandor tapped his mouth, muttering to himself. "There's a small town between Fort Jehu and Retrack City. That must be their destination." Without hanging up he turned to a panel attached to his throne and pressed to speak: "I'm sending you a destination for the Child. The objective has changed. Cancel the elimination order. Deliver him to the Core alive before 2330 hours tonight. No, I don't think the Ebon Shadow will be joining you—his last public video update tells me he's become quite distracted. You're authorized and encouraged to use any amount of force necessary—condition is unimportant as long as the target remains conscious and alive." Bricandor paused. "In fact, a bit of pain might even be preferable. Teach the creature a lesson for challenging your right to occupy this system. Yes. Goodbye."

Laaru stood in silence for a moment while Bricandor swiped a few more patterns across his panel. "What did I just do?" Laaru asked finally.

"Only good things, my child," Bricandor reassured him. "Joshua Ben-Belaran carries an insidious Contamination powerful enough to change the universe forever. He is a portal to another dimension, and once his tendrils have penetrated enough other minds, he will bring the interdimensional Njandejara upon us—the very being who wipes out planets and creates death itself. We'll harness this power with the Core and solve two problems at once. No more evil energy, no more evil portal."

"Do you—still need me?" Laaru asked, his voice a bit weak, and hollow.

"Absolutely. You are the key to my universe, and my comfort in my old age," Bricandor said. "I cannot guarantee the blitzers will not fail—you've seen the corruption among the ranks. Come and prepare yourself for the Core. You may yet be the one to power it."

"… Okay." Laaru hesitated. "Is this all—really going to help the most people?"

"Ah yes, my faithful compassionate one, ever weighing the needs of the many over the needs of the few. Come, and I will show you everything," Bricandor said. "But there is a greater blessing for those who believe without seeing, you know."

As Laaru hung up, thoughts flooded my mind with such intensity I thought I'd pop a headache—it was like I'd held my breath for a very, very long time. First off, filk Bricandor for quoting something I'd definitely heard Njande say about that "believing without seeing" shyte and making it about being *stupid* instead of about seeing with your inner eye. Filk him so much. Filk him for the nasty pause before he told the blitzers to rough up a kid before bringing him in. Next, poor Laaru! Poor stupid Laaru who I'd *definitely* gotten into this mess by teaching him how his shyte worked! Who knew it took ten minutes to damn the universe!

And finally, oh, Bricandor, *I will bring your end on you like a locust swarm, an earthquake in the mountains. The ghosts are coming for you, our blood crying out from the earth where it's spilled on every world, screaming to the stars and beyond.*

Sterba was glowing in my eyes as I resumed my chase after Laaru; Diebol was mad, and a poetry that didn't belong to me flared within me, a parting gift from the girl who dreamed of magnetic ghosts and the boy who held her memory.

I called Carl and Lark to warn them about the blitzers en route to their reptilian friends—I couldn't break Masha and Cinta off from their mission, and I needed to meet them here. They didn't answer. I managed to hear something from Carl's communicator at one point, but it sounded like it'd been opened by accident, like a butt-dial, because there was screaming and hitting and by the time it hung itself up, again without anyone hearing me, I'd guessed they had their hands full. *They're probably why the Ebon Shadow's "distracted."*

So I called Reise. "Are you able to get off base?"

"With an escort, perhaps," he said. "The cure works."

"That's awesome! We've done something right, then. Hey listen, Bricandor's sent blitzers to Realm—you remember the little town with the ice cream shop?—to kidnap Joshua. Cinta's kid? The Frelsi aren't going to help."

"Not for just one person, no. It's not like in our hero days when they'd have teens running anti-trafficking ops for civilians."

"Right. But Bricandor plans to use Joshua to power the Structure. The Frelsi don't get why we'd need more manpower for it —we're basically a sabotage crew for them—"

"A mere side dish of resource harassment to the main course of their intersolar influence."

"Yeah—right, I think. So I don't have anybody to go stop this."

Reise's voice went quiet in my earpiece. "Is this akin to the repugnant child sacrifice scenario with our sister?" he asked.

"Something like that," I said.

"Degenerate pervert," he said. "Well, I still remember the old days. I will retrieve him."

"Thanks, man. I owe you."

"You do not." He cut the line.

Okay, this was good. And as long as I got to Bricandor before Joshua did—since they wanted him alive—we had a backup plan here. Redundancies. I hadn't gotten up that morning planning on sending my little brother into danger, but this "little brother" had bulked up. Captivity left him bigger than me with absolutely lethal stealth stats. Even if he stayed totally out of sight, he could save a reptilian species from elimination; the blitzers weren't going to care about the last three surviving Allpersons in the galaxy if their orders included "any means necessary." As long as Reise didn't think Joshua had any real link to Njandejara—and so far, Reise didn't—I'd rather put Joshua's life in his hands than mine alone. After all, I hadn't rescued the boys to keep them *safe*—I'd rescued them to keep them *free*.

We were talking about the fate of the universe, here.

I'd managed to swipe some more blue serum from the Frelsi base—I couldn't take much without someone seeing, but I had enough for a lightning storm. The entire Structure was EMP-hardened—from Cinta's blueprints it looked like the Core was suspended in Guetala's upper mesosphere at the end of a space elevator, surrounded by a small blockade of weaponized satellites to protect it from outside. If I could arrive with some lead time, I could EMP-out any weapons down below to make it easier for Cinta and Masha to sneak up the elevator cables, like they'd planned. I wasn't going to be firing any biogenic laser blasts into the part of the Structure that literally existed to use energy from people like me: I had no idea what that'd do. But if Cinta and Masha could bomb the outer ring and send the whole thing crashing down to the planet surface, I figured we could call it a day.

I could see it through the shadows of the lower forest canopy as Laaru and I approached. Shyte, it was well guarded. They'd cut a huge gash in the jungle to make a lifeless field of earth, bleeding stumps, and tanks. Rows of blitzer battalions literally stood in formation doing nothing but staring into the woods. Behind them loomed a wall with gun turrets and razor wire, and behind that a silver polymerwall orb, the actual building at the foot of the thin space elevator piercing the heavens. Combat cranes stretched beside the space elevator, and airships circled overhead.

I was probably going to have to EMP blast just to get *in*. That sucked. I'd wanted to get in first so Bricandor wouldn't know I was coming. I needed to keep eyes off me so I didn't get Death Glare'd, and who wanted to waste power on all these scrubs?

But then, Laaru surprised me. Instead of walking up to the perimeter—encircled, by the way, with an EMP shield—he stopped. He looked at his bound hands and calmly walked over to the sharpest branch he could find, and began to saw.

Why didn't he just ask a blitzer ...?

Seemed like he wanted to go in without talking to anyone. Severe social anxiety after dealing with the blitzers on Bijou? Maybe planning on taking me up on my challenge after all, and digging through the computer system without someone spoon-feeding him? Just tired of being babysat?

This was one of those Diebol independence moves I liked that I hadn't seen from the Beryllian graduate before. Out of curiosity, I ducked behind the trunk of my tree—where he wouldn't see me—and tossed my laser-edge pocketknife down by his feet.

I heard a rustle as he jumped. "Hello?" he called—not too loud, so the sentries wouldn't hear. I didn't answer. "What the galaxy …" It took him a while—as if the knife might be a trap somehow—but eventually he picked it up and cut himself free. I peeked back around the tree trunk and watched his furtive glances here and there as he backed behind a thicket like somehow the Growen could still see him from here. He brushed dirt and leaves away with his bare hands, digging until he'd reached an uglier, greyer soil, with less organic material than the loam above it.

And then he blasted the ground.

Mineral mass shot out behind him like someone had taken a giant hose of brown and shot it past his ear. Shyte, no wonder he tried to get behind a thicket—any Biouk worth their salt, if the Growen had any Biouks in their ranks, would've heard that earth-shower. Dirt pattered against the leaves and thumped into two long hills behind him on the ground. He was gone with the next blast almost before I could blink again, burying the bushes behind him almost up to human shoulder-height. That would've taken filking ages to do by hand—he was actually faster now than some of the mining equipment I'd seen back on Beryllia.

Now I did send a call to Cinta and Masha. "Guys, there's a tunnel on the"—I checked the sun, and the compass on my Jei-wristband-pendant—"south side of the Core. If you want to use it to get in."

"We are already in," Cinta said. "Sewage line. Did you not pay attention to the blueprints?"

"I paid attention to my part," I said. "I'm way too big to fit through a sewage line."

"This is true. See you soon," he said.

"Roger."

Shyte. I was starting to feel better about this whole save-the-universe thing. Seemed like I was surrounded by competent people. For once in my life, out here alone in the woods, I didn't feel alone.

CHAPTER TWENTY-FOUR

Cinta

A ROUGH GRUNTING HUM INTERRUPTED THE OTHERWISE QUIET vibration of the building around the space elevator. Cinta's spine stiffened. He and Masha stood on their hindlegs, backs against the wall to minimize their shadows. The curved wall behind them had slots in it at various intervals like doorways with no tops, and it did not reach the high, transparent ceiling domed above them—it seemed designed only for blitzers to use as cover should the room come under attack. On the other side of this curved series of walls lay an open circle of floor—no cover—surrounding the entrance to the space elevator.

And patrolling this circle, Cinta heard footsteps carrying a low, humming voice that reminded him of razors, and Jaika's scream of despair, and the path of chains that ended in the cage where they took his claws. He had not thought of this voice in a year, and he did not want to think about it now, and its finger-pads gripping his shaven skin, and its empty sockets staring down at him—

It cannot be. It cannot.

It could, though. They had never killed Okl, the self-blinded, deafened, and smell-mutilated Bichank Awakener who sold the

Guetala Bichank stronghold to the Growen. Because of him, that city lay empty. Because of him, Cinta's cousin had died. Because of him, the Growen Stygge ranks surged with able-bodied Bichank land-walruses suddenly burgeoning with new powers, while their weaker family members floated frozen in space. The kind of electromagnetic ability that allowed one person to affect the biology of other people—did that even count as electromagnetic? Did that even come from this dimension?

This is prejudice and superstition now. Perhaps he has interdimensional help, perhaps not. Perhaps he sensed me with his abilities, perhaps a ba-eater told. I am a scientist and should not assume anything I do not know.

Scientist or not, Cinta did not want to poke his head around the edge of the wall to look. His ears stood straight up on his head; his nostrils flared as he checked and double-checked that the scent of the sewer system had not followed them when they left their outer set of atmosphere suits inside the grate—that, at least, the Frelsi had given them gladly—*they should have given me a missile!*

"I'm on my way, little one," the land-walrus grunted.

Nope. No. No thank you, forever. Cinta pushed Masha with his forepaw and dashed on all fours to the other edge of the wall.

Masha poked her head out before he could stop her, and looked back at him in confusion.

"He can't hurt us," her mind said. "They've left a mutilated Bichank and no blitzers here in the inner circle. We're fine— let's go!"

Cinta shook his head. Oh, the Bichank's paws made so little sound!

"Huh. He's walking this way," her mind said.

Cinta shoved his paw into the face of his suit, pushing the excess material into his mouth so he could grab with his muzzle —the suit allowed for species who used their mouths like humans used hands—and grabbed Masha's ear between his jaws. He yanked her out of the way just as the Bichank suddenly charged through the space where she'd been. Okl turned and lunged at her with a hoarse, barking laugh. Cinta kicked with both of his hind legs to push her out of the way and bounced onto Okl's face. Huge paws came up on either side of him, grabbing—he slipped down Okl's back and ran.

The land-walrus dropped on all fours after him. Its tree-trunk-like hind legs thudded behind its webbed, handlike forepaws: *thud, plat, thud, plat, thud, plat—*

Cinta led it in a circle making as much noise as he could. Behind them Masha dashed between the outer walls and through the clearing to the space elevator. Okl suddenly swerved left, leaving Cinta—the giant creature climbed the wall, paused atop it with all four paws together like a sabertooth cat, and then pounced at Masha. She yelped as he landed almost on top of her, big paws swiping at her, just missing her hind leg. Cinta steadied himself and fired, pistol clutched in both forepaws. His weapon swerved last-minute—Okl redirected its aim—it almost shot Masha—she squealed—the weapon suddenly tried to leap from Cinta's grasp. This, this was what Jei Bereens had called an em-pull, redirecting polarities in the world around the user to create temporary magnetisms—and Okl was good at it.

Cinta held on, and found himself sliding toward the Bichank. He did not want to let go and give the creature his weapon, but he also did not, absolutely did not, want it touching him again with those cold paw-pads—

So he ceased struggling and dashed toward Okl. The change in balance threw the Bichank backward, and it released him for a moment. Cinta dashed with Masha into the transparent tube of the space elevator, and holstered his weapon as she smacked the button with her paw to turn it on.

"Never have I met someone who did not fear me enough to run the other way," Okl growled. "Perhaps you are a fool."

The elevator did not want to move. It asked for a code, and DNA access.

Cinta would need both from Okl.

Okl had both paws on the outside door of the space elevator, prying it open. They would be trapped in here. Masha dashed out between his legs as soon as she could fit—Cinta leapt into Okl's grasp as he reached for her, again throwing the Bichank off balance as it swung for something and a different weight barreled into him. As he stumbled, Cinta climbed his shoulder and smashed him in the face with his pistol. Blood spurted from the Bichank's snout.

DNA.

Cinta leapt off the giant as it grabbed at him again. "Where is your fear?" the Bichank roared.

"I fear something else more than I fear you," Cinta spat, sliding to a landing behind him. The momentum of his slide turned him to face the beast's back. "What is the code for the elevator?" he asked.

The Bichank stood still, tilting its head to the side. Its ears twitched. Its shoulders began to shake, and a chuckle grew into a roaring guffaw that bounced off the dome and filled the space. "I remember you," it said as it turned. It licked the blood dripping from its snout with a long slurp.

"And I you," Cinta said.

"Who is this with you?" the Bichank asked. "You perform defense like a male in heat."

Cinta laughed. "Enough stalling. Tell me the code for the elevator. Or call your masters to come save you."

The Bichank snorted. "I have sounded no alarms because I do not need them. I am playing until the end of all things. Do you not want to play with me, little naked worm? Is it frightening to play with no claws?"

Cinta saw Masha staring incredulously at the pair of them,

creeping back into the elevator with her ears flat like a "T." "How do you *know* this monster?" her disgusted mind cried.

He could hear her thoughts, but not Okl's. *If I worked for Stygge Bricandor I would keep a mask over my thoughts as well,* he noted. Questions had not made answers appear.

Cinta motioned with his muzzle for Masha to get on the elevator, speaking to cover up her footsteps. "Are you not afraid I've returned for my claws?" Cinta asked as he undid the seal between his paw and his suit and stowed the glove in his waistband. "Or perhaps I have returned with better ones."

"Ah, I see you want to play, too," Okl snarled, turning his head this way and that, as if to see what Cinta had covered up with the inane sentence. He began to back toward the elevator. Cinta slid in front of him.

Three things allowed Cinta to hear better: seeing no mouth, touching his target, and pain.

The moment Okl opened his mouth to speak again Cinta jumped into it, just missing his tusks. "Elevator code!" he yelled, as the surprised Bichank bit down on Cinta's shoulder, flailing to get suit and animal off its tongue. Cinta gripped the creature's scarred muzzle with his bare paw, wincing as the dull grinding teeth bruised his skin—

"19050931!"

Cinta shouted it out as the Bichank flung him away. He threw his pistol at the elevator ahead of him as Masha punched in the code, smeared the blood from the gun on the panel, pressed her worried ears back against her head—Cinta raced for the opening as *thunk-plat, thunk-plat, thunk-plat* thundered behind him again, and hot, wet breath flared against his heels, and—

He made it inside as Masha closed the door in the Bichank's face. The elevator started up—the Bichank pulled away just before its head would have been sliced off. The pair zipped toward the stars, panting, as the enraged creature roared after them.

Masha checked Cinta's suit for tears. "Bichanks do not eat meat like we do," Cinta said. "Their teeth grind, and should not tear."

"You're not bleeding under there?" she asked.

"I do not feel wet. I will bruise," he said, resealing his glove to his paw.

"He'll sound the alarm and stop the elevator soon," Masha said, looking down.

"I do not know," Cinta said. "He will look like he has failed if he does—he who, I am sure, assured Bricandor he could guard this room alone with the huge army of blitzers outside."

"But how can he get us down from here on his own?" she asked. "If he breaks the elevator they won't be able to get their power-person up to charge the Core."

"Maybe he has gone to set the emergency stop himself," Cinta said. "Oh—no. He has not."

"What—oh."

They could only just make out the shape of a dead Bichank curled on the floor below with the burning staff of its own neodymium mace through its chest.

"Why would it do that?" Masha cried out.

"Perhaps it had done so much to be feared that when it could not be feared it had nothing left to be," Cinta said. "Or perhaps it has never known defeat. The first time can overwhelm."

"Well, they know there's a problem now," Masha said. It did not take long before blitzers flooded into the room, no doubt alerted by the cessation in Okl's heart activity on the monitor all Growen soldiers wore. They pointed and yelled, but it was not until Cinta and Masha could no longer make them out that the elevator ground to a halt.

They had prepared, and neither Biouk panicked—it was after all for this possibility that Cinta and Masha, not one of the humans, had taken the lead here. Masha now pushed the front of her atmosphere-mask in also, wearing the muzzle cover over her mouth like a human would a glove on a hand, and as Cinta opened the top of the elevator to the bracing cold of the mesosphere, Masha double-checked the straps on both of their explosive-filled backpacks. He could just see the rings of the Core above them at the end of the thick cable they must now climb.

"Cinta, one moment," Masha said, opening the side pocket of her pack.

She drew out two pairs of long, silvery forearm braces with intricate weld patterns etched across them. Cinta recognized one of the symbols from their marriage medallions. On the end, the braces had polymerwall-like sacks with thick metal lining bunched at the tip.

"I was a little afraid to give this to you. Because of what we talked about." Her voice wavered. "You don't need claws for my love. But these space suit designs lack traction. I always hoped you might take me to space. So this year I made us both climbing attachments that better mimic natural claws." She slipped her paws into hers, and they congealed to her shape. She flexed, and long metal claws extended with a delightful slicing sound. "Is that—okay?"

Cinta pressed his forearms into the braces she held out and slid his paws into the slippers. They compressed his forearms and ankles quite firmly, but it was not unpleasant. He eyed her paws; it looked like she had just used her normal toe motion to trigger the extensions. The thickness of these suits prevented a non-human mammal from tearing a hole from the inside if they panicked and extended claws for some reason, so Masha might have simply unsheathed her claws. He would try this.

With a deep breath, Cinta clenched where his sheaths used to extend. The socks squeezed his arm to hold the stabilizing metal against the shape of his bone—ah, this was so the claws did not just rip off with any weight—and lovely metal spikes speared out of his paw.

She had given him his claws.

Cinta almost could not speak. Years had passed since he had last seen slicing strength extend from his fingertips. He had not dreamed a mate, and a child, and claws, would find him. His chest surged with a gratefulness that felt almost like pride—a pride in his mate, and her mind.

"Thank you," he said, nuzzling her neck. "I love them."

Masha's rump wiggled, and her ears flicked. "I'm glad. Then let's climb!"

CHAPTER TWENTY-FIVE

Elitsza

THE ALIEN WORLD SEEMED LIKE ONE OF THOSE STRANGE NIGHTMARES where everything seems shorter, or just the wrong color. Elitsza recognized flora and fauna like back home, but with such violent purples and greens she thought she might have a headache. Accustomed only to wearing drapes and beads during her life, Elitsza felt trapped and itchy in the hazmat suit.

Every detail conspired to remind her that her world and everyone she'd protected, everyone she'd led, had become a horrible living mush. *You did this*, it screamed at her. *You didn't listen.*

It didn't help how excited Rizzt and Szizzle seemed all the time. Now they traipsed through the underbrush like children playing rock hunt back home, whispering this or that observation to each other like they'd discovered their grandparents' treasure maps. To Szizzle, every damn leaf seemed like a new mystery; to Rizzt, every color seemed like a new shade of freedom. At least they'd make a symmetric pair to repopulate the species, Elitsza thought bitterly: science and religion, the same disastrous enterprises that'd destroyed them in the first place. When Elitsza rebuilt, the people would focus on simple things, the kinds of old traditions that'd existed in the prehistoric days, long before their grandparents or great grandparents, before Njandejara and the Age of Flight—back to the innocent golden age of Hunt they only heard about in their lessons.

After the fifth excited hiss about the same flying lizard, Elitsza had it. "We're fleeing from an alien predator to an alien science facility so we can breathe on a horrible alien planet. Why are you frolicking on the graves of our people?"

Szizzle dropped her head, flushing an ashamed beige. Rizzt spoke up, "Does it help them at all if we punish ourselves?" he asked in the severe voice he'd used as Highest Priest. "Somehow I don't think that will bring them back."

"You just don't care because you were mad at all of us for infecting you with that Thing," Elitsza snapped.

"I never stopped loving my people," Rizzt said. "At first, they were the reason I didn't resist. Over time, I watched the Pit oppress them through me, and by then it was too late to fight. Who do you think I blame for that, if not myself?"

"So why are you happy?" she hissed.

Rizzt nodded to the bag he carried. "Because of him."

Elitsza could scream. She restrained herself. "I'm glad you've found someone who helps you understand the manuscripts in a new way. One might mistake your calm for callousness."

"I've never been happier or sadder in my whole life," he said. She could see his scales glow a somber sky-blue through the front visor of the hazmat suit. "I don't know how to explain it."

"I'm beginning to see that life, like sapience, is a spectrum, instead of integers," Szizzle piped up. "Even the computers that the mammals consider binary. At what point in the electromagnetic spectrum does the computer threshold decide 'this is on' versus 'this is off'? There is an on and off; there is a happy and sad; there is a right and wrong. But there's also right and more right, and wrong and more wrong, sapient and more sapient. There are other feelings we didn't know existed, just like there are other colors we can't see, and they're still light, even if we don't recognize them. There is a light and dark, but there are many kinds of light."

Szizzle checked the map, and shifted course a bit; then she said, "We may only now be learning what right is, like how in some of the manuscripts Njandejara allows things to happen we later realize clearly were wrong. Joshua says they were allowed because Njandejara knows the darkness of our eyes: only he knows how much light we can handle at our place in history. Eyes adjusted to dark shrink away from light, but eyes gradually seeing a light starting little by little may not even know what light is."

"I don't see your point, at all," Elitsza grumbled.

"Among other things, she's saying there's so much we don't know," Rizzt said. "There's something bigger going on here, something that'll save the whole universe and make it all worth it. We thought the war with Aliash was something, and it's nothing compared to all this. It's not just our world that's been touched by darkness; it's all worlds. But now there's a new way forward dawning—we may actually see our people again, Elitsza." He nodded down toward his bag again. "And he's the key to it."

"I think to say other worlds have suffered like ours is foolish as well as offensive," Elitsza snapped.

"More died on Burbura and Skraeli two years ago," Szizzle said. "I've been listening to the young mammals talk about their homes that they lost on this planet, too. I don't think we need to be suffering more than other people for our suffering to be valid. Our suffering is terrible. That's why it's so important—and why I'm so grateful—that there's a way to bear it."

Rizzt nodded.

"I'm very happy for you," Elitsza said, stilling the fluttering frustration in her abdomen with as much stoicism as she could muster. *Listen. Listen to your subjects, self.* "You're right. As long as our species is around, there is still some hope. If you find he helps, then that's good."

Rizzt stopped short and signaled for silence—he sniffed the air with his tongue out of habit before apparently remembering he couldn't smell in that hood—and pointed into the distance with his foreclaw. Round white and brown buildings crowded an ugly dirt street that stretched into more ugliness as far as Elitsza could see: these wicked mammals had cleared out all the trees rather than building under them.

"I'm going to leave you here by this bush for a moment," he whispered to Joshua, almost stuffing his slender snout into the hole in the bag as the translator repeated his words. "I want to make sure we're safe up ahead before we carry you in there."

"Okay." The little creature's voice sounded sad, and—scared? "I'll miss you, Rizzt."

"I won't be gone long!" Rizzt answered.

"Will one of you stay with me?" Joshua asked.

"I can," Szizzle said. "I'm the only one who can open the bag, anyway."

"But you have the translation pad," Elitsza said. "We have to stay together if we want to talk."

"You can take it."

So Elitsza and Rizzt crept into the alien town, staring at all the mammals and amphibians and even occasional morphed, ugly reptilians wandering the streets. No one really looked at them—a few other people wore hazmat suits, too. Those people, like them, seemed to be following maps to the transition hospital.

I hope we'll be able to tell what it is when we find it. Some of the houses had thatch or natural materials like stone, like back home, but most of the buildings were a hodgepodge of cement and that ugly hardening goo the male Bareskin had put Joshua inside.

After some time, they came to one street with a gathering

crowd and a lot of yelling. Most of the people in the crowd had the same armor the Bareskins had stolen from their enemies on the cold moon. They seemed to be stopping and searching people with hazmat suits trying to get into one of the buildings.

They were targeting reptilians.

Rizzt and Elitsza didn't even look at each other. No need to say anything, either. They both turned around and started to head away from the crowd.

"Hey! Get back here!" That was what it sounded like—it was too far away for the translator to be sure, and the reptilians didn't plan on sticking around to find out. They ran.

But suddenly Elitsza felt a sting in her back, and the world disappeared.

Elitsza awoke to find herself and Rizzt in the dirt surrounded by gray-armored bipeds with those horrible, mirrored helmet-heads. She could smell such an awful confluence of powerful things—something sharp and acidic, something rotten, something too green like trampled vegetation—

"They've punctured our suits!" she cried.

Rizzt didn't answer. He lay beside her, breathing, but breathing so, so slowly. There was a tear in the back of his suit— Elitsza could see white scales through it. *Oh no. Our male! Our species!*

"It doesn't seem like he's handling the stun cartridge well," one of the Bareskins said, crouching down by Elitsza. She didn't know what a stun cartridge was, but it didn't sound good. "Or maybe that's our atmosphere. You'd better get him inside the transition facility soon, huh?"

"What do you want with us?" she asked.

"Why did you run?" he asked.

"Because it looked like you were discriminating against

people like us, for some reason. Why wouldn't we run?" She tried to calm her voice. She had negotiated with the ruthless Aliash, she could negotiate with aliens.

"Well, I was wondering if maybe it was because you'd seen a small furry, about yea high, black and brown," he suggested.

"Do you mean a Biouk?" she asked.

"Well look at that, you don't even speak our filking language and you're already lecturing people on slurs," the Bareskin mocked.

"I really don't understand—"

"Yes, I mean a Biouk, scaly," he said. She didn't have to know their slurs to know he meant to call her one.

"What would it be worth, if I'd seen someone who'd seen him?" she asked.

"Well that guy could live," said the Bareskin, nodding toward Rizzt. "Shyte, who knows, we could even pay you. See these?" He pulled three small translucent rubber bags out of a pocket in his utility belt and handed them to her. "They're currency here. This is enough to live on for a year."

"All right," she said. "Follow me." She stood up—wow, she was unsteady. The Bareskins laughed. She wondered for a moment if this was how her favorite Bareskin, the male who'd saved her, felt when they'd had him do tricks for them in the cage.

She would undo all those mistakes now. She would save her people, this time.

Rizzt didn't even stir as she stepped past him. "Won't we bring him?" Elitsza asked.

"The faster I get what I'm looking for the faster you can come back and help him," the Bareskin said, crossing his arms.

She swallowed. She didn't like walking with these aliens behind her with their rifles. But she was a leader. "When we get there, don't kill the other reptilian," she said. "She may try to run. But she's the only one who can open the case."

"You're the boss," the Bareskin leader sniggered. Fluttershies, she hated their tinny voices.

They didn't have to worry about Szizzle running—when they arrived she was asleep, drooped around a tree root, and Joshua was sniffling in the bag with a low frightened whine. The whine faded to soft breathing as the Bareskin boots clomped and crunched through the underbrush toward him—unlike the deliberate Bareskins who'd brought them here, these plowed through everything around them like herd animals with no shepherd.

One of the Bareskins went to kick Szizzle as soon as they walked up; Elitsza pounced to wake her instead.

"Szizzle, open the bag," she said, shaking the scientist's shoulder. "Szizzle!"

Szizzle nodded awake with a yawn, smacking her jaws and tongue together. "What—"

"Open the bag," the lead Bareskin repeated, in a much less friendly tone.

"He's in there," Elitsza pointed, looking over her shoulder to reassure the Bareskin. "She'll open up for you, just give me a moment."

"Elitsza … what do they want with him?" Szizzle whimpered, rising to her feet now.

"He's under arrest, scaly," the Bareskin said.

Szizzle flashed bright orange. "They're the enemies of our rescuers," Szizzle hissed to Elitsza. "Why did you bring them here?"

"I'm doing this for you!" Elitsza snapped. "Rizzt is injured, and they'll have no problem killing us. It's better that one person die than an entire nation perish. We can die, or we can accept their payment and have enough funds to live a year!"

"But then what is the point of our species, if living is all we live for?" Szizzle begged. "That's just eating. We eat so we can work, we don't just eat to eat, and if we just live to live, and we don't stand *for* anything, what is the point?"

"You're babbling. This is an order!"

"This is for you, isn't it," Szizzle spat, her scales flashing black. "You need power, and when your Being of Power died, there wasn't any anymore. So now you're killing mine."

"Beings of Power? Are you listening to yourself? I'm taking care of you. You're insulting me for being a consumer, but there are no producers if we don't consume. We all need to eat."

"Then your belly and your pocket have become all you are, until you can't see when you've discovered a new kind of sapience."

"Shut up, fool." Elitsza snatched Szizzle's arm, and shoved it into the bag, rubbing it along the seam like she'd seen their nobler male Bareskin do. The black goo melted open like a wilting flower to reveal the little furry mammal in the center.

The Bareskins suddenly stepped backward as if frozen. *Why?*

"I will come with you," Joshua said, rising to his hind legs. One couldn't even tell he'd been whimpering earlier. His small voice seemed to boom through the forest; the lizards hidden in the trees stopped singing as if in reverence. "But you will not harm these people as they leave."

"But Joshua—" Szizzle cried.

"You can come with me, if you like," he said. "We won't be fighting them, though."

Szizzle trembled. Even she couldn't agree to that.

Joshua stepped toward the Bareskins.

They stepped back.

Elitsza took the opportunity to grab Szizzle's wrist and run for the town. She was stronger than Szizzle, and anyway the younger girl didn't fight anymore; she covered her eyes with her claw, and the black faded to brown. Perhaps Szizzle, like Elitsza, remembered the faces of her people crying up to her as they melted—perhaps Szizzle had to make a show of fighting this for the sake of her conscience, but still knew, deep down, that Elitsza was right. Elitsza didn't have the luxury of hiding behind conscientious objections. When the consumed called up to her from the river of flesh, they'd cried that *Elitsza* led them down this path of extinction. She wouldn't let them be right.

As they left, the spell around the Bareskin tribe broke, and Elitsza could hear them jeering as they snatched up the small mammal and carried him off.

But, in keeping with his promise, not a single one fired on the reptilians as they fled.

CHAPTER TWENTY-SIX

Reise

Reise zipped through the forest on a borrowed Frelsi air-rider, pushing against its compuwall windshield to drive it faster into the wind. His legs squeezed the bike body between its folded sparrow wings as he wove through the trees, trying to ignore the frustrating blinking tracker on the lower right-hand corner of his compuwall. Dr. Loylan had managed to procure transportation for him, but certainly not without conditions.

The molecular 3D printer hadn't taken long to produce a vial of the new endorphin in Nathan's blood, and the dose Dr. Loylan had injected into Reise's veins greatly exceeded what Nathan generated drop by drop in his body over the course of weeks. Her control panel had lost influence over Reise's movements within an hour. Nathan's imaging studies had returned as well: the mind-control graft itself would likely shrivel and fall out over the next few weeks.

With that crisis solved, Reise had risen to leave so he could keep his sister's friend from becoming a space-laser component. He hadn't even requested assistance with the mission—he knew he wouldn't obtain it—but Dr. Loylan had almost stopped him.

"We'll still need to monitor you for reactions. We can't afford to have you disappear."

"Three hours have transpired, and I remain healthy. I'll return by morning—it's the solstice tonight. We could also sit around and hope Bricandor's space laser is harmless, or poorly constructed, but I fail to see intelligence in that. No matter what happens you've already proven the efficacy of the cure. What should stop your colleagues from initiating tests on your Turned on their planets now? At what arbitrary hour of my survival will you know it's time to expand trials? Other people need this."

Dr. Loylan had agreed on the condition that Reise wear a new wristband to monitor his vitals—along with a sensor in his blood, currently wrapped in gauze under his uniform sleeve. Reise suspected her fear of his death or capture abated when she realized a second Turning could provide scientific data on interactions and long-term effects of multiple darts in the same once-treated subject.

Whatever her motives, Reise had escaped. Reise had called Jake to escort him off base—one should not traipse alone around a Frelsi base with a Turned dart in your neck unless one wanted a gunshot wound in the head—and made for the town of Realm.

They'd used to get ice cream there all the time.

Reise saw the blitzer troop before they saw him; he slid his hand up on the compuwall windshield to send his air-rider vertically into the tree above him, and killed everything except its most basic levitator engine. The quiet rumble was essentially inaudible under the continual song of the day-lizards and the stomping revelry of the blitzers through the woods.

Reise drew his rifle and waited for his prey to approach. The patterned shadows and reflections cast by the leaves onto the gray armor and mirrored helmets made it much harder to pick an accurate kill shot than in fields of ice and snow. A hostage complicated matters.

Reise had overheard much of the conversation on the bioship surrounding the rather remarkable but narcissistic Biouk youth. He knew Lem both wished and feared that he might believe this person somehow formed or had formed or would form a physical part of the interdimensional being that still had her under its thumb. Reise would have only minor qualms about placing a cartridge into Joshua's forehead if he *truly* believed him an incarnation of evil, but he required a great deal more proof of guilt than some magic tricks and wild statements, especially in a universe of rather more spectacular electromagnetic beings. Certainly if an interdimensional being wanted to ingratiate itself to a populace, it would prove its identity more dramatically. Lem herself was a more interesting candidate for interdimensional spokesperson than Cinta's adopted son. Her request for his rescue, however, fully disproved the possibility of Njandejara's involvement: Njandejara was supposedly eternal and could not perish.

In the meantime, Reise would go to great lengths to destroy those who hunted innocent life, no matter how foolish or grandiose that life itself.

They were close enough for him to hear their words now. He could see blood trailing down the side of Joshua's face, and a tear in his ear.

"The Counselor wants you alive, but that doesn't mean in one piece," someone was taunting.

"Have you heard of hardening?" Joshua asked softly.

"What?"

"My mother is a scientist," Joshua said. "She tells me about plasticity in the brain. The more you use a circuit—like to store a thought or action, basically—the more the brain releases signals telling its neuroimmune system that circuit is important. The less you use a circuit, the more that circuit releases a chemical that tells the brain, 'Hey, I'm not needed, you can remove me.' The space in your head is finite, so this way your brain naturally cleans out talents and thoughts you don't need, and strengthens the ones you do."

The blitzers seemed confused; their incessant noise quieted.

Joshua spoke with the calm authority of an esteemed convocation speaker and the warmth of a friend huddled over the counter—not like someone who'd clearly been treated like a living sports-ball, fur matted in blood and spit. "So the more you think a thought, the easier it is to think a thought, and the less you think a thought, the harder it is to think it. In a way, your past self creates the programming that controls your future self."

"I don't know if I need a science lesson right now, furry," someone growled. "You're not superior to us, you know."

"Well, Masn"—Joshua seemed to know the blitzer's name—"because of rigid, thick circuits in their programming, it's harder for someone rich or powerful to find and be stored in my Pali's dimension. The poor don't have that problem." He looked up, and Reise could swear the big round eyes stared directly through the treetops to Reise's. "Neighbor, the more you use the same circuit over and over, the harder it'll be to break out of it, until your brain can't fight it at all. Be careful how you choose to think, and walk, that you don't make it impossible to choose Njandejara at all in the future." Reise's mind stalled, trying to process, but his trigger finger remembered his mission, and his chest took its necessary breath, as Joshua finished. "To him who has, more will be given, and to him who does not have, even what he has will be taken away."

"Shut him up, will you?"

Reise saw a flash of underarm as someone raised their hand for a slap. Breathe, trigger pull—he sent a flayer cartridge through the side of that chest. He knew killer's anatomy: the blitzer dropped dead, hit sideways through the heart. It took just a tiny second for anyone to notice.

In that fatal second, the guy who first noticed went down with a cartridge through the front of his neck—a hard shot, with the reinforced material there now, but no manufacturer could create a perfect joint.

"Sniper!" someone roared. They hadn't seen the direction of the shot. They scrambled for cover, weapons spinning in all directions. Reise picked a target on the far side of the group from himself. A little underarm as he raised his weapon, there—

It wasn't as clean a shot, but it put the blitzer down screaming. "This side, this side!" They fired away from Reise.

Joshua raised his paws in the air. "Reise, stop!" he called—eyes closed, not showing Reise's direction.

Stop? Reise's finger twitched on the trigger; his eyes scanned another target—

"I know where I'm going!" Joshua cried. "Pali can send me help if I need it. He could even send you again. But not right now. This warrior's timeline will kill you."

Reise scowled. What a strange, insulting—

A shot whizzed into the bark right beside the barrel of Reise's rifle. It wasn't a kill cartridge, whatever Joshua might say: the white flash of stun serum melted into the tree branch. Someone saw Reise. And that someone had also gotten up a tree.

And that someone wanted to Turn him.

The cartridge had hit the left side of the branch—*approximately*—

Reise peered into the canopy in that direction and saw nothing. The reflective blitzer helmet confused his view—he had to be staring straight at it. But something was definitely moving through the branches above him, trying to get behind him. Another stun cartridge whizzed through the leaves by his head. Shyte. He swiveled to fire toward the movement, but hit nothing. Shyte! Had he been a big fish in a little pond on Bijou? This was a big fish.

"You can come with me, Reise, but you can't fight," Joshua wheezed—just before someone grabbed him and wrapped wire around his muzzle. It enraged Reise—he knew the gag well—but

—but also he knew 259 Growen slaves created by his emotion, his failure to let one person go down. *"You can't fight?"* Filking what was that? No. Last time he made that mistake—of bowing down—his friends spent a year in captivity.

This time the stun cartridge hit the bill of his patrol cap. Filk this. Reise wasn't going to Turn for this. He could still rescue Joshua later—they wanted him alive after all. Maybe this path did lead to his demise. *The demise of my liberty.*

Reise slung his rifle over his back and shoved both hands hard into the compuwall windshield. His air-rider roared to life, weaving through stands of trees too thick for the blitzers' cartridges to penetrate. He would've stayed, fought through, suffered anything for the cause of freedom—but this was not freedom's cause.

At some point, before he disappeared, he looked back to see Joshua helping the blitzer Reise hadn't quite killed back onto his feet.

CHAPTER TWENTY-SEVEN

Lem

I'D ACCUMULATED A LOT OF EXPERIENCE CRAMMING MY BIG STRONG self into small spaces.

I'd never been a small girl, and the equipment locker wasn't exactly designed to hold broad-shouldered, big-hipped warrior beauties. The little shelf behind me dug into my spine, and a box of wires and random shyte pressed against the side of my face. But I was waiting my turn.

Laaru's tunnel had taken him up inside an empty computing center—he apparently knew the layout of this place as well as Cinta did, and with every single person on guard duty for the solstice, no one had time to check their messages or waste eyes on paperwork. I'd waited a decent amount of time before following Laaru into his tunnel, so by the time I arrived in the computing center he was already swiping and scrolling across multiple documents on the large me-height compuwall in the corner. I'd crept behind him into the locker without quite shutting its door—less noise that way, and a girl likes to see what's going on.

My collection of interstellar software was basically burning holes in my utility belt. Sure, I'd sailed my skiff through wreckage and stardust to scavenge for our living, but I'd also become a collector. Something about how Sterba destroyed my home with our own appliances just stuck with me even though I hadn't been there. Or maybe *because* I hadn't been there. Cyber-attacks were a thing on both sides, but no one did it like she did. *Shyte, imagine if she'd turned that brain to solving sapient trafficking or energy inequality.*

I didn't exactly have humanitarian motives myself. Right before I rescued Jei from Mera, I'd retrieved Sterba's mace from the floating debris of her station above Alpino, and I'd managed to find a single hard drive of hers that still kind of worked when I took it in to my Forge software guy later. He didn't just like me because I brought in that good metal for him to sell—he liked me because I paid, and paid well, for fun and interesting "theoretical" problem-solving "for a video game." I think by the time he figured out the video game was called "real life" he either didn't care or just decided to make his brain dumb on that point. Throw in a few chips gathered from abandoned satellites, and I'd assembled an arsenal.

One of the most important programs I'd acquired was a nice little encryption-busting brute force algorithm—and it came with a little something to prevent security programs from detecting it, too.

So when Laaru started to pace—pissed about the password locks on some of the documents he wanted—I threw a little spark over by the entrance to the room. The snapping sound spooked him. He dashed behind one of the other compuwalls further from the entrance—Stygge or not, he didn't want to be caught snooping.

Excellent. While Laaru couldn't see me I slipped over to the computer he'd left open and slid my chip into it. By the time the kid decided he was safe I'd opened his documents for him and ducked back into the closet. I wasn't trying to be his fairy godmother or some shyte: I wanted to nudge him in the right direction, but I really needed him to hurry up so I could load the rest of my software into the building's control systems. I also figured I'd rather not hunt through every filking room in this building trying to find Bricandor when I could just follow Laaru straight there.

I drew Diebol's holopen out of my pocket, clutching it at the ready. After I brought it out of the ravine Masha had removed the tracking, and I'd asked my software guy to help me understand what I'd need to remote control a room with it like back in the Stygge training center. When Cinta shared his blueprints of this Core place I'd paid attention to shyte like temp systems and central polymerwall locks. I didn't have Diebol or Sterba's expanded control powers, but with the right software I could approximate it just long enough …

Diebol kept a lot of notes on his holopen—probably so he could remember his thoughts without holding them in his mind where Bricandor could find them. He wrote some personal stuff, like about how Stygges got their names from dead Stygges, and how he never got to understand how his namesake died or how he came into Bricandor's custody. But he'd also written a long analysis on Bricandor's abilities and weaknesses. Aside from the biological conjecture, I was most interested in the fact that Bricandor's ability was actually more receptive, like Mera's—and as a result, Bricandor needed to *see* you to Death Glare. Once he did, it didn't take long for your nervous system to shut down —a few seconds, in some cases. He was strong enough with his em-push that he'd stopped bullets before, too. This meant I needed to overwhelm his mind and stay out of sight.

Diebol had also come up with a way to survive the Death Glare, if you couldn't hide. He'd tried it out—it was like a philosophical "dance" where he canceled out electromagnetic attacks.

Our skill sets didn't exactly overlap: he had enhanced action potentials that looked like seizures and I had weird shock-generating capacitors in my skin like an electric eel. But I'd tried to learn the thing anyway, and at one point while practicing, I'd sort of successfully redirected the current of a small broken generator so it didn't electrocute me. I wasn't going to trust this ability I'd never really proved, but at least I had some kind of fail-safe.

And last, but not least … Diebol had left his voice. Old messages my software could emulate and AI could mimic. I wasn't the only one who'd feel weird hearing him again.

Laaru finished up and slouched out of the room, his shoulders hunched and hood up like he needed armor for his brain. I plugged in the rest of my chips, synced the screen to Diebol's holopen, and locked out the computer. I took the risk of leaving them to install while I followed Laaru—I just didn't want to somehow get locked out of wherever he went to find Bricandor.

The main hallway actually had a lot more cover than I was used to in a Growen facility—seemed like they'd designed it specifically with alcoves, pillars, and low walls for blitzers to crouch behind in case an encroaching army forced them to firefight inside the building. They'd expected the Frelsi to care more—and care enough to maybe even drive them to fighting inside. I dashed from pillar to pillar behind Laaru, syncing my steps to his to mask the soft tap-tap of my boots on the tile. He paused before a large, gold-plated polymerwall, shoved his hands in his pockets, and sighed.

Diebol's holopen flashed a small blue light to let me know my software installation had finished. Sweet.

It was judgment day.

LAARU

Laaru found Bricandor in his room, just down the hall from the space elevator. His mobile throne lay partially reclined, surrounded by the jade fronds of elegant plants. Bricandor's dry lips cracked a smile below his closed eyes.

"You are upset," he said.

"The Structure. It's some kind of model of a giant laser core. It's impossible for it to 'generate energy' the way it's built," Laaru said.

"All energy generators transform energy from one state to another," Bricandor chuckled, eyes still shut, hands folded across his chest. "This only transforms suffering into peace."

"That's like saying a gun is a windmill because they both use mechanical force! Bloodseas, what else did you lie to me about?" Laaru asked, voice cracking. "The mind control? That you blamed on the guy before me—the Stygge Diebol guy? People are saying that if he'd lived, the Growen would already have won the war. There are even factions of his fans left on the High Counsel who want peace with the Frelsi, and others who think you've stretched out the war to fund the Structure." He pressed his palms against his forehead as his voice rose. "Winning *quickly* would've been so much more humane. Are we failing on purpose?"

Bricandor sat up now. "I have hidden many things from you, but that I would not hide," he snapped. "Those who claim Diebol would have already triumphed underestimate the Frelsi and know nothing of the complexity of keeping the Independent planets out of their ideological clutches. I will allow conjecture about flaws in my leadership, but I will not stand for accusations that I would sabotage my own cause." He spat into one of the plant pots embedded in the ground beside him. "Who knows," he groaned as he eased himself to his feet. "Perhaps Diebol was a better strategist than I. But I am the one who will save the universe."

"So why don't *you* power the Structure, then?" Laaru asked. "What actually happens to the person in the Core?"

Bricandor laughed; his eyes twinkled. He still looked so innocent and kind, so incapable of malice—it was so confusing. "So that is your real objection, then," Bricandor said. "Not the cause, or the cost of sapient life, but your own skin. Laaru, I'm surprised at you. You were about to obtain your new Stygge name."

Laaru pressed his fist into his forehead. "Look, I thought it might not be pleasant, but I agreed because—because I want this all to—shyte, I did terrible things on Bijou because I believed this was going to save enough people to make up for it!" He hadn't heard this aloud before, and as his own words reached him he felt the blood drain from his face. He'd refused to set the Turned free for *weeks*. Some of them had been beaten, basically tortured, and as much as he'd tried to prevent that, *he'd* kept them captive. He'd—he—"I may have killed someone when I brought down the cavern to save the Structure. I didn't care, and I didn't care because *you said this would help the most people*." What was this pressure in his chest, his forehead—? He couldn't cry, or scream, but something needed to happen or he might explode. Or pass out? Or was he screaming, actually? Everything sounded so quiet, so far away. "I chose to help you because I trusted you knew what you were doing!"

"Boy, did you really think your choice mattered?" Bricandor chuckled again. "I was going to have you for my ends whether you wanted it or not. I cultivated your choice for *your* sake, that you might not suffer as you walked with me into inevitability. I could have dragged you along terrified, but I chose to make you comfortable instead."

Such horrifying words in such a dulcet tone. Laaru stammered. His mind was so blank.

"I've helped you," Bricandor added. "Even you can admit

I've showered you with comforts. I've provided for your family, and I've freed you from the shame of your Thought. You're brazen with it now, unafraid of who you are, yes? I broke that internalized bigotry for you. Meanwhile your predecessor lived years in a wooden cage."

"I thought that was like—an imprisonment for breaking the law or something," Laaru croaked.

"No. He was a child," Bricandor said. "It was for his good, of course. You don't understand the severity of a love like mine."

A clap sounded outside the room, requesting entrance. Bricandor stepped back to his throne and pressed the small compupad affixed to its armrest. The polymerwall unlocked, softening to let any and all DNA pass, and soldiers entered carrying Joshua, the Biouk from the bioship who could move asteroids.

He was bloody, with small chunks of fur missing, and a piece torn from his ear.

The clarity of that moment was so painful Laaru begged his mind to go dark, to bring him back into the fog, to let him believe the lie, so he didn't have to see this truth. He wanted to believe the injured Biouk was some evil portal masquerading in goodness, that this was necessary, that they needed to plug his aberrant power into the Core to end suffering—he didn't want to live in the reality where he'd told Bricandor where to find some-one, and the result was innocent blood.

He physically closed his eyes and, overcome, sat down on the floor with his head in his hands.

Laaru barely noticed when Bricandor left the room. Some issue with the space elevator. He overheard orders given to shoot him if he tried to leave—not that he knew where he'd go. Apparently

Bricandor liked to have back-up options when he sacrificed people to the void. Laaru wished he could summon the kind of indomitable rage Reise had. He could only muster emptiness.

Presently he felt a small body pressed against his side. It was warm, and safe. He lifted his head to see Joshua leaned up against him and at least fifty rifles trained on them both. They were probably set to stun, but no one was taking any chances with Joshua's movements given what Laaru had said about him.

A wire was wrapped around the Biouk's muzzle, digging into his skin. Laaru hated that. More gags, more tongue-cutting, more hiding what Laaru needed to know. Why were they so afraid of speech? Were words that powerful to them? For a moment, nothing mattered to Laaru in the whole universe other than getting rid of that wire.

Laaru lifted his hands to show he had no weapons and peeled the wire off Joshua's face. The Biouk winced, but smiled. Laaru tossed the wire across the room and looked away out the window.

The little snout nuzzled Laaru's ribs again. "I *know*, you know," Joshua said.

"I hope—you don't," Laaru said. "Which thing?"

"Both things," Joshua said. "Both your Thought, and what you told Bricandor."

"One of those I don't care about so much anymore," Laaru said. It wasn't what he was supposed to say, but it was—a wall, something he could put up to shield the emptiness. He didn't need more shame right now.

"Should you?" Joshua asked.

Laaru shrugged. His stomach was so, so heavy.

"I set you up to tell Bricandor," Joshua said. "You didn't know what you were doing."

More confusing shyte. It was true. That had been the only time the cub spoke to Laaru during the flight—to show off what he could do. But he couldn't mean he'd wanted to get kidnapped—?

"I don't want this," Joshua said. "But if it's not me, it'll be you."

"So you know what happens in the Core." Laaru lifted his head, peering at the Biouk through the hair falling over his face.

"Yes," Joshua said. "I don't want you to die. But Laaru—" He sighed, snuggling closer. "Your Thought is going to kill you, even if Bricandor lets you go."

"It's helped me get a lot done," Laaru said. "It's not like Bricandor was the first person to teach me what it could do."

"Pele didn't know how you were charging your powers," Joshua said. "If she knew what I know, that lesson would have gone differently."

"It seems like it's something that's always been a part of me, if I really think about it, though," Laaru said. "Even before I really recognized it."

"Whether through genetics or through experiences, we all have things we've been given that are part of us that aren't good for us," Joshua said. "An alcoholic person may have a problem in their ADH1B gene. People who choose sex lives with higher disease exposure often have low oxytocin. But healthy cognitive tricks can help you escape addiction, and healthy bonding can increase your oxytocin. The universe has a set of mathematical and biological rules for how it works. If every organism kept to those rules, there would be no suffering."

Joshua's bound little paws tapped Laaru's elbow. "I'm not saying everything will go perfectly for you if you keep the natural law. Someone else's bad decisions can still affect you, like the way a cheater can carry a disease home to a faithful person. But the faithful person in general has lower disease risk, just like the cheater in general has higher disease risk. Does that make sense?"

"It does," Laaru croaked. "Are you saying the Thought is against those rules?"

Joshua's eyes shone with such pain and sympathy Laaru almost thought he might apologize. But he didn't. "Yes," he said.

Laaru dropped his head between his shoulders. Something about him was always wrong to someone, wasn't it? He missed the days when his grandmother used to sneak him sweet oyster cakes back on Burbura, when the only thing wrong about him was that sometimes he stole sweets or stayed up too late.

"You are fearfully and wonderfully made, you know, Laaru," Joshua said softly. "You're a self-portrait of the most amazing Life in all dimensions, and eyes for the universe to observe itself. What you do isn't what you are. It just changes what you can become."

After months of constant criticism and years of self-doubt the softness was too much. A heavy shudder struggled to escape Laaru's chest; he squeezed his eyes shut to keep tears out of them. People in militaries didn't cry. Not if they wanted to stop being worthless as soldiers.

"It feels like right and wrong are always changing," he breathed through gritted teeth.

"Sometimes, when you find yourself Becoming something new, it's harder to tell what's right and wrong because the people around you don't know what that is for you anymore," Joshua said. "That's why you need a guide that's actually synced into the rhythm of the universe. You want to do what's kindest for everyone, but what is kindness? And who decides that?"

"Not me, apparently," Laaru sniffed, swallowing and staring ahead to steel himself against the emptiness. "It just seemed like —well, like they say, you calculate the cost of each life, and sometimes you have to make the hard decisions."

"The cost of innocent life is always death, Laaru," Joshua said. "To return to the universe the *nefesh* energy you've stolen."

"But then death just leads to more death," Laaru muttered. "Where's the solution in that?"

"It doesn't lead to endless death if sapients only punish the rare cases when more than two people prove they saw the whole crime. The land punishes the rest," Joshua said. "But it gets more complicated than that, and there are many complicated things about this universe. Which is why you were deceived, Laaru. Because you don't know how the universe works. And how could you, on your own?"

"Does anybody?" Laaru asked.

"My Pali does," Joshua said. "He can show you what you need to know for your part of it."

Laaru hung his head again and shook it. He wasn't interested in more soft voices selling him their side, especially not when they asked him to do impossible things.

Joshua stirred beside him; Laaru looked up and followed his gaze. A lot of the blitzers had left the room for some reason. There were whispers about the elevator room, and about helping Bricandor, and ambushes.

Joshua looked back up at Laaru. "You're not alone, you know. I've been hunted by the same Thought you have. It attacks me at night sometimes."

"Fighting it really doesn't work," Laaru said.

"No, it doesn't," Joshua said. "Soon things will change, and I'll be able to give you my power to help you resist its tyranny. But for now, there is a brain trick called sublimation, where you take the Thought, and figure out what unmet need you actually have beneath it. Then you choose a different thought or action that still fills that need but won't hurt you."

Before Laaru could answer, Joshua looked back over to the polymerwall that led to the space elevator. So did the blitzers. All but two suddenly received orders in their helmets and rushed out into the elevator room.

The lights flickered.

When they came back on, the two remaining blitzers who'd stayed behind lay on the ground. Lights flickered again as Pele—or Jaika or Lem, apparently—knelt in front of Joshua to cut the binding on his paws, and laid a hand on Laaru's shoulder to point him to the polymerwall on the other end of the room, away from the space elevator. "Your credentials should still work on the launchpad outside," she told him. "Get out of here."

"Thank you—" Laaru said, but the lights flickered again, and she was gone.

CHAPTER TWENTY-EIGHT

Bricandor

Counselor Bricandor usually preferred to delegate, but the moment he heard of Okl's death in the elevator room he left to resolve the issue himself. With less than an hour to the solstice, he could not afford an underling's incompetence.

But when Bricandor stepped into the elevator room, the lights switched off.

The blitzers could see—most of their helmets carried the infrared modification—but the words they shouted to each other about "image interference" made very little sense. And why should they make sense? The room itself suddenly didn't. Bricandor felt a soft mist come over him, and with it an intense desire to sleep, and obey.

"Say hello to Mera," said Jared Diebol's voice over the intercom.

He's dead. He has to be dead! His vitals monitor said—

But they had not recovered an identifiable corpse, and vitals monitors could be fooled, and—

Bricandor's heart would have raced if his body had allowed; he could just barely register his own terror under a blanket of sweet, overwhelming weariness. *Why fight?* said the mist. There was no point.

Yes, Morda could do something like this. He'd seen her carcass, however.

"Leave and secure our guests," Bricandor ordered, wheezing.

Blitzers shouted to one another about locked polymerwalls. Some new recruit panicked and tried to shoot his way out even as the others screamed to him about the repulsion—stray cartridges flew through the room. Someone was injured. Bricandor saw a lavender mace light up, and a posed female form, but before he could identify her the mace hurled toward his face. He deflected it with an em-push. It spun back to him. He caught it in an em-pull this time, holding the staff up in the air without touching its surface. The dancing spikes of light on the weapon's tip cast shadows across the blitzers near him, but the mace was useless as a lantern in a room so filled with purple haze.

"We have a cheeky intruder who thinks quite highly of themselves," Bricandor said, taking a gas mask from one of the blitzers. He felt something invisible tugging on the mace—if he could only follow the direction of the em-pull—

Sparks flickered in the darkness.

"Sterba greets you as well, 'Father Wolf,'" Diebol said. "Pity, she still won't tell me her real name. You erased that part of her."

The fire system engaged, and the room began to fill with water.

Father Wolf? Only Diebol knew to call him that. Oh, the terrible look on his face when he'd blocked the Death Glare, the nightmares he'd left behind—!

The temperature control sensor hummed; frigid air burst through the room, spraying the water like sleet. Even in the cold, even with the gas mask on, Bricandor had inhaled too much obedience serum to shiver. The fear seemed trapped in his mind, incapable of registering with the rest of his nervous system. He was going to die, the fear said—and it sounded so logical, the mist said, to surrender, then, didn't it? Why not lie down?

"I have learned something new today," Bricandor said, still swirling the captive mace through the room from this shadow to that, still searching for the intruder in the increasingly chaotic crowd. "Terror plus surrender becomes something quite like despair. Well done."

The water had risen to his knees. Someone gave a joyful shout—the hallway polymerwall had become permeable again— not the one back to the throne room, unfortunately—

The shout ended in a curse, and then a scream. Low figures rushed in from the hall, thick battering rams barreling into the crowd. Blitzers tripped—crunching followed. A cloaked figure lit up in the corner—yes, cloaked like Sterba.

A white mace sailed for Bricandor's face. Mera's mace began to fight him again; he hissed at her to obey and managed to block with her weapon before Sterba's could strike. Ear-blasting static blared from the intercom. Blitzers screamed about Fort Jehu as Bricandor dueled the floating staff—he saw another burst of sparks—

The maces flashed as they slammed against each other and Bricandor managed to identify the "hunched figures" now: waterproof trash bots. They rolled through the room, whirring teeth grinding whatever they found in their path—only appliances, easy for blitzers to destroy, but the mist was so *thick*—and as the water rose to waist-level it covered the bots. The blitzers could no longer see to shoot them. This soldier, then that, fell under the water and rose roaring in a pool of red.

Bricandor gritted his teeth, threw a hand down, and shoved himself up out of the water. He levitated, still fighting off the white mace with one hand out, and watched for the next blitzer to go down. *There!* He threw out a palm to draw everything there to himself. The bot flew out of the water, dripping—he hurled it in the path of the white mace.

One after another he found and threw the rebellious machines. He was irritated when his bones began to shake—he was escaping Mera's serum somewhat, and he despised the cold —but he could manage this. He was beginning to see patterns. His attacker could not maintain this level of concentration without repetition. But the mist, the blasted mist, and the rain, and the darkness—!

The water churned, kicked up by blitzers peeling off armor to avoid sinking as the room filled. Multiple blitzers tried to get a message outside so a tech team could lock down the central computers to stop "Sterba"—the screaming intercom made voice-talk difficult, and looking down to write was dangerous, but …

"There's a cyber team on the way," someone shouted finally.

"Good," Bricandor said, weak heart now racing.

More good news—the polymerwall to his throne room became permeable again.

But before anyone could leave, more blitzers rushed inside.

"We received the order from your account about alpha squad's betrayal, Counselor! We'll escort you to the evacuation point!"

"No, you fools, I sent no such thing!"

The lavender mace escaped Bricandor's grasp in his distraction as he screamed to be heard over the din. A fatal error—he expected Sterba's white one to strike—

But both maces fell into the water, sinking as if momentarily exorcised from their controlling ghosts. Their faint glow called to Bricandor beneath the dark waves; he floated in the air over to the polymerwall—a shadowed someone escaped the room under the water as the last blitzer rushed in. He tried to follow—but the wall was hard, locked under his touch.

"We used to play such complicated games against each other,

didn't we?" Diebol's voice interrupted the static on the intercom. "It took me so long to realize how much you took from me. Where I came from. My name, even."

Explosions outside shook the ground. The army had begun to fight itself. Bricandor reached into the water for the glowing maces so he could smash the polymerwall and leave, but bodies kept swimming in his way as they tried to tread water—what he wouldn't give to fight this person *alone*!

"Even what you gave me, you destroyed. I was almost jealous when I found out that as soon as you realized how Jei and I had formed our own mind-channel, you figured out how to bond Sterba and Morda the same way. It took me so long to figure out why I felt that way."

The transparent skylight showed fighter ships attacking each other overhead. As Bricandor raised the maces above the water, he thought he saw someone swim back in here from the throne room—he lowered the maces back down to see, but the person had disappeared somewhere among the other kicking legs. Both maces began to pull against him again.

"I never really got to introduce you to Jei, at his best, when every enemy made him stronger. Every single blitzer in here right now increases his power against you."

A green mace smashed down toward Bricandor's head. He couldn't identify the figure swinging it, but as Bricandor blocked with the two maces his hands couldn't hold, and also levitated himself above the water, and also tried to grab for his attacker's throat—

An enormous field of sparks hurled him across the room. Bricandor just managed to stop his frail spine from slamming against the wall. The figure in the darkness made sure the blitzers could *just* see where he or she clung to the cable of the space elevator in the middle of the room. Before Bricandor could stop them, they opened fire. With another flash of sparks, all those weapons swerved toward Bricandor—some set to power an electromagnetic down, some set to kill, some set to stun—

"And, well, then there's me. The child you kidnapped and erased. I think I've made it clear what I do."

A flayer cartridge hit Bricandor's shoulder, and another his thigh—he'd *just* managed to divert the other weapons away from himself. The three maces slammed down at him again. He got control of all three with great effort and hurled himself toward the figure in the center of the room.

"Bricandor … meet Jared."

Bricandor whirled almost too late as the familiar ultraviolet mace zoomed toward his back.

JAIKA-LEM

I was trying. I was really trying. He couldn't hear my mind, with all the others in the room, and I'd done everything I could to disorient him and throw off his abilities. But I was starting to think I'd screwed myself with this plan. He was incredibly hard to air-duel, and faking an em-push with my static cling on all those blitzer weapons almost made me fall off the elevator cable. I'd shot him. He didn't seem to care.

As he flew toward me with three of my maces sailing before him like spears, I put all my effort into Jared's mace behind him. Both hands, static pull, letting myself fall—

He turned to the side—Jared's mace sailed past him toward me—I slammed it back at him—he tried to catch it on Mera's mace, and slipped, *just* sliding Jared's weapon across his own face.

I hit the water first, firing my static repulsion so it didn't break my back. My splash, then liquid murmur filled my ears; his agonized scream still reached me. I knew he wasn't dead. I ripped my blue serum out of my pocket and let it spill around me. I kicked out of the water to breach like a whale, threw my hands down to call my maces back to me, and dove for the polymerwall, two in each hand. I rolled out into the empty throne room, yanked the bomb out of my belt, armed it, and shoved it back through the wall.

I dove for cover behind the throne.

The explosion in the elevator room bulged the polymerwall outward with a muffled roar—

The wall popped, spilling blitzers and blue juice and purple cloud everywhere.

He had better be dead. I could hear the combat quieting down somewhat outside as the cyber team fixed my spoofed message —I didn't actually have access to Bricandor's account. The "rain" was stopping, the floor draining, the building warming up—not heated by the temperature control system, but the jungle outside, because now my EMP shield bloomed, shutting off all non-shielded electronics throughout the room.

Just room. Not the building. Not great. I'd used up so much energy already throwing maximum effort into both of those "em-pushes," hoping to strike a killing blow; he'd responded so easily. I hoped I hadn't miscalculated, spending my power where it wouldn't work …

Help me, Njande. I breathed, summoning my strength. I floated Sterba and Mera in the air above me and gripped Jared and Jei in my hands. My angry Biouk self and patchwork Sterba stepped into the blue lights beside me.

Bricandor stumbled out of the elevator room covered in blood.

"It's not mine, little ghosts," he smiled. Shyte, he'd responded to the explosive by cushioning himself in a pile of blitzers. And he could read my mind.

But not—see me? "Where is your master, little ghosts?" he asked, facing my angry Biouk self as if he could see it instead.

Master? Did he mean me? I didn't know, but I didn't care. As Bricandor stepped into the starlight, I could see the blistering burn across his eyes. There would be no more Death Glares. He could see the room only through me and my mind.

Guess I'll avoid mirrors, then.

"I haven't been trying to torture you, Bricandor," I said. "You're just very hard to kill. Surrender now and it'll be over."

His head jerked as if pulled by a string; he snarled and flew toward me, hand extended like a claw. I stood my ground and sliced with all four maces like two pairs of scissors. He dashed backward; I missed. *Fine, laser time.* I yanked my maces back toward me and floated three of them, gripping Sterba's in my wet fists. I started to disassemble it—

He em-pulled her crystal out of my hand. I tried to grab it back with static, but couldn't see it suddenly—had he thrown it into the mess behind him? Shyte, I really needed that back. It was like he'd decked me in the gut, taking what remained of the only other girl who understood my world. *It's fine. You have more. Breathe!* I floated Sterba's husk and hurled Jei and Diebol at him, snatching Mera in my fingers now. Crystal, I needed a crystal to fire my laser—

"I see the ghosts have stolen my power sources," Bricandor said, looking around the empty room from which Joshua and Laaru had escaped. He deflected Jei and Jared with a wave of his hand. "Fortunately, it seems we still have an excellent power source here."

His burned gaze fixed on me.

Uh oh.

My throat flew toward his hand. I drew Mera's crystal and aimed. He ripped it from my grasp, nails tearing my palm, and hurled it—where? *No!*

"Guarding a memento of the Lady for a brother-at-arms, were we, little ghosts?" Bricandor jeered. "He must be so disappointed you've lost her."

Jei, I'm so sorry. I gasped, pushing back on Bricandor's pull, holding my neck just out of his grip. My whole body strained, my ribs and abs stretching with the force of my clench. My electric field bloomed across the building, stretching outside, climbing the cables toward the Core. Bricandor grinned at my surge—was he trying to power me up more?

Bricandor raised a fist. The space elevator creaked to life above us as he yanked it down to the ground. The door opened; his pull suddenly shifted direction, and he threw me.

My back slammed into the elevator tube. Sterba and Mera clattered to its floor, empty; I gripped Jei and Diebol in my fists again to smash my way out.

But I couldn't move my weapons. Bricandor rode in the doorway of the elevator, leering in at me, one hand pointed down as he shoved us upward, the other extended toward my active maces, pinning them to the ceiling. How the filk was he still so strong? His right leg almost dangled, flayer cartridge still embedded in his thigh as he rested on his left.

"You all burnt out so young, little ghosts," he chuckled. "But power matures with age. You should have rested more, worried less."

Shyte, I shouldn't have used the filking explosive—I'd needed all those blitzer minds to keep me hidden. Why had I doubted myself? What the filk was I supposed to do now, with him using my brain to see? I needed to blank out, I could blank out my mind, blind him completely, then take him down—I mean, it took a crazy amount of electromagnetic power for him to move the filking elevator. I could still do this.

I gutted Diebol's mace next, snatching the crystal out as it hung suspended mid-air.

"We'll all freeze to death in this mesosphere, little ghosts, if you fire your bio-laser," Bricandor hummed. "Only Sterba's electrical field warms us here now."

"Good," I said. I had an atmosphere suit on.

Bricandor released the elevator; it slid, and its brakes engaged, knocking me against its ceiling. *Green. I'm thinking color green*, I decided as I tumbled, wrestling against his em-hold again as his hands grasped for mine. He couldn't see Jared's crystal in all my mind's green; Diebol's shadow flickered in the walls of my field. The young wolf still hungered for the alpha's throat.

Shyte, that was a thought.

"She's too attached, little ghosts," Bricandor said. "She can't let go."

He threw a hand out toward Diebol's shadow in my wall. "What the filking—" I gasped aloud. Jared flew toward him with a lost cry and shattered against his fist into the crimson mess I remembered at the bottom of the cliff. My ears rang. *I can't breathe. Filking shyte, I can't breathe!* There was an emptiness in the back of my head, like an ever-present voice had been silenced. What had he just done to me? I tried to scream, and no sound would come out. My palms opened as I fell on my knees. *Pick it back up. Pick up the crystal that's next to your hand!*

"He was a special ghost," Bricandor murmured, kicking Jared's crystal out of the elevator. "I hated him, though."

The elevator started again. I squeezed my eyes shut, gasping. *Okay, green. Overwhelming emerald green. Nothing exists but green.* I saw no elevator. I saw no Bricandor. You couldn't erase things by thinking "don't think of this thing"—to clear your head you had to put something else in it. I filled my world with green. With the deep green leaves of Luna-Guetala's top canopy in the sun, and the tiny lemon-green blossoms flying on the wind when Njande-jara spoke to me, and the *ache* of life begging to press through the soil where the seed lay left for dead—

My fingers worked on their own without my mind. I sheathed Jei's staff back on my hip—Bricandor released it, unable to find it among all the other green things—and drew my own. I didn't try to gut it. Only an idiot does the same thing over and over expecting different results. My hands fell back on habit —on the instinct to melee smash.

The elevator docked at the top of the Structure with a jolt Bricandor wasn't ready for. He tripped backward onto the catwalk to the Core. I strode forward as he crawled backward—

"It seems one of your ghosts was destined to destroy the universe here all along," Bricandor wheezed as I raised my crimson mace. "Jerusha-Lem Benzaran—I'd completely forgotten about her."

The Core. It floated at the end of the grated metal plank, a glowing orb, a shifting mirror of black and white and silver suspended in the center of enormous rings. My field encompassed it now, and it danced in my blue light, sizzling where my walls touched it.

"It's happy to see her," Bricandor said.

I roared and slammed down my mace. He yanked it toward himself and slid to the side—it stuck into the catwalk—I stumbled past him with my momentum, almost trampling him. I whirled to face him, my back to the Core as he eased to his feet.

"Hit him while he's weak!" cried the patchwork Sterba from my dreams. I swung before he rose.

He suddenly dashed to the left, pouncing on Sterba where she floated mid-air. My throat burned as he stabbed her in the neck—he could see her, he could see her and somehow this was more horrible than if he'd been able to see me.

"It is sweet of your killer to keep you alive," he hissed in her ear as she gripped his wrists. I'd never seen her afraid. She was cool, marble perfection. But she was terrified.

How had she looked when she died?

Again, I couldn't breathe—again, the silence, like he'd lobotomized me—I pushed myself forward with the staff end of my mace like a spear, struggling to recover, calling the angry little Biouk into my fingertips—

As Bricandor killed him, too, I suddenly understood why

he'd been angry. Longing dreams of home in the canopy, of the Biouk world safe from the intrusion of the outside, flashed across my vision. That was my childhood self, the place I could never return to. That was why my inner Biouk was angry.

Because he knew all along he was doomed.

With this one, as my blue field faded and disappeared around me, I could scream.

CHAPTER TWENTY-NINE

Laaru

LAARU TOOK OFF HIS VEST AND WRAPPED IT AROUND THE BIOUK cub, clutching him to his chest as he crossed the outside courtyard in the humid dusk to the evacuation craft parked outside. No one cared about him. They were busy defending the perimeter from something, or roaring about Bricandor's whereabouts and the locked space elevator. The egg-shaped silver ship welcomed Laaru, accepting his DNA when he touched its side.

His chest was sticky with the blood on his shirt as he slid into the pilot's seat. There were only four seats in here; he lay Joshua gently on the front seat beside him. The pleather creaked under his touch.

"Laaru," Joshua whispered. Laaru winced—that voice sounded weak. The guy'd lost a lot of blood, and Laaru had no idea under all that matted fur where to press or what to do. Medical first, then evacuate? No, they always taught—

"Laaru, take off," Joshua said.

Laaru swallowed, pressing his palms against the front compuwall that formed the windshield.

"Laaru, I need you to fly me over the Core," Joshua said.

Laaru wanted to argue. He was tired of being a pawn for

everyone's grand mission and purpose or whatever. But he slid his palms upward, and the silver egg sprouted wings; rocket engines deployed underneath it, and it blasted off.

"Everyone serves someone," Joshua said. "Even those who think they serve themselves are slaves to something. Food, power, intellect—something. Choose who you serve instead of letting others choose for you."

Laaru said nothing. He knew, somehow, what Joshua wanted with the Core. He didn't understand it, but he knew. "I don't want to go there," he whispered, as the evac ship rose toward the mesosphere.

"Then I must go alone," Joshua said.

"That's not fair, either," Laaru said.

"I have a friend who is about to fall in," Joshua said. "I want her to live. I want the universe to live. There is something I can carry into the Core that no one else can."

"You sound so unsure. Maybe we can—" Laaru stammered. "Maybe I can take Bricandor, and you can get her away—"

Joshua shook his head. "You can come with me, but you cannot fight."

Laaru bowed his head and slid his hands across the dashboard to bring the evac ship around.

LEM

Bricandor bore down on me with my mace, floating it centimeters from his hands as he shoved it across my chest; I blocked with Jei's mace, both palms on either end of its staff.

"Ah, and this is the last ghost, isn't it?" Bricandor nodded toward the shimmering green weapon as I dug in my heels, groaning with my full force against the crossbeam our staffs formed. "The only one who could have killed me. What a pity for him that he chose to trust someone less qualified."

Yeah, that hurt. I stepped to the side with a shout, suddenly releasing the pressure—Bricandor stumbled forward, swapping places with me on the catwalk. My hands shifted automatically to swing Jei's spiking mace tip toward Bricandor's midsection. He blocked, planting my mace like a tree in front of him.

"You're perfect for my purposes, though, living ghost," Bricandor said. "One might say my interdimensional friends planned this."

"Shyte, I wish you'd shut up," I groaned, striking again. Again, he blocked. *Die, you, why won't you die?*

"Anisotropy, isn't it?" he said. "You're charged by disorder, and you fuel order. That's your Paradox."

He'd lured me another step closer to the Core as I stabbed. *I can't think. Shut up.* The words I'd said myself echoed in Bricandor's.

"Eh. I might actually be destined to bring about the end of all things, so."

"According to Njandejara," Sterba had said. *"But that's the narrative from the losing side."*

"It is not a cold person who will chill the universe, because they draw energy into themselves—it is a warm person, who discharges it," Bricandor said.

I didn't think that made any physical sense, but whatever he meant I could see one thing for sure: this assassination attempt had been great bait to get me near the Core. Was that the Accuser's plan all along? What sequence of awful choices had brought me here?

Nope to all of this. I slid back from Bricandor, back toward the elevator. He'd follow me, if he needed me. I could kill him somewhere else.

"Voltage is merely *differentness*, potential energy caused by heterogeneity between two bodies. Your capacitance—"

Bricandor em-pulled me. "When *you* create that separation in charges to discharge a spark, it is not only a potential difference between your cells."

He yanked; I held out Jei's staff again so he'd impale himself on it; he let go just before it could. "Yours recruits the very planetary energy fields beneath you into that capacitance chain."

He pointed toward the brightest pinpricks in the sky above us as the planets aligned behind each other. "So today, as the differentness of many fields align in harmony across the solar systems—well, today is your birthday, isn't it?"

Filk that! I stabbed—he sidestepped, and my momentum carried me past him toward the Core. I tried to cover my exposed back, spinning Jei's staff over my wrist back toward Bricandor's head behind me—he em-pushed me forward—

I tripped and found my face staring into the void as Jei's mace flew out of my hand into the Core. It fizzled and disappeared in the white mirror.

Shyte, how'd I get here? My chest heaved. I rolled over, metal grate digging into my back—I clung to Bricandor with my static as he fell almost on top of me, trying to shove me just that last meter off the catwalk.

I saw them then, above us. Two small Biouk figures balanced on the stabilizing outer ring that held up the Core. Lumps of explosives trailed behind them.

"Do it already!" I screamed. "Blow the filking thing!"

I heard Cinta cry my name as Masha reached for the detonator.

"This is who you are," Bricandor hissed, centimeters from my face, in my Accuser's voice. I grabbed the railing now as he tried to drag me by my collar. I didn't want to risk kicking him into the Core to power it, either. "Don't you see? This is all there is. This suffering, this pain. It's not worth it! They're not worth it! They're monsters, all of them, like you and me!"

"Let me kill you and you won't have to feel that way

anymore," I grunted. Shyte, my grip was slipping. He was throwing the weight of everything that'd ever hurt him onto me.

"I can take your suffering, both of you," a small voice said.

We both looked right. Here, balancing just beside us on the inner ring around the Core, crouched Joshua, trembling, his chest puffed out and ears laid back like it took great effort for him not to flee. A small escape pod hovered a few meters away, unimportant to the defense ships because of the spoofed Bricandor signature I'd given it.

"Filk everything and everyone," I groaned, dropping my head.

Bricandor laughed. "I don't want you anymore," he said to Joshua. "Watch and weep."

He gave me one more solid shove. I couldn't hold on anymore.

Joshua jumped full force into my side, knocking me away from the Core—my stomach slammed into the inner ring. I caught onto it like a wet cat, cursing Joshua out for being so stupid as Bricandor's em-push flowed over him, and he tumbled into the white mirror.

"Cinta, take care of Mali for me!" Joshua cried.

Njandejara's agony echoed across all worlds.

CINTA

Cinta wrapped himself around Masha and jumped for the space elevator as the outer ring supporting the Core exploded. Masha could not cry out. Her eyes fixed in horror on the center where her child had fallen. Her stiff body seemed dead in Cinta's arms, and she gripped her chest as if stabbed.

They landed on the catwalk by the elevator with a painful

thud and roll. The Core bloomed out toward them; a bright light consumed Bricandor and Jaika in a screaming flash.

"Get in!" cried a small human voice behind Cinta. He turned—the young Stygge that Jaika had kidnapped held open the side of an evacuation pod for them. Cinta dragged Masha inside. The polymerwall closed behind them. The Stygge floated the ship a short distance away from the energy bloom, orbiting it as Cinta squeezed his mate. The support structure creaked, tilting toward the earth below. Perhaps—perhaps the Core would not stabilize?

But it did not matter when the supports fell away. They had taken too long. Scarlet light shot out toward the other pillars of the Structure—toward Skraeli, Bijou, the Allperson moon, and a fourth unnamed world Cinta's crew could never reach. The blossom around the Core faded, leaving a portal suspended in the center of the red matrix with Joshua's silhouette stretched across it. On either side of the portal floated two small cracks—as if cracks in the fabric of space itself—where Jaika and Bricandor still battled.

Cinta sat down, cradling Masha, and whined, his ears collapsing down the side of his face. His shoulders shook. Joshua had not saved Jaika—he had trapped her. Cinta had not protected Masha from the one fate worse for her than death. And the Structure now held the most powerful creature in the universe at its source. Cinta believed with all his being that Joshua was the sum of Njandejara's connection with sapient life, the unity of matter and interdimensional energy, and with that connection crushed—what would the universe become as it drained into the ba-eaters' world? This universe drew on Njandejara like a child on its mother's breast, and the mother had been ripped away.

REISE

It made sense that the path ended here—it could not have ended anywhere else, really.

Reise stood in the shadows of the trees just outside the perimeter of the Growen encampment around the Core. Dead blitzers and broken tanks littered the field ahead of him—a short battle had occurred here at some point tonight.

Reise's strategic retreat and return had taken longer than intended. He'd almost run out of flayer cartridges, and now his fingers expertly cranked to recharge his rifle while he watched the light at the end of the space elevator.

Not far from him in the brush Reise saw two of the reptilians from the bioship, the despairing browns and shadow-greens of their hides almost undetectable by non-sniper eyes—Rizzt and Szizzle, if Reise recalled correctly. They wore no atmosphere suits; white patches of bandage wrapped around their upper front limbs, likely from a transition center. How they had found their way here, Reise did not know, but they had clearly fallen out with their leader.

The anomaly at the center of the Core was so bright, and so—displaced, in space—it seemed that no matter where Reise stood he could see into it as if right next to it. An ice storm raged around the Biouk inside. He was so small and—bare, as if shaven by a razor in a hurry. Almost-invisible spectres seemed to be sucking something out of him—life, or—essence.

"It is evil that this would be the solution you choose," Reise said to Njandejara. "You're a sadomasochist. You didn't just allow this to happen. You chose this."

Joshua met his eyes, sharp teeth gritted. "You'll see," Joshua said. "I can do this. I can stop the drain you created from your dimension. I can close the gap."

"You shouldn't have to. It should have been designed with fail-safes," Reise said, voice hard, but not unkind. "The mind shouldn't have the ability to lock itself away from change. The cause and effect in this universe punishes people who don't know, and don't choose."

Joshua did not answer—he cried out as something like an eagle dove for him and clawed into his right side. Reise turned away to give him his honor.

As he did, Reise heard a small voice on the breeze, as if inside his Reason itself.

"If the mind didn't work this way you hate, there could be no learning," it said. "Learning requires circuits that self-strengthen over time. There could be no focus. Focus requires eliminating that which isn't needed. There could be no trauma recovery. Recovery requires removing false lessons from the event that make its memory more painful.

"There is a risk to the way brain-hardening works, but it is possible to self-program in a healthy way. Like all mechanisms in the universe, there is a purpose, and a correct use, for the law of the mind."

"What about people who are too far gone?" Reise asked. "What if my circuits are so fixed, there's no breaking them?"

"As long as you're able to ask for help, there is hope," said the voice. "I can rewire anything to be truly free."

"If you were really like that, we could talk," Reise said.

Reise slung his rifle over his back and walked back into the forest to keep his promise to Dr. Loylan. After that—he'd need some time away from both the Frelsi and the Growen. Whether or not the universe continued on its current course of decay, he needed to find his own way without any more mind control, direct or otherwise. Perhaps he would find Laaru and help him retrieve that friend of his whom Bricandor had marooned. At any rate, Reise did not need to kill Njandejara—he'd killed himself.

What that would mean for Reise was yet to be seen.

CHAPTER THIRTY

Lark

LARK SCRITA AWOKE WITH A SHARP ELECTRICAL JOLT—NOT LIKE A knock-out blast, but like that nasty sting from those prods what Alpinoan farmers used on unruly dragons.

The first thing she saw was K'arl's face against a backdrop of stars and an obsidian-colored ceiling. She was still on the *Empress*, but in its cockpit now. *Good on you, Carl.* At least they'd done something right, then, and kept the hunter off Joshua's back.

"It's quite the nap you've had, beautiful," K'arl said. "It's hella late now. Check out the sights."

He pointed out the viewscreen behind her. "That's the Structure," he said.

Bright red paths shot across space, converging on a mirrored door to nowhere. Beans, it had to be at least forty klicks away, but that portal seemed right here, if you looked at it right.

Oh no.

"Joshua!"

Lark jumped to her feet—pain shot up her leg, and she cried out as she fell back into the navigator's seat. A scar on the back of her knee—looked like she'd just had medbots working on her.

What could she do for Joshua? Beans, they were sucking the life out of him! Could she—she reached for the controls of the ship. *Fly over there and save him!*

K'arl grabbed her wrists. "I think your little melting Biouk buddy's probably the least of your concerns right now, lovely," he said. She walked up his body, flipping upside down and wresting herself out of his grip. Her knee screamed, and she almost fell as she landed—*get that weight on the good leg, lass—* nah, landing on one leg wasn't a problem. She dove under his arms for the controls.

He grabbed her around the waist with a laugh. She elbowed him instinctively—*ouch, lass, armor, armor you dolt!* The strong arms tightened around her hips, and suddenly fear shot through her body in a physical wave. She didn't have any weapons on her. She was *much* smaller than he was, and injured.

She panicked, throwing her arms down and her legs up, somersaulting herself in his grip to whack his face with the back of her boot. He shouted and dropped her on her shoulders.

"What do you want, mate? Pay?" Lark cried, scrambling backward away from him. "Why do you bloody care if I rescue my friend?"

"You're not very loyal, are you," K'arl smirked, crouching now to get on her level.

"What the beans does that mean?" she snapped.

His gaze shifted to the back corner of the bench that lined the passenger area just behind the cockpit. She followed his eyes—

Carl sat in the collared shirt and long trousers blitzers wore underneath their armor, arms crossed and bare feet wide-set firmly on the floor. The yellow glow of a stasis collar let Lark know he couldn't move from the neck down. She knew she was supposed to feel guilt for not thinking of him first, but honestly, she could only feel proud of how in control he looked despite being a prisoner.

"You all right mate?" she asked.

He nodded. She got herself to her feet, struggling a mite with that bad knee.

"What would it take for you to let him go?" Lark asked K'arl. "How much for him, lad, and how much for the Biouk?"

K'arl rose and stretched. "I'm afraid they're not for sale, lovely," he said. "Oh, come on, don't make that face. You're prettier when you smile."

Lark took off her boot and threw it at him. "I said, how much?" she yelled.

K'arl stumbled backward, looking quite silly and frustrated at her rudeness. "Wipe that shyte grin off your face," he hissed to Carl behind her—apparently the "prettier when you smile" rule didn't apply to Carl. To Lark, as he pulled a pistol on her, K'arl said: "Don't do that again, please."

Then, with the deliberate and casual air of a torturer K'arl swiveled the pilot's chair with his other hand and took a seat facing Lark. "Come here," he said.

That wave of repulsed fear tingled across her skin again. Still, he had a gun, and she didn't, and if he wanted to be the dolt who let her get close enough to take it from him, that was fine.

She took slow, even steps forward. Beans, what a low, nasty, throbbing feeling this fear was—not that excited terrified high she rather enjoyed. This was like what she'd felt her first time infiltrating the lair of that Tridian gang, with all those big eyes on her, and those sharp teeth licking their tongues as tentacles brushed over hungry lips.

"Over here." K'arl pointed with his free hand, aiming his weapon at Carl to keep it well out of her reach as she walked to his other side. "I'm a pretty fast trigger finger by the way, if you want to test me."

Lark stood in the spot he wanted, a few centimeters from his right knee, as he removed his glove. The wave intensified. His warm, rough hand rested on her thigh as he looked over at Carl; she winced. She clenched her jaw to keep from screaming and fixed her eyes on the pistol. Why did this scare her so much? It was nothing. This was nothing. She'd handled worse to get a good lead. She'd played the odds that K'arl didn't want to hurt her before, and she'd won.

But beans did he want to hurt his brother. Much, much more, she realized, than he wanted to keep her.

"So Ms. Scrita, let's chat," K'arl chuckled, stroking a tiny pattern in her tights with his thumb. Tights? Bloodseas, she wasn't wearing armor anymore—down to a jumpsuit, she was, with one leg long, and the other cut off at the knee. Had he—had he really removed her blitzer clothes while she was out in stun-gun-land? No wonder her body was recoiling. Had anything—else—

"It's rude not to answer questions," K'arl said.

"Sorry, mate, I didn't hear you," Lark said, her stomach binding itself into a knot. "Can't believe you took my armor, is all. Thought we had some kind of respect, we did."

"It was only so the medbots could work on you," K'arl said. "When did you become shy?"

"I'm not." She tossed her head, playing nonchalant for strength. "I'm just surprised you're letting your feels get in the way of a payday, mate. You know I'd give you my life's savings for a trip over to that Structure."

"We're not negotiating right now," K'arl said, squeezing down on her leg. Lark clenched her teeth again to fight the tremble. "We're chatting. Which you used to love to do. Pretty much every single night, actually." He gave Carl a smirk, sliding his palm oh-so-slowly across her quad to the inside of her thigh. *Don't react. Don't react!* "How has your month been, Lark? From here it seems like I leave you alone for a moment and you destroy half a moon."

"This'n't a joke, lad," Lark said. "You fed me a bloody bioweapon."

"It's not a bioweapon." K'arl smirked. "It really does do what

I said it does. You must've overheated it or spilled it into something caustic or something."

"No, mate, blasted stuff left droplets in the vial that—" But Lark interrupted herself. None of this helped right now. Mayhaps she could sweet-talk him. "Forget it. Look, Jester, I appreciate what you tried to do. That's actually genuine from me there, mate, not a lie. Just wish you'd checked some safety boxes first."

"I can get you more, you know," K'arl said. His voice dropped the threatening timbre, and he stopped making hate-eyes at his brother. This was him in earnest: bloke clearly liked the idea of being her noble ally. "I can get you to a treatment facility, Lark. You can see it was working." He gestured toward her reflection in his armor, where that scaled crack split up her right cheek. "You can be what you are, right?"

"I can already be—" Well. No. She couldn't say it aloud. It still didn't feel true in her skin.

"You're still suffering in there," K'arl noticed. His hand traveled now down to the side of her knee. "We can make this better. I can't let this freak get away again." He nodded toward Carl. "He'll just steal you from me. But you and I can spend a little time together and see how things work out once you're in the right skin. What do you say?"

"Mate, I'm sorry, but I'm really turned off by blokes who commit genocide," Lark said coolly. "Benzaran told me about the Watchers. Then there's Joshua."

Her throat tightened. She shouldn't have said his name. Beans, every second they were here, what was—what was happening to him? What were they draining out of him? And the flames that seemed to flicker through reality in that looking glass—her head dropped. Bloodseas, she couldn't keep up this game. She couldn't bloody pretend. She'd felt truly known for once in her filking life, and they were eating the one who truly knew her.

Tears suddenly started to roll down her cheeks.

"Aw, how sweet," K'arl said. He snapped to his feet, leaning over her with his chest against hers as a scowl slid over his face. "It's great that you can turn on the waterworks at will, but right now your second-string manipulation just pisses me off. You can take me up on my offer, or I can kill you in front of brother dear here so your scream is the last thing he hears. Like I said, I like you better when you smile, so cut the faucet and filking smile." He emphasized the last word by squeezing her against himself.

"You're a full-on nutter, mate," Lark's mouth coughed before she'd planned a response; something cold and hard within her suddenly froze her tears and killed the wave of fear. Bloke wanted to threaten? "Mate, you're not going to kill him or me. I've kicked the Ebon Shadow's ass before and that was the premium model. I think I can take the discount version."

That bit was calculated. And it worked, cutting too deep for him to just shoot her or Carl straight now, because yeah—the bloke *could* be manipulated.

Now he wanted to hurt her.

Lark rolled with K'arl's enraged backhand and let its force spin her around—didn't even really sting like that—to knock her against the hand holding the gun. It misfired into the wall. She jumped his arm, throwing him off balance, wrapping her legs around his biceps, embracing his wrist in her crossed hands as she peeled his fingers off the grip—keep that pistol pointed over her shoulder, not at her face—

The problem with armor, mate, is that it's got to have joints.

She thrust upward and snapped his elbow with the full force of her torso. He screamed and dropped the weapon. She picked it up and fired at his head. Missed—shyte, hit the console behind him. *Blasted*—

"You *witch!*" He tackled her. The force of his full weight against her belly knocked the wind so far out of her she wondered if her ancestors could still breathe. The pistol went spinning across the floor. She reached over his shoulder, straining for the gun strapped to his waist. He lifted her with one arm and slammed her back against the floor. *Ooh I'll feel that tomorrow.*

"It's not you I'm supposed to face off against!" K'arl screamed. "I'm supposed to be your ally—it's him, brother and brother!"

"I'm not here to further your story arc, mate," Lark wheezed as her spine throbbed.

"I hate that you're making me do this!" Bloke just couldn't stop screaming, could he? He tried to smash her jaw with a left cross. She caught his wrist and went to get her leg up again for another arm-bar. He headbutted her, putting the full weight of his knee down on her inner thigh to pin her in place. She yelped —*beans, don't whine like that!* Sounded too bloody hurt for Carl to hear when he couldn't do naw't—

"I'm fine, mate." She looked up at the better Shadow. The room was spinning, but she could tell she was right by Carl's feet now. "Don't worry about me."

He tried to nod back at her, but sweat beaded on his forehead; his jaw ground. Beans, this killed him. Like when the Pit made him say that tosh he hated, or when he'd begged her not to spit out the medication bag. He bloody *needed* to defend her or he'd just die, he would, cut to the core of the bloke he was.

Lark was getting a mite sick of people attacking that part of him. The ice inside her firmed up. She was frozen iron, a shield for her mate. "'Ey, daft-punk," Lark spat, twisting her body toward the crushed leg to weasel it out from under K'arl. "I asked nicely, I did."

A thrash of her hips put her on his side, then up on his back. She slid her small forearm under his rough chin and snapped her other arm behind his head, locking him into a choke. She lashed her leg over his good arm, pinning it before he could claw at the vice around his throat—she squeezed—

He smashed himself backward—hard. The shock of his weight loosened her grip; he grabbed her arm and before she realized what was happening she'd flipped over his shoulder onto her back. A thick hand grabbed her throat.

"Really, mate? You're a bloody stereotype, you are," Lark choked, kicking her legs up toward his neck in the hopes of a triangle hold. He ducked and pinned her with his side across her chest, snarling as if she was inconveniencing him somehow by fighting. Again he jolted to slam her on the ground for compliance; he turned her to face his brother as he tightened his grip.

"Why aren't you reacting?!" K'arl screamed up at Carl. "I'm going to wring the life out of your girl by your feet and you're the same as you always were! Why does nothing matter to you? Why can't I get anything out of you?!"

"I'm sorry!" Carl's voice had as much tremble in it as it did growl, and Lark felt K'arl's hand loosen in surprise as the man of stone ran his mouth ten klicks a second. "I'm sorry I ruined your chances at being normal. I thought if we were both hard and unforgiving we could survive. Then we were just broken and making ourselves worse. I'm sorry. You don't have to forgive me. *But please stop.*"

K'arl screamed something wordless. Lark elbowed her way out of his grip and leapt for Carl. She just managed to get her finger on the unlock of his stasis collar before K'arl ripped her away by the leg. She heard the swoosh of a pistol drawing—*you're about to get one in the back, lass,* she realized—she whirled on her back and kicked his hand with the free leg before the trigger pulled. He fired into the back of the pilot's seat instead.

Finally free, Carl smashed into his brother shoulder-first with enough force to smack him against the other side of the room.

CHAPTER THIRTY-ONE

Carl

CARL PINNED HIS BROTHER'S WEAPON HAND TO THE FLOOR AND ripped the pistol from his grip. With the broken elbow K'arl couldn't go for the last two guns strapped to his side—Lark rushed up to grab them. K'arl thrashed and went to kick her. Carl shoved the tip of the pistol under K'arl's chin.

"Stop," he warned.

K'arl kicked again anyway. "*Empress*, engage scorched earth protocol," he sneered.

"Engaging scorched earth protocol," said the ship.

No. Carl whirled to shoot the hatch in the corner before the first machine gun popped out behind Lark. He hit the support gear and the gun fell limp, pointing at the floor. He hit the next three corners before they could activate, milliseconds apart. *Two. Three. Four.*

K'arl's armor closed back over his head, encasing him in an impenetrable heat-shield. He kicked again as Lark snatched at his pistols again—but this time she got them. Carl fired on the wall behind K'arl for the other weapon hatches. *Five. Six. Seven.* He backed off K'arl to be able to hit them all. *Eight.*

"To the galley," he told Lark, firing on K'arl to keep him

down. K'arl raised his forearm to protect the weaker armor around his neck, pushing back against the force of the cartridges punching his chest as he got up.

They had twelve seconds to disable the nerve gas before it filled the ship. "The silver valve behind the water system under the first storage cabinet," Carl said, reaching up behind him to unlock the polymerwall for Lark. She dove through; he followed backward, still firing. *Eight. Seven. Six.* K'arl broke into the galley after them, laughing. *He's really broken this time.*

"She was the only kind-of-innocent thing I was looking forward to, you know," K'arl said, tearing the utility axe off the galley wall.

"Beans, mate, then you shouldn't've dropped me off naked on an alien moon with your brother!" Lark cried out. "Got it," she told Carl.

"To the hold," he said. "The canister will explode from the pressure now if it's not ejected." They had about three minutes. Lark plunged through the wall behind them. K'arl brandished the axe at Carl; the narrow kitchen left almost no room for either man to swing or dodge. Carl couldn't stay close enough to get the pistol up under that blocking arm for K'arl's neck—he valued all his limbs.

The step backward down into the hold caught Carl by surprise—"You really didn't fix that?" he grumbled, tripping back against the railing.

K'arl laughed. The axe came down, ringing against the banister as Carl slid out of its path. It stuck there for a second. Carl took the opportunity to whirl and fire on the machine gun turrets just about to ease out of their hatches in the corners.

"Where is it?" Lark cried from the bottom of the stairs.

"Starboard to the waste tank," Carl shouted back. *One, two, three, four—and four—*the last turret took a second shot before he could knock its mechanism loose because K'arl had yanked his axe free again. Carl turned back to him and fired; he heard the scrape of a floor panel, and a *ker-thunk* as Lark found the ejection lever. Goodbye tank of nerve gas.

Backing down stairs was difficult when someone kept trying to behead you, and Carl fell. K'arl pounced on him. Carl tried to roll—the blade caught his shirt, pinning it to the floor. Stupid material refused to tear away as K'arl got the mount on him— Carl dropped the pistols and gripped the handle of the axe as it swung again. It trembled in their joint grip. K'arl jerked; the sharpened edge scratched Carl's cheek.

"Kill the engines," Carl grunted to Lark. "They're about to vent into the ship."

"What? Why?!" Lark ran-limped for the back of the hold near the old-fashioned loading door no one ever used. There was a mechanical fail-safe there to cut off engine power in case of fire. "Nutter wants bloody columns of flame just shooting through all his rooms?"

"That's what 'scorched' means, honey," K'arl said. Carl managed to plant a heel into the floor with enough force to give his hips a good thrash—he knocked K'arl off him onto his side, squirmed out of his guard, and yanked the axe away.

K'arl snatched for one of the pistols lying beside him—Carl hurled the axe. It bounced off K'arl's armored wrist, but still stung enough to stop him. Carl swiped the gun—and its twin— and dashed backward, firing on K'arl's neck again. He missed.

"Beans, the blasted flimflam's rusted solid," Lark groaned. "I can't move it!"

Carl glanced over to see her pulling with her full weight against the mechanical lever to disconnect the left engine from the fuel tank.

"Aw, she needs her big strong man to come help her out," K'arl mocked.

They both ignored him. With enough space now to avoid the axe Carl ran backward on his toes to Lark, shoved a pistol in her hands and ripped into the lever. "Get the other one," he grunted, sending her to the right engine. "K'arl, do you *never* do maintenance?"

The lever broke off in his hands. Lark screamed in frustration. "Just eject them," Carl said. "We have less than a minute."

"Eject the engines?" Lark cried, sprinting away from the loading door toward the front of the hold now as K'arl caught up to his brother. "Beans, it's a regular masterclass in here for mechanics who are also psychopaths."

"Under the front stairs by the loading door controls!" Carl shouted. "Where the emergency masks are—"

The axe came down again. Carl "blocked" with a gun; it bent inward—he let go and dove right as the oxidizer chamber burst. Hot material sprayed across his left side. It burned, but a quick self-assessment as he leapt to his feet found him still fully functional. He grabbed a heavy toolbox off the wall and swung it for K'arl's face. K'arl took the ringing hit without blocking and brought down the axe. The blade slid across the outside of Carl's shoulder, drawing blood, but didn't manage to bite down.

A thundering mechanical groan vibrated through the ship as Lark ejected the engines. Carl jumped backward and grabbed onto the bars of one of the nearby holding cages fixed to the floor. Lark clung to the support pole at the bottom of stairs. K'arl fired up his rocket-boots and took to the air.

The engines had fallen loose, and not two seconds later they fired a full burst of rocket exhaust in all directions.

The force shoved the *Empress* forward. The whole hold sloped—anything not held down fell toward Lark and the front stairs. Loose tools, a random drinking orb, a huge duffel bag of weights for some reason—*do you never clean?*

Carl released his grip and jumped for the girl. His palms stung as he caught the pole she clung to and wrapped himself around her. Something sharp stung into his shoulder blade. Something heavy bounced off his right rib cage. He felt Lark slide an emergency oxygen mask over his face—she was wearing one herself now—as K'arl rocketed toward them on his boots.

"Hold on," she said as she reached over to open the old loading door.

The back of the ship split open. K'arl and everything else not tied down shot out into space to collide with the rocket engines. An icy blast punched through the ship. Just as the door snapped shut again, Carl saw his brother smash into an engine intake— the explosion threw the ship forward again.

Lark whacked the stabilizer to keep the ship in orbit, and eventually it stopped rocking, and with a warm hiss life support took over in the hold again.

It was quiet.

The pair collapsed to their knees in relief. Carl grabbed Lark and crushed her against him, burying his face in her hair. *No,* said the survivalist in him. *Check and double-check.* He released her and jogged to the back porthole.

"Is he—" Lark asked.

"Yes," he said.

"Are you sure?"

"Very." He turned away from the pieces of person outside and leaned against the wall, closing his eyes to breathe. *I'm sorry I never tried to save you.*

Lark hopped and limped up the stairs to the cockpit; Carl let her run out her grief. But she wasn't going to be able to fly over to Joshua. Even if they hadn't just jettisoned their rocket engines, they'd shot flayer cartridges into the navigation console. They weren't going to fly anywhere without a repair team, and the fastest delivery out here would take days. K'arl didn't keep a life raft.

The Ebon Shadow found Lark Scrita curled up on the pilot's seat crying.

"That's it," she sobbed. "It's the end of the world."

He lifted her in his arms and carried her to the cushioned

passenger bench by the portholes. With one hand he cradled her shoulders as she pressed her face into his chest, gripping his shirt; with the other he wiped his thumb across her cheek, pushing tears and hair off her face. He wished he could carry some of the weight of what she felt, for her. "There's no one I'd rather spend the end of the world with," he said again.

She cried for a while.

When Lark ran out of tears, she wrapped her arms around his neck and hid her face by his throat. "I lied to you about one more thing," she said, muffled.

He tilted his head to look at her.

"The reason I can't be Frelsi isn't moral or whatever," Lark said. "I tried to join up. Captain Rana blacklisted me after what happened with the assassination list three years ago."

He allowed himself a slight grin. "What a truly devious lie," he said. "We'll have to break up."

"Is that sarcasm from the Ebon Shadow?" Lark asked, peering up at him.

He shifted to lay her down on the bench. "I'm learning your language," he said, leaning over her. There was just room for her on her back, and him on his side. He shivered. He recognized the continued post-combat burn of adrenaline, and with her against him his body didn't want to calm it down. It wanted to comfort her. "I'd like you to learn my language now," he said.

"And what language is that, mate?" she asked.

In answer he traced his hand down her side, pausing to clutch her leg, to say she was his and she was safe from everyone else. Her chest heaved as her breathing slowed; he felt her muscles melt beside his as she relaxed, and a small, almost inaudible sigh escaped her just-parted lips.

"I've been dying to chat with you," she whispered, lifting her cold hand to the stubble on his face. "You're injured though." Her fingertips hovered above the scratch on his cheek, the burns down his side, the cut on his shoulder. "Saw a wee mite of blood on your back, too, I did."

Carl didn't care, and he told her so with his teeth against her neck, fingers kneading into her back—the sting of the flesh wounds only made him hungrier. She bit her lip and arched into him with a little shudder. "Is this something people do when the world ends?" she asked softly.

"The world has always been ending since it began," he said. "This is what keeps it going."

Her fingers tightened behind his neck and in his hair; she clung to him, pulling his lips to hers with a little cry, and he felt all her grief, all her joy, all her worlds of incomparable emotions sliding into his mouth, and with a soft, overwhelmed growl he slid on top of her and set the beast free.

CHAPTER THIRTY-TWO

Lem

I'D BEEN HERE BEFORE. THE COLORLESS EXPANSE. BUT THIS TIME JEI wasn't here to meet me.

When Joshua fell into the Core, Bricandor and I tumbled into each other—a searing pain shot through me like I'd been ripped in half, or maybe torn out of my skin, and I fully expected to find myself missing limbs when I opened my eyes.

But as the torment slowed to a slow burn, I found myself in the almost-blinding nowhere, gripping Bricandor's collar with both hands as I tightened it around his throat.

"We need to get out! We need to get out!" He was hoarse from screaming.

A handsome voice laughed. "Neither of you are leaving."

We both turned to see a figure lounging on an ornate chair behind us—not that different from Bricandor's throne. He held a long pen in his hand and chewed on the end of it.

"No, meat-piles, you're not in my dimension—thank goodness, because you're both disgusting," he said, hopping to his feet. "You're too stupid for me to really explain the science, but basically, you're trapped in a pocket world. Kind of like he is."

He pointed with his pen. Directions were all off. I was on the right, suddenly; Bricandor was on the left; in the middle, hung Joshua. I could see us as other people must be seeing us, three cracks of despair in the wall of the world.

"Only he's literally standing between your dimension and ours," said the Accuser—because that was what he was. I was surprised to see him bother to take what looked like a physical form. "*You two, on the other hand, a*re just idiots stuck in a bubble you made yourselves."

"How do we get out?" Bricandor asked. You could hear him forcibly calming his voice to negotiate—the transition was freaky.

I started to walk toward Joshua. Only there was no toward— there was no direction at all. I grew dizzy watching him as a million worlds with a million stories flew over him, and he screamed into the driving rain.

"Let me help you!" he begged. "Why won't you let me help you?"

Was he talking to me?

Couldn't be. Must be billions of people in his sights. Shyte, no way his mind wouldn't break now. I bowed my head and closed my eyes. Poor Cinta, and Masha. My bones ached, but Joshua—even with my eyes closed I could hear the ba-eaters sucking life out of him into their world, giggling and shrieking with glee. How much did he have? How long until he drained? Then it'd be our universe next, right?

I looked back over my shoulder to Bricandor and the Accuser. "You can escape if she goes with you," the Accuser said to him. "You broke your universe a little bit. It's not a real tear, not like that." He pointed at Joshua's portal again. "Your rift will repair itself in a couple of days. Or, for you, in a couple of—well, you're too stupid to understand time here anyway. But once it closes, bye-bye to both of you." He jerked his pen at me. "She can open the tear enough for you both to fit through to go home, though. Channeling her chaos to order, and all that."

I almost laughed. Or cried. Shyte, everyone had wild ideas about how my abilities worked. Wouldn't making holes in things be less ordered? I definitely didn't want to risk making the tear worse so more energy leached away from our dimension.

But in some ways, that energy shyte was all beyond me now anyway. Me, my only job was to keep Bricandor down so he couldn't continue to destroy people's lives. I was a warrior, not a hero. So I couldn't leave. I sat down with my wrists on my knees, head bowed.

Shyte. This was actually the end of me.

"Look, I know you're all very stupid, but it should be obvious," the Accuser snapped, dragging Bricandor and me together with his telekinetic pointer fingers. "You're two ends of the poles. There's your voltage difference, right there."

I could see us, suspended in space, like a positive and negative node. I didn't understand what to do with that, but I didn't really want to understand. "No thanks," I said. "Bricandor's not going back."

"You'll die here, too!" Bricandor hissed.

"I know," I said. "But I can't let you go back. And anyway, I'm going to wait for him." I nodded toward Joshua.

Bricandor leapt at me, screaming. "You monster! You evil monster! You torment me, then lock me here—"

"My guy," I laughed. Shyte, my gut hurt. I coughed; blood came up. I spat it on the ground, and the colorless void became red. "I was trying to kill you. I don't think you're going to make me feel bad about succeeding."

"I will make your time here a living torment! You will—"

"I mean, what, did you think heat death wasn't going to include you?" I sidestepped as he clawed at me.

"I was supposed to rest, be reborn in *their* world, become one of *them*!" he hissed.

"That may still be possible once he's drained." The Accuser

pointed at Joshua. "If she lets you out." A grin played in the corner of his fake mouth. He was playing with us.

"Shyte, man, he's using you for something," I said to Bricandor.

He ignored me. "What can I do? What can I do to make her scream?" Bricandor shrieked.

The Accuser tapped his lips with his pen. "Well, it's a blank canvas, really. Imagine what you want, both of you. Let's see what you can do."

My timeline compressed suddenly—I was being skewered by Sterba, crushed by Jei, getting my fingers broken by Diebol, and stabbed in the back by Mera. Man, I did have a way of getting everyone to hate me, didn't I? The Accuser wasn't here anymore —not in physical form, just in vicious equations I didn't understand.

"I was never that great at math," I wheezed, reaching for Bricandor through the memories. *Don't power up. Don't use your abilities.* I could imagine crushing him, impaling him, flinging him into space, but what was the point?

I imagined a wall, hiding me from him. Then a cliff, rising above him, carrying me away. Then a little cottage, the one Jei had told me about in the bamboo hills above Retrack City, the one for Mera.

Bricandor smashed the little door on its hinges. My head exploded, and then came back together. I coughed, gripping my chest as it bent in on itself and my ribs cracked one by one. "Shyte, you're such a loser compared to her," I breathed as tears of pain sprung to my eyes.

"Compared to who?" Bricandor hissed. My skin tore off. I imagined holding it on and closed my eyes, hiding in the memory of her.

"You would rather die in a glorious blaze of fire than fizzle out and betray what you stand for. We are alike in this. We know each other's souls, and will not change the glory we see in each other."

"So because we're such good pals, and we respect each other's beliefs, we gotta kill each other," Lem quipped.

"Sarcasm has no place here," Sterba answered.

"Maybe I filked up somewhere, there." I was on my hands and knees now as every bone in my body snapped. It was agony, but he was so angry it was all so quick. "Was there any way I could've beaten her, and you, and Diebol, and Mera, without all this?"

I was there a hundred years and I was there an instant, building planets and forests and wombs to hide in. Everything shattered around me, over and over. I couldn't save anything. I couldn't. Everyone who came to me would eventually die anyway, because that was the way of the universe. The universe itself was on borrowed time. So what was the point? What did I do it for?

The angry little Biouk with the torn ear roared. He knew what to do it for. Chases through the treetops in the dappled sunlight, cuddles in the family nest, libraries full of books, hallways frankly magnetic with the ghosts of history as the earth remembered them, wrists clasped in warrior pride just before that moment when two sparring friends hit the dirt together, laughing—

But that beauty just made it hurt so much more to lose.

For another eon or so I tortured Bricandor back. I wasn't as bad as him, I told myself. I stopped short each time of doing what he did to me—and each time, I refused to do or think anything that would trigger whatever my ability really was. He tried electrocuting me for a time, so I might shock him back—I didn't.

I stopped trying to hurt him when I saw Joshua curled up in the fetal position in his trap, hissing against the cold. I longed to reach in there and scoop Joshua up, and I suddenly didn't want to hurt anyone anymore, because a part of me wondered how much interdimensional energy *I* was spitting out of our universe, and how much Joshua then had to absorb. I knew it wasn't wrong to fight, in and of itself. But I didn't know where the line was anymore.

And there just wasn't any point.

One day, I was riding my air-rider through the Luna-Guetala jungle when I almost crashed head on into a paradox—not like, a moral paradox, as in "Paradox Warriors," but like a space-time issue. A physics thing. I only saw it because the chronometer on my wristband slowed. Somehow I caught that before tumbling head-first into it.

I dismounted outside the field. My boots crunched on dry leaves as I stuck my hand forward, and—yeah, my clock straight up stalled in there. Took like minutes for one second to pass on my wrist—and a few feet away, while I marked time, a domed building materialized.

Or didn't. It was there and not there, a mess of particles and waves. It ... flickered? Blurred? Like the center of the anomaly was moving at a thousand kilometers an hour—but actually it'd slowed down so much the atoms just stopped, and now I could see matter as it was, frozen in two states at once.

Everyone inside was trapped in an eternal second.

I sucked in my breath. Matter stopping—well, matter also stops when energy's gone. That's heat death.

Is every isolated moment without a flowing timeline actually just a tiny heat death?

I waded forward. I was hot enough, chaotic enough and ordered enough, to keep my atoms flowing, my energy alive. Shyte, these people weren't even conscious of being trapped. They stood at their desks, or scribbled their messages, or wagged their fingers, all still, all lifeless. Are we not conscious, not sentient, without the passage of time to unite one thought with another into soul? Is *time* life?

"Come on, Lem," Jei would've laughed.

But Jei hadn't materialized, no matter how I willed or prayed.

I was, I am, the universe's lone Paradox Warrior, the fireball now freezing in time and the cat both dead and alive as I slowed toward the center of the silly domed building with its bureaucrats and fools. In those eternal moments he and I had both walked away from the edge of the cliff into the place we call now. Each moment died as another second was born. It takes many points on a graph to make a line; many instantaneous deaths to make eternal life. Then and here, I contaminated the present with the past I hated putting into words. He died! He died to keep me alive. And I'd failed anyway.

There was a pit in the center of the anomaly—literally a dirt pit in the office building in the frozen bubble of time in the jungle.

Jei lay unmoving and broken at the bottom.

Oh, Jei. I sighed. The anomaly wanted me to stretch out my powers, to snatch him back from the brink, to heat his molecules back up—I didn't. I wanted to, more than anything else in the universe, but I shouldn't. I almost couldn't remember why I shouldn't, but I shoved my hands in my pockets and closed my eyes.

"Very clever, Bricandor," I said.

Somewhere, outside it all, the silence broke as a boy cried out.

"Hey, hey, sister, I've got you."

"I'm not going to kill you! You're sick, not evil! I've been there before, I spent years there before you and I became friends."

Someone else was crying my name. Cinta? "You're not allowed to die for me," I told Cinta again. "No one is, ever again."

I lay down and let the nightmares flow around me. It sucked to see Jei and be unable to reach him. It sucked to keep being drowned and shot and exploded and shyte. But this would be over at some point. I just needed to wait.

"Let me help you!" the voice screamed. Not Cinta.

No. I was very done. I was just going to wait out Bricandor. I was done losing things. I was done loving things. I would embrace the pain and wait. I wanted heat death for myself, just not for everyone else. I was selfish like that.

"Let me help you!" he screamed again.

But oh, this was the one thing I couldn't let go, because he wouldn't let go of me.

I found myself wrestling with Njandejara in the sand, pinning him on his back. Grit dug into my ankles under my pants, sneaking into my boots, and dust filled my nostrils. We'd been wrestling all my life, hadn't we? He shrimped out of my grasp and almost got a leg over to get me in guard—I slipped over onto his back, and tightened my forearm in front of his neck, and my hand behind his head, for a blood choke. "I won't let you go," I cried, choking myself. "I won't let you go until you give me the goodness I've been fighting the whole filking universe for."

He pressed his fingers into my hip, and a sharp pang shot down my leg. I didn't let go, and I realized he was gripping my wrist, clutching it to his shoulder, so I couldn't. He was why I didn't let go. "Your new name is One Who Struggles With The Highest Power," he said. "And the goodness I can give you is me."

It was over then, between Bricandor and me. I beat Njandejara, and I beat him. The old dictator wasn't going home through me. I lay down next to Joshua's portal and curled up, waiting for him. I was so tired. Maybe, I thought, I was a million years old now.

Bricandor gave up on me, but he didn't give up on escape. He crawled right to the edge of Joshua's portal, screaming into it: "What do you think you are? Come out of there! Come out of there and get us all out! We can *see* the surplus energy on you. You can get out of there! So why don't you? Why are you putting up with the torment of a broken world that isn't even your problem? Prove yourself and get us all out before we all perish!"

"Dude, stop," I croaked, kicking at him with a weary boot. "He hasn't done anything. You and me—we deserve to be here. This is what we do. We live by the sword, we die by it. He's good. Filking—leave him alone."

Joshua smiled at me through some pain I couldn't grasp, and I realized suddenly he'd been the one calling for me all along. And I did want to let him help me. Shyte, though, I could barely move. I reached out to him. "Please remember me after you've won and made a new world," was my dying whisper.

"You'll see it today," he said. His paw gripped my fingers, and I closed my eyes.

CHAPTER THIRTY-THREE

Joshua

WHERE IS THE DOOR?

Joshua drooped, fur dripping and bones aching, before a jury of those who considered themselves his peers. Stars glittered through the hall of justice over stone floors punctuated with spots of gleaming wood paneling in seemingly random patterns —as the equations as old as galaxies conferred—while the dying Biouk scanned the room for a way out.

"We're going to hang them all," the equations said. "Actually —you're going to hang them all. Because that's justice, isn't it? They don't even know how to make a filking shoe without oppressing someone."

Do you know where the door is?

A confused and trembling reptilian sat down on the cold stone bench beside Joshua. "So I get that he's the Accuser," the reptilian nodded over at an almost-perfect cloud of mathematical law. "So are you the Defense, then?"

"No." Joshua shook his head. *Where is it?* "I am what once was part of the Judge. Now I'm the Accused. They don't really like the matter hybrid that I am."

"It goes all the way back, doesn't it?" the little reptilian asked. "We can say it's our parents' fault, or the fault of whoever hurt them, or so on, but everyone adds a string to the web, don't they? This goes all the way back to that first mutagenic plant."

Joshua nodded and winced. He was feeling dizzy, actually. The Accuser again flashed before his memory every single horrific thing that old being had ever seen—from the kinds of tortures people couldn't even voice without blanching to the little dumb mistakes and seemingly harmless nothingnesses that rippled out into the timeline to enable them. And Joshua could see the future evils the Accuser couldn't. The screams echoed again through his skull until blood trickled from his ear. *Let me help you*, he begged inside. *Please unchain me and let me help you.* The little reptilian mopped Joshua's forehead with a damp rag— the reptilian had closed his eyes not even a hundred years into sapient history to keep his mind from shattering.

"This isn't who we were meant to be. This isn't who we *are*, is it?" he asked, burying his face in Joshua's fur.

"It is who you are," the Accuser snapped. He pointed a long string of numbers at Joshua. "What do you have to say for yourself?"

Joshua shook his head, peering into the shadows under the table at the far end of the room. He'd been through the entire loop of history twice already. They'd eaten his liver for days. Pali had promised him there was a way out. Where was it?

"You won't speak? Then I will. I say you care more about matter than energy—about biological rules than spiritual truths." The Accuser spread another piece of timeline out before the audience—not an actual piece of the timeline, but rather a recording, for like the other interdimensionals he was as trapped inside history as the sapients were. "See her?"

"You're mad at me because I want her to love her biology," Joshua said. The chains on his fore and hind-paws clinked. Where *was* it?

"Yes. Sex, race, species, nuclear membranes separating

perfectly compatible molecules from each other—these disgusting little details oozing with sputum and saline—" The Accuser spat. "Let's put aside for a moment the fact that all this nastiness should have been erased in the first place for something more uniform. Even if you assume any matter is good, look how quick they are to pervert these things! See here, in this history, all I have to do is point her in this direction, and she—I mean, look, look how she twists this 'good' thing! It's disgusting." He laughed. "Then she blames me for pointing her that way, but it was clearly in her all along. I didn't *make* her do that. They'll do anything for any one of their nasty holes."

The Accuser flipped to another life. "Look at this one. You told them not to put our names—the names of interdimensionals who hate them—on their lips. That's sweet of you—they're still too stupid to realize some of us can travel through the electric portals of thought like the Old One can." He held the moving picture up to the light like a prism. "But what's most pathetic is they don't need us and our names to ruin the world. Sure, in lands where they're weak, we have a lot of power. And places where they're stronger, with the kinds of philosophies that breed medicine and science and engineering, there we're weaker. But then the greatest evil happens in those same places where they have all this power, and we have none. Not in cannibal dances around screaming spits, but in board rooms and hospitals and temples where we aren't mentioned at all!"

Joshua glared into the ice, and the fire, and then the silent emptiness, as they all washed over him again, each in their turn. He gritted his teeth, closed his eyes, curled his toes—whatever he needed to do to see himself through each loop of pain—but he was becoming desperate. Where was it? Where was the way out?

Now Joshua was trying to roll this huge boulder into place. First up the hill, and then, maybe, into some fourth-dimensional space. The little reptilian crouched beside Joshua again, offering him a drink, as sweat and blood dripped down his muzzle. "Why is it like this?" the reptilian asked.

"It'll be worth it," Joshua breathed. "You, and what you can do, are worth it. Imagine what a shriveled insect you would be if we stayed in our cocoons, without the stretch and pain of the struggle."

The hill flipped upside down as the land danced like the sea, and the rock rolled away without revealing any door. Joshua chased it down, and again put his paws against it. Could a person even shove a rock into the fourth dimension, actually? That didn't seem right.

"But why does the butterfly *need* to struggle to exit the cocoon? Why is everything built on the paradox, the light and dark, the good and evil, the particle and the wave, when you could've just made it all good?" the reptilian asked.

He wasn't being helpful right now. Joshua himself was feeling the full weight of what a mess the universe seemed to be, and it took everything in him to pant, "What I am building this way is worth it. Because this is who I am, and I am worth it."

He pressed his shoulder into the rock and groaned with effort. No door? Was he supposed to just explode with love and shatter the whole realm or something? He couldn't hear Pali here, and not being able to hear the other self that had been so close to him—it was like someone had cut off his ears and skinned him. Everything seemed raw, and silent, and so *lost*.

"Pali, where is it? Did you forget?" he found himself murmuring. "Is this forever?"

Again the little reptilian was beside him. "Where are we?" he asked, as Joshua shivered on the mountaintop again, waiting for the eagle.

"That is a good question," Joshua said, trying to calculate it for himself using a metaphor. "So a being is traveling down a road. They look out at the trees outside their vehicle. Those trees seem to be moving backward. From the traveler's reference plane, they are. From the reference plane of the trees, the traveler is moving forward. Which plane is correct?"

"Neither," snapped the Accuser from the courtroom. Ah. It looked warm in there, and Joshua took his little reptilian and began to trudge that way through the snow. "Only the speed of light is constant in each reference plane. Light's reference plane is correct. Ours."

"Is that where the ba-eaters live? In the reference plane of light?" the reptilian whispered. "If that's true then when they try to mess with our world, it's like trying to hit a target outside of a moving car, with all the different speeds and planes constantly changing."

"Maybe it's kind of like that for the Brightest Ones," Joshua said. "But light's reference plane isn't constant. Its speed is: it adapts for each reference plane."

"Is light from outside of time, then, where Njandejara lives?" the reptilian asked. "Because that's what I'd expect from something Outside stuck into time—it would be constant while everything flows around it, like a finger in a stream."

"That's an interesting thought," Joshua said. He crawled under the stone bench, tapping the courtroom floor, blinking back the fourth round of the horrible history lesson as his stomach churned. *Door. I will find this door.* The Accuser stared at him, trying to understand—as old as the Accuser was, he didn't know the future with any real certainty except with dark trickery: spending blood and tearing energy from the stars to tell the matter-beings bits and pieces he could suck out of the timeline. He could see a lot of patterns, but in the end, no one could *really* see the patterns of the world from down here any more than an electron can see the order in the chaotic storm around it to realize it's part of a lattice. This was why Njandejara's rules didn't make sense to these people sometimes—all the molecules he was aligning, in the balance of energy and entropy, couldn't really observe themselves from down here.

Which was why it was such a problem that Joshua couldn't hear Pali. He couldn't see the pattern. Where was it? Where was the door? He'd done the first part of his mission already. He'd died. Now Njandejara would live this moment of death, forever, because he was outside of time, so all of it was present, or already static, in front of him. That was part one: fill the huge interdimensional energy suck left by the matter-beings with Someone who was infinitely energetic, who could in one moment of time fill the eternities of all other beings; essentially disconnect the universe of those he loved from the leeching null and connect the null to Njandejara instead.

Joshua had done that. He'd brought death to the deathless one.

This was the part the Accuser had been counting on.

But the Accuser had also been counting on the fact that if he could sever Njandejara's connection to the matter-universe at any one point of the timeline, then *because* Pali was outside of time all the older connections back into time could not count, and in fact ceased to exist. It was strange, but simple: the time-line relied on Njandejara for existence, so if he ceased touching the timeline at any one point—well, no more timeline. Every conversation, every breath on the wind, every memory, would unravel backward, and eventually the entire timeline would never have been.

And the best way for the Accuser to make sure that happened, that Njandejara let go of the timeline, was to undo Joshua, the frail and finite matter holding the infinite energy inside—because Joshua had matter, and matter could be harmed enough to despair.

Njandejara had created a weakness for himself, and delivered it directly into the Accuser's hands.

But because Joshua was matter, he had a place in the time-line. So that was hopeful, right? He wasn't in the outside where Pali saw all things at the same time—he still existed in the world of choice. Unlike Pali, he didn't have to suffer every moment forever. This moment was eventually going to end.

He really needed it to end.

Joshua sat in the fire and melted again, grinding his teeth as his throat screamed without his permission. *Where is the door?!* The Accuser loved this. "You could always just withdraw, you know," he said. "They're really, really not worth this. Just say the word. Say you're done. You can undo yourself, shed this dead matter, and go home."

No. This body was his, and he would hold on to it. He kept his promises. There was only one way this risk worked out for him: he made one connection, from death to Njandejara, and made the second connection from Njandejara's life, back to his people. A completed circuit.

Where was the door to Pali's house of life, so Joshua could connect them to him?

The little reptilian who had walked with Joshua walked with him no more. Joshua was alone, and in the darkness his body felt every cruelty suffered by every victim in history, and he began to cry, a shuddering tearless, weary cry. He was so tired. Where was Pali? Where in this whole dimension of death was the Progenitor of Life?

"Just let go!" the Accuser begged. "I hate seeing you like this. You're really so much better than this. Let go! Don't you realize he's suffering, too? If you disconnect—let go—out there, he is freed. Freed from this timeline shackling his hands. Freed, too, from the eternal moment of this death you've bonded him to. You are hurting the self you love the most for people who can never actually understand love at all! Let me set you free!"

No. Joshua laid his ears flat, bit down against the inner scream, and closed his eyes.

There in his mind's eye, he played pictures of his beloved ones. Of building Pali's home for them. Of their expressions—he imagined what they'd say when they saw the world remade, or even when they saw him, again. He imagined the blossom at the end of the stem that was the timeline when Pali's energy filled their universe bit by bit until it was unrecognizable, and they never needed to cry or ache again. He ran his mind over every line in every dear little matter face, kissing it in his heart.

And as he did so, he remembered one little couple he loved, and looked out across the stars to where they floated in their dead ship and saw the end of the world, and wept for him, and comforted each other with their matter forms. And he remembered where the door was.

The door was in the way *differentness* came together across both matter and energy, with the two opposite kinds of Being loving each other not despite but *because* of their differentness, taking the risk of vulnerability and pain and responsibility and future, shielding it in promise, and creating a rhythm of bare knowing, giving and receiving, entering and holding, and sacrifice. The door was the union of male and female animals creating life; it was the electron and the proton, joined to make matter; it was two races of people marching down the street for one cause; it was the harmony within each person when their opposite selves found peace; it was the bond between Njandejara, the perfect energy being, and all these ridiculous matter people he loved.

"I'm the door," Joshua realized. "I can't believe I forgot."

CHAPTER THIRTY-FOUR

Cinta

NO ONE TOOK ANY ACTION AROUND THE STRUCTURE FOR ABOUT three days. Without Bricandor, the Growen soldiers on the installation itself had no orders until Laaru took command—which he did almost as soon as he landed. It was not difficult. Jaika and Bricandor had killed all the soldiers who would have known Laaru as prisoner, and the last written documentation listed Laaru as a high-ranking Stygge with almost Diebol-level clearance. Disappointment about the Structure had swept the Growen ranks—it did not seem to *do* anything particularly helpful from a military standpoint, at least not anything that justified how many blitzers had died for it. Laaru was declassifying thousands of pages of documents on both the mind-control debacle and the Structure, and the faction of the Growen High Counsel that did not want peace with the Frelsi now faced the wrath of the Independent planets. The Bont homeworld rebelled, Burbura held emergency elections, and Skraeli opened negotiations with Frelsi leadership. There was serious talk across the systems about how to end the war.

Masha and Cinta stayed in the escape pod Laaru had lent

them, sleeping and holding each other. Occasionally one or the other would let out a soft whine and hide his or her nose under the others' ears. They did not eat. Every few hours they took the pod's silver wings up to circle the Core—this was Masha's quiet demand. Cinta did not think it healthy for her to haunt her son's resting place like this, but what could he say?

"I have to wait for him," she said. "It's all I have. Please wait with me."

So they waited. Cinta did not know what for. At one point, he received a cryptic message on his transmitter from the Watchers about a living door. He was too tired to understand, but at least he and Jaika had done something right—at least some of the Irin had survived.

On the third day, Cinta's mercenaries joined them, their ship finally repaired at Laaru's behest. The two Allperson survivors, Rizzt and Szizzle, arrived on foot bearing mourning wreaths in their tradition—Szizzle now pregnant with eggs—and that afternoon found almost the entire bioship crew, Laaru, Nathan, and Jake included, sitting on the sloped roof of the building around the space elevator, watching the glow of the Core far above them. Reise was not there.

Cinta had not known how to tell Jaika's brothers about what had happened to her; Reise had not even wanted the rest of the family to know she'd survived Forge—if he could, he said, he would keep the secret of her return to Luna-Guetala between himself, Jake, and Juju. As the oldest brother he did not see a purpose in doubling everyone else's pain, and would rather bear as much of it himself as he could. But Cinta had begged Reise to let him tell the Frelsi she was responsible for ending Bricandor, and rumor had already flown ahead of them anyway. Her name, at least, had been redeemed.

It was Szizzle who first saw when the Core went dark. "What's happening?" she cried, pointing a long-clawed finger.

"Something's coming out?" Rizzt asked.

"Nothing good ever comes out of a rift," muttered one of the humans.

But by the time Cinta reached the mesosphere with the escape pod to check the Core, there was nothing there—only a cold black stone floated suspended in the paths where the mirrored portal had been. A hologram flitted above the stone for just a moment, Cinta thought—or perhaps he was dreaming, seeing shadows in the stars and recordings of memory in the magnetic field?

"I want to say goodbye to Cinta," she said. "I want to tell him when you said sometimes he's the rescue, you weren't talking to him about sacrificing his life, but living it. I want to talk to him about how we're never enough and that's when we're exactly enough. How right now on this timeline, no matter how helpless he feels, if he isn't the answer you've placed there you'll give him someone else who is. He has such a journey ahead of him still, and I don't want him to be tired."

"I'll tell him for you, Jaika."

The space elevator was already moving. Cinta raced it down —was it—he couldn't be sure of what he saw through its clear tube, but—he almost crashed the little ship in his hurry to land, and stumbled out of the landing pad and into the building with his heart pounding and his breath rasping like a bandsaw.

Everyone gathered around the space elevator, and of course —of course, Cinta realized, because how could it be any other way—Joshua stepped out, fully furred and a bit older, but still Joshua, with bright eyes and perky ears, and the loveliest grin in the galaxy.

"Hey Mali," he said, falling into Masha's arms. "I'm really hungry."

The Accuser

"But I had you!" the Accuser cried. "You must pay for their energy loss, or they must pay it, which means you must die, which means they must disappear! I had you in the perfect paradox!"

The Old One laughed. "Will you join me now?" he asked.

"No! This has accomplished nothing! They will go on destroying. This has not stopped their will to consume, not in the least!"

"Are you completely missing the chemical reaction I've started here?" Njandejara rose above the cosmos with a joyful cry, for even as he was always in the moment of his death, he was also always in the moment of his triumph. "What I've done won't just stop the transfer of energy out of their universe. I'm not only paying for the energy they've siphoned. A Le Chatelier reversal, a complete change in equilibrium back toward the other direction—that's what we've done. Give the chemical equation an eon or two to use up its initial substrate and every single one of them will be so infected by the change in their world they produce more energy than they consume. There will be backward steps sometimes—horrors and tremors and birth pangs—but in the end state, the entire universe will be my home, and it will be beautiful."

"And the ones that don't? You have their will in this equation still!"

There, Njandejara nodded. "They'll be yours to prosecute," he said. "Ours to judge. You underestimate my anger. At some point I cannot be me and allow their imbalance to go uncorrected—for the sake of the energy in the universe, for your sake and mine, and for the little ones whose hearts ache with the tearing pull of a stretched universe in the very fiber of all their cells. They sense it, you know, that this is not where they were meant to live—it is animal instinct, the scent of a broken environment. I will honor them. And then, Accuser, I will also prosecute you."

The Accuser snarled and took his equations to another corner of space to sulk. But Njandejara's promise lingered behind him: "What I have done is once for all time. But time is complicated. In all realities, at the same time, I'm always doing this, somewhere—I've done it before, and I'll do it again. Because I'm outside of time, and what I do once crosses all universes. And there is no universe where I am not madly in love with the beings you hate."

CHAPTER THIRTY-FIVE

Tziyyon, Jaika, or Jerusha-Lem Benzaran, Beloved of Njandejara

I WAS MASS, THEN ENERGY, THEN MASS AGAIN. WE ARE LIGHTS along a timeline, and if all energy is only mass accelerated, that pattern of mass contains information just like a string of lights in a computer. Everything is a metaphor for everything else; as our neuronal impulses contain our programming, so also there's actual information stored in our energy at certain positions and times in history.

The information that made up *me* coalesced under the shade of an enormous Bangla tree with thick roots almost made for my shape, embracing me like a throne. The bark wasn't rough on my hips—that was kind of strange.

Actually—huh. I leaned back with an odd little grin—I was more comfortable than I'd ever been in my life. Even when I'd stayed the night in the pillow-fort in that rich person's house on Retrack City. It actually felt like something was missing from my body. Like a stiffness or a—smell? Or pain?

Shyte, had I always been in pain and only just now realized it?

The tree and I were planted on a cliff overlooking a ravine into a void; I saw two figures in the ravine I thought I recognized, and for some reason I thought I needed to scramble to my feet and bow, or fight, or both.

A calming, jovial elbow nudged me to stay seated. "It's okay to chill for a moment, Benzaran," Gideon said. My brother's friend leaned against the thick tree beside me, his arms crossed —not like a defensive person, or a tough person, but a very comfortable person who's so in charge he can really go to sleep whenever and wherever he wants. He wore his sleeves rolled up, thick biceps stretching a casual shirt peppered with what looked like glowing gemstones across his torso. A long-haired human girl I didn't recognize slept beside him with her head on his shoulder, a tiny smile across her face as her parted lips fluttered with soft, unconscious breath. She was draped with glittering shapes, too, but most of hers stretched in long stripes across her ribs. I recognized those patterns from somewhere, but I couldn't quite place them; whatever they were—probably too light and beautiful to be gems—they looked like they'd been bought at a premium.

"Fulfill your duty as a witness, real quick, and then you're cool to go find him," Gideon said.

Find ... who?

The ravine opened up below us into a field of stars. Njandejara was there—you couldn't see him, or you'd go blind, but there was a rift through reality into the place outside of time, and as he opened it he pointed to a long string of pictures sparkling and trailing into eternity, winding around to expand into where we were. We were part of the string, somehow. It was a little dizzying to look at.

But for the person down in the ravine it was more than dizzying. Bricandor clung to a rock above an abyss, screaming. "This is a permanent punishment for a temporary crime! What I did was finite! How can my sentence be infinite?"

"The blood of the children will always call to me, infinitely." Njandejara waved his hand over the string of time; scars appeared across his fingers, each one weeping as the skin peeled back. "Every action you took permanently changed the choices available to those around you. I live forever in what you did. What else can I do with you, then? My presence is torture for you, even now searing your inner being. You have to leave."

"But if you contain all goodness, then when I leave, there will be only meaningless suffering, with no goodness at all!" Bricandor cried. "Why is the universe like this? Why can I not have some other option where you are not involved, neither you nor not you? Let me be nothingness."

"There is no such thing as nothingness," Njandejara sighed. "Neither matter nor energy are actually created or destroyed, only transformed or displaced. So you cannot disappear into nothing. You must leave."

Bricandor protested more, but Njandejara didn't answer him again. The Progenitor Being turned his back on the pitiful creature, and the tormentor of my ghosts evaporated into the void with a horrified scream.

But as the rift closed, and the ravine sealed after it with a thundering finality under a lavender meadow, I saw a slouching to Njandejara's—shoulders, if you could call them that. You really, truly couldn't look at him, although you really, truly got the sense that you wanted to—you had to try to steal glimpses of him reflected in the grass or the sky as he passed. You felt him, more than anything.

And I felt that he seemed somber about his judgment.

"You cared about him," I said, shielding my eyes with my head low. "Is there—is there still hope for him, somehow?"

"That is a secret between myself and him. All evil is permanent. All damnation must be permanent to match it."

"But nothing with you's that simple," I said. "You're Master of Paradoxes."

"Yes. But the whispers of reversal, the hints of healing in

belief, are for each person to hunt for themselves, not for others —in this you must be selfish."

"I am so confused," I sighed.

"It will become clearer in a few eons, little one." He stroked my chin with a gentle chuckle, I thought, but then I couldn't see him anymore—or I could see him everywhere? It was like he was the sun for the whole world. "I gave all of his people warnings, you know—the original Diebol, the original Sterba, all of the old namesakes—I sent them disease and tragedy to let them feel what they were doing to other people, to beg them to come to me and become healed, but they ignored it and pressed on. They didn't care about the warnings."

"I'm sorry," I said. I didn't know exactly what I was apologizing for, actually. I did know I couldn't see where Njandejara had gone—except, wasn't he here still, in this tree, and in this pale blue sky? I blinked, confused.

"You get used to it," Gideon laughed. "Here comes Joshua."

Oh, Joshua. My brother from the rift, the dear one fading with me as I faded—somehow that moment made him infinitely more precious to me than even all the lovely whispers Njandejara used to send me in the breezes and babbling brooks. This manifestation was *with me* in a way they couldn't be, and I cried out and leapt to my feet to meet him. He'd kept his promise! I was here, I was *here*, and like he said he would, he'd answered my question about my brother's friend, too. I scooped him up and squeezed him, and when I set him down my fingers ran all through his fur in delight. Every scratch and tear and burn from his ordeal had healed with glowing kintsugi—for that was what the "gems" were, I realized, on the two humans—and his once-torn ear flicked with the loveliest patch of gold.

"You're back!" I laughed.

"I took some time to go talk to our friends in your universe," he said, nuzzling my chin with his snout. "They're going to be all right. There's energy flowing from here—well, the future 'here,' technically—into your universe now. And Pali's stopped the drain. In just a while the whole place will be beautiful."

"Yeah, about that—what is this place?" I asked, sitting up on my knees and looking around. The lovely Bangla tree grew at the edge of a jungle that seemed so familiar, but then—these plains of wildflowers creeping up to its root seemed so foreign to me.

"It's not quite done yet," Joshua said. "Right now, it's more like my dream still. But we'll have the best of all your planets, basically, when it's done. Only better."

"I mean, it's pretty sweet now," I said. I laid my hands on his shoulders. "Thank you for letting me come here."

Joshua patted my hand without taking it off his shoulder. "Thank you for letting me bring you. I like being the noble gas to your cation."

"I have no idea what that means," I said.

"Look it up!" he laughed. "There's a lovely library off that way." His muzzle pointed to a mountain range—floating above the highest peak I could just see something golden and ivory with pillars and spires. "In the meantime, go explore! I'll have an important question for you when you're done." He scampered off, and as I looked back toward the tree, I saw Gideon and his friend were just leaving, too. "Say hi for me!" Gideon called. "We'll hang out all together later. I'm going to go wait for Nathan."

Hi to who?

So I walked through the prairie wilderness of a strange world alone. But not lonely. The sunlight-that-was-also-Njandejara was very warm, like a constant gentle massage on my skin.

There's a settlement up ahead. There were no guards on the edges of the town—it was hard to see where the settlement began, actually, because of how gradually nature faded into it. Grass grew on roofs, and fruit trees lined the streets. Most people were barefoot. Each building—even the simplest ones—seemed designed for a particular person, or a particular purpose, with a personality. *Someone who actually loves their job built these.* No two structures were exactly the same, and as I wandered, I couldn't really find a "poor" or "rich" part of town. When I found the marketplace, I heard laughter, not bartering.

Was it even a market?

People of all species displayed things they'd made. Ceramics. Tapestries. Paintings. Musicians frolicked and chattered in alleys and on roofs, each playing their own strain of music here and there under their scattered conversations, somehow all harmonizing even when they weren't conscious of each other, as if they just naturally paused to do something else when it was their time, plugged in to a song that ran through all of life from the humming of the celestial spheres to the chirps of the insects who would never suffer another winter death. There weren't any farmers. People who showed off plants they grew seemed to be doing it because they were excited about a new corner of nature they wanted to share with their friends, not because they needed to eke food from the ground. Because they didn't—anyone could eat from any of the trees lining the way at any time. Mothers and fathers and chefs and children ran here and there under the shade of colorful booths and cool leaves with platters of—appetizers, I guessed—so elegant I'd only seen the like on light-channel shows or that one intrigue mission I'd had in the Luna-Guetala pleasure station. Elderly people who weren't elderly—all of the scars of age transformed into effervescent jewelry that streaked their strong bodies like warpaint—knelt over cauldrons while they regaled clusters of friends with old histories, so the scent of comfort food danced under the wafting creativity of gourmet cuisine.

Everyone was working because they wanted to create, not for need, and nothing clashed with anything else no matter how foreign or strange. From where I stood at a distance even the way people moved around each other or bumped into each other seemed coordinated—but they were so completely unaware of it, just being themselves, just happening to fit into where they were in time. Skin colors and feathers and scales seemed deliberate, too, brushing the canvas of each moment in space as if every still frame of reality, isolated, was someone's greatest painting. Fat dragons and sleek Crajk-beasts lounged in the sun without muzzles or cages, and peacock guinea pigs ran across their backs completely unafraid of being eaten. I thought I recognized the first one I'd killed, and I knew I recognized the Watcher sleeping in a snowdrift with a red mark through its belly, shielded from the heat by a glittering glass dome. No one preached, saying "know Njandejara," because everyone knew him, and the snippets of conversation I overheard where people taught each other something sounded less like lessons and more like treasure hunters conferring as they uncovered the deepest secrets of the universe from each other's minds.

Every single thing in the market seemed to have Njandejara's touch on it. Not like a mark or a brand or something, and definitely not like a picture of him. Just—it seemed like people wanted him to see their creations. Like children with a parent, completely brazen and self-assured and happy.

I stood there at the head of the marketplace and almost cried.

"Lem-Lem," said a warbly voice beside me. "Is it your first time at the market, the market—your first time?"

Captain Rana, my first commanding officer, stood beside me on his thick webbed feet, his huge round Wonderfrog eyes staring down the street with me. I would've hugged him—but most Wonderfrog culture frowns on that. I bowed instead, restraining the giggly thrill in my belly. I hadn't seen him since Bricandor Death Glare'd him in his ship years ago.

"Yes, sir," I said. "First time."

"Have you been to the tavern? The tavern, the tavern," he croaked, his wide mouth grinning. "The others will be happy to see you, to see you, to see you."

"I'll follow you, sir."

Ah, the tavern. The tavern was comforting in its darkness, full of rich oak smells and colors. Some people sang. Some regaled stories. There were no bar fights or drunken rows. Rana wound on all fours almost like a sidewinder past living tables with bark still intact—again, of many shapes and sizes, for many kinds of people—his feet *plat-plat*-ing across the smooth floor. I suddenly had the intense desire to take off my boots and feel the wood, which seemed alive and unharmed somehow—and no one stopped me, so I did, and carrying my shoes, tip-toed to the table in the corner.

Colonel Win, my Hoernig commander after Rana, raised a huge amber glass to me. I nodded my greeting. There were three Bichanks at the table—two seemed to be wide-eyed newcomers like myself, one with a glowing golden mark on his neck and Frelsi Bijou winterwear, and the other wildly and gorgeously striped with ruby and topaz across her entire chest and face. One of her legs was completely glowing like this—I guessed at some point she'd lost the leg altogether, but it was hard to tell, really, because the marks weren't really gore, or even like—scars. They were praise, higher than medals of honor.

"I'm Kola," she said. "I think I know your brother, maybe."

"Maybe," I said. "I'm Jaika. Or—for some reason I feel like my name is Tsiyyon, here. I'm pleased to meet you."

A Bichank chef leaned on the chair behind Kola, one of his arms almost entirely covered in a lovely emerald sheen draped across flowing fur.

"We've worked together, you and us," he said. "All of us. To stop the mind control. Just at different times. It's good to finally meet you, across time."

He patted the shoulder of a thin human wearing the warpaint of age; the gentleman kind of jumped with a laugh, laying down a scientific article whose title took up the entire first half of the page. "We were some of the first," the human admitted, folding his glasses, which seemed decorative rather than necessary. "The chef here, and me. Kola and her team took care of Nathan the year after. And you brought him home."

"Wow," I said, scratching my head under my thick hair as I sat down. "Uh, it's an honor."

There were so many happy Frelsi here. Graap, the Sailfin from Kola's team, and a charming Biouk who kissed my hand like a human knight, and at one point a little Bont kid ran by. "She was the first bait for the Turned on Forge—the body the scouts went out to find." Kola nodded, pouring some of her glass into mine. "Try this."

"Diebol did that, right?" I asked.

"Yeah, I think so. She's a really happy kid. It's amazing how there's no—trauma—here." Kola shook her head. "You know how back in our home universe, when everyone *looks* all happy you kind of keep expecting something horrible to happen—or like, you wonder if maybe they're hiding some Growen dystopia shyte under their filking perfect smiles—you know what I mean?"

"Yeah. I've been to Beryllia."

"It's just not like that here. There's not even, like, the worry of it, because the deeper you go, the more you discover, the more you meet the one who loves you. It's—it's so weird, in the best way. I'm still not used to good things actually being good." She waved across the room, and a human danced over carrying another round of drinks—I guess like a waiter, although everyone was a servant of everyone else there while being served themselves, so—

My eyes widened as the waiter neared. "Filking—Banks?" Was I really looking at a Growen blitzer from my squad, from my days undercover?

He started to laugh. "Holy—are you—are you the fake Frank Zej?"

"Y-yeah!"

"So the letter you wrote me about your change of heart—the one that introduced me to Njandejara, that got me here—that wasn't exactly factual, was it." It wasn't quite a smirk, but I immediately felt like I needed to defend myself.

"I mean, the Njandejara bit was true," I stammered.

"Obviously," he laughed again, gesturing around us. "Man, I owe you everything, Fra—un-Frank. That was the best thing anyone did for me. Just in time, too. Although I guess everything is just in time, since you-know-who is outside of it. But you know what I mean about just in time." He made a pistol gesture at his own face, which is I guess where General Johnson shot him a few days after my letter.

"I made sure your killer got his," I said quickly.

"I heard about the coup. But I deserved to die. We care about justice here, and I mean, you know what I was," he said. The closest thing to a shadow I'd seen yet passed over his face, with such somber severity it was like he was sentencing someone else, but the gratefulness never left his features. He shook his head and chuckled again. "But the letter! I bet you don't even remember most of what was in it."

"I—" I really felt I should, but I shook my head.

"I think you'll find it's that way with a lot of things here. It's the little thing that you don't even think about—oh, hold on, someone needs a drink over there. We'll talk later!" He disappeared around the bar, and I was dumbfounded. I knew he didn't deserve to be here. None of the Growen did. But if Joshua had reversed the drain from our universe, of course some of them made it. We all paid into the drain, and we were all bought from it. Joshua had filled the deficit Banks left and rewritten his programming, too, although in what eternal moment he did the latter I didn't know. Banks didn't have any of the beautiful gems everyone else did.

But he'd befriended Njandejara with the willingness to be rewritten, so he was here. The lowest of the loved was still loved.

My head was already spinning when, to top it all off, a familiar-looking Sailfin bounced over.

"Ahem, excuse me. I'm Braap—do you remember me?" he asked. "From Fort Tapiz?"

Yeah. I'd last seen him Turn the week the mind control took off.

Now I actually couldn't take it. Tears flooded my eyes; immediately it was as if the air embraced me to tell me it really was all okay—as if a soft, strong hand wiped my face, and whispered in my ear that no one who lived here would ever suffer again. I wasn't being told not to cry, to buck up—the tears were just being wiped away.

Braap wrapped his scaly arms around me in the similitude of a hug, trying to show cultural respect to me as a mammal. "Oh, Benzaran, I'm not here for a sad reason," he cooed. "When you and your friend broke the Forge control panel, you set my city free. I wasn't Turned anymore. I'm only here because I was free enough to save my family when our house fell in. I have pictures of them!" He reached into the canvas pouch slung over his shoulder, and showed me his daughters, and his mate. "Look! They're all doing amazing things. Because I had the choice to give my life. I wouldn't have had that choice if I was under Growen control." He tapped my shoulder, approximating a mammalian petting motion with his cool scales on my warm human skin. "So I just wanted to thank you, and let you know— I mean, I know from watching you out there you've felt like nothing you've done has mattered. But what you did was worth it to *me*. I'm just one person, but you know. I matter, too," he laughed. "There are a lot of people you'll be surprised you touched—that's one of the best things about being here, is connecting with people you never knew you knew across the ripples. I'll tell you my whole story sometime, but—" He looked behind me, and his narrow vertical pupils dilated. "I think someone has been waiting for a while to see you."

The others at the table looked up at me, expectantly. My chest tightened, and my muscles tensed—not in fear, but with that blazing hope I'd hated because of how much pain it'd caused me unfulfilled. I almost couldn't turn around in the overwhelm between anticipation and so much past grief. I knew who Gideon had suggested I was looking for. Would it actually …? Oh—

I turned, and there standing behind me, beaming with his hands in his pockets and hair falling over his face, was Jei.

CHAPTER THIRTY-SIX

Lem

I ALWAYS THOUGHT IF I'D SEE JEI AGAIN I'D JUST CRUSH HIM WITH A hug. But here, now, the joy was so somber, so—thick in the air, almost noble—that I found myself standing still, my chest simultaneously bursting and feeling just—safe, like everything was finally okay, like I was cuddled up under a thousand blankets with rain pitter-pattering on the tree-home roof outside. Or like standing in the lightning with my staff raised, but I was the lightning, too.

Jei was all right. He was all right, and he was happy. I'd buried him pale in a world of washed-out sand, and here his colors from skin to eyes glowed with such warm, saturated, brilliant *life* I wondered if we'd lived in greyscale before. His shoulders sloped, relaxed; his eyes shone with the triumphant wisdom of someone who's fought monsters and won so hard they work for him now, just grateful to lie conquered at his feet. He seemed to be at the same time burgeoning with energy—like he might suddenly run a marathon or wrestle a sabertooth—and completely overtaken with that pure, childlike calm that had hurt me so much to see on his dead face. There were no lines on that face now—the ever-present struggle was just gone—and a gleaming mark of honor burst like an exploding star across the center of his chest.

I couldn't speak. I dropped my chin for a bow to the decorated warrior, my friend. Jei returned a slightly deeper bow I didn't think I deserved, then nodded his head toward the back door.

I followed with a goodbye wave to the other Frelsi.

It was quieter out behind the tavern. Jei and I walked away from the town into the taller prairie brush. My toes dug into the dirt, pressed against rough blades of grass, but nothing cut me. I hopped up on this rock and then that as we came upon them, just enjoying the feel of the warm stone on my skin. Jei stayed on the ground, of course, boots swishing in his own comfortable, steady rhythm, and every now and then he took a deep breath and sighed—a full-chested, oxygen-hogging sigh, happy, and content. He chuckled when I lost my footing on a particularly slippery rock, but when I fell it didn't hurt. It was like the earth was laughing with me.

I didn't ask where we were going, and he didn't say. It was just nice to have the quiet, and a goal, and the fluttershies overhead, and in the distance the whinny of Pegasi who would never again be any Growen officer's steak. The wide prairie and lofty sky seemed like the kind of expanse that would have given us both panic attacks after the Stygge training center—but so full of Njandejara's embrace, this infinity had no emptiness to fear.

I could see the sandstone cliffs in the distance before we approached, and hear the thunder of the surf. I expected to be afraid—terrified, even—when we came up on the edge. I didn't want—it—to happen all over again. Even if it—didn't happen—I didn't want this to be a dream. That's how the real world works —all things that are beautiful turn out to be secretly awful, and that leaves people like me who've seen shyte always on alert waiting for the hammer to drop.

But ... I actually wasn't afraid, here. In some ways, it didn't matter now if the cliff suddenly crumbled and I had to live all the horribleness of it all over again, because—it would be okay, in the end. We could handle it. It was cliché, but it was so real: in the end, no matter what happened, my invisible friend would in fact hold my hand through the end of the world. As Jei and I sat there, dangling our legs over the edge with the green-grey waves lapping at the white rock below, it seemed like that other cliff was replaced with this one—like it was always supposed to *become* this one, so that like me, it could be healed.

"Was it worth it?" I asked him. "Saving me, I mean."

"Yeah," he said. "Thanks for taking down Bricandor for us. I know it was a higher price to pay than you expected."

I hung my head a little. There wasn't really—shame—but— I'd kind of filked that.

"Justice is important to people here, Lem," Jei said, fiddling with a blade of grass between his fingers. "Even if we're happy here, we want the universe to be right. There's a part of us that's crying out until it's fixed. That wants Njandejara to care enough about what happened to us, you know?"

"There's a difference between justice and revenge, though," I said.

"I know. But you got the job done. I'm grateful." His eyes lit up. "There's so much I want to show you. You know there's no meat here? There's all kinds of weird, savory fruit that's—well, better, actually. So then out of curiosity some of the local scientists thought they'd brew petri dish meat, which sounds disgusting, but you have philosophers from thousands of years ago geeking out with moderns who just got here, and—well, this death-free meat's far better than anything *I* remember from the old worlds, anyway. People have so much time to invent and explore and discover when they don't have to fight wars or scrape for food. Even the bloodsuckers here don't transmit disease or make you itch. I've kind of wondered if they're actually sharing neurotransmitter bursts—ideas, feelings, that kind of thing—from one person to another, but so far no one's told me."

I lay back in the grass and looked up to the sky, just listening while he talked. He'd never been shy, but I was always the partner who shared paragraphs; it was cool to think about him living this whole life here that—should have been? Well, no—it couldn't be beautiful like this, it couldn't feel like this, if we'd been born into it. Evil should not have been, but this—this, with all the pain it cost to get here and all the loss of what could have been, was actually exactly what should be. Things both were, and were not, right the whole time.

"I don't think I've ever seen you this quiet," Jei said.

"It's weird, isn't it?" There really was no sun, but the clouds were white and puffy and gleaming, glorious and huge. "To be honest, I still don't really understand where we are," I said. "I mean—I know you died. I'm actually not sure if I did. Like is this a dream place, or … because Joshua said—"

Jei dug around in the grass for a stone—he found one and hurled it over the water with what looked like a super wild em-push, skipping the pebble at least sixteen times despite dropping it from an unskippable height. "The dead sleep," Jei said. "That's why we don't like séances and things like that. We need our sleep. We dream about the living, and sometimes we might share the same dream with them, like I did with you, but—yeah. We need to sleep."

"So this is you dreaming?"

"It's more like a staging area—from our reference plane, at least. We're all waiting to step into the future where this is final-ized. You know how a person in a coma will experience time in the coma, but also, when they wake up, it's like no time passes at all?" He found another stone—eighteen skips this time. "When we wake up, it'll be in this better world. And it'll also be like no time passed at all. But in the meantime, in the reference plane of the old worlds—from their point of view—we're sleeping, still waiting for justice, while our people live and die back there. Some people die and join us in the wait; some people meet up with us at the end, still living, once this universe replaces that one."

"So it was like an infection all along," I said. "His universe bleeding into ours."

"Maybe more the opposite of an infection. A marriage. A healing."

"'Healing doesn't change who you are—it restores what you're meant to be,'" I quoted, looking up at his silhouette against the sky. I couldn't remember if he'd said that to Mera, or she'd said that to him.

He nodded.

"Are they here?" I asked softly. "I guess Jared can't be."

"Well—I wouldn't rule it out one hundred percent," Jei said. "I have this patient feeling I'm going to find Mera."

"He—but there isn't any *time* when you die. To change your choices. Especially not if you've locked your brain into it after years of bad ones."

"That's true," Jei admitted. "But Njandejara's outside of time." He laid down in the grass too, his hand folded on his belly. "I'm not saying he's definitely here. Our will in our dimension still—decides things. Permanently. But I'm saying if Joshua can go talk to people in voids and time-loops shut away from Njandejara, he can also talk to people in that weirdly time-dilated moment of death. You never know."

He tilted his head to look at me through the grass between us. "I think that's what Joshua's coming back to talk to you about, soon."

"About them?"

"About people like them. Like you said, this world is bleeding into the old universe now. The old worlds will need heralds—messengers to cover people with Njandejara so they'll be compatible with the new universe—able to live in it safely—when it's done."

"Like the clownfish and the anemone," I murmured. "So the anemone doesn't sting."

"I guess?" He looked up to the sky now, too. "Joshua's staying here so he can build the bridge from this end. This comforting air that's everywhere, like Njandejara in fluid form? Joshua's sending that—or him, rather—to our home universe, so he can talk to everyone at once instead of being limited by his physical body."

"I think I've felt this air before," I said. "I thought that's what I sensed when I'd—hear him. Isn't that like how it was for you?"

"Yeah. I don't really understand it. I know Njandejara being outside of time means that what Joshua did ripples backward, too." Jei reached for another pebble, and this time threw it high above him, playing catch with himself like a kid. "But this is going to be different. More—alive, spilling through everything everywhere."

I listened to the breeze, and the far-off roar of a dragon, and the surf. Far, far away I could hear singing day-lizards. "So you're saying maybe I'm supposed to go back and work on prepping the universe," I said. "Cuz I'm not actually dead." I didn't know if I felt disappointed by that or not. Cinta was back there. My siblings were back there. I'd heard from some of the other Frelsi that Laaru was doing great things. There was a lot of pain back there, but … my sweetest connections to the people I loved had been forged by healing pain.

Jei stiffened, looking at the sky—then sat up, tapping my shoulder. "Look, Lem," he said. "Some evenings around this time we can see into the Finished Universe on the horizon."

I sat up with him. Other people gathered on the cliffs now, scattered at respectful, pensive distances from one another, all gazing into the sunset. Jei pointed—just where the sky and water met you could see figures and trees, and gem-encrusted walls. You could see pretty far in the clear air if you squinted.

Cinta and Masha were there with their children. So many, many children. "Good for you, buddy," I laughed. I saw Lark getting the white stone with her new name on it—her complete identity, everything she ever wanted to be. She had a kid. Carl had new clothes on—it wasn't like I'd noticed him covered in blood or anything before, but he just seemed comfortable, and humble, and, well—like he had new clothes.

I strained my eyes for my siblings. I didn't get to see all of them, but I knew their stories weren't over yet, and it might be some time before any of them walked to the edge of the water where I could make them out. I saw a few Frelsi faces I knew, including some of Reise's friends—I was surprised to see a few more Growen soldiers I recognized from my time on Alpino, too, one of them clutching a copy of my note.

I sighed. Jei stared off into the sunset, one leg draped down the cliff and the other knee up to support his chin as his arm wrapped around it. His hair flickered in the breeze. He was okay! They were all okay.

"I think what Joshua's going to ask you, Lem," Jei said. "Is if you'd like to step into the Finished Universe with us today—or I guess, from their point of view, sleep, and wake up at the End— or go back to the old worlds and help them."

I looked at him. I'd waited so long to see my buddy finally. If I left now—shyte, it could be decades before I got to see him again.

"Is it cool if we sit back to back?" I asked suddenly.

"Sure. There really is nothing to lean on here, is there?" He turned, still watching the sunset. I leaned back against his spine and dropped my head back on his shoulder, looking away into that blazing orange and pink with him. The back of his ribs expanded against mine almost imperceptibly with his breath. We'd sat like this after Sterba and Mera, floating alone in that tiny Maggot spaceship unsure of where to land—because no matter where we went we'd face punishment. We'd failed the worlds and hurt each other brutally. It'd seemed like nothing would ever be right again.

But it was. It was right again, and better.

"I'm going to ask Njande to decide whether to send me or not," I said. "If he goes with me, I can take it. It'll suck. I'd rather stay here with you and Joshua. But I do love the people back there, and—I mean. Love just does shyte like that. Crossing dimensions and shyte. There's a special joy in that. I'll be okay with either one."

He bumped my head gently with his—just a wordless affirmation that he heard me and believed in me. Shyte, what a different Jei from the Stygge training center, I smirked.

The music from the settlement drifted over to us on the breeze; even as night fell, if you could call it that, it wasn't the kind of darkness where consuming shadows could hide, but just a different kind of light, a shade to rest under, punctuated with fireflies from fertile forests untouched by pollution. Joshua came by presently and gave me my marching orders. They were good, and I was at peace with them.

I was going home.

INDEX OF TERMS AND CHARACTERS

Air-rider: Single or double-rider hovering transport vehicle, popular among civilians and Frelsi warriors for its low cost of construction, safety profile, and ease of operation.

Allperson: A species of sapient reptilian that inhabits the crater of the third Bont moon. At war with the **Aliash.**

Alpino: Neighboring planetary system to Luna-Guetala. Its various biomes range from arctic tundra to temperate zones, but due to extensive landmass, with oceans comprising less than 50 percent of the surface area, much of the planet is covered in volcano-strewn prairie or cool desert. Bereens's home planet. Contested Zone.

Angela (Last Name Redacted): Frelsi soldier in her thirties taxed with protecting and freeing the Bijou settlement from the Growen. After becoming Turned, works in kitchen duty with Kola, Graap, and other defenders of Nathan Peter.

Ba-eater: A Biouk term for an interdimensional being that devours the human psyche. Used to describe gods and demons of multiple religions.

Bangla: A species of wide, many-trunked, vine'd tree common to Luna-Guetala jungles.

Baricella: A species of bipedal mammal characterized by long, black, fuzzy growths around the mouth that resemble the pedipalps and legs of spiders. Habitat includes Luna-Guetala jungles and the moon of Baricel orbiting Gas Giant 3; small colonies were transported by Growen slavers for cheap labor to the Northern Continent of Alpino. Visual spectrum includes high-acuity infrared but does not include much of the color spectrum. Communicate verbally with an extremely high-pitched language, most of which is outside the range of other mammalian hearing; emotionally, communicate with motions of the growths around the mouth.

Bichank: This people group, called "land-walruses" by many humans, bear more similarity to a sentient grizzly with tusks. Habitat includes the Luna-Guetala jungles, but actually likely originated on the cooler planet of Alpino. Culturally similar to Biouk peoples, communicate verbally with a throaty, roaring language, and emotionally with eye movements and wrinkles of the muzzle, like humans.

Biouk: See space-lemur.

Bijou: Cold planet currently undergoing terraforming, characterized by large diamond and neodymium crystal deposits. Home to a few Frelsi settlers, mostly Bichanks and humans, prior to Growen invasion for construction of a major leg of the Structure.

Blitzer: Member of a Growen heavy infantry unit, characterized by silvery armor and large, reflective, space-capable orb'd helmets.

Bont: A wide-snouted sapient reptilian species characterized by a second brain located near their thighs, similar to the second brain in a cockroach's back.

Bricandor: Leader and supreme diplomat of the Growen Unification Forces. Human in appearance and appetites; rumored to have appeared in the galaxy, or at least developed his Stygge powers, after the Black Comet.

Burbura: Independent planet with over 90 percent of its surface area under water, a condition many scientists attribute to a past global warming crisis. Highly technological trade, media, and political hub home to most of the sentient species in the known universe—"Where Burbura goes, so goes the galaxy." Independent planet/Uncontested, with both Frelsi and Growen diplomatic presence.

Cadet Commander: The highest rank available to a child in the Frelsi guard, preceded by Cadet 3, 2, and 1, and Enforcer. Followed in adulthood by Lieutenant 2 and 1; Sergeant 5, 4, 3, 2, and 1; Captain 3, 2, and 1; Colonel; and Admiral. Unlike the Growen Unification Forces, which separate rank into three chains—Officer, Enlisted, and Stygge—the Frelsi separate rank only into the child and adult chains.

Captain Rana: Wonderfrog officer over the Eighth Combined Battalion in the refugee base at Fort Jehu, overseeing both children and adults in self and community defense. Former commanding officer for Lem Benzaran, Jei Bereens, and Lem's siblings. Contaminated.

Cinta Belaran: Space-lemur from Luna-Guetala, 29 revolutions old, currently studying interspecies biomedical science to become a healer. Formerly a pacifist, joined the Frelsi Unification Forces three years ago after capture by the Growen, and advanced quickly to the rank of Lieutenant. Lem Benzaran grew up as his little sister for a few years, and they have since remained close. Adopted father to Joshua and public mate to Masha.

Contaminated: A derogatory term for a matter-based, sentient being who speaks to interdimensional energy beings such as, and usually specifically, Njandejara.

Contested Zone: The areas not covered by the Spaces Treaties. On Contested planets, the Growen and the Frelsi fight for dominance. On Independent planets in the Undecided or Uncontested Zones, neither is authorized outright displays of force. The Growen hold that all Frelsi allied-planets fall within the Contested Zone, but that Growen-occupied planets do not.

Draconian: A winged human subspecies, *Homo sapiens draconus* instead of *Homo sapiens sapiens*, marked by scale-like growths on the forehead and ridges of the zygomatic arch. Originally from Alpino, live in a symbiotic cultural relationship with the hunter-gatherer and herder "Blue" humans, trading off land every season so the latter can herd dragons. Jei Bereens' electromagnetic trainer was a member of this subspecies.

Dr. Patti Loylan: Physician assigned to the Eighth Combined Battalion at Fort Jehu. Also supervises the biological research program to improve artificial habitat compatibility, travel comfort, and optimal combat ability of diverse species. Shy. Contaminated.

Ebon Shadow: Bounty hunter alter ego for brothers Carl and K'arl Hampt. The most feared mercenary in the galaxy, the Ebon Shadow was often hired by the Growen for plausible deniability with assassinations or kidnappings that would otherwise break the Spaces Treaties. Following the events of the Battle of Bioumatta, chronicled in *Neodymium Exodus*, and the presumed death of K'arl, the Ebon Shadow began exclusively accepting anti-Growen contracts, working in tandem with the young Bont bounty hunter Lark Scrita.

Electrogenic: An electromagnetic being that can generate electric charge, similar to the electric eel on the rumored human homeworld.

Enforcer: The second-highest rank available to older children. See Cadet Commander.

Firebase: The largest Frelsi base on Alpino, located in the South Central continent about three hours' journey from Growen South Central by air-rider.

Forge: Generally habitable arid planet orbiting the second sun in the Bioumatta system. Resource-rich, but characterized by generally toxic colorful sands throughout much of the planet's atmosphere. Some portions of the planet are terraformed, or are only habitable underground, due to the planet's proximity to the sun and certain past meteorological events.

Fort Jehu: One of the larger Frelsi bases on Luna-Guetala, about an hour's journey by air-rider south of Retrack City. Destroyed during the machine apocalypse caused by Stygge Sterba.

Frelsi: Conglomerate of militarized special interest groups and refugee bases organized to protect people groups punished for refusing to join the Growen Unification Project.

Gideon Horn: 17-year-old male freedom fighter, ward of the Frelsi refugee system. Orphan. Special skills in ground combat and weightlifting. Known for cheerful, occasionally insensitive demeanor. Best friend of Nathan Peter and Reise Benzaran. Contaminated.

Gray: Frelsi slang for members of the Growen Incursion under the Growen Unification Forces.

Grenblenian: Common trade language throughout Luna-Guetala, adopted by most planets with a mammalian presence.

Growen Unification Forces: Interplanetary social organization forcefully uniting all sentient beings under one centralized government. Supported by various economic and social causes, including interest groups that propose eliminating Contaminated people to defend the universe from interdimensional invasion through their brains.

Jaika: See Jerusha-Lem.

Jake Benzaran: 14-year-old male ward of the Frelsi refugee system, below fighting age. Brother to Jerusha-Lem, Reise, Juju, and others. Special skills not yet known. Sustained significant childhood injury leaving him limping, and prone to epileptic attacks; as a result, can be quite skittish. Contaminated.

Jared Diebol: Deceased male soldier in the Growen Unification Forces who advanced early to commander status due to his Stygge training, electromagnetic abilities, and unusual voracity. Specialized knowledge of the Frelsi electromagnetic pair due to his close mental relationship with Jei Bereens. Not contaminated; obsessed with curing contamination. Would have been 24 years of age at the time of this chronicle.

Jei Bereens: Deceased male freedom fighter, ward of the Frelsi refugee system. One of two known electromagnetic humans in the Frelsi forces. Highly trained, with specialized knowledge of Growen systems and technology due to his childhood in Growen captivity. Arch-enemy of Jared Diebol; Paradox Warrior partner of Jerusha-Lem Benzaran. Contaminated. Would have been 21 years of age at the time of this chronicle.

Jerusha-Lem Benzaran: 18-year-old female freedom fighter, ward of the Frelsi refugee system. One of two known electromagnetic humans in the Frelsi forces, also known by her Biouk name, Jaika. Highly trained, with specialized knowledge of Biouk space-lemur society due to childhood living among the space-lemurs. Contaminated.

Joshua: Child of Masha, who claims he is parthenogenetic in origin. Has reached the age needed for much of Biouk maturity, but speaks with knowledge more common to someone thirty years older than him. Possibly the source of the contamination and a matter-based representation of Njandejara.

Juju Benzaran: 12-year-old female ward of the Frelsi refugee system, pre-fighting age. Quiet, with talents in early communication, and an unusual protection spell from Njandejara. Sister of Lem Benzaran. Contaminated.

Laaru (Last Name Redacted): A 17-year-old human graduate of the Beryllian Academy of Excellence, an electromagnetic with strong connection to mineral deposits and a highly technical knowledge of geology. Learned how to unlock his powers from Lem Benzaran (Pele), and joined the Growen under Stygge Bricandor in order to save the life of his Contaminated schoolmate, Xunst. Contamination status unknown.

Land-runner: A sleek, heavily armored, spiked vehicle that uses wheels to move along a planet's surface, most commonly employed by the Growen.

Lark Scrita: 19-year-old human living her life as a famed sixty-year-old Bont bounty hunter. Child of a Contaminated couple killed by the Growen. Takes missions from the Frelsi along with Carl Hampt, the Contaminated version of the Ebon Shadow. Contamination status unknown.

Lechichi: A fruit common to Luna-Guetala jungles. Grows

in clusters of small, translucent white orbs with rough reddish-purple husks.

Lev (Last Name Redacted): 22-year-old male Draconian freedom fighter, co-leader with his mate Nefesh of the squad that included Reise Benzaran, Nathan Peter, Gideon Horn, and Jake Benzaran following the collapse of Fort Jehu. Gentle, mildly philosophical with slightly socialist tendencies. Contaminated.

Lieutenant Seria: 23-year-old female freedom fighter, ward of the Frelsi refugee system, highly trained in communication and investigative skills. Testified extensively against Lem Benzaran in an investigation that culminated in Benzaran's exile. Formerly romantically interested in Jei Bereens. Not contaminated.

Lift: A floating platform with one solitary railing and a compuwall for light transport of goods and people within a short distance.

Luna-Guetala: The only known habitable binary or "double-planet" system, differentiated from a simple planet-moon system by the sheer size of the smaller celestial body. Luna, the smaller, more temperate twin, is often mistakenly called a moon by LG inhabitants. Neighbors the Alpino planetary system.

Masha: Exact age unknown; between 28 and 30. Sanitation worker at a large neodymium glass factory on Forge. Artistically and scientifically talented, but limited because of her gender and social status. Pro-Frelsi. Highly Contaminated.

Meat-man: Frelsi slang for perpetrators of sentient trafficking, whether through slave trade, brothel ownership, or actual sale of sentient beings for edible consumption.

Mera: Deceased at 20 years old. Female soldier for the Growen Unification Forces, thought to have been originally rescued from abuse as a sky-dancer by Diebol. Graduated from the same Stygge training program Lem and Jei rejected. Tasked with solving the problem of Jei Bereens when he becomes super-charged. Special skills in tracking electrical fields with a sense organ similar to the ampullae of Lorenzini in sharks; releases a calming pheromone and neurotransmitters that allow her to control others' minds. Outgoing, insecure, warm. Not contaminated. Diebol experimented with her biology to produce a mind-control dart for mass production.

Morda: Diebol and Bricandor's name for Mera.

Nathan Peter: 18-year-old male freedom fighter, ward of the Frelsi refugee system. Recent orphan. Special skills in compassionate organization and negotiation. Known for small size and quiet voice. Best friend of Gideon Horn and Reise Benzaran. Possibly contaminated.

Nefesh (Last Name Redacted): 22-year-old female Draconian freedom fighter; co-leader with her mate Lev of the squad that included Reise Benzaran, Nathan Peter, Gideon Horn, and Jake Benzaran following the collapse of Fort Jehu. Strict, professional, and serious, she was managing comms from home base when the rest of her squad was stranded on Bijou. Her name is also a word for a sentient form of life energy. Contaminated.

Njandejara: Interdimensional energy being interested in befriending matter creatures. Differentiated from other energy beings by existing outside time, as well as outside space; rumored to be the ancient origin of all life. Considered a mental illness by Growen scientists, and a dangerous invasion force by Growen philosophers.

Pele: An underground name used by Lem Benzaran during her time in exile on Beryllia.

Reise Benzaran: 16-year-old male freedom fighter, ward of the Frelsi refugee system. Brother to Jerusha-Lem, Jake, Juju, and others. Special skills in sharpshooting and piloting. Known for unusual, highly educated speech pattern. Not contaminated. Yet.

Retrack City: Large, cosmopolitan area occupied by the Growen forces during latter period of the Growen-Frelsi conflict for Luna-Guetala. Most populated and culturally celebrated spaceport on LG. About an hour's ride by air-rider north of Fort Jehu.

Revelon: Planet in the Uncontested Zone with fairly low gravity, mostly cool climates, and thin mountain ranges, inhabited by tall mammalians with keratinized, thick, rock-like skin.

Skraeli: Any of a number of sentient life forms comprised of complex carbon-nitrogen clouds. Require extreme gravity to maintain protocellular oxidation and life, and must wear atmosphere suits on the lower-gravity planets inhabited by most sentient beings. Language comprised of flashes of color punctuated with occasional sounds; emotions often communicated with scents.

Space-lemur: The human slang term for the Biouks, a sentient tree-dwelling race of omnivorous mammals characterized by small stature about half the height of an average human, enormous ears often as large as the head, powerful claws, a lack of tail, fangs that extend to the chest in adult specimens, and an extended lifespan often over a hundred Luna-Guetala revolutions. Divided into "moon" and "planetary" subspecies, with the "moon" species dwelling on the Luna twin of the Luna-Guetala twin planetary system. Language comprised of harsh, throaty sounds and snarls; emotions often communicated with ear movements.

Sterba: Deceased at 30 years old. Female soldier for the Growen Unification Forces. Trained and tortured by Bricandor to force an artificially strong bond with Mera, who is viewed as her sister. Special skills in heightened concentration and cognitive processing allow her unprecedented control over computing and machinery with incredible range. Cold, perfect. Shared nightmare bond with Lem Benzaran, who still feels deep connection with her. Not contaminated.

Stygge: A person gifted with electromagnetic abilities who has allied themselves either with the Growen, or with another force bent on eliminating the Contaminated.

Suns: There are two suns locked in an unusual binary system, one much larger than the other, which almost orbits it. These two suns support all known life in what is called, by Biouk scholars, the Bioumatta system. Luna-Guetala, Burbura, and Alpino orbit the first sun at the same rate as the second sun follows beside them, allowing for an almost-perfect temperature alignment from both sides. Forge orbits scorchingly close to the second sun, yet still at a distance to sustain some life, and the Bont homeworld close behind, with its many moons. Revelon, a smaller, cooler planet with less gravity, orbits further from the second sun, passing between the two suns into proximity with Luna-Guetala every few years. Further out, orbiting the entire double-sun system, is the resource-rich gas giant Skraeli, and beyond that, Bijou.

Turned: A Frelsi term for a soldier affected by a Growen mind-control device.

Undecided Zones: The areas protected by the Spaces Treaty; also known as Uncontested Zones. See Contested Zone.

Wonderfrog: The human slang term for the Bwangam people, a semi-amphibious sentient group with a body plan similar to a human-sized frog. Native to Luna-Guetala, but population range also includes the Burburan swamp systems. Language comprised of rounded, guttural sounds, with frequent repetition; emotions communicated with changes in skin color and aggressive, expressive body language.

Xunst (Last Name Redacted): A Contaminated teenager, age unknown, marooned on an unknown moon when Stygge Bricandor found him on Beryllia. Originally slated for execution, he was spared when his schoolmate Laaru joined the Growen. Member of a human tribe known for intricate circular metal weapons.

TRANSLATOR'S NOTE

The manuscript you have read was translated for your esteemed eyes from a time-shifted language that appears itself to be a Biouk translation from the original Grenblenian. Our lead specifically requested it be delivered to you personally, claiming it contains a communication relevant to your role in the heat death of your dimension. Because of the nature of translation, the reader should understand that many idioms such as "Prince Charming" or "homework-eating dog" may not exist in the original, or if they do, they exist in rather different contexts.

The entire work caused a number of us a great deal of trouble. The original manuscripts of these chronicles appear worn and aged, but dating with radium, argon, and carbon produced wildly inconsistent and unusual values, and electron microscopy revealed the presence of compounds and genetic material not in existence on our planet. Some have theorized a universe pre-existing ours; others on our team have discussed the possibility of a different version of our universe. All of this conjecture is not immediately relevant to the reason our lead specifically requested your eyes, and because we value our positions in the scientific community, we have brought the finished work to you as fiction containing truth instead of fact containing reality.

I hope in this understanding you will forgive any apparent anachronisms in the text.

ABOUT THE AUTHOR

Jen Finelli is a world-traveling sci-fi author who's ridden a motorcycle in a monsoon, swum with sharks, crawled under barbed wire in the mud, and hiked everywhere from hidden coral deserts and island mountains to steaming underground urban tunnels littered with poetry. She was once locked inside a German nunnery, and recently had to find her way through swamp-filled Korean foothills dotted with graveyards on Friday the 13th under a full moon without a flashlight. On her quest to rescue stories often swallowed by the shadows, she's delivered babies, cradled the dying, and interviewed everyone from prostitutes to Senators. If you want cancer-fighting zombie fiction, dinosaur picture books, scientists jumping into volcanoes, or talking cars and peyote legislation, you might like Jen—and if you liked the Neodymium Chronicles, you can download a secret companion book on her website at byjenfinelli.com/stories-from-my-other-universe-secret-update-page. Jen's qualified as a Fellow of the Academy of Wilderness Medicine (FAWM) adventure physician and sexual assault medical forensic examiner—but when she grows up, she wants to be a superhero. You can follow her journey to build a clinic for the needy in Paraguay on her site.

IF YOU LIKED ...

If you liked Neodymium Apocalypse, Part 2, you might also enjoy:

Other WordFire Press Titles by Jen Finelli, MD
Neodymium Exodus
Neodymium Betrayal
Neodymium Sacrifice
Neodymium Apocalypse, Part 1

Our list of other WordFire Press authors and titles is always growing. To find out more and shop our selection of titles, visit us at:
wordfirepress.com